STUPID
GIRL

A New Adult
Romance Novel

By Cindy Miles

eISBN: 978-1-937776-90-9
ISBN: 978-1-937776-96-1

Interior format by The Killion Group
http://thekilliongroupinc.com

OTHER BOOKS BY CINDY MILES

The *Stupid in Love* Series:

Stupid Girl
Stupid Boy (February 2015)
Stupid Love (Coming Fall 2015)

The *Cassabaw Island* Series:

On Morgan's Creek: A Cassabaw Station
Novel (Book 1, April 2015)

Other Titles:

Forevermore (Young Adult, Scholastic books)

Visit Cindy on her website, Facebook,
Twitter, or Goodreads!

Contact her at
cindymilesbooks@yahoo.com

DEDICATION

To Deidre Knight, for Believing
To Keith Urban, for Inspiring
To my mom, Dale, for Encouraging
And to Lyndsee Homberger, for Reading

"I have loved the stars too fondly
to be fearful of the night."

-Sarah Williams

Prologue: *Before*

WAKE UP! WAKE UP NOW!

Inside I shook, and my teeth chattered uncontrollably as my body ignored my mental command to drag itself out of the fog I wasted in. My eyes felt glued shut; my lips stitched together. Instead of waking fully, my breath came out in short little puffs between clenched teeth. Not from cold. The air around me was warm, humid, and my fingers slipped against my sweat-dampened skin as I crossed my arms tightly around my body, knees drawn up against my chest. *Where am I?* I lay on my side, the soggy ground earthy, pungent and gritty against my cheek, my ribs, hip. A grinding ache, low in my stomach, was accompanied by a burning sensation between my thighs. I tried to sit up, to shake my head and clear the haze from my thoughts, but I couldn't budge. Couldn't remember, couldn't speak. It was as if invisible fingers dug into my skin, freezing all movement. The taste in my mouth sickened my stomach, and it reminded me of when I was little and had hidden a handful of pennies from Kyle's piggy bank in my cheeks. Metallic. Cold. Bitter.

Finally I forced open my eyes and blinked. Two beams of light shot over me through the darkness. A motor growled. Then, furious voices rose above the sound in angered yells.

"I'm gonna fucking kill you, man! What the hell'd you do to my sister?"

"What'd you give her, Evans? Where is she? Open your goddamned mouth and tell me!"

Recognizing my brothers' voices, I peered into the misty light and tried to focus. What were they doing here? The images were blurry at first, but the longer I stared, the clearer they became. My oldest brother Jace held someone by the throat against the hood of the truck. Kyle, two years older than me, took a swing at the body on the hood. Knuckles crunched against flesh and bone, and the body slammed into the metal of the hood, then grunted and swore.

"Fuck you, Beaumont. Liv knew exactly what she was doing—"

Kyle punched the body again, and a grunt escaped Kelsy Evans' throat. Kelsy? My brain worked furiously, scrambling to think past the haze inside my head. Kelsy Evans. My boyfriend. We'd been going out for almost a year. There was a party. At Lawson's Lake. That'd been tonight. Right? My lips tried to move, my tongue pushed against my teeth as I inhaled and forced a shout from my lungs. "Jace!"

My brother let Kelsy go with a jerk and in seconds was on his knees at my side. Calloused fingers pushed the wet hair from my eyes. "Olivia? Wake up, honey. It's gonna be okay. I'm here, I'm here. Kyle!" Jace hollered. "Let him go, bro. She's over here and her lip's busted." Jace's hand gently gripped my jaw, turning my face toward the light. "She needs stitches."

"I ain't asking again, Evans," Kyle shouted. He grabbed Kelsy's jaw and shook it. "What'd you give her, man? Look at her! Look what you've done!"

Straining my eyes to hold focus, I peered past Jace to where Kyle held Kelsy against the truck, forcing him to look in my direction. Kelsy's gaze held mine for several seconds. What *had* he done? Kelsy wouldn't hurt me.

"Ecstasy! Just a half tab, bro—"

Kyle swung, his fist connecting with Kelsy's jaw. His head whipped back, and Kelsy sputtered. "I was drunk, man! Come on!"

My insides grew cold as my brain began to work, fitting the broken pieces of the past several hours back together. Grasping at Jace, I held onto him, pushed myself up. My eyes drifted down my body, and I noticed one of the spaghetti straps to my sundress hung loose and torn. Beneath the material, my bra was pushed up and over my breasts. My feet were bare; my panties bunched awkwardly between my thighs.

Oh, God. Jesus God, what did Kelsy do to me?

I needed no confession. I knew then, the burning pain between my legs a tell-tale sign. My body began trembling again, and sobs escaped my throat. The way my cries sounded in the night air, as if everything else around me had stilled to allow my voice to echo through the trees and off the creek? It was as though the world had died, and only I was left alone to shout and scream, praying for someone to hear me. Anyone. To save me.

No one had. Because I had only screamed inside my head. No one heard me.

Every muscle between my legs ached, but I drew in a lung full of air and forced my voice out in a long, echoing wail as the truth crashed over me. "*Nooo!*" I clawed at my dress, the one intact strap hanging limp over my shoulder. Yanking hard, my breath came faster. "Get it off! I want it off me!" It felt filthy, soiled. It was disgusting! I wanted it off!

"It's gonna be okay, honey," Jace crooned as he pulled me against his chest and held me there. With his palm, he pulled my head tightly to him, and I finally stopped clawing at myself and sobbed into his tee shirt. I blocked out the sounds of Kyle beating the bloody pulp out of Kelsy Evans as best I could, and my fists worked Jace's shirt tightly between my fingers.

"Take me home," I sobbed, my breath hitching. A souring pit formed in my stomach, and a wave of nausea dumped over me. My voice dropped to a cracked whisper. "I just want to go home."

Jace rose, and in the next second he'd bent down and lifted me in his arms. As I drifted through the night air, the one thing I'll always remember is the fireflies. Dozens and dozens of fireflies blinked over the creek bed, like a million stars littering the heavens.

"Everything's going to be okay, Olivia," Jace's deep voice soothed me. "I swear it will."

Glimpsing the blinking fireflies once more, I closed my eyes.

And prayed when I woke up in the morning, I'd realize this had all been just a terrible, sickening nightmare.

1. Slammed

A year later ...

THE MOMENT I SPIED the ***Welcome to Killian*** sign at the outskirts of town, my stomach dropped and my hands gripped the steering wheel hard. The small Texas college town sat half-way between Lubbock and Amarillo. Two hundred and forty-eight miles from home. Three hours and forty-four minutes by car, going the speed limit.

I hoped to God it'd be enough.

Peering through my shades, I noticed Killian's *Sonic* parking lot was filled to the gills with rowdy boys, souped up trucks and hot rods. As I passed by, I eyed several girls sitting on the backs of opened tailgates, laughing and flipping their hair. Reminded me of my hometown of Jasper. What was it about a *Sonic* burger joint? Always seemed to be the popular hang-out spot. Part of me wanted to pull in, tell the hair-flippers to get a grip and leave. But the bigger part of me kept my foot on the accelerator. Stay low, keep quiet, and no one will even know I exist. Just the way I wanted it.

Slowing down, I hit my blinker and pulled into the massive brick entrance of Winston U. Flanked by huge magnolia trees and planted mounds of petunias and other annuals, a little of my earlier somberness over leaving home eased out of me. It was replaced by an excitement I was sort of surprised by. Things would be different here. I just felt it. No more stares, no more whispers. No more muffled giggles. No more rumors. No one knew me here. I'd just melt in to the population and be a big nobody. Invisible, like a ghost. Perfect.

I started down the main drive leading to admissions, and scanned the grounds ahead of me. Large colorful banners stretched across buildings that said WELCOME FRESHMEN, along with several home-made Greek signs for Rush Week. People were everywhere, on the lawns, the sidewalks, the parking lots. Maybe I should've taken up Mom's offer to come with me today. My brothers had offered to come, too. Even Grandpa Jilly. I'd turned them all down, insisting I could—no, *needed*—to do this alone. What was I thinking? *Stupid, stupid girl*. Too late now, I was in it up to my gills. No turning back. Drawing a deep breath, I pushed my self-doubt aside. *I can do this*.

While not super huge, Winston was mostly well known for their successful baseball and football teams. The Silverbacks. But I'm not exactly a jockette or even into sports, so that's not what drew me. Winston also had an extraordinary astronomy program, with a mega-observatory to boot. They called it the Mulligan, and when it was first installed in 1910 it had been the largest scope in the country. I'd been lucky enough to gain employment in the Science complex through the financial aid department. It was geek-girl heaven, and I'd be right smack in the middle of it.

Literally. I loved the stars, constellations, galaxies, and all that went with it. Staring through my scope at the seemingly infinity heavens had helped me get through the last painful year of high school. To a certain degree, it'd healed me, right along with my family. We Beaumont's all stuck together— except for my dad, who'd pulled a disappearing act long, long ago. Other than my family, astronomy was my life. All I'd ever wanted to do was study the stars, ever since I was a little kid and Jilly had given me my first telescope for my sixth birthday. Finally, it was happening. I just prayed the past would leave me alone. That the nightmares would stay gone, that the relentless fear which had for a while replaced my fearlessness would recede somewhere deep, deep inside of me. And would stay there. Forever.

As I kept my eyes on the street signs, my hand fumbled around on the bench seat of my truck until I found the campus map. Holding it up eye level, I navigated my way through several streets until I found my dorm. Oliver Hall held three stories, double occupancy dorm rooms, each with a private bath, and a common room. I'd been assigned to the second floor, dorm room 21. The parking was split into two sections, with Oliver Hall in the center. I pulled into the not-too-packed left side lot, found a spot closest to the front, and parked.

I pushed my hat back off my forehead and for a moment I sat, just looking out at the red brick building, manicured with boxwood hedges lining the walkway up to the dorm. A huge cottonwood tree, probably a couple hundred years old at least, stood tall and off to the side, casting an arc of shade over the hall. People milled about—mostly girls, since it was a girls' dorm. Laughing. Hollering. Going in and out of the door, everyone loaded down with bags and boxes and belongings from home. Mid-August, it was hot and humid as Hades. And I was here. Alone.

This was my new life.

Somewhat intimidating.

I gave Mom a quick call to let her know I'd arrived and promised to call later. Then, after a big, calming breath, I opened the door and climbed out. The heady scent of freshly cut grass hit my nose, and it actually helped me feel a little less anxious. *These people don't know me. They don't know what happened to me.* A little more apprehension eased out of me. Shoving the truck keys into my bag, I made sure I had my dorm keys, and pushed my cell into my back pocket. I slipped my shades off and tossed them onto the dash, shouldered my backpack, and shut the door. Reaching over the side rails of my truck bed, I grabbed a box filled with astronomy books and desk supplies, and started across the lawn. Not super light, but manageable, and I'd rather get the heavier boxes in first. Looked like I'd be making a few trips to get all my stuff inside anyway. My boots dug into the grass as I made my way to the entrance.

"Heads up!"

Just as I turned, a sudden, powerful force slammed into me, taking me down, and I hit the ground with enough vigor to make the breath *whoosh* out of my lungs. The box flew out of my arms, and I was a little stunned at first, lying in the grass. It wasn't an unfamiliar feeling; I'd been thrown from so many horses over the years, I'd lost count. And this is what being thrown felt like. Maybe worse. My hat had shifted and now shaded my eyes. I concentrated on breathing.

Then, suddenly, my hat was pushed off my face, and *he* was over me. Arms braced on either side of my head. Looking down. Frozen in place, I couldn't do anything else except stare back at him, and I watched his smile fade as his gaze fixed on mine. He looked about as surprised as I felt.

His face took me off guard. It was … shocking. Not handsome—almost frightening. Rough. The lightest, most startling blue eyes

I'd ever seen stared down at me. One of them had a really recent black and blue shiner marring the otherwise fair skin. A whitish half-moon scar started at the corner of the other eye and curved around his cheek bone. Another white scar jagged down from his jaw, just below his ear, halfway down his throat; it was met by a black tattooed inscription that disappeared down his shirt. Super dark hair—almost black—swung over his forehead, and equally dark brows furrowed. We both stared for a few seconds.

Then, his head lowered, and full, firm lips covered mine.

And he kissed me.

One, two, three seconds passed as my brain reclined in some hazy fog where I didn't know anything or anyone. Only this kiss. Strong lips pushed mine open, just a bit, and a velvety tongue barely swept against mine. A faint trace of spearmint lingered. For an instant, I was completely lost.

Then, the shock wore off, and my brain worked again. Almost too well. Between reality and old panic clawing at me, I reacted.

I reared my knee up and sunk it straight into his family jewels. "Get *off* me," I said in a low firm voice. I put my palms against his chest and shoved him.

"Ah, damn!" the guy wheezed. He grabbed his crotch and fell over onto his side. He groaned in pain. I leapt up, stepped over him, and started grabbing my books.

"Jesus fuck, Sunshine." The guy laughed and wheezed at the same time, and still clutched himself. "What'd you do that for?"

His voice wasn't too deep and sort of raspy. Heavy accent. He looked like a gangster, only he wore a WU Silverbacks tee shirt, with the number 14 at the upper left chest. *Whah'd you do that fah?* Definitely not from Texas. He'd kissed me. And for a moment, I'd let him. What was wrong with me? I spared him a harsh glare. "Are you crazy? Why do you think?"

Male voices caught my attention, and I looked over to my left. A group of guys— jocks, all wearing Silverbacks tees—were laughing. One was on the ground, howling like a total fool.

Apparently, college would be just like high school after all. Maybe worse.

"Christ, I'm sorry. Was just goin' out for a pass. I didn't even see you there. Then," his smile was slow and lazy as his gaze raked over my mouth, "well, I just couldn't fuckin' help myself."

I shot him a hasty, embarrassed glance. Heat flooded my cheeks. "That is just plain psycho." Dropping to the ground, I flipped over the box and started shuffling my stuff back into it as fast as I could. The guy rolled, groaned, and swore again, then slowly went to his knees and started helping me. I didn't look up. "It's okay. I've got it." God, I wanted him to just leave, walk away, join his buddies and pretend the whole thing hadn't happened. People were already looking, and I didn't want them to. I didn't want to be noticed. At all. *He'd kissed me.*

The guy ignored me all right, and continued to pick up my scattered belongings. My eyes avoided his face but noticed tattoos snaking down one arm. The other was inked, covered with random works of art, and a dark band tattooed around one wrist. Black letters were inked onto the knuckles of both hands, but his nuts apparently had recovered and he was moving too fast for me to read them. I didn't want to get caught staring just to see what they said. For that matter, I really didn't care what the words said. I wanted to be out of the situation. It wasn't happening, though. Instead, it was dragging on and on.

The group of jocks were still laughing and now calling him names. He glanced over his shoulder. They laughed harder. He shook his head and continued picking up my books. "Ignore them," he said. He was a little closer now. "Fucking retards." *Fahkin retahds.* I stood with my box, and he rose with me. Grabbing my hat off the ground, he plopped it onto my head. He inclined toward my loaded arms. "I'll get that."

I flashed a determined look at him. He was about six feet tall, lean, broad shoulders. A piece of tattooed art poked out of the collar of his shirt and crept up his neck on one side. Probably more beneath the shirt. Definitely not your average clean-cut college athlete. I shook my head and started walking. Typical inked-up punk big mouth bad ass. Surely he had better things to do. "Thanks, I've got it," I threw over my shoulder. *Pushy guy* ...

I didn't get three steps before the box was lifted out of my arms. The guy gave me a crooked grin, and it made the scar at his eye pucker. "Least I can do for slamming into you. Least you can do for charging my nuts with your knee." *Chahgin'.*

My gaze slammed into his and held steady.

"Look. I don't need or want your help, and you don't have to make anything up to me. It's no big deal." I wasn't too sure about him, but apparently he liked to fight. And he was a major flirt. Or he was a lunatic. Either way, he was trouble. It was so obvious. "Your nuts will survive."

"I'm taking the box to your room, Sunshine, and that's that. No need for hostility. So lead the way."

Godalmighty, he wasn't giving up. I could kick him again, but that'd just cause another scene. The last thing I wanted to do was draw more attention. I'd just gotten here! With a final hard glare, I turned and started toward the dorm.

He followed. Whistling.

I thought the best thing to do was ignore him, pretend he didn't bother me, so that's what I did. I walked the remaining few feet to the dorm entrance, fished my key card out of my pocket and pushed it through the slide. His big tattooed arm held the door open for me. I shook my head and passed him. We walked in together, hit the stairwell, and started climbing. My boots scruffed against the old concrete steps; his Nikes made no sound at all. I slid a guarded glance toward him, just to make sure he didn't shank me or something. I pretended he wasn't there. Kind of hard since all I could think about was that stupid kiss.

"So you got a name, Sunshine?" he asked.

He was one step below me, and I glanced over my shoulder, pushing open the door to the second floor. "Yes."

A few yards down the corridor, he chuckled, throaty and full-on male. "So you gonna tell me what it is?" His accent was unique and sharp. "Let me guess? Ballbuster?"

I spotted dorm room twenty-one and, digging the key from my pocket, unlocked the door. I shook my head. Everything about him screamed *player*. Well, actually, had he not been wearing a WU Silverbacks jersey, everything would've screamed *thug*. That thought was going against what Mom had always taught me—not to judge by looks alone. Kelsy Evans had proved that theory our senior year when he'd slipped what Jilly had referred to as *sex poison* into my drink. Never would his all-American good looks, family upbringing and incredible charm have raised suspicion that he was really a perverted asshole. Not until it was too late. Jilly hadn't liked him from the moment I'd first brought him to the ranch, and he'd never missed an opportunity to remind us all about that. This guy? Open book. He wasn't trying to pretend he was anything other than a badass heart-breaking flirt. There could be something said for honesty, anyway.

Still. I was in a new place, with new people, away from the safety of my very familiar home and protective brothers. I was on my own and needed to be careful. My brothers and grandfather had already threatened to drag me home at the first sign of trouble—which was something I avoided at all costs. Until now, apparently. I'd noticed a haunted glint in this guy's unusual eyes when he'd looked at me, though, and it had unnerved me. Big time.

"You're killin' me here, Sunshine. What's your name?"

But now his pushiness was making me want to retreat. Making me on edge. I really just wanted to be alone and get settled without any problems, scenes, or incidents. Having been sprawled across Oliver Hall's lawn was bad enough. Heaving a big sigh, I met his startling stare with a bored one, and relieved him of my box. Surprisingly, he allowed it. "Apparently, Sunshine," I answered. Leaving him standing in the hall, I shut the door. A breath of relief eased from me, and only then did I realize I'd been shaking a little. Had he really unnerved me that much? Of course he had. He'd *kissed* me, for God's sake. There was no way he knew what kind of line he'd crossed with me. Good Lord, I hoped he couldn't tell. With another cleansing exhale, I stared at my new living space.

The room was empty, except for the double occupancy school-issued beds, dressers, and desks. I set my box down on the far side of the room, closest to the window, and glanced around.

The now-familiar male laugh sounded from the other side of the closed door. "Um, pardon me, sweetheart, I'm not leaving until you tell me your name. You've made it an issue now, see?" The way he said sweet*heart* came out like sweet*haht*. Pardon, *pahdon*. "I'm sitting down. In the hall. Against your door. And I got patience, Sunshine. A fuckin' lot of it."

With a long breath, I closed my eyes. What was his problem? There were easily fifty girls in the common room downstairs. Why did he want to know my name so badly? He hadn't even told me *his* name yet. Not that I wanted to know it. What I wanted was for him to leave me alone. My eyes raked over my room. Of course, I had a lot more stuff to get from my truck, which meant leaving my room, which meant coming face to face with him no matter what I did. *Hell.* There was no way out of this, unless I shimmied out of the window—and I was heavily weighing that option. With an aggravated sigh, I took my hat off and flung it onto the bed, swore under my breath, crossed the room and opened the door.

As promised, there he was; sitting on the floor, knees pulled up, tattooed forearms resting against them. He was *right* in front of my door. Tilting that shocking face and arresting eyes upward, he gave me a half-grin that troubled me more than I'd like to admit. White teeth flashed. "Name?"

My gaze settled on his, and I held it that way for a few seconds before stepping over him and heading down the hallway. Six months ago I might have been intimidated. Now? Okay, sure, I was ... a little. I couldn't afford not to be. My entire future was at stake. I couldn't put my old scared self out there for anyone to see. That would open doors I never wanted opened again. Down the stairwell and out of Oliver Hall, I crossed the lawn, pulled open the tailgate of my truck and climbed up. I knew he was right behind me. I shot him a hooded glance.

"This is a wicked ride—especially for a girl." He was standing by the wheel well, arms resting on the side of my truck, looking casual and unaffected. Like he hadn't knocked me over, hadn't kissed me. Like he did that sort of thing every single day. He rolled his gaze skyward, as if concentrating. "I thought people from Texas were supposed to have manners." His eyes drifted back down to mine. "You're like some, I don't know, mean ass fuckin' road warrior or something, with this tank. With zero goddamn manners."

I was stunned by my gut reaction; I actually fought the urge to smile. His accent

was strong and vulgar, yet ... charming. I
don't remember the last time that thought
crossed my mind. I wondered where he was
from, but wasn't about to ask him. I kept
shuffling my stuff around, lining boxes up to
carry in. Glancing over my shoulder at him, I
continued working, and opened the big heavy-
duty plastic toolbox my brother Jace had
bought me for my birthday, containing my
telescope bag. I said nothing. Those blue eyes
had a wildness to them that made me wonder
what hid behind them. They were so strange
to look at. Especially with that big shiner
circling one of them.

"Brax Jenkins." He half-turned, and I saw
the name *Jenkins* across the broad back of his
jersey. "I'm not a fuckin' serial killer or
stalker, I swear to God. I'm a baseball player.
And I'm gonna help you unload this truck.
Then you can tell me your name." He
shrugged. "You know, even trade for me
slammin' you to the ground and you sackin'
my nuts. What do ya say? And don't kid
yourself, sweetheart. I saw that smile you was
tryin' so hard to hide."

I studied his determined look for a second.
Hahd to hide. His strong jaw was set, and the
muscles there flexed. He wasn't giving up; no
time soon, anyway. Hard to believe that the
very first person I met at a school where I
didn't know a single solitary soul was *this*
guy. Intense, oozing with sexuality, and
something else indefinable, he was exactly the
very thing I needed and wanted to avoid. Why

did he want to know my name so badly? I couldn't figure it out and it made zero sense. Girls all over campus probably kept tabs on him, and he could easily have his pick. Probably a different girl each night for weeks on end. So why bother with me, even if only to get my name?

"Come on, it's just a name, Sunshine," he continued, and glanced at the sky. "Not like I'm proposing to you or anything." He shrugged. "It's just a name." His eyes drew back to mine, and his lips pulled back further, making his already-wide grin dangerous and wolfish looking. "And I'm not fuckin' apologizing for that kiss. It was natural hot-blooded male gut instinct." He shrugged. "Couldn't help it."

Couldn't help it? So yes, to answer an earlier question to myself: He was kookoo. But if I simply gave him my name, maybe he'd just be satisfied and be done with it. He'd knocked me over and spontaneously kissed me; he'd make up for it by helping me. Done. Although I could easily unload the truck alone, I pinned him with a hard stare. "Only if you leave me alone afterward."

He clapped his hands together sharply once and leapt into the back of the truck, and it bounced with his weight. "Sweet." His gaze drifted over the contents in the bed, and then to the big black bag I'd shouldered. "What's that?"

"Telescope," I answered in a quiet tone. I noticed he hadn't promised anything. I pushed another box closer to the tailgate with my boot, stepped off, and lifted it into my arms.

"So what are you, a weatherman or something?" His lips parted with another half-cocked grin. He grabbed a couple of boxes and balanced them, and jumped down beside me.

"Yes," I answered in a quiet voice. "Or something."

"Ah, I see," he said. He walked close enough that our shoulders brushed.

I glanced at him but said nothing.

"You're one of those wicked smart girls, aren't ya? Like some foxy cowgirl Dexter's Laboratory scientist or something?" He was smiling, looking down at me. *Smaht.*

Crude as he was, I couldn't help the smile that pulled at my mouth. I shook my head and shrugged. *Foxy?* "Something like that." I pressed my lips together hard, trying to make the grin go away. I didn't want it to be there, and I didn't want it to encourage Brax Jenkins. It was nearly impossible.

When we reached the dorm entrance, Brax caught the door as a group of girls filed out. They all slid me an odd look, and one said, "Hey there, Brax," in a husky voice, and then stared hard at me as she passed. Almost … challenging me. Daring me to interfere. *Daggers*, even. It was always so noticeable when girls flirted, and it looked and sounded stupid and immature. They never really knew what might lay behind good looks. Or an arresting pair of eyes. No matter how jolting of a kisser. I knew that first hand.

"Ladies," he said. They all walked away, giggling and whispering. He held the door open for me, his eyes never leaving mine, and I pushed through.

"Fan club?" I asked as we hit the stairwell. At least people knew him; maybe I wouldn't get shanked after all. Kissed, apparently, but not shanked.

He chuckled and turned that odd gaze on me. "Something like that," he said pointedly.

A half hour later, Brax set the last box down in my room. He rooted himself in front of me, his tattooed arms folded over his chest. Those eyes regarded mine, determined. One of his brows lifted. "Name?"

"Olivia Beaumont." I stuck my hand out to shake his, like I'd been raised to do. "Thanks for the help. You can leave me alone now."

Brax took my hand but his gaze stayed on my eyes, and his strong fingers wrapped around mine. The jolt of excitement that shot through me at his touch surprised me, but it was accompanied by alarm. I pasted a grin on my face and prayed there were no tell-tale signs of either. He actually seemed a little stunned that I'd even offered a handshake. Although he didn't squeeze too hard, I could feel his strength radiating in his grip. A smile lifted one side of his mouth as he regarded me. "You got a middle name, Olivia Beaumont?"

"Were the first two not good enough?" I

asked. When he continued to silently stare, I shook my head. Strange request, I thought, but I answered. "Grace," I said, and then remembered to drop my hand.

His smile was full-blown, and it transformed his harsh features of scars and crudeness into something ... else completely. Something that made my blood surge within me. It took me off guard. It could also possibly be the origin of his fan club. "Well, Gracie, I'll see ya around."

Brax turned his swaggering, lean form sideways at my open door, allowing a curvy brunette with blonde highlights to pass through. He looked over her head at me, winked, and left. The girl just stared after him, then turned to me, wide-eyed. She wore hot pink shorts, a white tank, and wedge sandals. Her hair was super straight, parted in the middle, and fell nearly to her waist. She carried a big zebra striped purse that rested against her hip.

"You're Olivia Beaumont, right?" A light, tinny voice fell from her mouth. "I'm Tessa Barnes, your new roomie." She glanced out the door once more and pushed her palm to her forehead. "Oh my God, do you know who that was?"

I nodded. "Said his name was Brax Jenkins."

Her big blue eyes, rimmed in dark liner, bugged. "You *know* him?"

I shook my head and sat on the bed I stood closest to. "No, I just met him about an hour ago. He knocked me down on the lawn then insisted on helping me carry my stuff in. Why?" I purposely left out the kissing part.

My new roommate slowly shook her head. "Oh, girl. Oh ... *girl*." When I didn't respond to her exasperated remark, her eyes popped open even wider. Then she muttered what sounded like a stream of Spanish under her breath. "That's *Braxton Jenkins*, my darling. Sophomore. Kappa Phi brother. Winston's big dog starting pitcher. Total man slut." Tessa shook her head. "Bad *ass*, and not in a good way. He's dangerous. Trouble with a big fucking T. If you've got any sense at all, you'll stay far away from him."

I briefly wondered what my new roomie would think if I told her Winston's numero uno man slut had kissed me on the lawn? It didn't take long to decide that was something better kept to myself.

2. Big Dog

WHAT A TOTALLY STRANGE way to start an introduction with my new college roommate: a warning to stay away from Brax Jenkins. A warning which I really didn't need. Tessa plopped down on the end of my bed. I looked at her and lifted a curious brow. "What do you mean by dangerous?" He looked it all right. I'd thought the same thing myself. Man slut? That much was completely obvious.

The serious expression on her face made her arched brows tug forward. She crossed her tanned legs. "He's a total punk. From Boston," Tessa began. "Has a short fuse and as you can tell, gets into a lot of fights." She pointed to her own eye and made an air-circle around it, referring to his shiner. "Lots and lots of fights. Starts most of them, from what I've heard. It's even rumored he killed someone when he was younger." She rubbed her arms as though the mention of Brax chilled her. "And those eyes are so freaky creeping weird." This time, she physically shuddered. "Scary."

Funny, those eyes of his had been scary, but I'd also thought they were—

I regarded my roommate, who seemed to be a little on the dramatic side, and smiled. "He definitely looks like trouble, but being from Boston or anywhere else doesn't make a person a punk or a murderer," I said. "You can't speculate on rumor." I realized I was defending him, when minutes ago I'd been thinking him a thug, too. Grandpa Jilly would call that being a *goddamned hypocrite*.

Tessa leaned forward, unaffected by my subtle chastising. "Fair enough, girl. But he *is* a man slut. Certifiably sound sources have told me that much. Sincerely."

I just stared at her and waited, knowing she'd give full disclosure. I wasn't really sure why I wanted it, but I listened anyway.

Tessa sighed, as though irritated that I couldn't just take her warning at face value. She cleared her throat pointedly. "Braxton Jenkins isn't just Winston's top dog starting pitcher for the Silverbacks." Her slight Texas drawl was made even more dramatic by her intense storytelling of Brax. "He is top-dog over the dating pool. His ego is … epic. His female conquests? Legendary. He's all about the hootch chase, Olivia. Once he's caught his prey, stolen the goods, he releases, just like a pro-Bass wrangler at a fishing tournament. *Bang 'em and throw 'em back*." She scowled.

"More than one reliable source claims to have heard him say those exact words, too. I mean, how sanctifuckingmonious is that? Bangs and dumps, and does it with no shame. Trust me, he's heartless. Boy's like a damned horny hound looking for a bitch in heat."

I couldn't help but grin. Tessa's drama was … entertaining. "That describes about, oh, probably most of the guys on this campus, I'd imagine. But how do you know all this about him? Aren't you a freshman?"

Tessa bobbed her head. "My older brother is on the baseball team with him," she said. "He warned me away months ago. Says Brax is an arrogant ass."

I rubbed my chin with my knuckle. "Again, you just described probably ninety percent of all guys at Winston." I held her gaze. "So you don't *actually* know girls he's been with?" I asked. Some of what she was relaying sounded more like hearsay, rather than firsthand experience like she wanted me to believe. Gossipy, and having been on the other end of that word, I totally hated it.

"Well"—she cleared her throat again and her face screwed up— "let's just say I've heard plenty, and the sources I've heard it from are trustworthy. Besides, he doesn't try to hide it. He'll tell a girl he's a one-night-stander. That I *have* heard myself. And that means the same as bang 'em and dump 'em, right? But I *do* know guys he's beaten the shit out of. That's all the proof I need." She regarded me, and tucked her straight hair behind her ear. "I'm a little surprised that he came onto you, though. Oh," she said, catching herself. "Shit. No offense. That came out way worse than how I meant it."

I shrugged with indifference. "No offense taken. But he didn't come onto me. He was just being nice for plowing me down." That was mostly true. The kiss wasn't a come-on. He'd basically said so himself. It was a ... what'd he call it? A *reaction*.

"Right. Brax doing something just to be nice." She shook her head. "Maybe. But what I meant was: Brax Jenkins usually goes for a certain *type*." Tessa shrugged and glanced me over, from my dusty boots, to my worn, hole-in-both-knees jeans, white tank and thick wad of mousy brown braid. Not to mention, zero make-up. "You're about as opposite from that usual type as it gets." She smiled, and her white teeth shone bright against her tanned skin. "But in a totally good way. You don't want him bothering you, anyhow. Like I said, Olivia. Trouble." She twirled a finger by her ear. "Maybe even a little *loco*. You'll see. He's like, all over campus, flirting up a different girl every day, scoring a different girl every weekend. So says my brother."

I nodded. "Thanks for the heads-up, but I promise you—the last thing I'm looking for is a relationship. With Brax Jenkins or any other guy. My full concentration is on school." I gave her a hesitant smile, hoping that wasn't too much info.

"I'm from Lubbock. A lot of kids come here from there. What about you?"

And just that fast, Tessa changed gears, so I went with it. More than likely I'd never even run into Brax Jenkins from Boston again. Ever. I was pretty positive he didn't hang out at the library or the observatory, and that's where I'd be spending most of my time. Tessa didn't need to tell me how polar opposite I was from Brax; that was beyond obvious. And, absolutely no big deal. I certainly wasn't about to become his or anyone else's throw-backs, conquests, or whatever else you call it, that was a sheer certainty.

What I accomplished here at Winston would set the pattern for the rest of my life, as well as the future of my family's ranch. I had plans. And nothing—or no one—would stand in my way. That kiss? Yeah, it'd been shocking, to say the least. But now that I knew he'd probably done the same thing a dozen times that day? Chalk it up to experience. One I wouldn't be repeating.

I smiled, and answered. "Born and raised on a small horse ranch in Jasper. Just north of Abilene. Three brothers, my mom, and grandpa. " I was pretty sure all the gritty details of my small ranch life mucking out stalls, repairing fences and getting flung from insane horses wouldn't interest Tessa, so it was my turn to change gears. "Want some help getting your stuff in?"

"Thought you'd never ask!" Tessa leapt up and headed for the door.

We trudged downstairs and crossed the parking lot to Tessa's silver Jetta. It was loaded to the gills with clothes and shoes. More than I'd ever seen. In. My. Life. I shouldered several duffels and stacked three boxes high in my arms. The heavy scent of hair products and perfume permeated from the top one. My Grandpa Jilly would call her a girly girl.

"My brother Cole's bringing the rest of it with his truck later on," Tessa offered as we started back to the dorm. Made me wonder if Tessa had noticed how small of a space we'd be sharing. I wasn't sure a truckload was going to fit, on top of what we'd carried in from her Jetta already. I'd brought minimal stuff, all of it easily contained on my side of the room.

As we walked down the hallway, Tessa looked over at me. "My god, woman, what do you do? Work out 24-7? Your arms are seriously cut."

I gave a brief glance at my bared arms, which just looked skinny to me. I laughed. "Just a lot of chores, I guess. Ranch work. Breaking horses."

"Ugh. I hate chores. And I'm pretty sure I hate horses, too."

We dumped the couple of loads off at the dorm, and over the next hour and a half I got to know my roommate a little better. Tessa's mom was from Mexico, which explained her gorgeous tanned skin and fluent Spanish. A pre-nursing student, she still had all of her core to finish. Her eyes bugged when I told her how many core classes I'd completed before I'd graduated high school.

"Astronomy major? Damn woman, your brain must be the size of a basketball in there." She pointed to my head and her nose squinched up. "I hate science."

"Okay, let me get this straight." I smiled. "You want to be a nurse, but you hate science and chores?"

Tessa stared, blinked, then barked out a squeaky giggle. "Yeah, but I love people, and I want to be a labor and delivery nurse. Not much intense science involved there, right? It's all gravity, baby! Pretty much just a push and catch sort of deal!" She laughed, and so did I. Surprisingly, I felt at ease with Tessa. If someone had pointed her out and said we'd be friends, I'm not a hundred percent positive I would have agreed. We were just so very opposite. Yet, I liked her.

A tinkling sound came from Tessa's cell, and she grabbed it off the bed, her fingers flying over the keys as she responded to a text. "Cole's out front! Let's go!"

We met Tessa's brother outside, and for some reason my eyes slipped to the spot of lawn where Brax and I had fallen and met. Kissed. Brax had such arresting features, and Tessa was right about those eyes. Shocking. I mentally shook my head to push all dangerous thoughts of Braxton Jenkins out, and glanced at Cole. He and Tessa looked alike, for the exception that Cole didn't have blonde streaks through his hair. His was buzzed cut, and you could tell he was an athlete; strong build, tall, broad shoulders. He was a cute guy, and I was pretty sure he knew it. Tessa introduced us.

"Hey," he said quickly. He barely acknowledged me with a glance, and it had lasted all of a half-second. He turned to his sister. "Let's get this stuff out of here, huh? I got somewhere to be."

"Don't be such a shithead, Cole," Tessa snapped. She looked at me, rolled her eyes, and we started unloading Tessa's belongings. When she suddenly and loudly cleared her throat, I looked up and she winked at me. "Cole, by the way ... how 'bout Brax Jenkins was over here hitting on Olivia earlier?"

I laughed lightly, totally embarrassed, and passed a fast look at Cole over the top of my boxes. "He was definitely not hitting on me."

Cole glanced at me, and quickly weighed me in from my boots to my hair. It was so plain on his face that he, too, was doubtful Brax Jenkins had any interest in me at all. Still, he put in his two cents. "I'm not gonna talk shit about my teammate, but just like I tell Tess. Stay away from him. He'll hurt you."

"Uh, thanks for the warning," I said quietly. Not only wasn't I sure Cole had even heard me, he didn't seem to notice or care, which was okay by me. Staying well below the radar was my goal, and that seemed to coincide with steering clear of Winston's bad boy. And his teammates. And anyone else who knew him.

I glanced at Tessa, who shrugged, and I didn't say anything else as we walked back to the dorm. I hadn't planned on being around Brax at all, making it pretty easy to stay away from him. Besides, all these warnings and talk about Brax Jenkins was sort of ridiculous. He'd knocked me over. He'd reacted on hot-blooded male instinct and given me the briefest of kisses. He'd helped me carry stuff in. That's it. It wasn't a big deal, not a date, and he certainly wasn't interested in me. Not a proposal, as he'd pointed out. As Tessa had so delicately put it, I was not his type. Not at all.

So why did my lips still tingle?

At our room, Cole put down his load. "Later," he called over his shoulder. He was really speaking to Tessa and not me. He disappeared out the door.

"Sorry about that," Tessa apologized. "He's a butthead, just usually not so damn rude. Probably in a bad mood or something. I swear his PMS is worse than mine. Man Periods. They're a fucking beast."

A grin pushed passed my lips. "I've got three brothers. And a surly old cowboy grandpa. I know exactly what you mean."

Tessa's gaze assessed me, and she stared at my lip. "Where did you get that scar?"

My fingertip grazed it, and it felt as huge as the lie I was about to tell. I shrugged. "It was just an accident. I was thrown from a horse I wasn't supposed to be riding, and a barbed wired fence caught my face when I landed. Several stitches later, and, well, here it is." The lie came easier and easier every time I told it—especially since I didn't really remember *how* my lip got busted, only that it'd happened that night, with Kelsy. The taste in my mouth, like sucking on pennies, I remembered. Only later did I realize it'd been blood. The emergency room, and getting nine stitches in my lip? That memory will always be stuck in my head, no matter what. Forcing myself to shrug the awful recollection, I kept a casual gaze trained on Tessa.

"God! I bet blood was everywhere!" She cringed. "I guess you can't wear lipstick too often, huh?"

I pushed an uncomfortable laugh out and rubbed my lip. "Yeah, not so much, so I just don't wear make-up at all."

"I'd literally die without make-up." Tessa cocked her head a little and studied me. "What's that ring for? You're not married, are you?"

I glanced at the narrow silver band on my ring finger, and met Tessa's curious gaze. I'd had to answer the same question before, but it never failed to make me shrink a little inside of myself, making me question more than once why I continued to wear it. "No, not married."

Tessa's eyes grew wide. "Oh, shit. Is that an abstinence ring?"

I shoved my hand in my pocket. A familiar sick feeling pitted my gut. "Sort of. It's a pledge of virginity."

If possible, her eyes grew wider. "No fucking way. Let me see it." In two steps she was in front of me, grabbed my wrist and pulled my hand from my pocket. She lifted the ringed finger closer, turning it round and round, studying it as though it were some long lost artifact. "God, my mother would've given anything to have gotten one of these on me." She looked at me and smiled. "Pretty ballsy of you, Olivia. Especially here. Kudos."

I shrugged. "Just something I believe in personally. I don't make a big deal of it, just like I don't judge others."

Tessa's brow lifted. "You're not like, Amish, or Mennonite, are you? Not that there's anything wrong with that—"

"No, nothing like that," I interrupted her, and smiled. Inside, I calmed myself, making sure I didn't sound defensive. "It's just a decision I made in high school. That's all." Right now, that's all the information Tessa needed about me or the ring. I wasn't ashamed of it; completely the opposite. Yet every time I was asked about it, I felt as though everyone could see right through me. Could see that I was a fake. Didn't matter that my virginity was taken from me, and I hadn't given it away willingly, or rather, consciously.

Our stares held for a few seconds, and in that space of time, an understanding passed between us. Tessa nodded, and so did I.

"No prob. It's cool, Olivia. Sincerely. Let's unpack!"

The two of us spent a little more time talking classes and family and Tessa's latest boyfriend ordeal, which included a rather harsh dumping via text, while putting our stuff away. She didn't mention Brax, my ring, or vow of virginity again, which relieved me on all sorts of levels. The darkness that existed behind that little ring wasn't for anyone's ears at Winston. Ever.

Tessa was standing on her bed, hanging a poster of a muscled Calvin Klein underwear model wearing nothing but a pair of white boxer briefs and chiseled-in-stone abs, when a shrill chirp rang from her cell. She answered it and squealed. "Marcie! Oh, shit! I dropped a tack!" She bent down, searching for it, found it and stuck it in the corner of the poster. "Yeah, I'm almost done. I'll be over in a sec!"

She jumped down, grabbed the wedges she had on earlier, plopped onto the bed and pulled them on. She looked at me. "Hey, you wanna come with? I'll intro you to my girls. They're lunatics. We're all from the same high school. Shopping and dinner? There's a Welcome Freshmen party over at Cole's frat, open house, next weekend." She giggled. "We're all getting new outfits."

I gave Tessa an appreciative smile. I couldn't believe she'd even invited me. "You're not rushing?"

Tessa grinned. "Nah. Not sure my potty mouth could make it through the week. But I *am* hitting the Rush parties. You?"

I shook my head. "No. My schedule is way too full." I'd break it to her later that I just wasn't the shopping and spa, or frat party kind of girl. Not that there was anything wrong with that, but … it just wasn't me. Not anymore. Plus, it cost money to join, and it was money I'd rather send home to the ranch. "Thanks, but I've got a lot to do today. I'm meeting my new boss later this afternoon at the observatory."

Tessa stared into a little round mirror she'd put on her desk and ran a tube of gloss over her lips. "Not to sound spoiled, but I'm *so* glad I don't have to get a job. Even though one at an observatory might be sort of cool." She shook her head. "I don't know how you'll do it, with school work and all." She smiled at me, her lips super shiny. "You're gonna miss all the great parties! You know, the ones my parents won't know about?" She laughed. "Mom and Dad made me swear I'd keep my GPA up or else I *would* have to get a job. Until then, I get allowance. Next time?" Tessa grabbed her keys and zebra purse, and started for the door. She turned and flashed a wide smile. "See ya later, roomie!" The door closed behind her, leaving me alone.

I stood in the middle of the dorm room and took a deep breath in as the storm of Tessa dissipated like a funnel into the sky. Tessa and I might have very different backgrounds and couldn't possibly be more opposite. Where I was a star geek and old for my age, she was a little immature. No, a lot, actually, as if she'd never left high school. Yet, we somehow clicked. She was nice. And, just as I'd noticed her differences, I'm pretty sure she'd noticed mine, too, and hadn't judged. I appreciated that about her.

After a few minutes of looking around the room and through some of the stuff I hadn't unpacked yet, I decided to put together the three-tiered bookshelf Jilly had bought for me as a going-away present. Within a few minutes I had all of the disassembled pieces out of its box, each part and the matching hardware displayed on my freshly made bed. After a brief glance at the instructions, I dug my wrench and screwdriver out of the small toolbox Kyle had given me, and set to work. Jilly had made sure the desktop shelving was made of solid oak and not that *cheap shitty particle board crap*. Just the thought of my grandpa and his old cowboy foul mouth made me laugh out loud. I already missed him. Crazy old man.

Within a half hour I had the oak shelves assembled and atop my desk. Quickly I arranged all of my astronomy books, and stepped back to inspect my work. Deciding to hang my own inspirational poster, I knelt on the floor and fished in the toolbox for my tacks, found them tucked into a small corner, then grabbed the rolled poster I'd taken off my wall from home. Toeing off my boots, I climbed onto my bed and stood, then slid the rubber band off the paper. I'd tacked up two corners when a knock at the door startled me.

My mind scrambled as I stepped off the bed and made my way to the door. I knew absolutely no one at Winston. Except for my roommate, and she wouldn't be knocking. Maybe it was the dorm monitor for Oliver Hall. Tessa mentioned earlier she might be stopping by to introduce herself. Or, it could be someone looking for Tessa. Pulling the door open, I blinked in shocked surprise. I felt my gaze widen. *Not* the dorm monitor.

Brax Jenkins's peculiar eyes stared down at me from the doorway. His forearm rested against the jamb in a cocky stance. His pitch-dark hair fell in soft messy curls that had no pattern or symmetry and brushed his collar. A phantom smile tugged at his lips. What in the world was he doing here? I wanted to ask him just that, but I didn't. Didn't need to.

"Seems I can't get that kiss out of my head, Gracie."

Instead, I shook the surprise from my head and shrugged, trying to hide my embarrassment. "What do you want, Brax?"

Brax's lips spread. "Is that something you really want me to answer?"

My face flamed, and I started to shut the door. His hand and quiet laugh stopped it.

"Calm down, Sunshine." He glanced over my head. "What'cha doin'?"

I folded my arms over my chest. "The same thing I was doing the last time you saw me." I forced myself to look at him. "Seriously. What do you want?"

"Last time I saw you, Gracie, you were in the grass and I was lookin' down at ya. After you kissed me, that is."

His sharp accent and cocky remark took me off-guard, but I bounced back quick, trying to mask my awkwardness. Something about Brax made me lose all wittiness I'd accumulated over the years, scrapping with my sarcastic brothers. But Brax wasn't my brother. He was a strange guy I knew nothing about. I corrected him. "You kissed me. And the last time I saw you, you were right where you are now. Leaving."

Brax laughed, thoroughly amused, and the sound came out raspy and husky and as completely male as his speaking voice. Although he made me nervous, I was surprised to find I liked hearing that laugh, his voice. Now he leaned against the door jamb, crossing his tattooed arms over his chest. It didn't appear that he was going to leave anytime soon. "Yeah, got me there." His gaze moved over my face, lingered on my mouth—the scar on my lip, I imagined—and then lifted. I waited for him to ask me about it, my scar, but to my surprise, he didn't. "Who's that?" he asked instead, inclining his head to the poster I'd been hanging.

I glanced over my shoulder in the direction of his stare and turned back to him. "Maria Mitchell. One of the first female astronomers. You agreed to leave me alone, remember?" He really never had, but I'd hoped to convince him otherwise. I couldn't even begin to imagine why he was here. I'd been pretty blunt before, just trying to get my point across. I wasn't one of those giggly girls who swooned as Brax Jenkins held a door open for me. Hadn't I made that clear enough? "Did … you forget something?"

"No, but you did." Brax reached into the back pocket of his jeans and held out a cell phone.

My cell phone.

My hand flew to my pocket where I'd earlier stuffed my phone. Empty, of course. He handed it to me, and I looked at him.

"You must've dropped it when I sacked you on the lawn," Brax said. He rubbed his jaw with his thumb, and my stare was drawn to the black inked letters on his knuckles. I still couldn't read them since they were upside down. His brows pulled together. "I picked it up with your other things and forgot about it until I sat on it."

My eyes flew to my phone and flipped it open, to see if it still worked. The backlight flashed green. I breathed a sigh of relief. The last thing I wanted to do was spend the money for a new one.

Brax laughed. "Where the hell did you get that thing anyway? A fuckin' yard sale?"

I snapped the phone shut. The way Brax said *fahkin' yahd* was kinda funny. Crude, but funny. Suddenly, I felt a little self-conscious. "It's fifty dollars cheaper per month than an iPhone." I shrugged and stuck my old fossil phone into my back pocket. "I pay my own extra-curricular bills, so I save where I can."

An appreciative light glimmered in Brax's eyes, almost making them lighter than they already were. "Smart girl. Kinda figured you were different than the others."

The others? He'd already summed me up? Only fair, I suppose, since I'd summed him up pretty fast, too. That I was even on his mind once he left here took me off guard. Well, no, I guess that wasn't completely accurate. He had to return my cell phone. That's all. Again, I tried to throw off my slight anxiety of him being here by diverting the conversation off of me. I nodded to his black and blue eye. "What's the other guy look like?"

Brax's mouth lifted at the corners, a sly smile, and I couldn't help but be drawn to his mouth. It'd been on mine, after all. To my horror I noticed how perfectly shaped his lips were. The one feature on his entire face that wasn't frightening or threatening or beat up or scarred. And my gaze zeroed in on them. What was wrong with me? Clearing my throat, I hurried and shifted my eyes back to his, only to find a knowing gleam in those strange blue irises.

"A lot worse than me," he answered. His eyes again settled on my mouth, then rose, looking me square on, and pushed off the door jamb. His tall, broad shouldered frame leaned toward me. "So you gonna leave me standing out here, Gracie, or let me in so you can tell me how you got that scar?" His eyes dipped to

my hand. "And why the hell you're wearin' a
wedding band."

3. Suckerpunched

Brax's bluntness stunned me for a second. I knew he'd seen my scar. It was kind of impossible not to. From being in the sun most days, my skin had tanned, and the scar that slashed through my top lip had turned white over the past year, and was about a half-inch long. Not exactly disfiguring, but it stuck out like a white silky sore thumb. Instantly, I pulled at my lip with my teeth, trying to cover it. How many more times would I have to tell the lie about how I'd gotten it? Usually, no one bothered to ask. It's not something I'd ask a virtual stranger, yet Brax and Tessa had both pointedly and bluntly asked me about it.

The ring, though? I'd never tried to hide it. I just didn't have too many people ask about it, either. The kids back in Jasper had known exactly why I was wearing it. Again, this was a new place with new people. And one of them now stood in my doorway, waiting for me to answer. I knew he saw the hesitation in

my face. I didn't even know him. I only had
Tessa's point of view, which had been a pretty
crappy one. But with a known reputation and
a black eye to boot? Not to mention the bold
kiss he'd planted on me? I definitely didn't
want to be alone in my room with him. *This
isn't high school, Olivia. You're not drinking,
this isn't a party, and you're not with a pervy
deceptive boyfriend who wants to get in your
underpants. You're in total control. Get a
grip.*

"I brought your phone back, don't forget,"
Brax urged. *Fahget.*

Sheer curiosity and something else I
couldn't explain drove me to create my own
point of view of Brax Jenkins.

"Just for a minute," I offered. I forced an
air of irritation into my voice that I was pretty
sure didn't quite measure up. I didn't want
him thinking he put me on edge, although
that's exactly what he did. Now that the words
were out of my mouth, I wished I could take
them back. Glancing around, I searched for …
something. A weapon, just in case? I wasn't
sure what, but just that thought sounded
absurd as I looked at him. All I knew was that
being alone with Brax made me jumpy.

A ghost of a grin, barely there, pulled at
Brax's lips as he pushed my door open wide,
resting it against the wall. Shamelessly, he
swaggered into my room. He must've felt my
trepidation and thought to let my dorm door
stay open. Still, there was something in his

eyes, his body language that made me leery.
My room suddenly felt crammed full.
Crowded. Smaller, just with him in it. He
passed by me, then glanced briefly over his
shoulder. "Scar? *Scah*. "An accident." I
answered.

"What happened?" Those strange eyes
were fixed on mine. Waiting.

I tugged at my lip again with my teeth. "I
was thrown from a horse into a barbed-wired
fence." *God, please forgive these stupid lies I
keep telling!*

"No shit," he said, his mouth pulling into
that sly side grin. "Tough girl, huh? You don't
look it. Now Southie girls? You can tell right
away they don't take no kinda shit. From any
damn body." Those eyes regarded me
curiously, and for far longer than felt
comfortable. "But braids and freckles don't
usually stir the fear of God in people, Gracie.
Or horses, for that matter."

It struck me odd, his comment. Although
my mom never talked bad about our estranged
father, she'd told me something not too long
ago. Something he'd said, before deserting us
all. *I need more, Sadie. This braids and
freckles life on the ranch? It's sucking me dry.
It's just not for me. It's not enough. It'll never
be enough.* I vaguely remembered my father,
but the thought of his weak cowardly retreat
from our family and his responsibilities made
me angry, filled my mind with a blazing red
color that heated my cheeks. I shook the

thought away and inclined my head toward Brax's scar. I needed to veer the conversation away from me. "What about you?"

His eyes changed; hazed over. "Broken bottle." Just that fast, the glimpse faded, and his lip curled up. "Just a little scuffle with a guy who had one too many lagers. As you probably have noticed, I'm not from here." *Lahgas.*

"Kinda hard not to," I said. I already knew where he was from, but I didn't want him knowing Tessa and I had been talking about him. "Where?" I asked, avoiding his direct stare.

"South Boston," he clarified. He inclined his head to my hand. "Married?"

Instinctively, I twirled my ring with my thumb, then sighed. "No, not married. It's personal."

Brax shrugged. "It's an easy question, Gracie. Just answer it."

Easy it definitely was not. I stared at the thin band of silver on my finger, then the clear blue of his odd eyes. I lifted my chin. "It's a pledge ring. A vow I made."

His eyes widened, his face shocked. "Jesus Christ, you're a fuckin' nun?"

I blew out a breath. "I'm pretty sure you're going to hell for saying all those words in the same sentence. No, it has nothing to do with the church. It's a personal vow. Of virginity. My decision." I made my gaze stay on his, forced it, unafraid and unashamed. Well, that last one was another lie. Shame crept into every corner and crevice of my being, filling me like some dark silhouette that shadowed me, no matter where I went. But no one here would ever know that about me. Not if I could help it.

Brax studied me hard for several seconds. Haunted eyes penetrating mine. One side of his mouth lifted into that cocky smirk. "Well, at least you're not a fuckin' nun."

He moved toward my bed, and glanced up at my half-hung poster. "Got any more tacks, Gracie?"

And just like that, it was done. I'd guessed then he didn't want to talk about his past, and he must've gotten that I didn't want to talk about mine, either. A person doesn't get gashed and scarred by a broken bottle—or anything else—and not have a dark history behind it all. I decided not to pry. I'm glad he decided the same. At my desk, I grabbed two more tacks and handed them to Brax. When he smoothed the poster against the wall, I read the letters inked into his big knuckles. On his left hand, **g o i n**. On his right, **d o w n**. *Goin' down.* He pushed the tacks in and stood back to look at it.

"Maria Mitchell, huh?" He looked at it for a second, glanced over his shoulder at Tessa's Calvin Klein poster, then turned and held me still with his gaze. "I already knew that about you, Gracie. I could tell just by comparing you and your belongings to your roommate's." He moved to my bookshelf, and ran his forefinger over each volume as he read the titles. He looked at me. "Even without that ring I'd have guessed you're a virgin. But an astronomy student? You got me there, Sunshine."

Panic and shame rose from my stomach and into my throat, and suddenly my past felt splattered all over my face. I didn't want him to know, to guess, or to even stay on this conversation anymore. I knelt by my toolbox and started straightening its contents. "I can see why you have a black eye." My voice had dropped to a low pitch.

Brax's chuckle interrupted my thoughts. "Sorry—it's a God given talent that I have."

"Your rudeness?" An angry blush crept up my neck. If only he knew.

Brax grinned, unaffected, and wandered over to my tool box and squatted down, lifting a wrench. "Nah, that's been a long work in progress. Did I mention I'm a Southie? Rude is part of our DNA." He shook his head. "No, me. Spotting a virgin. It's a talent of mine." He shrugged and set the wrench down, and stood. "I haven't encountered many, unless you count the ones I knew in kindergarten, while I was still *in* kindergarten." His stare seared me. "But in your case it's a little hard to hide, Gracie. It's stunning on you."

The sharp realization that I was even having this exchange with a guy I barely knew blazed my insides further. Not to mention he was so way, way off. "I don't try to hide it, or advertise it," I answered in a quiet voice. "It's no one's business but mine." I closed the toolbox and stood.

With one hand, Brax reached toward me and flipped my braid. "Be proud of it. Not many can claim it at your age, ya know."

I wanted to melt into the floor of my room. Humiliation of the truth—and my own lies—swamped me. "I ... think you need to leave now, Brax. Thanks for returning my phone."

Brax pushed his tattooed hand over his heart. "I'm not trying to embarrass you. I said be proud. You wound me, Gracie."

"We're not friends, and we don't know each other like that. So could you just leave, please?"

His gaze pinned me, and there was a light that sparked there, and I couldn't tell if it was mischief or admiration. "We've already known each other now for, what? Several hours? We're old friends now." He stepped closer, his body angling toward mine. "We've kissed. That makes us something, yeah?"

"Not even close."

Brax rubbed his bottom lip with his thumb as he studied me. "I plan on changing that."

I looked at him skeptically. "Somehow I don't think I fit into your crowd."

"Who said I was gonna share you with mine or any other crowd?"

The heat from my blush stung my skin and I felt it rising like mercury in an old thermometer.

"That's cute, Gracie. Damn cute."

Exasperated, I breathed out, lifting my gaze to his. "Thanks again for returning my phone," I said. I felt trapped, caged in like a big cat at a carnival, and I wanted him to leave. "I've got to go, though."

Brax cocked his head. "Where ya headin'?"

Grabbing my boots, I sat on the bed to pull them on. Brax was borderline pushy. An irrational, irritating, irresistible kind of pushy. "To meet my boss and go over my work schedule. I've got a job at the observatory."

Brax leaned his shoulder against the book shelf and crossed his tattooed arms over his chest, regarding me. His mouth pulled up at one corner. "A job, huh? Are you kicking me out, Gracie Beaumont?"

I looked at him. "I kicked you out five minutes ago."

The whites of his teeth gleamed as his smile widened.

Despite his bold acknowledgment of my supposed virginity, and blatant expression of pursuit, he was … more than charming. But I'd been warned of that, too, and I knew behind his charisma and witty comments and sexy Southie accent and too-sly smile, demons lurked. Scary ones. I wasn't sure he was as dangerous as Tessa warned me about, but I did feel he was just passing time with me. Fascinated, more than likely, because I wasn't twirling my hair, fake-sighing and throwing myself at him. Plus, he thought I was a virgin. That's a novelty to any guy. Something off limits, forbidden. It's like a red flag to a bull. A green flag to a race car driver.

I'm sure he thought that fact alone was intriguing about me, especially since so many girls my age had lost their virginity in high school. Some before that. But I wasn't here for anyone's entertainment. I didn't want to be his or anyone else's novelty. And ... I wasn't at all what Brax thought I was.

Yet a thrill shot through me at the thought of him not wanting to share me. At the way his presence crowded my room. And at the way he looked at me with those almost all-knowing eyes. That split-moment kiss and the energy it'd left behind lingered in my head way longer than I wanted it to. I didn't understand it, but there it was. I'd not had a boyfriend, or even a friendly date, since that awful night with Kelsy Evans. The thought made my palms clammy, and my insides jittery.

How had he affected me so fast? Now that *was* a real talent. Day one with Brax Jenkins, and I was already thoroughly kissed, charmed ... and nauseated at the same time? Someone needed to smack me right in the forehead. I'd never confess it to anyone, being affected by him. I'd take it straight to my grave.

Brax gave me a wide grin and straightened. "Lucky for you I've got practice in thirty minutes, or I'd argue with you. I'll show you a shortcut through campus to the observatory." *Ahgue.*

I stood, and grabbed my truck keys and small patchwork slouch bag that was my purse. "I can find it."

Brax's dark brows drew together in a frown. His black hair swung over his forehead. "Come on, Gracie. I know the way through campus. You'll end up going the long way." He grinned. "Trust me."

I regarded him. Eyes completely zoned in to mine. Eyes that carried a hint of ... something dark. Something forbidden. Something prom-ising. A small smile pulled at his lips, and I caved. "Okay. Thanks."

"No problem." He ran his hand over the bookcase. "You put this together yourself?"

"I did."

He gave me an appreciative nod. "Nice job."

I looked at him. For a second, the man slut was gone and he seemed truly impressed. I ducked my head, a little embarrassed. "Thanks."

I'd completely forgotten that Brax had pushed the door to my room wide open, and he stepped aside to let me pass through first. He'd managed to put me at ease—well, as much at ease as I could be put—after all. He pulled it closed, I locked it, and we started down the hallway. A couple of girls passed by, and their stares were first, of course, on Brax. Then they quickly turned to me. Their whispers were audible as they continued by, their words not.

"Not virgins," Brax leaned over and said in my ear.

I just shook my head, and he laughed.

Outside, we crossed the parking lot and at least half a dozen people spoke to Brax. Some girls. Some guys. They all regarded me with suspicion or at least extreme curiosity. I couldn't blame them. I looked about as far from someone Brax would be hanging out with that anyone could look. Which made me want to pull a blanket over my head while I walked. Or better yet, run to my truck, throw myself in, and speed away.

I also noticed how Brax's presence seemed to crowd not just my dorm room, but the very space I walked and breathed in. All around me at once. It astounded me and made me feel jittery. And curious. Which I ignored.

"So when do you start work?" he asked.

"You ask a lot of questions," I answered. When he continued to look at me, waiting for an answer, I sighed. "Monday. Five to nine, I think. The professor works around my classes and lab."

Brax looked down at me. "What lab do you have? Aren't you a freshman?"

We reached my truck and I wasn't at all surprised to see a motorcycle parked beside it. "I am, yes."

Brax's ghostly stare locked onto mine for several seconds before answering. "What classes are you taking?"

I noticed then that the letter R simply didn't exist in Brax's vocabulary. I avoided directly looking at him, fiddling with the truck keys instead. "Intro Astronomy and a lab, Physics 301, Literature Humanities, and

American and Texas Government." I finally glanced at him. "I ... have to go. Thanks again."

Brax lifted a brow. "Well then, Gracie, we might bump into each other after all, then." He nodded toward his bike. "Follow me."

I climbed into my truck, partly relieved to be out of Brax's direct stare path, and started the engine. I watched Brax as he straddled his bike and braced it with his legs on the ground. The make and model was foreign to me, since I didn't know bikes all that well, but it was older, with a silver tank and black leather seat. When he started the engine, it rumbled and roared like some loud, pipeless beast. Pulling a black half-helmet down over his head, he tightened the straps under his chin, pushed his shades on, threw me a lop-sided grin, and waved me on.

I followed behind Brax, through the school's many avenues and magnolia-lined streets. Students were everywhere, and Rush stations lined the sidewalks. After making a few turns, we ended up at the back lot of the Science complex and observatory. I parked and got out, and Brax pulled up beside me. His eyes were hidden behind his shades.

"Thanks again," I said. "For the help, the phone, and the route."

Brax's lips pulled back into a full-blown grin. "Anytime, Sunshine. Talk to ya later."

I watched him pull out of the parking lot and leave the way I had followed him in.

Talk to you later. Which meant he *planned* on talking to me. Later. As I walked along the paved path that led to the observatory's wide front entrance steps, I considered my weird, extraordinary day. From the moment Braxton Jenkins knocked into me, nothing else afterward made a bit of sense. Why me? What could a baseball playing, fraternity brother, tattooed Southie sophomore who got into frequent fights and could keep company with any number of gorgeous leggy college girls, want anything to do with me? A plain, no make-up wearing, star-searching scarred-up in more ways than one cowgirl Geek?

Oh yeah. He thought I was a virgin.

Guys *were* douchebags.

As I rounded the walkway and climbed the steps, I pushed through the side-by-side front glass doors, and left behind the sweet, humid August air. With an inner determination and vigor, I set aside the silly giddiness Brax Jenkins had managed to stir inside me, and in a very short time. I was pretty sure I hated that. And I probably wouldn't have to worry about it, either. Once the virginity ring novelty wore off, I'd drop right off of Brax's radar. Which was fine with me.

The cool, air-conditioned interior of the observatory's main entrance swept over me as I entered the foyer and walked up to the help desk, situated in the center. I looked up to the domed building's painted tiled ceiling. It was beyond spectacular, and speckles of light filtered in and glittered against the walls like so many chipped diamonds. After glancing around, I noticed a, well, really cute guy, early twenties if I had to guess, seated behind the horseshoe desk. He wore a long sleeved white shirt, buttoned up the front, sleeves rolled over his tanned forearms. Plastic boxes sat before him, filled with free flyers and maps of the building. A donations jar also sat, half full. I walked to the desk, and the guy looked up. "Hi, I'm Olivia Beaumont. I'm here to meet with Professor Callander about a job?"

The guy rose from where he was sitting and smiled, and it was warm and easy. I was surprised at how comfortable it made me. He stuck out his hand, and I shook it. "I'm Noah Hicks. Professor Callander's TA. He's asked me to show you around, if that's okay?"

I returned the smile. "Sure, that'd be great."

"Let me get someone to watch the desk." He picked up the phone and made a call, and I stepped back and waited.

With Brax and his interruption of my first day pushed to the back of my brain, the thrill of being in Winston's fabulously large observatory washed over me. I'd worked so hard to get here, and finally, amazingly, I was.

Soon, a young guy around my age hurried toward us. He was tall, bone-thin, and glasses sat on his flawless pale face. He grinned at me through shaggy, reddish brown hair that flipped over his ears and stuck out his hand. "I'm Steven," he said, and his toothy smile was wide and unembarrassed. "Guess you're the other honors grad scholarship financial aid job recipient?"

I shook his hand. "Wow, now that's a mouthful. But yeah, I'm Olivia. Beaumont."

"Anytime you need to switch a shift, just let me know," Steven said. He moved to take Noah's position behind the desk. "But we'll be working a lot together, too."

"Okay, great. You do the same," I offered.

"Ready?" Noah asked.

"Sure."

Noah Hicks led me through the observatory, winding our way from the first floor, where three large auditoriums held multiple exhibits, all the way to the top observation platform outside and the dome that contained the Mulligan scope. Round, almost like the top of a lighthouse, it had a double railing around the steep drop off, and the public was allowed in on Wednesdays and Saturdays. The Mulligan was … epic. I could barely wait to get a nighttime look.

Along the rest of the tour, he told me more about my duties, responsibilities, and participation in arranging the planetarium exhibits. All very exciting to me.

Then, Noah went over his position with Professor Callander. Noah had an impressive resume and sounded like a brilliant astronomer. Tall and clean cut, he had close-clipped brown hair, strong features and soft brown eyes that reminded me of suede. Noah looked like an athlete and carried himself with confidence and answered all my questions. I was glad to be working with him. Very non-threatening—a characteristic I seemed to inadvertently siphon out with people now. After the tour, he accompanied me to his office, and we went over my work schedule Professor Callander had coordinated for me. They all matched perfectly with my classes.

"So have you always been into astronomy?" Noah asked.

I smiled at him. "My whole life."

He nodded, and returned the warm smile. "It shows in your eyes. See you in class, Olivia."

"Bye," I offered, and I waved to Steven on my way out. Like I'd suspected, my shift would be from five to nine on Mondays and Wednesdays, and three to closing, which was ten-thirty, on Saturdays, as well as any special events the observatory hosted. Professor Callander had promised if I thought I could handle more hours after school started, he could always add me into the schedule. The pay was decent, and I'd be making more than plenty to live on. Plus I'd have enough to send some home to Mom and Jilly.

I treated myself to a loaded burger from an on-campus fast food joint on the way back to my dorm, and overall I thought the day was ending up pretty decent. Noah and Steven both were nice enough, and neither felt threatening. It irritated me sometimes, the unconscious measuring of people—mostly guys—that I couldn't seem to help measuring.

I was powerless to stop it. Ever since Kelsy Evans, it's what I did. My conscience always on guard. My intuitions constantly tuned into anything, any one trait a person might have that made me feel trapped. It was as solid in my character now as a handshake. Yet Brax Jenkins had slammed me to the ground, kissed me, and I'd allowed him right into my dorm room. I'd lost my damn marbles for sure.

Tessa was still gone by the time I got back. I had kicked off my boots and was sitting on my bed, eating my messy but delicious bacon cheeseburger when my phone beeped, signaling a text. Probably Mom, wondering why I hadn't called back yet.

I glanced at the small screen on my phone. The name SOUTHIE popped up in all capital letters. Butterflies immediately swarmed inside of me, at the same time my guard shot straight up. *What did he want now?*

Surprised for only a few seconds, not only at the text but at how my heart leaped at seeing it, I shook my head. Brax had apparently sent himself a text from my phone and hi-jacked my number, before bringing it back to me. Then entered his number into my phone. I glanced at the text:

```
Brax: Hey Gracie, how'd the i-view
go?
```

Wrestling with the decision whether to answer or ignore, I just stared at the screen and Brax's words. So taken off guard by his persistence, I couldn't do anything else. I set the phone back down, stared at it. Picked it back up. Set it back down, closed my eyes.

The phone chirped again, and my eyes flashed open. Grabbing the phone, I looked at the screen.

```
Brax: I know you're there, Gracie,
probably staring at the screen. I-
view?
```

I pushed out a frustrated breath.

```
Me: It wasn't an i-view. I already
had the job. I didn't drop my
phone. You pick-pocketed it.

Brax: You dropped it. Opportunity
arose. The job?
Me: Swell. I work Mondays,
Wednesdays, and Saturdays.

Brax: That's a lot of damn work,
Gracie. I think we should meet to
go over our schedule. ☺ And did
you say the word swell? I think I
heard that once on an old fuckin
PopEye cartoon. How old are you,
anyway?
```

Cahtoon. Since no one could see me, I smiled. It was just too hard not to.

```
Me: I'm old-fashioned. My grandpa
says swell all the time. One of my
favorite words. We have no
schedule, Southie. We've known
```

each other less than twenty-four
hours.

Brax: Old-fashioned? What, do you
make jelly and pies, too? And
that's why we need to meet. So
we'll have a schedule. See?

Me: Jelly and pies—yes. Every
season. And I'd think the infamous
Brax Jenkins would already have a
loaded schedule. Why me?

Brax: Infamous, huh? You been
hearin rumors about me, Gracie?
And why not you?

Me: Rumors? Plenty of them. Why
not me? Because I don't play with
players. And I definitely don't
play your game.

Brax: Now I'm a player? An
infamous player, even. With my
very own game. You're a lot braver
on text, Ms. Beaumont.

I squeezed my eyes tightly shut. Maybe he
was right? Would I really be standing in front
of him, boldly having such a conversation?
Probably not. I sighed.

Me: No, I'm not. I feared you'd
shank me earlier. But I had time
to think about it today.

Brax: Shanking you didn't even
cross my mind, Gracie. A few other
things, def, but not that. So
you've been thinking about me
today? Swell. It must've been that
kiss.

I sucked in a breath as my heart sped up.
Why was he so blunt with me?

Me: You just hi-jacked my word.
What kiss?

Brax: Haha, good one Gracie. You
know as well as I do you can't get
that kiss off your mind. I haven't
thought about anything else all
day. I'm infamous for hi-jacking
many things. A word is a first for
me though. I know a seafood joint.
It ain't Boston, that's for damn
sure, but it'll do. Tomorrow
night, after I get back from our
out of towner? Seven? I'll pick
you up.

Holy God, he'd just asked me out. On a
date. The two of us alone. My heart thumped
heavy against my ribs, and my palms grew
sweaty. Why oh why was he asking me out?
And what was I supposed to say? I didn't
know him, at all, and the thought of a date
made me so jittery. I couldn't do it. Brax
would be able to tell I was a bundle of nerves.
He'd eventually figure things out. Figure me
out. No, the less he knew of me, the better. I

moved my fingers over the keyboard of my cell, and noticed that they'd become clammy.

```
Me: Not a good idea, Brax. Thanks,
though.

Brax: C'mon, Gracie. It's dinner.
Not a marriage proposal. And why
not a good idea? You think too
much, maybe.
```

Why not? How about because you're a kappa phi sophomore man slut, for starters. There's just no rational reason for you to want to go to dinner with me. And the bald fact that there's something strangely attractive about you makes me react in ways I don't want to react. And, I don't trust you. How's that for why not?

```
Brax: My clothes just went out of
style. Are you in the bathroom or
something?
```

A grin tugged at my lips. Okay, so he had a sense of humor. Still …

```
Me: There have to be a thousand
other girls you could take to
dinner, Brax.

Brax: There is. But I'm asking
you, Gracie.
```

Staring at the words, I tried to make sense of them. Why did I have to deal with this so soon after arriving to Winston? Never, ever did I expect this. I didn't want this, no, I really didn't. I liked the way he called me Gracie. No one ever called me that. But, he was still a guy, and I didn't know a thing about him. My heart thumped heavy against my chest. *Not all guys are Kelsy Evans, Olivia ...*

Me: If it's because you ran over me on the lawn today and humiliated me, forget it. A mercy date isn't necessary.

Brax: I never mercy date. Ask anyone. And I'm sorry I humiliated you. It wasn't intentional, although I admit I'm glad it happened. The kiss was unavoidable. Just like the next one will be. Seven?

I swallowed hard. *Holy God.*

Me: No way.

Brax: Give me one good reason.

Me: You don't know me.

Brax: That's the reason for a date, see? Another reason.

Me: You have a bike.

Brax: It has a big seat. Don't worry, your skinny ass will fit. Seven?

My mind whirled for a few seconds. All in the space of one day, I had arrived at my first day of college, got plowed into by the school's most infamous bad-boy starting pitcher/womanizer/party animal, and that same said crazed bad-boy had kissed me and was now asking me out. It sounded like a movie, a romantic comedy from the '80s. I'd managed to make it through my senior year of high school despite the harassment and rumors. I'd kept my grades up, secured an academic scholarship, and ... hadn't dated anyone since the incident. Now, the most opposite of opposites had asked me to go out to eat with him. I was insane for even considering it. But I was. Considering it, not insane. Well, maybe both. As long as we just kept things friendly. That was the only way I could make myself comfortable enough to go out with him. Friends only. I had no room in my life right now for anything more than that. I wasn't ready to face anything else. And unless my radar was wrong, Brax Jenkins certainly wasn't looking for a relationship with me. Sex, maybe, but not a relationship. And while part of me balked at the thought of a date, the other part couldn't shake the feeling of Brax's lips on mine. And he did make me laugh, even if I hid it.

Me: Okay. As friends.

Brax: I got plenty of friends, Gracie. See ya at seven.

Me: I'm not stupid, Brax. Your
charm will not turn me into a
blabbering soupy pile of mush like
most of the silly girls running
around campus. Believe it or not,
I'm really and truly here for my
education. My future. I don't have
room in my life for anything else.
Friends only, or I won't go.

Brax: Shit. That's the most you've
said all day. But okay. Friends it
is, although I hope to change your
mind. And I'd never think you were
stupid. L8R

Me: Bye

I closed my phone and set it on the
bedside table. Had I just agreed to go to dinner
with Braxton Jenkins? Why had I said yes?
This was too much distraction. I should text
him back and cancel. I stared at my cell, but
my hand didn't move.

I shook my head. I had a date with the
very guy I'd been warned not once, but twice
about, in the same day. I closed my eyes, and
Brax's image came to mind. Those peculiar
eyes, staring at me in a way no one else ever
had. His mouth against mine, no matter how
brief, had stirred something inside of me. Was
I that starved for attention? Redemption?
Love? In any form, even if just sex? I pushed
it away and heaved a sigh. I'd sleep on it and
see how I felt in the morning.

Friends. That's the way it would stay.
I couldn't afford it not to.

4. Nutcracker

"HOLY SHIT. SERIOUSLY? Have you lost. Your. Fucking. Brains?"

I gave a half-grin, mostly because she was right. "Yeah. Probably so."

Tessa's reaction was nothing less than I'd thought it would be after telling her I was probably meeting Brax for dinner the following night. I'd just finished showering and was lying on my bed in a pair of gym shorts and a tank top, hair wrapped in a blue and white striped towel. We had our own bathroom, which was a nice privilege. Had my scholarship not been so lofty, I would've been sharing with three other girls in a community shower. Depending on the girls, that could be a disgusting disaster. I wasn't obsessive compulsive, but I was definitely a neat person. I had a suspicion, though, that my present roommate was not.

Tessa plopped down onto my bed, and I sank and shifted a little with her weight. She looked at me, dark brows furrowed, then she rolled her eyes. A string of Spanish flowed from her lips. I could tell they were probably pretty decent swear words and it kind of made me wish I'd taken Spanish in high school instead of French. She looked at me again, and shook her head. "Why did he ask you out?"

My laugh was light, barely there, and a little embarrassed. "I don't know. It's nothing, really," I assured her. "Probably the fact that I'm not falling all over him intrigues him?" I sighed. "Don't worry. I insisted it would be on a friend-basis only, or I wouldn't go. I made it perfectly clear I wasn't falling for any of his wily charms or sex lures. I wouldn't even be surprised if he cancelled."

"Ha! As if. And what did he say when you said *friends only*?" Tessa asked. A slight growl was in her throat, and her blue eyes flashed. I almost laughed again. Tessa was definitely a formidable foe. Glad she was on my side.

I shrugged. "He said ... okay." I pushed up, crossed my legs, and leaned against the wall. Actually, he'd said he had plenty of friends, and that he'd hoped to change my mind, but Tessa didn't need to know that. "Seems kinda harmless to me—"

"Why do *you* want to go with *him*?" Tessa interrupted. Her anger was palpable in the room, and part of me knew she was right. Had I lost my mind? I didn't know Brax Jenkins. Not at all. "You could've just said no," Tessa continued. "Or screw you. Something. *Anything*, other than yes!"

God, she was absolutely right. I could've just said no. Why hadn't I? Was it because somehow Brax had put me at ease almost immediately? How had he done that? He was pushy and flirty and definitely not my type. Did I even have a type? Either way, the last thing I wanted was for my roommate to think I was unstable. A baby. Incapable of handling myself, in any situation. I'd keep the fact that I was more than nervous to myself.

I shrugged. "I don't know. I did say no at first, but he convinced me it was just a friendly dinner. He seems all right. Funny. Different." I held up my ring finger, and the band burned a circle where it sat, filled with lies. "Besides. He knows I'm out of commission."

"Oh my freaking god," Tessa said. "I'd forgotten about that." She reached over and thumped my forehead, right in the middle of it. It took me off guard, and I blinked and jerked my head back. My toweled head hit the wall. "As if that will stop him? It probably eggs him on! That's how he gets you! Charm! Olivia! Sincerely. Text him back and cancel."

A sincere laugh popped from my lips and I rubbed my head where she'd flicked me. "It's okay, Tessa. Really. I can handle myself." I smiled and patted her knee. "Trust me. I cold-balled him when he crashed into me on the front lawn. He won't mess with me." I leaned back and looked at her. I pulled my knees up and locked my arms around them, forcing myself to believe the words I was saying. "Brax has a whole university of gorgeous girls at his feet, all willing to do God-knows-what with him. I'm sure he doesn't see me that way. I've made it *clear* I'm not that way. Maybe for once he wants to hang out with someone who isn't drooling all over him." That was my rationale, anyway, and I honestly couldn't believe it was coming out of my mouth. Was I nervous or confident? Which one? I couldn't be both.

Tessa's blue gaze narrowed and bore into mine. Several seconds ticked by. "That's the most retarded thing I've ever heard in my life. Text him back. Cancel. Here, I'll do it. Give me your phone." She reached for it.

"No, Tessa, it's okay. Seriously." Palming my phone to keep it safe, I shook my head. Then I studied her, and gave a hesitant smile. "Have we known each other for less than a day, or has it been a lot, lot longer?"

A small hint of surrender tugged at Tessa's mouth. "Seems like a lot longer." Now she regarded me with a critical eye. "I still think it's a big mistake. Epic. At the very least, please ask him for his medical papers. That famous dick of his has seen a lot of action, Liv. No telling where it's been." She frowned. "Cold hard truth: He wants in your bloomers. Ring or no ring. Game on. Nothing more." She took in a long breath. "His brain … he thinks with his big, ole, egotistical wiener. All guys do. It leads Brax Jenkins around like a magical porn radar wand. It has now honed in on your virginal hands-off hootchie cootchie. Guard it well, chica. He'll snatch it right out from under you like a fucking bandito if you don't."

I sat and stared at my roommate for several seconds in shock before bursting into laughter. I fell over onto my side, buried my face in my pillow, and howled. I couldn't stop! I hadn't laughed that much with anyone, except my family, since ... I couldn't remember when. A long time. Finally, I peeked out. At first, Tessa just stared back, frowning, but then she, too, broke. We laughed until we both cried. Where did she come up with this stuff? Magical porn radar wiener wand? How would I now look Brax in the face and not burst out laughing just thinking about everything Tessa just said?

Finally, she rolled off my bed and changed into a pair of shorts and an oversized High School Musical tee shirt. She plopped down onto her bed and pulled her long hair into a floppy ball on the top of her head. It slid crooked, but she ignored it. Now she was again totally focused on me, and serious.

"All joking aside, Olivia. I know we've only just met, but I like you. You're a little weird, but I like you. And as a girl, roommate, and sister female struggling to make it in this hounddog guy world, please. Watch Braxton Jenkins with both eyes wide open. Don't blink, not even for a second. I don't know him personally, only what I've told you, and that's been enough for me to keep clear of him. Don't let him get to you. You'll only get hurt in the end." She eyed my ring. "And as far as that goes, it might represent a vow to you. But to guys like Brax?" She sighed. "A beacon. Guard you hootchie cootchie, sí, but guard your heart as well."

I nodded. And I knew she was right. "I will, I promise."

Tessa narrowed her eyes. "You gave him the knee to the cahones, huh? Pretty cool. But I think we need a code word. A safe word, maybe. In case things get out of hand and you need me to rescue you, or visa versa. Even just to put yourself at ease in an uncomfortable situation. You can think of it and it'll make you feel better. Or text it to me, along with a location."

I pulled my towel turban off, and shook my damp hair loose. "I'm sure he'll keep his magical porn radar wand to himself, and I seriously doubt I'll need a safe word, but okay. It's nice to know you'll come screeching around the corner in your little Jetta to save me. Or at least make me feel better. What's the word?"

Tessa put her hands on her hips and scowled. "I could just use your big old Army tank truck out there and run Brax's cocky ass over with it," she said. She tapped her forefinger to her temple, and paced our small dorm room. "Hmm. Let me think. Safe word. Safe word." After a few moments, she stopped, snapped her fingers, and her face lit up. "Got it. Nutcracker!"

I grabbed my wide-toothed comb from my bedside table and pushed it through my hair, eyeing Tessa. "Okay. Nutcracker it is. Safe word. Got it."

"Good. Don't forget it. I swear it'll work. Now I've gotta get some sleep. I promised I'd meet my parents at sixfuckingshootme o'clock in the morning to go to Cole's baseball game—out of season, might I add. If I don't rest, I'll be a total bitch the whole day. Plus, Brax is pitching. I'll keep my eye on the horn dog. 'Night, Liv." She clicked her lamp off and shuffled under the covers.

"'Night, Tessa,' I answered. I turned my lamp off, too, and tried to go to sleep. Instead, I laid there, thinking, my mind wandering aimlessly around.

My first night, on my own, away from home. New sounds, new job, new people.

One new person in particular. Completely unexpected.

Brax's image crept into my mind, behind my eyelids, and there he was, almost as if I was holding up a picture of him in the dark. I could see him plain as day, looking down at me with those ghostly blue eyes as I lay on my back in the grass. Those eyes, that unusual scarred face. And those perfect lips cradling mine for a nanosecond. His crude but funny accent. His painful expression as my knee connected with his family jewels. The whole day flashed before me then, from the moment I left my home, until Tessa clicked off her lamp. Especially all the stuff in between. Just then my phone vibrated, and it startled me. I grabbed it off my nightstand.

SOUTHIE flashed in the window. Guilt, like I'd been caught doing something wrong, pinched my insides. Guilt for what? Thinking about him? Maybe he'd had time to think about it—about me, and was canceling.

I flipped open the phone, and the green backlight made me squint. I blinked a few times, braced myself for his rejection, then focused on the words.

```
Brax: Did you change your mind
yet?
```

He wasn't rejecting me. He hadn't changed his mind. This was so crazy.

```
Me: Yes. Just now. After you woke
me up.

Brax: Liar. You weren't asleep
sweetheart. You were lying there
thinking about me. And my charm.
And that kiss. So are we still on?

Me: I'm not convinced Winston is
large enough to contain your ego.
I had lights out and was trying to
go to sleep. Yes, we're still on.
Unless you wake me up again.
```

Brax: Winston held my ego last semester. It's cool. Glad to hear you haven't chickened out on me. What are you wearin'?

Me: I think your ego grows daily. I'm anything but a chicken. And only stalkers and weirdos ask girls they've just met what they're wearing at one in the morning.

Brax: Your scientist cowgirl mind is in the fuckin gutter, Gracie, which interests me. What I meant was, what are you wearin' tomorrow. Not a chicken, you say? That gives me things to think about.

Fahkin' gutta. His accent, even in text, rang heavy in my ears. Strangely enough, it brought a smile to my lips.

Me: Sorry. I'll try to keep my mind out of the gutta. Jeans and blouse. Don't think about my non-chickeny ways, please. Ever.

Brax: You makin fun of my southie, Gracie? I like that. Blouse? Who are you, I Love Fuckin Lucy?

A giggle squeaked past my lips, and I slapped my free hand over my mouth to stifle it. My eyes shot to Tessa's side of the room, and I listened. Still asleep.

Me: Yeah, I wear blouses. Why, is there a dress code?

Brax: No code, just curious. Haven't heard the word blouse since 1940. Right along with swell. Now go to bed. Stop texting me in the middle of the night, Gracie, for Christ's sake. I gotta pitch tomorrow.

Me: You mean today. Happy pitching. 'Night Brax.

Brax: I'm impressed. Happy pitching vs Good luck. I like that. Cuz it ain't luck, I promise you. Wicked skill. 'Night, Gracie.

Me: Ego. Epic. 'Night.

I closed my phone and set it aside, and stared at the ceiling in the dark. A smile tugged at my mouth. God, he was crude. But funny. The way I clicked with him left me speechless. Like Tessa, had I only known him for a day? I had to wonder, though, how many other girls he'd texted before he'd reached my name. Okay. *Damn*. He was charming. And I'd be lying to say his promises of kisses and more wasn't just plain sexy.

Get a grip, Beaumont. Remember. He's a player. This is what he does. He's probably been up half the night texting a dozen other girls and flirting their panties off. Buck up and get real. Or do you need a reminder of what kind of harm guys really can do to girls?

After that thorough scolding from my inner self, I sighed, kicked the covers off because I was a little warm in the room, and closed my eyes. My inner self, and Tessa, was right. Jesus, don't let Brax Jenkins get under my skin. Take him at face value as a womanizer. It doesn't make him a bad person. Just don't let your heart get involved. *You're not special, Olivia. You're just another challenge. Keep it friends-only, and you'll be safe. You've got plans. Remember? Plans that don't include mending a broken heart over some university loverboy.*

With that last inner self advice, even though I thought it a bit harsh, I felt my lids grow heavy, and I drifted off to sleep.

It felt as if I'd only been asleep ten minutes when Tessa's alarm clock from her iPhone screeched. In the dark I heard Tessa as she fumbled around for the phone, knocked it on the floor, and grumbled.

"Jesus God!" she griped. "Sorry, Liv."

My eyes felt gritty, but I was used to getting up early. Just not used to being kept up until three in the morning. "It's okay, I'm awake."

"Why? It's only sixsshutthefuckinrooster-up o'clock in the morning." She yawned and flipped on her light. I squinted over at her. The floppy ball on her head was down by her ear. "You got something going on?" she asked.

I stretched and sat up. "No. I'm going to go up to the rooftop and check out the pre-dawn celestial view with my scope."

Tessa stopped pulling her hair loose from the ball, shook it out, and stared at me. "That's the weirdest thing anyone's ever said to me. Ever."

I laughed. "It's okay Tessa. I'm a Geek and proud of it."

"You're not a Geek. You're a weirdo freak of nature. Go back to bed."

Already wearing a pair of plaid boxers, I pulled a long-sleeved tee over my head, a pair of socks, and my boots. I grabbed my telescope bag, stood and grinned. "See ya—"

The flash from Tessa's iPhone camera went off, making me squint. "What are you doing?" I asked.

Tessa grinned. "Classic dork Geek in plaid shorts and cowboy boots? I'll show this to Brax today. You'll be safe, then, that's for damn sure."

"Nutcracker!" I hollered.

Tessa busted out laughing.

I grabbed a wrench from my toolbox, left my roommate and slipped out into the still-quiet corridor. I made my way to the stairs and climbed to the rooftop exit. Outside, the air hung heavy with humidity, like a sopping wet blanket draped over me. From past rooftop experiences, I knew I'd better stick something in the doorway, just in case it locked behind me. I jammed the wrench between the door and jamb on the ground, and found a clearing not too far from the exit. Quickly, as the darkness was fading fast, I set up my pod and attached my scope. The pre-dawn sky was breathtaking; stars littered the heavens, and I zoomed in on several. The thought crossed my mind: What would Brax think of it?

I pulled my eye from the scope and shook my head. Breathed. Then focused again. The moment my eye touched the eyepiece, a shooting star blazed a glittery line of dust, then faded. My mouth pulled into a content smile. I never grew tired of meteors. Ever. Was it a sign, this one particular star, its tail ablaze and zerping across the sky? What had given me this, I don't know, sort of peace and confidence that less than twenty-four hours ago had been absent for the past year? Was it Tessa and her ridiculous yet easy-going camaraderie? Was it finally being away from Jasper, from Kelsy?

Or was it Brax's cocky, this-is-what-you-get attitude that made me not so skittish? Or rather, the promise of intimacy between us? He seemed to have a way of putting me at ease either way, and it had taken him less than a day. Pretty impressive. Despite his flirtations, I didn't feel threatened by him. Not at all. And I liked that feeling. It almost seemed … foreign. Yet it was a piece of my old self, pre-Kelsy, that I'd truly missed.

The afternoon dragged, so I did what I could to pass the time before Brax would pick me up. My appetite faded after the apple cinnamon muffin and pumpkin spiced latte I had at the on-campus coffee house. I went for a run; stopped at the massive library and scoured the astronomy section. I also took another tour of the observatory, climbing to the platform and checking out the view, and spoke a minute with Steven. I liked him, and already I could tell he'd be easy to work with. None of it, though, took my mind completely off what was to come. And off the thought that I'd consciously made the decision to go out with a womanizer who bluntly promised to kiss me again. Insane. I'd lost my mind.

My thoughts drifted. It wasn't like me at all to be so distracted. Despite telling myself constantly that dinner with Brax was nothing more than, well, dinner with Brax, I still had butterflies. The jitters had taken over me, and I willed them away. *Go. The hell. Away.* Doubt infused with my too-easily-won confidence. Maybe this was all a mistake after all, just like Tessa had warned. Maybe I should cancel. Maybe I shouldn't.

By five, I called home, talked to Mom and Jilly, and told them about my new job. I didn't mention Brax or my dinner date. Lord, no. Talk about poking a stick in a hornet's nest. Telling them would only have led to a ton of questions I wasn't prepared to answer. After the hell of senior year, and the toll it'd taken on my mom, I wasn't about to stress her out right now. One day after getting here? No way. And if my brothers found out? They'd show up and cause a huge scene. I could handle myself, and I was pretty sure I could handle Brax. I had to. Because a Beaumont family scene was definitely something I wanted to contain. Besides, having a friend like Brax might be pretty useful after all. For sure there wouldn't be any other guys bothering me, and if they did, Brax could easily put them in their place. That thought gave me a little comfort. Not a lot, but some.

Finally, I twisted my hair into the usual braid, pulled on a pair of relatively hole-less low-riders, a floral baby doll blouse with capped sleeves, and a pair of brown leather sandals. Just as I'd finished brushing my teeth, my phone chirped. I found it on my bed. SOUTHIE. Against my will, my insides leaped. It was only 6:15. I flipped the phone open.

```
Brax: Bring a jacket or a long-
sleeved shirt or you'll freeze
your ass off. And shades to
reflect bugs. I got an extra
helmet. Have you thought about me
all day?
```

```
Me: Shades and jacket, I'll grab
them from my truck. Helmet,
definitely. I value my brain. And
yes, I thought of you, but only
when I pulled on my blouse. Did
you win your game?
```

The minute the words were sent, I'd regretted them.

Brax: Now you're comin' around, cowgirl. You ready? Yes, we won.

Me: Swell. That's not what I meant. And yes, I am.

Brax: Good. Get your ass down here. I'm starvin.

Stahvin. I smiled and shook my head. Why was he so early? Quickly, I grabbed my patchwork slouch purse, dropped my cell into it, grabbed my key card and dropped it in, too. From my desk I picked up my room and truck keys, let myself out, and locked the door behind me. Butterflies slammed against my stomach the whole walk down, and it irritated me. It wasn't just anxiousness about seeing Brax. It was just the idea of going out with a guy. Any guy. And the closer I got to the parking lot, the more nervous I became. The more I wanted to turn around, run and hide. No matter if it was just a friendly dinner, that I was now a freshman in college and not a dumb high school teenager. Why couldn't I just be calm, cool, collected? I willed those qualities to fall on me, and fast. To infuse in my DNA and make me full of confidence. After a few deep breaths, I had it together. I crossed the common room to the doorway, and pushed it open. And those newly summoned qualities fled the moment I laid eyes on him.

Braxton Jenkins straddled his motorcycle just in front of the walkway. His helmet was off, shades on. Faded jeans, the bottoms cuffed. Black boots. White tee shirt. Black leather jacket. I couldn't see his eyes, but I knew the moment he saw me. A wide, white smile split his face in two.

The butterflies returned, full force and rabid, with teeth gnashing.

Holy God. I couldn't do this.

Beaumont! Breathe, girl! Nutcracker! Nutcracker!

The entire silly conversation with Tessa from the night before poured into my brain and instantly calmed me. Just thinking the safe word made me smile. I couldn't help it. It was just so damn *funny*. Anyway, it eased my nerves. I walked up to Brax, calm and cool. Friends. Nothing more.

"Hey," I said. "So you won. How'd the pitching go?"

Whatever expression his eyes held was hidden behind those shades. "Bitchin' as always. We spanked 'em good. Nice blouse there, Gracie."

I smiled, and his face launched into another heart-stopping grin. I inclined my head toward my truck. "Thanks. Let me grab my glasses and jacket."

Brax said nothing, and I felt his eyes score a jagged blazing hole into my back as I walked toward my truck. It unnerved me a little, but I pushed it aside. I opened the door, and leaned in across the seat to grab my faded denim jacket and shades. Jamming the key in and locking it, I headed back toward Brax and his bike. His eyes were still hidden, but I knew his gaze followed me. I shrugged into my jacket, which, at this time of evening in August I highly doubted I'd freeze my ass off without. "Ready," I said. I slipped my bag cross-ways over my head and shoulder, and plopped my keys in.

"Come here, Gracie," Brax said.

My heart slammed. I stepped closer.

Brax reached behind him and retrieved a helmet. He slipped it over my head and snugged it down tightly, tucking my braid inside. I was glad he still wore his shades as his face drew closer and secured the strap under my chin. Those eyes, so close, would've made me squirm in discomfort. I stared at myself in their reflection, and at his fingers nimbly moving with the black nylon strap. I noticed a few scars I hadn't seen before, small nicks that had turned silvery white with age. Definitely a roughened face, yet I had a hard time looking away. He smelled good; recently showered, light cologne. I drew a deep breath. Then another. It barely worked to settle me. My lungs just kept filling up with … *him*. Unavoidably, my eyes dropped to that mouth. Another breath …

"Nervous?" he asked. One side of his mouth tipped upward and again, I noticed how perfectly shaped his lips were. Perfect lips set in an imperfect and scarred face. The balance between the two was breathtaking. The grin he wore stretched the scar that dipped below his eye, beneath his sunglasses. One of many, and I was curious to know how he'd gotten each one of them.

I slipped on my shades. *Of course I'm nervous! I don't know you but I'm about to get on the back of your motorcycle and leave the school!* Two could play the eye-hiding game. "You've obviously forgotten about my knee and how it introduced itself to your crotch. I'm just used to live horses, Brax. Not horse power. How safe of a driver are you?"

He gave me a full grin then, and all of his straight white teeth showed. "Wicked safe. Get on, Sunshine." He pulled his helmet on.

As I moved around to the back, Brax's muscular legs braced against the ground and steadied the bike. I placed a hand on his shoulder and threw my leg over the seat. Finding the foot pegs, I settled in, scooching as far away from Brax's backside as I could. Tessa's childish words about his magical porn radar wiener wand and my hootchie cootchie burst into my mind, and I pursed my lips together hard to keep from laughing out loud. Why had she put that vision in my head? Crazy fool. And here I thought I was mature. I must be just as juvenile as Tessa since it made me laugh so much. Physics and astronomy? Got it. Say the word doo-doo and I fall apart like a six year old. Great.

Now, what the heck was I supposed to do with my hands? I felt behind me, searching for a bar, a thick chunk of leather seat. Anything to hold onto. There was nothing.

Brax chuckled, grasped my one arm with his hand and pulled it around his waist. Then, the other. He secured both of my arms against his abdomen with one hand, and held them there. My arms, pinned by his heavy one. Heat flooded my body. A hard, ripped washboard stomach pressed against my fingertips through his thin white tee shirt. My insides squeezed, I pinched my eyes shut, and nerves made me shudder. I thought for a second I'd back out. Then, his arm tightened against mine, and I couldn't.

I gulped. The movement of it made my chin strap bob.

Brax laughed. "Hold on tight, Gracie. And don't let go."

5. Gripped

THE WIND PUSHED AGAINST my face as I peered around Brax's shoulder. We cruised through the tree-lined campus avenues, surrounded by century-old brick buildings, and I couldn't help noticing all the looks being thrown our way. I had no doubt people wondered what new stupid girl Brax Jenkins had lured into his web of womanizing charm. Well, the joke was on them. I wasn't lured. And I wasn't a stupid girl. I was fully aware of the dangerous situation I'd placed myself in by accepting a friendly dinner date. But I had it under control. *Dummy. You should've never agreed to go. Should've never let him in the dorm for that matter. You know good and well he sets you on fire like no one else ever has. Friendly dinner date my ass. Now what are you going to do?*

Brax's strong hand pressed my arms tighter against his stomach.

I swallowed. Hard. Maybe control wasn't exactly the right word. Determined? I was stuck now. On this friend-only dinner … excursion. Maybe it'd be the last one.

Once we hit the main street, Brax picked up speed, and so did my heart. He had both hands on the bars, and I didn't need him to encourage me to hold on tighter. I squeezed my arms around him. Warmth from his skin seeped through his jacket, his tee shirt, straight into my arms. His abs were ridiculously ripped and scored with muscle. Before I'd known what was happening, my knees were squeezing his thighs.

Brax picked up speed, and I found myself holding my breath. My brothers and I had grown up with dirt bikes, and we'd played on them our whole lives. But this was different. Fast. Exhilarating.

I was positive the driver had a lot to do with it.

Soon Brax slowed as we cruised through first one small town, then the next, passing local gas stations and grocery markets. I stared at Brax's back, his broad shoulders. A piece of his neck showed, between helmet and jacket collar, and again I noticed the black ink tattooed into his skin. I wondered what they all were, what they meant. As I peered over his shoulder again, I saw his hands gripping the bike bars, and the letters inked into his knuckles. The inked band at his wrist that barely showed beneath the cuff of his jacket. Brax Jenkins was truly an enigma. No doubt the same things intrigued every single girl he'd had on the back of his bike. Typical tattooed bad-boy. Every girl's dream—even if they never told anyone. Was I included? Apparently so.

As we rode down the main street of a small town called Campton, there were business establishments, mom-n-pop restaurants, and bars on both sides of the road. Brax pulled into a place called Tulley's Chowder House, and it had a big white clam painted on the side of a faded blue stained concrete building. He downshifted, pulled into a parking spot, and rolled to a stop. Killing the engine, Brax braced the bike with his legs. When I swung off he followed, knocking the kickstand with his boot heel, and his movements were as smooth and natural as his sly smile. He pulled his shades off, then his helmet, and turned to me. Dark curls hung in careless disarray. I nearly fell onto the concrete. I wasn't sure I'd ever get used to those eyes. They were secretive and clear and fathomless. What in the world had I been thinking, agreeing to come tonight? Brax Jenkins, even on my very best day, was way, way out of my league. Even as a friend.

That blue gaze regarded me as he slipped my glasses off my eyes, then unfastened my strap. Not wanting him to think I was, in fact, a chicken, I watched him as intently as he watched me. A small smile quirked his lip as he studied my face.

"You always had them freckles on your nose there, Gracie?"

Stupid freckles. They made me look like a child. I shrugged, and pulled off my helmet and handed it to him. "For as long as I can remember, I guess."

Brax hung it on the handlebar with his, then turned a focused gaze on me. "Are they just on your nose, or everywhere?" His mouth pulled into another sly, sly grin.

I narrowed my gaze and noticed his black and blue eye was a shade lighter today. "My mom would say, don't be so damn fresh." The freckles were just on my nose, as far as I could tell. But he didn't need to know the character of my anatomy. The hidden parts, anyway. "And you can ease up with all the flirting or I'll take a cab back to Winston."

Brax stared at me, then laughed. "Swear to God, Gracie, you're killin' me. Fresh? Blouse? Swell?" He laughed again and shook his head. The movement made his hair fall over his eye, and he jerked his head to move it. "I feel like I'm in some, I don't know, fuckin' nineteen forties Honeymooner's sitcom." His eyes lit on me, steadied, stared. "My charm is something I can't control, Sunshine. Don't take it so personal. It's all in good fun so just roll with it. You aren't callin' a cab, so let's go eat. You hungry?"

I watched him for a second or two before answering. At least he admitted it: Don't take it personally. He was flirty with all girls. Okay, I could handle that. I had a brother just like him. Brax wanted me to roll with it? I could roll; as long as I didn't feel closed in or threatened, everything would be okay. And so far, strangely enough, it was okay. Finally, I nodded. "Stahved."

A throaty chuckle escaped Brax's mouth, and he placed his hand at the small of my back. "What are you, crackin' wise, makin' fun of my Southie again? Let's go."

I smiled, and let him guide me to the front door. "Now I feel like I'm in some gangster movie, at a barber shop slash money laundering joint, slash ... horse gambling ring," I teased. *Teased*? Brax Jenkins had now coaxed me into teasing?

Brax rounded on me and held the door open. His mouth lifted at one corner, in a half-cocked, carefree smirk. "Hey, I know that barber shop. My friend's mother's Uncle Jackie runs it. It's is as reputable as they come, that place. And I know you wanna say *bahba* like me, but try to refrain yourself, if at all possible. No high-jackin' my Southie, sweetheart. I'm original."

I shook my head and walked through the door he held open. "Holy smokes, it'll be hard, but I'll try."

Brax laughed again, and was still chuckling when the hostess walked up to us. She was a pretty blonde, tall, with breasts she was obviously proud of since they popped out of the top of her v-neck shirt. Her gaze skipped over me completely and landed straight onto Brax.

"Just two?" she asked. Her eyes softened as she looked at him.

I felt Brax's hand leave my back. I couldn't help but lift my gaze to his.

And there it was; I saw it. Right before my eyes. Way different than the way he looked at me. The womanizing glint I'd been warned about. The cocky, devouring smile he gave the girl as he checked her out from head to toe. "For now," he said to her. "You new? I've never seen you here before, sweetheart."

I stood there, intrigued and scathing at the same time. Well, maybe not scathing, but ... something. Brax's flirting was going on right in front of me. And the hostess was flirting right back, as if I wasn't standing there, with him. Sexual tension rolled off him. Off of her. I could feel it where I stood, and it shocked and irritated me.

Really, though, I wasn't with him. We were there as friends—if you wanted to even call it that. I'd just met him myself. But *she* didn't know that. Which made her rude and tasteless in my book. But who was I to judge? Again. I'd been fairly warned.

Finally, the hostess passed me a quick glance. The look on her face revealed surprise, probably at why Brax was even with me. Maybe I should tell her we're brother and sister?

"This way," she said. She wore a snug pair of jeans, low-waisted, and her tight-fitting v-neck also rose just enough over her waist to flash tanned skin beneath. I followed behind her, and noticed the extra twist she put into her walk.

What girls did to get guys' attention was idiotic. If only they realized how ridiculous they looked. Stupid, stupid girls.

I threw a quick glance over my shoulder at Brax. His gaze was fixed on her backside. In some kind of trance. Probably his magical porno radar wiener wand was on full alert. I almost snorted out loud at the image that thought conjured.

To be honest, I was glad the whole flirty, bootie-shaking scene transpired in front of me, and right up front. That uneasy, giddy feeling I'd had earlier faded almost instantly. It made me feel very much like an idiot. Seriously. Brax? Attracted to me? And even if he was, it wouldn't have gone anywhere. My choice. It sounded ridiculous in my head. I now felt more relaxed, like I could be myself. No second guessing. Brax was what he was, and he'd claimed nothing less from the very beginning.

The hostess stopped at a booth, and I slid in. Brax pushed in across from me, and she handed him both menus. She smiled, and I could tell she was pooching her lips out so Brax would fix on them. "Enjoy your meal."

Under my lashes, I watched Brax's eyes follow her sexy sauntering figure as she left. Before he caught me looking, I snatched my gaze back to my bag, which I lifted off my shoulder and set aside. When I looked up, he was studying me. I smiled at him and held out my hand for a menu. His eyes narrowed, then he handed me one.

Setting the flat, two-sided piece of laminated plastic on the table, I started scanning the choices. "So what's good?" I asked, and looked up. "Since this is your place."

An intense glint flickered in the depths of those odd blue eyes as he regarded me. "Well." He set his menu aside and rested his forearms on the table. He leaned toward me. "As I said, this ain't Boston. You won't find any decent North Atlantic Scrod, that's for fuckin' sure." His grin was lop-sided. "Chowder's not bad. Lobster? Nah. Fried oysters, they'll do for central Texas."

I felt my lips pull at the corners. "Were you an extra in *Good Will Hunting*? I'm just asking." I widened my eyes, extra-like, star-struckish. "Oh my God, do you know Matt Damon? Mark Wahlberg?" I closed my eyes and sighed, then opened them and rapid-fire blinked. "Tell me you know Ben Affleck. Swear to God, I'll die right here in this booth if you do."

Brax stared at me, then threw his head back and laughed. Loud. He wiped his eyes with his knuckles. "Okay, smart ass. At least you got good taste. No, I don't know them." He leaned closer and raised his brows. "But I know someone who does."

"Swell!"

Brax rubbed his chin with his hand, and shook his head as his eyes found mine. "What are you? Bednobs and Broomsticks? Mary Poppins?"

I pressed my lips together and shrugged. "Maybe."

Our waiter showed up then, a cute guy, a little on the short and stocky side with blond hair, our age. He gave a nod to Brax. "Hey, man. How's it goin'?"

Brax looked at me. "Swell. Thanks for askin'."

I shook my head.

"Drink, ma'am?" the waiter asked me.

"Um, tea with ginger if you have it, thanks," I said.

Brax looked at me, lifted one brow. "Same."

The waiter left to get our drinks, and Brax leaned back and hooked his arms on the back of his booth. It pulled the material of his tee shirt tight across his chest muscles. He eyed me closely. "I'm pretty sure I've never been just friends with a ginger tea drinking virgin before. I kinda like it."

Anger rushed to my throat and cheeks. I glanced around, then back to Brax. "Would you mind not announcing it to the whole restaurant?"

The throaty chuckle that came from Brax was contagious, despite my horror at how loud he'd just stated my alleged virginity.

"Okay, I'm sorry. I won't say it out loud again," he said.

I frowned. "Make sure that you don't. And stop thinking about it, while you're at it."

His mouth pulled up. "No promises there, Sunshine."

Our waiter returned, and I ordered fried oysters and fries. Brax ordered the same, along with the chowder. *Chowdah.* The waiter left, and Brax leaned back.

"So tell me about this ranch life of yours, Gracie," he said. "You live far from here?" *Fahr.*

I drew a long pull of tea through my straw, and it was sweetened, with a hint of ginger, and perfect. "About three and half hours south. A little town, Jasper. Typical small-town Texas." I shrugged. "Not much to tell, really. We broke horses for ranchers—"

"We?" Brax interrupted.

I nodded. "Me, my mom, my Grandpa Jilly, and my three brothers."

"No father?"

Fahtha. I shook my head. "He left a long time ago. When I was three. I don't remember him at all." Well, only flashes of memory. Nothing worth telling, and more likely than not they were fixed memories from the handful of pictures Mom kept in her top dresser drawer.

Something passed in Brax's eyes then; I wasn't sure what it was. A glint of sadness? I couldn't tell. "Damn shame," is all he said.

Then he leaned forward, his tattooed hands rested on the table. "So let me get this straight. You get a horse. A wild fucking horse. And you get on it. And this horse, he runs around, bucking and crazy as all holy gates of hell, and throws your skinny little ass all over the place until what?"

The lights overhead were getting hot, so I slipped out of my denim jacket and set it beside me. I shrugged. "Until he either throws me off or stops bucking and follows my command."

For a split second, Brax's gaze softened, smoldered, just like it had when he'd flirted with that hostess. Fleeting, it faded quickly. "And how exactly do you make a wild horse ten times your size follow your command?"

"Simple. I squeeze my thighs around him."

A very slow, very deliberate, and very wily and sexy smile broadened Brax Jenkins' intriguing face. He laced his fingers together, and leaned forward. "Is that so, Gracie?" His voice, accent, was low, raspy. Ridiculously sexy. Totally fascinating.

Nutcracker!

I thought it, unable to help myself, then I smothered a laugh with my hand. Even though I felt the heat rising in my skin from my blunder and Brax's insinuation, just saying the safe word in my head helped. I didn't feel caged in or threatened. All I could feel was laughter bubbling up inside of me, all stemmed from that ridiculous conversation with Tessa, and the safe word. My eyes began to water, and Brax just looked at me, cocked his head, and grinned.

"Did I say something funny, Gracie?" he asked.

The waiter and our food arrived with perfect timing. Even knowing what Brax was doing—which was some serious flirting—it didn't really seem to matter now. It was like there was a separate part of my brain that wanted to do exactly what it wanted to do. Without my consent. And I think whatever it was, it made me lose all coherent sensibility. Despite the past year, Brax seemed to have the ability to make me drop my guard. No wonder so many women fell at his feet. The boy had serious talent. But I had a safe word. And it had worked. And I wasn't going to be one of his throwbacks. Not me.

"Do you know every time you get embarrassed, your skin turns pink?" Brax said. His lips curled around the fried oyster he'd popped into his mouth.

I tamped down my embarrassment, took a few bites, and downed some tea. "Do you realize you have no filter whatsoever?"

His brow lifted. "Pure skill." He dug into his chowder.

I nodded. "Really?" Inclining my head toward his hands, I asked the question that had been burning in my mind. "What do those mean?"

Something in Brax's eyes shifted, hazed, and I immediately regretted asking the question. With one thumb, he grazed the tattooed knuckles of the opposite hand. He shrugged, and lifted his profound stare to mine. "I don't know. I was just a kid, Gracie. A stupid kid thinking I had something to prove."

It was then and there I glimpsed a vulnerability I hadn't really noticed before in Brax's confident mannerisms. I couldn't begin to put a finger on it, but it was there, evident, still the same. Strangely enough, it almost reminded me of ... mine. I wanted to ask more, but something kept it inside of me. Those light blue eyes, rimmed by dark lashes, regarded me closely, almost as if anticipating I'd ask something. Anything. He waited, and held my gaze so long, I almost couldn't look away.

Before I could say anything, though, two guys slid into the booth with us. The one who sat beside me draped his arm on the bench rest behind my head. He regarded me with a hooded gaze.

"Bro, what's up?" the one beside Brax said.

I looked at Brax, and he bumped knuckles with the guy. The flirtatious look in Brax's eyes faded, replaced with something else. Arrogance? "Kenny, Jake," he said. He inclined his head toward me. "Olivia Beaumont."

I gave each one a quick glance. "Hi," I said to both. My internal human measuring device turned on, and immediately I could tell both guys made me feel cagey.

The one guy beside me, Kenny, lifted my braid. "We're Brax's frat brothers. He's just too rude to tell you that part. So, Olivia Beaumont. Where're you from?"

I shot a fast look at Brax, and I was surprised to see his eyes fastened on Kenny's hand—on my braid.

"Are all the girls from your hometown cute little things with freckles and braids?" Jake asked.

Kenny actually lifted my braid to his nose and sniffed it. "Or just you?"

Trapped by the small space of the booth, panic rose in my throat. Broken memories from the year before slammed into me, and pure fear and reaction shrugged over my shoulders like a sopping wet blanket. I reared my elbow back to ram him in the gut, but Brax's words stopped me.

"Get your fuckin' hand outta her hair, Kenny, before I break your fuckin' face against this table here," Brax said. His feral eyes flashed fury. He didn't blink, breathe, or flinch. He just stared fire at Kenny. It was the most intense, intimidating look I'd ever seen. On anyone. And every one of my brothers had a fierce look when they wanted. Brax's voice was stone-cold dead serious. Lethal and chilling.

It shocked me. My earlier reservations returned full force. Yes. Brax had demons. He hid them well, but not well enough. I was looking at them right now, and they were staring back. Hard.

Kenny dropped my braid fast, scooted away from me, and held up his hands in defense. "Whoa, bro, take it easy," he said.

"What the hell's gotten into you?" Kenny coughed. "Yeah, me and Jake was just riding by and saw your bike, thought we'd see what you were doing." He looked at me. "Sorry, Olivia. Just playin' around is all."

"No problem," I answered quietly, although I didn't believe him, not for a second. My heart pounded, and I struggled to keep them from noticing my breath coming faster. When I looked back at Brax, his eyes were still locked onto Kenny, angry and furious. Why, I wondered?

Kenny's lip curled in a not-so-attractive grin at Brax. "All right, we'll leave you two lovebirds alone. Jenks, I'll let Collins know we, uh," he glanced at me, "bumped into you two. Jake, let's bounce."

They both slid from the booth, and Jake glanced at Brax. "Kick ass pitchin' today, bro. You smoked the hell out of it."

"Yeah, I know," Brax said, still eyeing Kenny.

Without another word, Jake and Kenny left.

Brax's gaze stared them down until they were out of sight.

"What was that all about?" I asked calmly. I hope Brax hadn't noticed the sheer dread Kenny had caused in me; I didn't want to make a big deal about it. That would only raise questions, and I wasn't willing to give any answers. So I thought making light of it all and hiding the fact that I'd almost had a panic attack was the best route. "I thought he was going to start chewing on my hair." I laughed softly, forced, and it felt as fake as it actually was. "I was almost compelled to use my safe word."

For a second, Brax didn't respond. Those ghostly eyes were hardened, terrifying. Then, he took a visible deep breath in, closed his eyes briefly, and when they opened again and focused on me, they were clear, bright, and most of the fury had disappeared. But it was still there, the anger. Simmering in those odd blue orbs. "Kenny's a fuckin' prick, Gracie. Excuse my French, but he is."

Before I thought about it, I'd reached across the table and grazed his knuckles with my fingertips. "It's okay. Really. Forget about it."

Just that fast, Brax's eyes went from clear to smoky gray-blue. The cocky sly half-grin was back. He looked down at my fingers, then back to me. "What's your safe word?"

I lowered my hand and met his gaze square-on. "It wouldn't be a safe word if I told you, would it?"

A slow, wolfish smirk curled his sexy lips up in the corners. "You touch me like that again, Gracie Beaumont, and you're gonna need a helluva lot more than a safe word." He leaned back and studied me for several uncomfortable moments, and his eyes never left mine, never wavered, not once. "Now how 'bout you tell me why you got that wild ass look in your eye when Kenny grabbed your hair?"

6. Trouble

As those severe blue eyes examined me, awaiting my response, I realized something extremely important about Brax. His perception level was way higher than I'd thought. He'd seemed so occupied in staring down his obnoxious frat brother that I hadn't noticed the depth of intensity in which he simultaneously studied me. That relentless scrutiny focused, measured, weighed as he stared, and while those ethereal eyes promoted his peculiar looks I immediately knew one thing for absolute sure. Brax Jenkins was not an empty-headed, popular, tattooed man slut of a baseball jock. He was exceptionally clever. Intelligent. I could see it in his watchful, alert gaze.

But I was smart, too, and wasn't about to reveal my secrets to a virtual stranger. No matter how oddly drawn to him I was. Maybe, with a little luck, my apprehension could be successfully masked, because the less of my horrific senior year in high school anyone knew, the better. Pasting a smile to my face, I straightened in the booth, fixed a confident stare to my gaze and answered his question. "I told you, I'm not like the typical giggly partying flirtatious college girls you usually meet. I just don't like strange guys crowding my personal space, is all."

Brax studied me for several seconds, his eyes fixed and concentrating on mine. I knew he was trying to figure me out, and I hoped with all mighty hope he failed. Finally, he ducked his head, as if trying to get a better view from my chin up. "All right, Gracie," he said in an even, low tone. Then his crooked mouth lifted at the corner, puckering the skin around the scar on his cheek. It made him look fierce and sexy at the same time. He leaned toward me, eyes never leaving mine. "I crowded you."

Although I made a conscious effort not to fidget under Brax's scrutiny, I couldn't help the flush of fire that raced up my neck and pooled in my cheeks. The heat pouring through the pores of my skin actually stung, so I knew I was probably beet red. And by the way Brax's grin lifted a little higher at the corner, he hadn't missed it, either. Enjoying it a little too much, I'd even say. I did my best to shrug off my reaction, and drew a calming breath in, nice and slow. "I guess I just don't feel threatened by you," I smiled, "since we're only friends and all." Stranger yet, I actually *didn't* feel threatened.

Brax's smile didn't fade. "And all, huh?"

I lifted a shoulder. "Just a figure of speech." I shifted in my booth seat, tucking my foot under my bottom, determined to shift gears from myself. "So do you have any brothers or sisters?"

Something faint, ghostly, crossed Brax's features. He didn't look away from me, but I saw the change, and it reminded me of a fast storm brewing in the ocean. Bright and sunny one second, clouds swirling overhead the next. He rapped his fingertips against the table between us, making a thudding sound. "Three brothers, one sister," he said. *Brotha. Sista.* Then, the confident arrogance was back, and his eyes cleared. "They're older, doing their own thing." His jutted his chin. "I'm what you'd call the black sheep of the family."

My brows knitted as I gave him a puzzled look. "Not too black if you've earned yourself a baseball scholarship. Besides. You may be charming but you can't charm your way through academics." I pursed my lips. "I'm starting to think you're really just a geek beneath a tattooed gangster disguise." A seriously phenomenal disguise, too, I thought, as my stare drifted from one piece of inked body art to the next.

Brax's amused look made his eyes dance. "You think I look like a gangster, Gracie?" *Gangsta.*

My gaze raked over his inked knuckles, then I looked up and shrugged. "Yeah, a little."

"And yet you climbed on the back of my bike and left campus." Brax rubbed his chin with his thumb. "With nothing more than your little purse and a safe word. Interesting." He inclined his head. "Unless you're packin'."

I couldn't help but grin. "I said you looked like a gangster. Not that I thought you were one."

Brax's white teeth flashed behind his lips. "Looks can be deceiving, Gracie. Remember that."

From his tattoos, dark hair, and vaporous blue eyes, to the silvery scars that marred his skin, I absolutely wondered about that.

"Here's your check, guys," our waiter said. He was walking toward me and slowed just long enough to slip the plastic holder with the receipt onto the table. Just as he leaned, the platter of drinks he was carrying tipped, too, and a tall glass fell. A gush of ice and soda splashed over the front of my top and soaked my skin.

I gasped and jumped back in surprise.

"Oh, hell!" the waiter said. "Damn, I'm sorry darlin'! Let me get you a towel."

"I got it, man," Brax said, eased out of the booth and grabbed a handful of napkins from the waiter's stand. He handed them to me and embarrassment flooded my face once more as I patted my sticky wet chest. My blouse clung to my skin.

"Thanks," I told Brax. I glanced around until I found the restrooms. "I'll just go rinse off a little." Scooting from the booth, my eyes darted to Brax, and laughter danced in his eyes. I skirted the bar and down the hallway leading to the restrooms. Finding the ladies room, I couldn't get inside quick enough. It was just spilled soda. I'd been thrown face-first in horse poop my whole life, but this had embarrassed me just the same. Probably because it'd happened in front of Brax, and he seemed to think it was so funny. I stared at my reddened face in the mirror, then down to the soaked material of my floral shirt. Wetting several paper towels, I got the sticky off my skin and managed to mop up what I could of the drink. Balling up the used paper, I tossed them into the trash and pushed open the door.

"Hey, Livvy," a voice said smoothly, and my head snapped up. Even when my vision zoned in, I couldn't believe what I was looking at. Who, rather.

Kelsy Evans leaned against the opposite wall, arms folded casually over his chest, eyes dead on mine. Cold fear and panic replaced my easy-going spirit from before, and I froze. My brain scrambled around, trying to make sense of who I was suddenly face to face with. How could this be? God, how was he here? Inside, my brain jumbled into a ball of tangled barbed wire. I wanted to run, run fast and far, but that message didn't make it to the muscles in my feet, my legs. I couldn't move. Not a single inch.

And he knew it. Kelsy's mouth smirked

into what I once thought was a charming smile. "Funny running into you here, huh? God, it's what? Like four hours from home?"

My mouth went dry as no words formed. I could do nothing more than stare at him. The narrow hallway, with its blue stained concrete walls and old black-framed photographs of fishing boats, floated in and out of my peripheral. But my gaze remained mercilessly locked onto his. I didn't want to look at him. But I did.

Kelsy widened his eyes, and it made him have a shocked look on his tanned face. But I immediately knew it was as fake as that smirk. "Oh—don't tell me you're at Winston? Holy shit, no way." He pressed his big-knuckled hand to over his heart and leaned forward. "Now what kind of good fuckin' luck is that, huh? That we'd end up at the same school? Come here, girl, don't be such a stranger," he said, and the air completely stopped in my windpipe as he pulled my body against his into a tight embrace. I stood there as he squeezed around me, still as a scarecrow and just as lifeless. He buried his nose into the hollow of my neck and inhaled, exhaled deeply, and his breath rustled the curls at my nape. "Damn, Livvy, you still smell like daisies and sunshine." His hand felt its way down my arm, and his fingers brushed my ring. "Still wearing this old thing, darlin'?" He whispered. "Why didn't you return any of my calls, Liv?" He buried deeper into my neck.

"You didn't have to ignore me."

It started as a low, distant roar, somewhere deep within me like a brewing thunderstorm, and it built and built and rolled upward through my stomach until I felt it pounding against my chest. Without thinking, my hands found strength and before I knew it, they were between our bodies, pressing against Kelsy's chest. I pushed.

"Stay away from me," I said quietly, and weak. I couldn't look him in the eye anymore, so I stared past him, over his shoulder, and fixed my gaze on the square blue and white tiles on the floor. Without another word, I moved past him. I thought at first he'd let me go, leave me alone, but the second my body evened up with the end of the short corridor, his voice fell over me. Not loud. Deadly sober.

"Not in this lifetime, Olivia Beaumont." A stern yet mocking tone deepened his already-heavy Texas drawl, and it followed me around the corner, in my mind, even as I made my way through the tables and away from the restrooms. My insides felt washed out, and cold, and full of dread and that little thing you get in the pit of your stomach when you know something's just not right.

And never will be.

Kelsy Evans was here. At Winston. For a brief second, I stopped, and my hand grasped the wooden partition separating the dining room from the kitchen. Inside, I sagged, and tried to breathe, tried to look normal.

Unaffected. Just a few more breaths and I'd be good.

Oh, God ...

Across the room, I saw our booth, and Brax's dark head turned toward the window as he faced away from me. I had to go to him. Act as if nothing was wrong. It'd been a mistake, coming here, with him. Never should I have let my guard down. Class, school, study, repeat. No socializing. Not even with a smooth-talking Southie—no matter that he put me at ease and made me laugh. It'd been a mistake. Had I not agreed, and come to this place, I wouldn't have encountered Kelsy, and I'd have stayed safe. Now? Slowly, my feet moved, and by the time I got to the booth, I pasted a smile to my face and leaned across my seat, gathering my jacket and bag. "Thanks for dinner," I said, and my eyes skittered across to Brax's chest and tattooed forearms, which rested casually on the tabletop. Anywhere but his eyes. "I'd better get back, though." I huffed a sigh. "First day of school tomorrow, plus work." Standing, I shrugged into my jacket and fidgeted with my purse. I could feel his eyes on me, but I couldn't bring myself to look at him.

"You okay, Gracie?"

The raspy voice, tinged with concern, stopped my fidgeting, just long enough for me to slip a quick look in his direction. His brows were jutted together, narrowing his eyes and making the skin crinkle at the corners. He didn't believe me, I knew it. A slight noise bubbled out of my throat that resembled a strangled chuckle. "Oh, sure. I'm just tired, I guess. Kind of nervous about first day of class. You know?"

Back to the fidgeting, I adjusted the low waist of my jeans, smoothed my damp blouse, and glanced down at my toes, snuggled into my sandals. I looked out the window, then just … started walking toward the door, because Brax wasn't budging from his seat. And I had to get out. Now.

By the time I reached the exit door, Brax's tattooed arm reached in front of me and opened it. To his credit, he didn't say anything, but I could feel it in the air around us. He knew I was unsettled, and I could do nothing but silently pray he'd just let it go.

Just as I was pulling on my helmet, and Brax was already straddling the bike, a voice reached through the heavy, humid air of the parking lot. It sent a streak of fear down my spine.

"Hey, Livvy, see you at school, huh?" Kelsy Evans said.

My eyes darted to that voice, and Kelsy was standing at the door of his truck. The big, black obnoxious Ford was the same one he'd driven in high school. Quickly, I turned my gaze from him, from that truck, and from the horrible memories both stirred inside of me. Fear. Revulsion. Shame. Those things had bound to my DNA, and I had to fight every day not to let it take over me. My body moved to climb onto Brax's bike before my eyes registered the fact that Brax was no longer on it. He stood beside me, his presence looming and heavy and invasive and comforting, his large palm pressing against my lower back. I looked up at him then, and the muscles in his jaw flinched. Although he wore dark shades, I knew his gaze drifted toward Kelsy.

"You know that guy, Gracie?" His voice was scratchy and low, and a little edgy.

I didn't want to, but I couldn't seem to help it when my eyes moved to look at Kelsy Evans. And when I did, even from where I stood, I could see the whites of his teeth as his lips pulled away from them. He knew the reaction he caused in me. And he liked it.

My stomach plummeted, but I took a deep, inconspicuous breath. "He's just somebody I went to high school with." I turned away.

Brax stood there, though, staring at Kelsy through his dark shades, his body rigid and still, and right then I knew that my dirty little secret, the one I'd hoped to keep hidden from a school filled with brand new people, would not be kept for very long.

7. Brax

THE GUY WAS A douchebag. A fuckin' prick. I was one, too, so hell yeah, I could tell that about him. An arrogant fuck, by the way he'd stood with his chest bowed, next to his big hillbilly pick-up while smiling at Gracie. That alone was pissing me off. He'd rattled her in the restaurant; that much was obvious. I immediately saw the change in her. He was a lot more than just some douche she knew in high school. She came back from the bathroom on edge. Damn, she was skittish as hell when I'd first picked her up at the dorm. But then I'd turned on the charm and coaxed her into relaxing a little. Gracie was pretty damn funny when chilled and not on constant guard. I gotta admit—I actually enjoyed her company. Usually there was a game involved, where the girl was coy and pretended she wasn't flirting but she really was, and thought I didn't know it. I'd known Gracie less than two days and I could tell she was as real as they came. But when she came back, after that drink spilled on her? Scared shitless and nervous as hell, if I had to label it. Her gaze darted all over the place, and she wouldn't look me in the eye. Now? She wanted to get the fuck out of there. Away from him.

And that pissed me off even more. Made me curious. And that grin on his face? Made me want to drag his sorry hillbilly ass behind the dumpsters there and beat the living fuck out of him.

I stared at him through my shades, just long enough to let him know that I thought he was a prick. A silent challenge between two dudes. I didn't say a word, just looked, and took inventory. Rich pretty boy, that much was obvious. Pricey clothes and a ride he probably didn't have to pay for. My height, maybe my weight. But no fuckin' backbone. Well, except when it came to intimidating girls. He got off on that. Pussy.

Finally, he ducked his head, climbed into that ass truck and took off.

"Brax, can we go now?"

Her voice shook a little, even though she tried to steady it. She stood next to me, still as a goddamn statue, waiting for my answer. When I looked down at her, with those wide soft eyes of hers staring back at me, I was reminded of what a douchebag I truly was. What in the hell was I doing with her? What in the goddamn hell? Sweet and innocent, with her little freckled nose, flawless skin and full mouth made for hours of slow kissing. Not fast like the first one I'd taken from her.

Christ, I'd thought about nothing else since. That white scar in her lip was fuckin' sexy as hell. I took advantage of my shades and just stared at her. Innocent, but … not. I couldn't put my finger on it, but there was something about her, something she was hiding. Naïve, maybe a little, but she wasn't stupid. Far from it. Yet I felt protective over her for some reason, and that shocked the hell out of me. Kenny about lost his goddamn hand, just for touching her hair. It'd made her more than uncomfortable. And it'd scared her. The thought of Kenny or that rich idiot or anyone else bothering her boiled my fuckin' blood.

That thought made me take one last long look at Gracie Beaumont's questioning face. I'd introduced her to the guys as Olivia because Gracie was my name for her. I didn't want anyone else to call her that. Just me. I stared at her through my shades. Her head tilted toward the sun, her skin was the color of honey; healthy and alive. She'd trusted my sorry ass enough to climb on my bike and leave the school. Part of me felt lucky that she'd given me that trust, because I got the feeling she didn't hand that out too much. The other part of me, and the larger part? Felt like a bum. A goddamn bastard bum.

But hey—who was I? Who the *fuck* was I? I'd only just slammed into her the day before. And she'd never know what an unlucky meeting that was. For her, not me. Not until it was too late. So I guess it really didn't matter what I was doing with her now 'cause I was doing it regardless, bastard that I was. Regrets were a bitch, and I'd worry about them later. I could no more control my selfish streak than I could my Southie mouth. Regrets? Hell yeah, I'd have them. No doubt. But I could tell something about Gracie Beaumont. She was strong. Kick ass strong. And that, for some reason, made my regrets suck a little more. And retreat a little more, to a place far in the back corner of my fucked up mind. But like I said. I'd worry about that later.

Finally, I flashed a slow smile and reached to tighten her chin strap. Her long thick braid rested over her shoulder, and I picked it up. It felt smooth and heavy between my fingers. I pushed it aside, and just as I did the thought of kissing her mindless when we got to the dorm entered my head. That could wait. But not for long. "Sure thing, Gracie." I straddled my bike. "Hop on."

Gracie's lean body slid behind me, and her small hands timidly rested on my hips. Like before, I reached back and grabbed her arms, pulling them tightly around my stomach. I held them in place with my hand, just in case she had thoughts of pulling them back. Funny. I was used to chicks grabbing my crotch while we rode. There was something to be said about Gracie's shy touch, though. Different. Yeah, I liked her holding onto me this way.

"Thank you, Brax." She said this quietly, close to my ear, before I pulled on my helmet.

Her breath was soft against my neck, and her body pressed against my back.

For a split second, I closed my eyes. *Jesus Christ, Jenkins, you are a grade-A bastard. Far worse than that prick with the hillbilly pick-up. You sure you got the stomach for this?*

I had to actually take a deep breath in and think about it. Could I? Stomach it? I was in it now, with no fucking choice but to go forward. Gracie's trusting words of thanks stuck in me like a fucking knife. Dug deep into my gut. I shook it the fuck off and opened my eyes. Pulled on my helmet. Started the bike. Felt her arms squeeze tighter against me as we sped out of the parking lot. And I liked it. Fuck, maybe I'd just bang her and get it out of my system. Get her out of my system. I could convince her. Might take some time, but I could.

By the time we made it back to Winston, the last rays of sunlight streaked purple and gray across the sky. That's one thing I liked about Texas versus Boston. The sky. Here, it was a vast blanket of a million different things, day and night, stars and sun and storm clouds. Back home, only holes of it skewered through the tall brick and concrete structures of the city. All except the harbor, anyway. That was the place to go to see more than just circles and holes, and I'd hung out there a lot as a kid. Yeah, I missed the harbor all right. Missed a lot of things. Didn't miss a lot of things, too, that's for damn sure.

I cruised through the campus streets, and every time I rolled over a speed bump, I goosed the engine, causing Gracie's head to bump into the back of mine. Crack, her helmet smacked against my helmet. Goose. Crack. Goose. Crack.

"Brax," she said, and softly punched my arm. There was laughter in her voice, though, and it made me smile. Almost laugh. Just like a goddamn kid. I pulled up at the walkway leading to her dorm and stopped the bike. Before I killed the engine, she'd thrown her leg over the seat and was standing there, and I watched her long nimble fingers loosen the chin strap. When she pulled the helmet off, that wild thick braid fell out and over her shoulder. Why it fascinated me, I had no clue. But it did. It damn sure did.

"Thanks for dinner," Gracie said. Her voice had the perfect female pitch, and her Texas drawl was soft and easy on the ear. I liked it. "And for helping me unload my stuff." The smile on her mouth came hesitantly, and it was really just barely there, and she couldn't quite meet my eye. "And for showing me the back route to the observatory." A nighttime breeze had kicked up, and it brushed over her face and a loose strand of hair caught on her lip. She ignored it. Hell if I could. I reached over and gently knocked it loose.

Another embarrassed grin pulled at her mouth, probably because I was staring at her like some lunatic, and her gaze shot to the grass between her feet. It was cute as hell. "You're welcome," I told her. "Least I could do for knockin' the wind out of you yesterday." Wasn't going to apologize for the kiss, though. I'd already told her that.

"True," Gracie agreed. She gave a quick girl's laugh that sounded different from any other I'd heard. I liked it. She glanced over her shoulder then, toward her dorm, and kinda jerked her thumb in that direction. "Well, I'd better get going." She waved, turned and began walking, then looked back at me. The movement made that long braid of hers slide over her shoulder and fall down the middle of her back. "I'll see ya around, Brax."

"Yeah, you will," I answered, and another slow smile caught my lips and pulled. I slipped my shades off to better watch her, and hell. I couldn't keep my eyes off her. Not off that braid. Not off that ass. Not off those long legs. Not until she'd slid her dorm card through and pushed into the common room. She didn't turn around again, yet I still sat there, straddling my bike, staring.

My cell vibrated against my thigh. I grabbed it, tapped the screen, and raised it to my ear. "What's up, man?"

Cory Maxwell cleared his throat on the other line. First baseman for the Silverbacks, he was probably my closest friend at Winston. "Your presence is required at the house of awesomeness, dick wad."

I shook my head. "Of course it is." Tapping the screen, I disconnected just as

Cory was about to say something else. With a final glance at Gracie's dorm, I slid my shades over my eyes and started the bike. The engine rumbled as I headed toward the frat house.

Cars crammed the yard and parking spaces, and people drifted in and out of the front entrance. Another party, more booze-filled sorority girls and liquored-up jack fucks littering my living space. Freshmen year, yeah, I thought it was a blast. Partied every chance I got, game or no game. I took a goddamned whipping. Now? Over it. Bored. Sick as shit of it.

Yet, my presence was required. Silverbacks superstar pitcher. Badass Southie.

Not a single soul here really knew me. Besides Cory, anyway. Didn't know a single fucking personal thing about me. Assumed plenty. Like I was some sideshow carnie freak or something.

Gracie knew me, though. Not much, but more than these clowns, and I'd known them for over a year. Most were ball players, their girls, and random girls trying to hook up with ball players. The idea came fast to me that Gracie wouldn't fit in here, with these people, in this atmosphere. That thought, and how easily Gracie had slipped into it, took me off guard. Made me even more curious about her. About myself. What the hell?

I walked in and everyone yelled and clapped. Slapped me on the back and congratulated me on the game as if I'd single-handedly won it. A cold bottle was pushed into my hand. This, I was used to. It'd been my life for over a year. I'd liked it. A lot.

"Jenks, you asshole, that was some fine sick pitching today, son!" Cory said from one of the sofas in the common room. I sank into the cushion next to him.

Lifting the bottle to my mouth, I let the lager flow down my throat. I grinned, and raised the brew. "I know that." Everyone laughed as my gaze settled on most of my teammates, some on the floor, others draped over the furniture. Their girls draped over them. Same faces, same scenario. Different day.

A heavy body flopped down beside me, and I didn't have to look to know it was Josh Collins. I could smell his chewing tobacco. Third baseman and a junior, he was a fellow Kappa Phi brother from Austin. And a dick of many things. But he was a good third baseman and that was the only decent thing I could say about the guy.

Josh leaned forward and braced his elbows on his knees. His gaze remained straight ahead. "So." His drawl was long and irritating as hell. "How'd your date go?"

I took another pull on my lager. "It went."

Josh's shoulders shook as he laughed silently. "Yeah, I bet it did." He looked over his shoulder at me. "Kenny said she wears a fucking wedding ring. Priceless."

I took my time on the second pull of beer before answering. "Kenny says he fucks your sister, too. You believe everything he says?"

Anger rolled over his face like a wave, and I couldn't help but laugh. I took another swallow. Collins hated shit being said about his sister. Might be the only other redeeming quality the fuck wad had.

"Well, what the hell is it, Jenks?" Josh pushed.

I gave a casual shrug. "It's just something to keep pricks like you away, Collins." I lifted a brow. "Why do you care?"

Josh's lips pulled back and he grinned a gap-toothed smile, one only his mother could love. "Just curious, is all." He winked and punched my arm. "It'll make this semester's dare a little more interesting, huh, big guy?"

My gaze hardened as I looked at him. "Choose another one, Collins. She's not dare material."

Josh's teeth showed, and I fixed on that big gap in the middle. I wanted to make it wider. "Trust me. She really, really is." He pushed up, stood. "Totally opposite of you, that's for fuckin' sure. Besides, Jenks. You chose her. Remember? Picked her out the second we rounded the corner and saw her crossing the lawn. Anyway." He smiled. "It's just all good college fun. She'll get over it and you. Probably laugh about it later on." He headed to the kitchen, stopped and turned back. "Good pitchin' today, son." He nodded, then ducked into the other room.

The music thumped against the walls, some random local country rap band, and the smell of beer and sweat filled the common room. It made the inside of my skull ache, and I pushed my temples in with my thumbs. Goddamn, Collins was right. I *had* picked her. Honest to Christ, it'd been sheer impulse. Gracie had caught my eye the moment she'd pulled up in the parking lot, wearing that cute fucking hat and driving that old tank of a pickup. I knew she was tough the second I'd laid eyes on her, and that had initially drawn me in. Now? Jesus H. Christ, I'd only been out with her once. Seen a piece of who she really was. And I liked what I saw. Even the part she tried so hard to hide I liked, and it made me want to find out more. Which made me an even bigger prick than Collins because the only way to get Gracie out of this now was to come clean with her. I didn't know her well— not at all, actually, since we'd just met. But one thing I did know for a fact: She'd tell me, my fraternity and the semester dare to go straight to fucking hell. And to be selfishly honest, I just wasn't ready to give her up yet.

I stood, tossing my bottle across the room and into the trash can by the kitchen. I'd had enough bullshit chatter and drunken laughter and was headed to my room when fingers closed around my wrist. When I turned I was surprised to see the blonde from the Chowder House, staring at me with a vixen smile and a mile of cleavage popping out of her shirt. *Blouse*. That word and that thought of Gracie made me smile, probably giving Blondie the wrong idea as she pushed closer, and her hand crept up my arm.

"I knew if I asked around I'd find you," she said. She slid her body against mine, and I felt her breast brush my elbow. "You're kinda hard to miss. Not too many guys look like you. Where ya goin'?"

I looked at her. Any other given day I would have given her a panty-dropper smile and said *wherever you're goin', sweetheart*. She was hot. Stacked. A little drunk. And more than willing. Any man's dream.

I couldn't believe it. I wasn't interested. Yeah, I'd flirted a little at the restaurant, but that'd been for Gracie's sake. I'd wanted her to feel at ease with me, not so guarded. I didn't want to bang this drunk chick. I wanted to hole up in my room for the night, maybe send Gracie a text.

Text instead of sex. Sometime since yesterday I'd lost my fucking mind.

"Not tonight, sweetheart," I said, and gently pushed the girl's hands away.

She pouted her lips out and crossed her arms over her breasts. "But I drove all the way here." I looked down at them. Yeah, I'd lost my fucking mind all right.

"Well, why don't you go say hi to Josh Collins over there," I said, and turned her in that direction, and pointed. "Big guy, Silverbacks cap on backward standing against the wall? Tell him I sent you over, yeah?"

The girl stared at Josh, turned, gave me a playful, if not drunken slap on the chest, and waved. "Okay, I'll let you slide by this time. But just this once." She sauntered off and made her way to Josh, who looked over her head and gave a nod of approval. That guy's dick would rot off before graduation. But most said the same thing about mine. The difference was I knew Josh. His probably really would.

I made my way to the stairs and took them two at a time, reaching the second floor and my room without anyone else stopping me to talk game, sex, or beer. A fucking miracle. I locked the door, kicked off my boots, yanked off my jacket and pulled my tee shirt over my head. Then I grabbed my cell from the front pocket of my jeans and flopped onto my bed. I settled into the unmade covers and lay there in the dark, and the fluorescent light from my cell screen glared in my eyes. I tapped Gracie's name and typed.

Me: Stop layin there thinking about me. You've got class in the mornin. Priorities, Sunshine.

I set my cell on my chest and stared in the dark at the ceiling. I couldn't believe I'd slammed into her then … kissed her. When I'd told her it was spontaneous, that was the damn truth. I don't know … I'd looked down at her, had pushed that hat off her face and … I just couldn't fucking help myself. She'd tasted sweet. Warm. And it'd been too damn short of a kiss. It wasn't the first time in my life I'd been compelled to kiss a total stranger. So why had it affected me the most?

My phone vibrated, and I lifted it. Just seeing her name on the screen made me smile like an idiot. Jesus, what had this quiet cowgirl with secrets done to me already? Should've snuck a pic of her earlier. Maybe she'd send me one. I blinked and read her text.

Gracie: My priorities are in order, thank you very much. I was just getting ready for bed. Haven't you had enough of me for one night?

Me: Hardly. So tell me what spooked you in the restaurant, Gracie.

No one had ever accused me of being subtle. I just always found it better to get to the point, whether I'd known you ten years or one day. And the point was, whatever happened at the restaurant with Gracie bothered the hell out of me, and I wanted to know what was up. I waited, and thought maybe she wouldn't answer me. Then, she did.

Gracie: You're very pushy for a virtual stranger. Nothing spooked me. I was embarrassed by the enormous amount of soda that drowned me. Then I got a little dizzy in the bathroom. That's all. But thank you for your concern.

Me: You didn't look dizzy, Gracie.
You looked scared shitless.

Gracie: Quite an imagination you
got there, Southie. I kneed your
family jewels within seconds of
meeting you. Not the reaction of
your average scaredy cat. Do you
show this kind of heroic concern
with all the girls?

Me: Guess you bring it out in me.
Maybe you're tougher than you look
but I doubt it. Guess I'll just
have to keep an eye on you,
Gracie.

Gracie: Why do you call me Gracie?
Of course I'm tough. I'm a Texan.
And I'm not too sure you have
enough eyeballs in your head to
keep an eye on me, plus the other
gazillion girls you keep an eye
on.

My mouth pulled, and I grinned.

Me: I've got wicked eyeball talent
Gracie. Tough? You'll have to
prove it to me. I call you Gracie
cuz that's your name. Are you
wondering why I didn't try and
kiss you tonight?

There was a pause; I thought I'd scared
her off.

Gracie: It's my middle name. No
one calls me that. You didn't try
and kiss me bc you knew I'd punch
you in the nose.

Me: I'm original that way, see? I
call you something no one else
does. Punch me in the nose, eh?
That's interesting enough. Now
stop bothering me and go to bed.
I've got an early class in the
morning.

Gracie: You're so weird.

Me: Takes one to know one.

Gracie: 'Night Brax ☺

Me: Sweet dreams, Gracie.

I set the alarm on my phone and shoved it
under my pillow. Gracie was tough, yeah, I
could see that. But there was something off
about her, too. A vulnerability that she tried
her goddamned best to hide. Why did I care so
much? What was it about Gracie that made me
pass up a half-drunk piece of ass, just to lay
up here in the dark and send a few texts to a
girl I barely knew? How was it she'd already
gotten in my head? I'd been at Winston almost
two years and not one girl had managed it.

In less than forty-eight hours, Gracie
Beaumont had.

I punched the side of my bed, jumped up, and made my way to the bathroom down the hall. I stared at my face as I brushed my teeth. Turned my head to the side a little, and noticed how the scar on my cheek bone was more silver and less red. The skin around my blackened eye had turned the color of light purple and rust. Lifting my chin, more scars. Ink. How Gracie had even agreed to get on my bike in the first place still shocked the hell out of me. Girls like her? Usually they made a wide fucking arc to avoid guys like me. She wasn't a half-witted party chic in college for the sheer fuck of it. No sorority. No running the frat party scene with a group of over the top make-up wearing girlfriends. She wanted to be a goddamned astronomer. Worked at the observatory. Used an outdated cell phone to save money. And drove an old ass tank of a pick-up truck.

And every single one of those things intrigued the hell out of me.

I spit, rinsed, and threw water on my face. Pushing my fingers through my hair, I stared in the mirror. And the longer I stared, the more I wondered. And got pissed at myself. *What the hell are you doing, Jenkins?*

"I don't fucking know," I finally said to my reflection. "I just don't fucking know."

8. Curve Ball

Tessa's screeching alarm jolted me out of sleep and brought me to my first conscious thought of the day.

Braxton Jenkins. *Brax.* This couldn't be happening. I closed my eyes and breathed.

"Dammit! That noise is so freaking annoying!" Tessa said in a sleepy voice. Her voice was scratchy and groggy in the dark, and after a few seconds she found her cell and turned off the alarm. I pushed up and rubbed my eyes, and flicked on the lamp. Tessa's floppy hair ball was again slumped over to one side, and she was in full stretch/yawn mode. She peeked at me through squinted eyes. "Did you shower last night?" she asked. "Because I totally didn't."

By the time Tessa had made it back to the dorm it'd been close to 2am. She tried to tiptoe in, but tripped over one of the three pairs of discarded heels she'd tossed onto the floor before she left, and it took almost an hour for me to fall back asleep. No wonder her eyeballs were puffy. Crazy thing. I gave my roommate a grin. "Yeah, go for it."

"Sweet!" Tessa said. She leapt up, grabbed some necessities, and darted for the bathroom. "Thanks! I'll be out in a sec!" She slammed the door behind her.

I slipped from my bed, yawning as I cleared the nighttime cobwebs from my head, and padded over to my very slim fold-out closet. Stretching my arms way overhead, thoughts of Brax and our conversations filled my head. I'd had fun with him yesterday. A lot more than I even admitted to myself. So much that he'd managed to completely kick the dreadful thoughts I had lingering about Kelsy right out of my brain. I wondered if I'd run into Brax today? I'd be lying to myself if I said anything other than I hoped so.

First day of college. My anxiety from last night seemed to have dissipated, and eagerness filled its place. A familiar tug pulled at my mouth as I situated my gaze to the narrow rack of clothes. Thinking of Brax, his arrogance, and his Southie mannerisms made me smile. And I couldn't get his face, and those ghostly eyes, out of my head. Just as I chose a treasured E.T.-The Extra-Terrestrial tee shirt that my mom had given me, my cell phone chirped an incoming text. As unavoidable as breathing, my stomach flipped from anticipation. I knew it was Brax before I even looked at my phone. Was I the first thing on his mind this morning, too? It was dangerous to think it, to hope it. But I dang sure did, and I couldn't help it.

Brax: Wake your ass up, Sunshine. First day of college you know.

Shaking my head, I pulled at my lip with my teeth and grinned to myself.

Me: I'm already up, smarty pants. I'm an early riser anyway. What time's your first class?

Brax: Smarty pants, eh? You're wicked funny. Early riser, that's right you're usually out milking cows by now. 8am class for me. U?

Me: Same. Maybe I'll see ya around.

Brax: Not if I see you first. ;)

Me: Very funny. Bye.

Brax: Catch ya later Gracie.

Brax Jenkins was an anomaly. While he looked like he'd knife you in a dark alley and rob you blind, he'd treated me with kindness and respect. He was funny. He was sexy and knew it, but not in an idiot way, like Tessa's brother. And Brax might say his flirtations were part of his charm, but it was hard not to think otherwise when he point-blank asked questions like *were you wondering why I didn't try and kiss you?* That's something I'd tried really hard not to think about. Tessa had already warned me that he'd charm the pants off of me—at first. Is that what he was doing? And was I being naive enough to fall for it? It made my head ache thinking about all the stupid what-ifs. He seemed genuine. Real. Blunt and to the point. But was that all a perfected act to get what he wanted? The last thing I needed was to fall for some inked up bad boy baseball player, only to have my heart stomped on. Jesus, I hated doubts. Hated that I'd become such a suspicious person.

But did I really and truly want to go through any sort of hell again? Over a guy?

No, I wouldn't go there. Not this time. I'd keep Brax Jenkins at a friendly distance, despite my traitorous heart doing monkey-flips at the mere thought of him.

By the time Tessa's "sec" was over and she was out of the bathroom, I'd pulled on a pair of old soft faded jeans, my fave E.T. tee shirt, and a pair of All-Stars. After shaking out my hair and running a wide-toothed comb through it, I quickly re-braided it, brushed my teeth and washed my face. I was ready to go.

"God, I think I'm jealous," Tessa said, staring at me in the mirror.

I wiped my mouth on my hand towel, hung it up and gave her a curious look. "Why?"

She pointed at me. "You throw on a ratty old tee shirt and some holey jeans and you look gorgeous." She scowled at me, drawing her brows close. "No make-up. Low maintenance." She rubbed her chin with a forefinger. "Maybe I'll give that look a try."

I shook my head and grabbed my backpack. "This is definitely not a ratty tee shirt, Tess." I looked at her. "It's a classic." It was, too. I glanced down at it. My mom had preserved it from her teenaged years in the 80's. An original E.T. movie tee shirt, black, with the logo and E.T.'s long glowing finger pointing. I loved it.

She grinned. "What-ev, freak. Let's go."

Together we cut across the courtyard, Tessa chatting non-stop and me slowly eating the spoonful of chunky peanut butter I'd grabbed on my way out. At the pavilion Tessa was joined by two other girls. "Guys, this is Olivia, my roomie. Liv, this is Marcie and Kelly," she hugged them both. "My girls from back home." Marcie was even taller than me, with nearly black, perfectly coifed hair and wide full lips. Kelly was Tessa's height, petite, with a blonde stacked bob haircut that looked perfect on her. Her eyes were humongous and blue. Both smiled and said hey, but gave my big glob of peanut butter a strange look. Tessa waved. "See ya later." They left, huddled together and giggling. Tessa's laugh rose above the others, and I smiled and continued on my way to the Foster building and my first class of my college career: Lit Humanities.

The campus was alive and buzzing with students, even at this early hour in the morning, like ants pouring out of a mound. I continued eating off my spoon and weaved my way through sleepy-eyed and dreary walking college-goers, looking more like zombie extras from a horror movie than students. The scent of fresh cut grass rose from the ground and I inhaled; it reminded me of home and smelled clean and brisk. The air felt different this morning. An early onset of fall maybe? Or was it that I felt different? Either way, exhilaration filled me, and I trotted the steps of the bricked Foster front entrance two at a time. Inside, I shouldered my way down the hall to lecture hall 31, and ducked inside.

Winston was not a huge school, so the room wasn't auditorium-style. It was just a big classroom, which was fine by me. A huge dry-erase board took up the wall behind the professor's podium, and as I scanned the seats I noticed only three other students were there, spaced out, looking down at the handout that sat on every single desk.

"Peanut butter on a spoon, now that's just cute as hell, Sunshine."

Brax's warm breath brushed my neck as he leaned over and whispered to me, and I jumped and looked at him. His eyes were clear and snapped with mischief. The purple around his eye had faded to pale lavender. "You're in this class?" I asked, surprised.

Brax's white ghost grin dominated his unusual face, and his hand gripped my elbow.

He smelled good, freshly showered, hair still damp. Wearing a plain black tee shirt and jeans, he left me breathless. Which concerned me. "Weird, huh?" he said, and eyed my feet. "No boots?"

I narrowed my gaze. "You knew." A smile tugged at those lips I had a hard time not staring at. I cleared my throat. "Boots aren't functional for me here, Brax."

"You were wearing them the first day I met you," he said.

I shrugged. "They'd been functional earlier that day. When I'd shoveled horse poop."

His mouth parted even wider, his teeth straight and white He guided me down the last row of seats, and slipped my back pack from my shoulder. "Let's go sit back there," he dropped his head close, his mouth near my ear, "E.T." The whisper made my breath hitch. My gaze slipped over a blonde girl as we passed, and her eyes were glued to Brax. They grew wide and glassy as she stared, and I could in no way blame her.

His presence behind me made my nerves crackle. The place on my elbow where his fingers gripped turned warm, and that heat tumbled and shot all the way through my body. Awareness of his close proximity, and how he seemed to be hogging all the air around me, made my skin flush. Godalmighty, what was wrong with me? We took our seats beside each other and he draped my backpack over the back of my chair. He did the same to his, then leaned toward me, those perfect lips twitching.

"So what are you, some kind of a peanut butter eating Sci-Fi nerd?"

His voice was low, teasing, and raspy, and I liked it. I shrugged, smiled, gave him a quick glance, and turned my attention to the class curriculum on my desk. I licked my spoon. "The truth is out there."

Brax's laugh came straight from his gut, and I could tell it was real, one of those infectious sounds that inspired others to stop and join in. I peered at him, and his eyes were directly on me and he shook his head. He stopped laughing, but his eyes still danced. Grew serious. "You are so damn different."

I wasn't exactly sure how to take that remark, really, and it left me unsure how to even answer. So, I didn't. I just finished my spoon. I knew I was different. Always had been, and had always been comfortable with myself. Walking across a packed campus eating a spoon of peanut butter didn't seem all that strange to me at all. Different? Different than what, I wondered.

"All right, guys, find your seats." Professor Sentinel stood behind his desk, shuffling papers. He was late thirties, early forties maybe, with long brown hair. He wore glasses and a white button-up long sleeved shirt, the sleeves rolled to his elbows. Suddenly, my chin was gently grabbed and Brax pulled my attention to him.

His eyes narrowed in a mock frown. "Okay, Gracie, I don't wanna catch you cheating off me, you hear?" He glanced down at the syllabus on his desk. "Especially while we're studying Homer. Got it?" his lips turned up in the corners.

"I'll do my very best to restrain myself," I answered. Then, I casually moved my gaze around Brax's head. The room started filling up fast, but it was one body in particular that I noticed when I scanned the room. He'd just slid into a desk three rows over, and was now deadpan staring at me. My breath lodged in my throat. It was an expression that made my skin turn cold. I felt the blood drain from my face as Kelsy Evans looked first at Brax, then finally toward the front of the room. I eased back in my seat, facing forward, and breathed. God, how could this be? Kelsy in the same class as me? And Brax? Was I being punished for something?

"Hey."

I turned to Brax and tried not to look as faint as I felt. He rubbed his chin and kept his eyes on mine, the **goin** inked into his knuckles glaring at me. I could tell in Brax's expression that I wasn't fooling him. Not for a second. And before I could even say a single word, his head turned and studied the students in the room. I didn't think he'd be able to single Kelsy out so fast; he'd only seen him from across the parking lot. Once. But he did. I knew it from the angle of Brax's head, and from the way his broad shoulders stiffened.

Slowly, he turned back to me, shifting his weight, angling his chest, his body toward mine. Almost shielding me from Kelsy.

"Look at me, Gracie," Brax said. His voice was low, steady, without a trace of humor. Dark brows furrowed over those shocking, now-angry eyes. He drew closer, so only I could hear his words. "I don't know what happened with you and that prick, but I don't fucking like the way you go all pale and scared-as-shit looking when he's around."

I didn't say anything, and I focused on his chest instead of his eyes. He rectified that by lifting my chin with his knuckle. Brax ducked his head. "Did he hurt you, Gracie?" His finger grazed my ring. My pledge of virginity. My band of deceit. Between his tender gesture and protective, determined gaze, the fear once more slipped right on out of me. Amazing, really, how he'd managed that with just a few words, a look, and a slight touch. I breathed in, settled my eyes on his, smiled.

And lied.

"No," I said in a low voice, as believingly as I possibly could. I mean, yes, I felt a connection with Brax. Yes, we'd known each other for a very, very short time, yet he made me comfortable, aware, and disrupted. But no—I was not about to divulge my dirty secrets to him. To no one. Not even Tessa. "I'm just shocked to see him, is all." Then I straightened, forced my eyes not to drift to Kelsy. "What we had before was just a silly teenaged high school romance. It's been over for a long time, Brax."

Brax said nothing. Just stared at me. His eyes didn't flinch, remaining seared into mine so hard I was positive he could see through the shroud of lies that poured from my mouth. Before he could respond, if he was even going to, the professor began.

"As you can see, you each have your class syllabus in front of you. Follow it. You're not in high school anymore, guys, and your mommy can't send you a sick note as an excuse. I expect all homework turned in on the assigned dates. No make up dates for tests. And if you don't have a composition book, get one. You'll need to keep a personal log of the class, to be turned in for a grade at the end of the semester. And they'd better be individual." Professor Sentinel, whose longer hair curled at his shirt collar, grinned as his watchful gaze scanned the class through his rounded wire-framed glasses. "As you can see we begin with good ole Homer's *Iliad.* Peel open your text books, girls and boys, and let's see if we can decipher what the row between King Agamemnon and our poor unfortunate hero, Achilles, and the resulting tragic Graeco-Trojan conflict was all about, eh?"

My eyes slipped to Brax's. He gave me one last long stare, and then his head turned in Kelsy's direction. Kelsy must have sensed it because he looked over. Then he quickly turned away.

All during lecture, I felt Brax's eyes on me. It made concentration more than difficult, which meant I'd have to go back over the notes I furiously scribbled for the entire class, and more than once. I'd already studied Homer's *Iliad* in high school, but Professor Sentinel warned us his lecture would be very different. Despite that knowledge, my brain kept returning to the fact that the guy who had humiliated me in more ways than one was sitting across the class from me; the guy who had suddenly entered my life and felt like an inked knight in shining armor—or wolf in sheep's clothing—was sitting protectively beside me. All I wanted to do was escape the past year, start my new college life and begin the shift to my career in studying the stars. How did it end up being all about Kelsy Evans? God, why couldn't he have chosen a different school?

By the time Professor Sentinel wrapped up lecture, I'd started feeling cagey and wanted to escape. When he excused the class, I couldn't help but notice how Kelsy grabbed his pack and darted for the door, which made me feel somewhat better. Maybe the challenging looks Brax threw him had paid off. Maybe Kelsy would give up and leave me alone. So what if he thought Brax and I were together? That could only be a plus, right? That's all I wanted. Just to be left alone. I gathered my curriculum and textbook, stuffed them in my pack, and stood.

"Where are you headed next?" Brax said.

"Conner Hall." I looked at him, at the strange color of his eyes, and the scars that marred his skin. "U.S. and Texas government."

"I'll walk you."

As we stood facing each other, and relatively close, I realized how much of Braxton Jenkins there really was. He seemed to surround me. I put my hand on his inked arm and noticed for the first time that a rugged Celtic cross was one of the melded pieces of art tattooed into the myriad of objects. "I can walk myself, Brax. Honestly, I'm fine."

Brax's gaze drifted down to my hand, then he looked at me. Fury, like I'd seen at the restaurant when his friend Kenny had touched my hair, lit those blue eyes on fire. "I don't like that guy, Gracie."

I forced a smile, and shook my head. I was grateful for his concern, but I didn't want it to become an issue between us. To be an issue would draw attention to the real thing, the real hidden issue, and I wasn't going to let that happen. As Brax followed me out of the classroom, I threw him a goofy smirk over my shoulder. "I'm not helpless, you know. As a matter of fact," we stopped outside the classroom, "I'm probably the least helpless female you'll ever encounter. Besides," I said, and lightly elbowed Brax in the ribs. "Kelsy is an arrogant idiot, but he's not dangerous." I lifted a brow. "You're sure protective over a girl you barely know."

"Brax, my man!" A guy wearing a Silverbacks ball cap shouldered into him. "Is this the Betty, bro?"

Brax's eyes were still trained on me, even as he ignored his friend, who shrugged and walked off. Betty? I could tell by the way Brax's jaw clenched he was completely ignoring his teammate and still a hundred percent focused on me, deciding whether to believe me or not. In the depths of his eyes I could almost see wheels turning as he thought things over. "I know you all right, Gracie. In case you missed it, I hate shady pricks." He inclined his head. "But I'm still headed that way, so let's go."

"Not until you get that horrible mean frown off your face," I said, and tugged my mouth up. "You're scaring people."

Brax's face softened then, ever so slight of a shift that I was pretty sure only I could detect. "You're so smart, aren't ya, Sunshine?" A ghost of a smile pulled at his lips. "Come on, then." *Smaht.*

We stepped out into the early morning Texas sun and blended with the other Winston students as we made our way across the dewy lawn. The air wasn't sweltering, which was a good thing. At least every other person spoke to Brax. Some he acknowledged, others he didn't. For some reason I couldn't explain, his full attention was still on me. We were nearly to Conner Hall when we stopped, and he faced me.

"So you work tonight," he said. "Wanna grab a bite after?"

"There you are!" a tinny voice said behind me, before I could answer.

Tessa rounded on me, giving Brax one of the evilest dirty eyes I'd ever seen in my entire life—and I'd seen plenty of them. "How was class?" she asked me.

I tried not to laugh at Tessa's ferociousness. "Class was fine. Tessa, this is Brax Jenkins. Brax, Tessa's my roommate."

Brax turned that ghostly blue gaze on Tessa, and amusement made his lips turn at the corners. I stared at his side profile, watched the muscles pull in his jaw. "I play ball with your brother." *Brotha.*

Tessa's brows folded. "I know that. So Livvy," she said, and dismissed Brax immediately. She half-turned, facing me and giving Brax the back of her shoulder. Behind her, he shook his head and smiled. "You're coming with me and Marcie and Kelly tonight, right?" When I gave her a confused look, she lifted both brows. "Remember? You said you would?"

I'd said no such thing and Tessa knew it. When my eyes lifted to Brax's, he cocked one brow and grinned. "I'll pick you up after work, Gracie. See ya later."

Before I could answer, he'd turned and began to swagger through the crowd, heading to his next class. He'd shut Tessa's negotiations right on down.

"Gracie? What the hell's he calling you that for?" Tessa asked. When I met her gaze, and gave her a little shrug, her brows knitted into a disapproving frown. "Seriously, Liv? You're going out with that beast again?"

I shifted my backpack and gave my roommate an uncomfortable glance. "He's been nothing but respectful to me so far, Tessa." I glanced over my shoulder, then back to my roomie. "I'm not getting a sketchy vibe from him. Do you think he's that good of an actor? Or possibly the rumors are wrong?"

Tessa's frown deepened, and she shifted her weight. "I don't know but the fact is you'd better watch it, Liv. Sincerely. People are already starting to notice Brax is all up in your biz. You'll be the talk of Winston before you know it. Is that something you want?" She started walking, then looked back at me. "Don't say I didn't warn you."

I stared after my roommate for a few frustrated seconds, considering her words. While I tried to convince myself Tessa was over-analyzing the situation, I wondered if she was right. About everything. About nothing. Did I want to become the talk of Winston? Of course not. I wanted to go as unnoticed as possible. I highly doubted that would happen by going on friendly dinner dates with Brax Jenkins. So what to do? With a sigh, I jogged up the steps and found my next class.

U.S. and Texas Government was a breeze—especially since my grandpa Jillian had once been a Texas Ranger before he'd retired to busting horses for a living. He loved the law and had shared enough with me and my brothers that I'd actually liked the subject. Class was interesting to me, and the time flew by quickly.

As did the rest of the day. Intro Astronomy was a little repetitive for me but still perfect, and Noah Hicks had greeted me at the door with a wide, easy smile. Steven was there, too, and I grabbed a seat beside him. We basically went over the syllabus for lecture and lab, introductions, and since most of us would be taking a lab together, we chose partners; Steven and I signed up for that, too. Dr. Atwood started his first lecture with Basic Coordinates and Seasons. Steven had rolled his eyes at me and mouthed the words *basic coordinates*, and I'd stifled a laugh. Nerds, all of us.

Before I knew it, my classes were finished for the day and I was hurrying back to the dorm to trade my backpack for my telescope and camera. Noah had told me we could bring our own and take it to the platform after the observatory closed, which was something I'd been wanting to do since before arriving at Winston. In my room, I slung my scope bag over my shoulder, grabbed my truck keys and headed out. As I crossed the common room, a girl I hadn't seen before stopped me. Long brown hair, wide brown eyes accentuated with heavy make-up. She was pretty. She grabbed my arm and smiled. Three other girls clustered around her.

"Hey," she said. "Are you and Brax Jenkins together?"

My eyes flittered to all of them standing there, staring at me. "Uh, no," I answered. "Just friends."

Her smile broadened, and she looked relieved. "Okay. Just checking."

She immediately turned and began a private chatter session with her girls, and I eased toward the door. What an awkward moment. That thought plagued me all the way across the parking lot, at how bizarre some people could be. Just as I unlocked the door and set my scope bag across the seat, a hand slipped over my hip, and I jumped.

"I'd almost forgotten what a sweet ass you have, Liv."

My body jerked and I spun around to stare Kelsy Evans in the eye. His slow smile made my insides clinch. I took a breath in, and steadied myself. "Get your hands off me, Kelsy."

9. Unwanted Attention

INSIDE, I WAS SHAKING. But fury gripped my muscles as I stared hard at Kelsy. "Now."

He did let my hips go then, and held his hands up, palms facing me. "Chill, wildcat, chill." His lazy smile settled on my eyes and he shoved his hands into his pockets. Then he let out a big, exaggerated sigh. "Come on, Liv. We got too much history to be like this. Quit acting all Ice Queen on me, now." He ducked his blond head, to catch my averted gaze. "Talk to me."

That cagey feeling returned, and I hated it. I hated the way Kelsy made me feel dirty, like I'd done something wrong and was being an *ice queen*. Was he that oblivious to what he'd done to me? Or had a year dimmed his reality? I forced my breath to even out, so I wouldn't seem as scared as I really was. I looked at him, tilted my chin up. "There's nothing to talk about, Kelsy. You have a whole college full of girls to talk to." I put my hand on the door handle, and he stilled my movement with his hand over mine.

"Don't you run, Olivia," he warned. His face had reddened, and his brows were now knitted together into a frown that transformed his golden boy athlete looks into a monster. In my eyes, anyway. "Don't you be some ice queen chickenshit runner like you were our senior year. Talk to me, goddamit! I don't want to talk to other girls." His head drew closer. "Just you."

His raised voice sent my hackles up, and I snatched my hand away from his. Several people crossing the parking lot noticed, too, and stared in our direction. "This conversation is over, and I'm leaving now. I ignored you during our senior year for a reason. Go away, Kelsy." I hopped up into my pick-up and glared at him. "I mean it. Don't bother me again." Memories of that last year in high school flashed before me like a bolt of lightning with pictures. Kelsy had secretly hounded me, begged me to take him back. But in public? In front of his peers, others? He'd treated me like dirt. Like I had done something wrong to him. God, Jesus, I'd thought it was all over.

Kelsy's face darkened, then he barked out a harsh laugh. "You're letting him fuck your brains out, aren't you, Liv?" A small grin curled his lips. "That tattooed loud mouth thinks he's a badass prick in our class. That's why he's panting around after you, huh, like some fucking hound dog?" He slammed my door, and I jumped in my seat, but he drew his face close to the glass. "He doesn't know you like I do. What that dumbass ring really means. What a fucking *ice* bitch you can be, does he, Liv?" Kelsy laughed as I turned the engine over. He pounded my window with his fist. "He will. Soon." Then, he cursed, kicked at the ground, and looked at me. Just that fast, his mood shifted. No longer angry, his features sagged, as though saddened. He'd done the same thing in high school, when no one was around. It was as if he had a split personality, and it was scary as hell. "No, wait. Olivia, I'm sorry. I didn't mean it, you make me fucking crazy is all. Liv, turn off the goddamn truck. Olivia!"

Without another look I threw the truck into drive and Kelsy punched my fender as I sped off. My heart slammed against my ribs, and my breath came in harsh puffs as I hurried out of Oliver Hall's parking lot. I didn't glance behind me, not once. I knew Kelsy stood there, staring in my direction. I had every single line on his face permanently etched into my brain, going from fury to forlorn, and no matter how hard I tried to purge both, his image wouldn't fade. Wouldn't go away.

Neither would the memories.

A sob crept up in my throat, and God, I wanted to let it out. Scream. Cry. Dirty swear to the top of my lungs. But I didn't. I felt trapped, foolish, running away from Kelsy Evans yet again. Like a coward. I couldn't escape him. I'd thought big, bad ass thoughts when he wasn't directly in front of me. I became strong, brave, untouchable, when alone, or with my family. But now Kelsy Evans was here, I was alone, and he was poking around in my brand new life. Touching me. Cornering me. Threatening to let my secrets out. Then every ounce of bravery I thought I possessed flowed out of me like a bloodletting. Kelsy wasn't a serial killer. But he was definitely unbalanced. What did he want with me? Why *me*? He'd always had a temper but his behavior seemed crazy and uneven. This was my life, my college career. My scholarship. The *first* day of class. What the hell was I doing? I couldn't continue to allow Kelsy to rattle me so badly. I needed to get a grip. And I needed to get it fast.

By the time I pulled into the Science complex, and found a parking spot close to the observatory, I'd slowed my breathing down. My hands still shook as I gripped the Chevy's big steering wheel, and for a brief second, I closed my eyes and concentrated on deep breathing. I couldn't go into my first day of work shaking and breathless. I leaned forward and rested my forehead on the wheel, and the cool steel pressed into my skin. It felt good, and I pushed harder, trying to force the incident out. Away. *Breathe*. Just a few more minutes—

A knock at my window made me jerk

upright, and when I turned my head, I met Brax's strange gaze staring back at me through the glass. What was he doing here? Butterflies replaced the panic I'd felt seconds earlier. Quickly, I pasted a smile on my face, cut the engine, and opened my door.

"What's wrong?" Brax said this to my back as I grabbed my scope bag.

When I turned and glanced up at his face, I noticed it was taut, unamused, and a muscle tugged the scar at his cheekbone. His acute perception rattled me almost as much as Kelsy's unbalanced character. Brax saw too much of me. Kelsy knew too much about me. And both scared the hell out of me.

"Nothing, why?" I said, and closed my truck door. When I shouldered my scope bag, Brax eased it right back off and slipped it onto his own. He wore his silver and blue Silverback's uniform, his hat was stuffed into his back pocket, and long dark socks that went from just below his knees to his cleats clung tightly to muscular calves. No clay or dirt, he must have been headed to practice.

We walked, but his eyes stayed on me, more likely than not weighing what I'd said. "Feeling dizzy again?"

I lifted a brow. "Dizzy?" My eyes were back on the ground, and I watched Brax's big cleats hit the pavement as we crossed to the old brick observatory's front entrance. At the steps, we stopped. I tilted my head, staring at the weathered white dome that housed the Mulligan.

"Yeah, you know, with your head on the wheel?" His harsh yet comforting Boston accent soothed me somehow.

I looked at him then. "Cat nap before work?"

Brax's eyes narrowed. Those crazy blues were slits surrounded by ridiculously long dark lashes. "You were breathing too hard for a nap, Sunshine." *Hahd.*

I sighed and peered at the sun. "I don't want to be late on my first day." I paused at the steps. "On your way to practice?"

His gaze still pierced me. "Nah, sweetheart, I wear this uni all the time." He winked. "Chics dig it. Of course I'm going to practice. So are you going to get something to eat with me after work, or go do that *thing* with your girls?" He lifted my scope bag off his shoulder and eased it onto mine.

I climbed a few steps, leaving Brax at the bottom. I turned my head and gave him a look. "There is no thing with the girls. Tessa just doesn't want me to go anywhere with you. You've a sketchy reputation, you know."

Brax nodded, and his mouth tilted at one corner. "I figured that. So?"

I stared at him, the late afternoon sun shining on one side of his face, making the scruff stand out on his jaw. That barely-there grin pulled at his mouth. "I get off at eight tonight," I said. "You can meet me inside by the front desk."

He shifted his weight, and I again noticed his muscular thighs, calves. "Yeah? Why inside?"

I continued up the steps. At the door, I paused once more and looked at him. "I've got something to show you."

His white teeth flashed. "Now you're talking, Sunshine. See ya at eight."

I watched Brax swagger away, and noticed how his muscular legs bowed a little. A strong, sexy, athletic-type bowed walk. Completely arrogant, male and confident. He broke into a trot across the Science complex and disappeared through two buildings. I couldn't quite figure out what he wanted with me, but somehow, I was glad for his interest. Despite his reputation, and the rumors, he was nice. Really nice. Somehow he'd mastered a way to put me at ease. Not an easy feat by no means. Which is why I'd thought to show him a view through my scope after work. I'd Googled the weather and it promised to be a perfectly clear and starry night sky.

I pushed through the double doors of the observatory, and the cool air flushed over my skin. Noah was seated at the front desk, and gave me a broad smile as I walked toward him. Before I reached the desk, he stood. I noticed the blue Winston U Observatory collared shirt he wore, with a silver celestial logo on the left upper chest.

"Hey, Olivia," he said, and reached beneath the counter. He handed me a blue plastic draw-string souvenir bag. "Three work shirts. Just like this one," he said, and tugged at his collar. "Do you remember where the employee break room is?"

I took the bag he offered and nodded. "I do."

"Great. There's a restroom in there where you can change, and I see you brought your scope." He eyed my bag.

"I can't wait," I confessed. "A friend is going to come by after I get off work. Is it okay—"

"Sure, no problem," Noah interrupted me. He rubbed his chin and grinned. "As long as there's no horsing around, as Dr. Callander calls it. But I don't take you as someone who horses around too much."

I grinned. "I do try to contain it if I can."

"I'm sure you do." Noah inclined his head toward the hallway that led to the employee's lounge. "When you finish changing you'll find Steven in observation room #3, cleaning the planetarium display." He smiled. "He couldn't wait for you to get here to help."

I raised my brows and headed down the hallway. "Oh boy," I said, then waved. "Thanks, Noah."

"You bet. Oh, and my office is just across the hall from the lounge. You can stash your scope behind my desk."

I took a few minutes in the employee restroom to change shirts and wash my face, then found a place to store my scope in Noah's office. After heading down the wrong hall, I found my way to observation room #3. Steven was just climbing down from a ladder situated beneath an enormous Saturn model when he spotted me.

"Whoa! Olivia!" he said, and hurried over to me. His dark shaggy hair swung over his eyes, and he flipped it to the side. "I got here an hour ago so I could leave an hour early." His chin lifted. "I have a stargazer's meeting. Amateur and off-campus, but don't worry. It's only once a month. Anyway," he pointed overhead, "we need to get all the planets wiped down, as well as the upper and lower rows of recessed lights. And auditorium seats. I've already cleaned the left side of each, plus three planets. There's a presentation this upcoming weekend." He pointed. "Come on, your cleaning stuff's over here." He walked to the side wall where sure enough, my planetarium cleaning supplies sat in a plastic bucket.

"Okay, no problem," I answered.

"I'll get your ladder set up," he offered.

"Hey, that's all right," I stopped him. "Steven, I'm used to hard work. I can handle a ladder."

He gave me a long look, then nodded. "I like a nerdy girl with a strong back. We'll work great together, Olivia."

I chuckled, found my ladder and situated it beneath Mars. I grabbed my bucket and dug in. I was pretty sure the planets hadn't been cleaned in a while, and the tacky residue on the metal exterior wasn't easy to remove. Steven and I talked about class, our observation logs and upcoming night observations, and his weird roommate Curtis who ate orange peels. It passed the time and soon, the planets were finished, as were the recessed lights.

"I'll finish up these seats if you want to go ahead and leave," I told Steven.

"Sincerely?" he asked. "Thanks! I owe ya one." He grabbed his supplies and stopped at the door. "When you're finished you can leave your bucket in the tool closet, just down from the lounge. See ya in class."

Over the next hour I cleaned the remaining auditorium seats, my thoughts unavoidably drifting to Brax. I pondered the rumors. And I also reflected on the time we'd already spent together. I felt conflicted. One second fearful and nervous that the rumors were true. That I'd let my heart get tangled up in a mess like Brax Jenkins. The next second I felt butterflies, anticipating our dinner date. Thinking about he'd shown up in the parking lot before work, just to talk to me. It made my head spin, and my insides stung just thinking about it. A little immature sounding, I knew that—but since I was the only one I'd confessed it to, I guess it was ok. He was so … enigmatic. I knew next to nothing about him, yet a pull, an electrical draw existed between us. At least, on my end. Yes, there was his unique physical appearance. Not just his strong, sexy athletic build, cut from stone jaw and clear blue eyes. And not just the scars and ink. Something else drew me to him. Something deeper. It mesmerized me and frightened me all at once. Neither of those reactions would I ever let him see.

I was on my hands and knees, almost finished scrubbing the last few seats when a voice startled me.

"So being friends with a geek gets me first class into the planetarium, huh?"

I jumped, squealed, and hit my head on the metal arm rest.

"Whoa, Sunshine," Brax laughed from across the room. "Easily spooked, yeah?"

I rose to my feet, saw him moving up the center aisle, and my body immediately reacted; my heart started pounding a little harder. Brax no longer wore his uniform; in its place was a pair of faded ripped jeans, a white tee shirt, and boots. No doubt about it now. Brax unhinged me. But I was pretty good at hiding some things. I hid my reaction and grinned. "Gosh, I guess they just let any ole riffraff into the observatory these days."

Those muscular thighs and easy bowed swagger moved Brax closer, and he stopped in the aisle beside me. With his arms folded over his chest, he inspected me. "That TA tried to be a dick about it, but I convinced him to let me back here."

I eyed him. "You didn't punch him out, did you?" I really only half-teased.

A look of amused exasperation settled on Brax's features, and in the low light of the auditorium, he looked even sexier than he did in full blown light. Which was a pretty incredible feat. "No, Gracie, I didn't punch him out." His lips twitched. "This time."

I shook my head and dropped to my knees to clean the last seat. "Good. I need this job, Boston."

Brax laughed, crouched beside me and ducked his head, bringing us to eye level. His elbows rested against his knees, and I shifted my gaze to the tattoos on his forearms. "I wouldn't jeopardize your job, Gracie," he said. "Unless someone pissed me off and did something to you I didn't like."

I raised my eyes to meet his, and through the strange light the color of blue shone sincerity. He meant what he said.

I dropped my supplies into the bucket and leaned back on my heels. "Why is that?" I asked with a little discomfort. "Exactly."

Brax stared first between his feet, then slowly lifted his head. His gaze pierced mine; he didn't blink, only searched. A muscle flinched in his jaw. "Hell if I know."

I wanted to fall right over onto my backside. I felt that weak. The way he stared at me, talked to me—I swear I almost believed it. Almost believed every single word he said, without question. But deep inside, I knew better. It just couldn't be real.

How could it be?

"So what'd you want to show me?" he asked.

I calmed myself with an inconspicuous breath, rose, and grabbed my supplies. "Follow me." He did—and right behind me, until we reached the auditorium entrance doors. I paused and looked at him over my shoulder. "Want an inside celestial view first?"

In the low lights, a curious, dark gaze filled Brax's eyes. He leaned closer. "I'll take anything you're offering, Sunshine."

"Good Lord, Brax. Stay here," I said, setting my supplies down. I hit the lights and crossed the auditorium to the main planetarium switchboard. Steven had shown me how to operate it. "Ready?" I asked into the pitch darkness.

"Always."

"Dork." I smiled and shook my head, then threw the switch. Within the simulated night sky, each planet, situated in the correct coordinates and hanging from the ceiling, illuminated. Stars blinked.

"Damn, Gracie," he said slowly. By his tone I could tell he was genuinely impressed. I'd been, too, when Steven had shown me earlier. The auditorium had turned into a replicated pitch-dark starry sky, complete with illuminated and finely detailed planets. Suddenly and quiet as a stealth soldier, he was beside me. His hand found its way to my lower back, his breath on my neck, and my eyes drifted to his profile. With his head lifted, he stared at the stars and planets overhead. His fingers felt heavy against me, and I fought the urge to lean into him. "Christ, it looks so real. Is that the Milky Way?" he asked.

Although the illumination from the display threw the room into a yielding blush, it was still shadowy enough to hide my reaction to Brax. I drew a breath. Slowly released it. "Sure is," I answered. I elbowed him gently. "You're really a geek buried under all that." I looked at him and grinned. "Aren't you?"

Brax's gaze left the celestial display and turned to me. His hand stayed on my back, and the sharp scent of earthy guy soap filled my nostrils as I inhaled. His head ducked, and he cocked it sideways. His hair was still wet from a recent shower. Those perfect lips twitched. "Under all what?"

Talk about poking a caged tiger with a stick. Had I lost my mind? My *damn* mind? I blinked, and hoped I'd erased the unease from my face. "Under all that cockiness and ink," I countered. Narrowing my eyes, I nodded toward the door. But Brax's gaze stayed focused on mine, sharp and soft and ghostly and sexy at the same time. I shoved that thought away. "Now do you want to see something cool or not?"

One corner of his mouth lifted—a habit of his that was addicting to look at. "Cool, huh, Sunshine?" Still, his hand splayed over my lower back, and I swear, I found myself not wanting him to remove it. Then, he lifted my braid, played with it between his fingers for a moment, then flicked it over my shoulder. "Yeah, show me something cool. Although it's gotta be damn good to beat what's right in front of me."

I knew Brax was doing exactly what he did with all girls: flirt like a hellion. He'd even told me it was all in fun and part of his character, and for me not to take it personally. It was harder than I thought. A pent-up exhale slowly released from my lungs, through my pursed lips, and I laughed nervously. "It's way cooler. I promise." I hit the exhibit display lights, and the room darkened. "Come on, Boston. Follow me." I started up the aisle toward the door, its EXIT illuminating red hue the only light in the auditorium. Brax walked behind me, guiding me with his strong hand, and each of his fingertips left an impression in my skin, I was sure of it. At the door, he grabbed my supplies bucket, reached around me and pushed it open, and I stepped out.

Noah Hicks stood just beyond in the foyer, as if he was expecting us. He smiled at me, but his gaze turned questioning and cautious toward Brax. "I see you found Olivia with no problem," he said. "How'd you like the display?"

Brax's body closed in toward mine. "Fucking spectacular." His fingers dug into my back. "Never seen one like it before, man."

Noah gave a brief look at me, then nodded. I wondered if he got the gist of Brax's words that had nothing to do with the display. Or was I kidding myself again? Noah then smiled at me. "You're going to the platform, I guess? Clear sky with a decent lunar slice to observe. I just unlocked my office, if you want to get your scope." He moved past us then, and brushed his hand over my shoulder. Brax pushed closer, and I felt his chest against my back. "I'll start locking up in about an hour," Noah said.

"Okay, thank you," I replied. I glanced back at Brax. "I'll be right back. Wait here."

I left Noah and Brax sizing each other up and hurried down the hallway. What was that all about? The energy pouring off of Brax had taken me off guard, so potent and possessive. How could that be? And Noah? I knew him less than I did Brax, yet I'd noticed a total change in his demeanor, as well. Like two big cats facing off. It couldn't be that I was bringing a friend to the platform; Noah had already approved that. Was it Brax he didn't approve of? No doubt the rumors surrounding him didn't exclude the faculty.

In Noah's office I grabbed my scope bag, slung it over my shoulder and hurried back. "Okay, let's go," I said to Brax. He and Noah were staring each other down like a couple of gladiators. Brax looking like a street thug, Noah like a, well … a manicured professional. Neither moved or said a word, so I stepped closer, grabbed Brax's hand, and tugged. "This way, gotta hurry." Brax's body shifted toward my pull, and I threw Noah a friendly smile. "Thanks again. We'll be back down shortly."

Noah nodded at me, turned and disappeared down the hall and into his office.

Brax lifted my scope bag from my arm and shouldered it, and we curved around the hallway and came to the doorway that led to the observatory's dome and massive platform. My heart raced ninety-to-nothing, and confusion warped my brain. I stopped, dropped Brax's hand, and turned to him. I kept my voice low. "If I invite you back here you'll have to leave that Southie badass disposition behind, Brax. Noah is one of my bosses. A TA for the astronomy department. And, he's nice. So whatever got your hackles up with him, relax. No bullying. Got it?"

Crystal blue eyes snapped with mischief, and his lip twitched. "You got it, Sunshine. No bullying." He rubbed his jaw. "This time."

10. Sunshine

Brax DUCKED HIS HEAD as if to get a better look into my eyes. A slow smile crept over his mouth. "God, you've got the cutest accent. Damn, Gracie. I like this side of you."

I opened the door and turned to him. He made me feel comfortable, brave, safe and cagey all at once. It was a disconcerting hairball of emotions to say the very least. "It's not a side, Brax. It's just me. This job's important, okay? Not only to me, but to my family. So don't get me into trouble." I forced my eyes to stay on his. "I'm not working here to make extra money to go on a spending spree at the mall, you know. I send what I don't live on to my family. To help with the expenses of the ranch." I sighed. "I've trusted you so far, and that doesn't come easy for me. With you or anyone else. So please don't make me regret it. And just about everyone here has the same accent. Texas."

A softness settled across Brax's face then; like many of his expressions, it changed the contours of his face, shifted harshness into marbled perfection, into something I thought I could stare at for hours on end. Something else flickered in his eyes, though; misconception? Curiosity? To try and read it, or his thoughts, was ridiculous. He was as inscrutable as a guy could be. But when he lifted his hand to my jaw, grasping it with his thumb and forefinger, and forced me to keep my sight on his, I had to swallow past the humongous lump in my throat that had grown in a matter of seconds.

"You're different from any girl I've ever met. I could tell that the second I looked down at you on the lawn. And you know what?" He pulled even closer. "Regrets are little bastards, Gracie, and we all have them, only," he drew closer, his voice quieted, "you won't have them with me. And I can't help that I don't trust the guy. Unlike you, I see through his stiff-collared play-by-the-rules prickness. Like it or not, he's a dick. Just a cleaned up dick with a title. You watch him. I fuckin' mean it."

I stared at him for a second or two. Was Brax crazy? Like mentally unstable? I felt no threat whatsoever with Noah Hicks. He was courteous and professional, nothing more. Wasn't he?

I'd thought the same thing about Kelsy Evans at one time, too. *Don't you let your guard down, Olivia. With Noah, Brax, or anyone else for that matter. You'll just get your teeth kicked in.* I gave a nod, agreeing with my inner self, and opened the door. "Will do. Now let's go. We're running out of time."

Brax said nothing more as he trailed behind me, but his presence filled the narrow stairwell. We could've taken the elevators, but I liked how my body felt after a vigorous climb; how my lungs felt exercised, alive. Brax's breath was smooth, even, barely noticeable. I'd figured he could handle the seven story sprint, as fit as he looked.

At the top, Brax reached around me once more and pushed open the door, and I led us both out to the platform. The night air wasn't as still and heavy as it had been lately, which was a sheer Texas blessing and as close to pre-fall weather as we'd get. A soft breeze brushed my cheeks and cooled my skin, and Brax set my bag on the platform by my feet. The three-quarter moon offered a strange filtered radiance—just enough to see my way around the platform without the use of a flashlight. Brax's head moved with his gaze as he took in the impressive tower. He pointed to a row of mounts, close to the ledge.

"Basic scope mounts," I offered. "For the general public's use." Kneeling, I unzipped my bag and pulled out first my tripod, assembled the lower aspect, and set it upright. I knew my scope so well I could do it blindfolded. Then Brax was kneeling with me, and he studied as I collected my scope pieces and locked them onto my tripod mount. We were still crouched, and I knew he watched me, and suddenly, I felt shy. Conspicuous. Peculiar and totally out of my element. Like maybe it was a bad idea, sharing this part of my life with a virtual stranger. Especially one like Brax Jenkins. I mean, he was a star athlete. Big shot Winston bad-boy athlete. I was ... an astronomy geek. We were about as different as night and day. And I was an idiot for even entertaining thoughts of anything more than friendship. I started to rise, but his hand to my wrist kept me in place.

"You," Brax said, and again, ducked his head, "are one badass lady. Smart and beautiful. I like that."

I looked at him and even under the cover of shadow, my face grew hot with embarrassment and I knew he could tell it. My eyes drifted down to a spot between my feet, but Brax's knuckle lifted my gaze right back up. I swallowed hard. His dark brows, so conflicting against the fair color of his skin, lifted, just before he grinned. "No shit, Gracie. Look at you. You just threw that scope together like it was nothin'. You put together your own bookcase. You have a tool box. You drive a fuckin' Mad Max tank for Christ's sake." He rubbed his jaw as he studied me, then grazed the scar on my lip with his thumb. "Your cell phone's a relic, and you send extra money home to your folks. Like I said before. Different. And different is pretty goddamned appealing to me."

I was speechless. Frozen in place. Uncomfortable. Ecstatic. Yet, my mouth opened, and I spoke. "Funny. Those were all qualities that set me apart from other girls in high school. Made me about as much of a novelty as this," I held my ringed finger up. "I was made fun of. People talked behind my back." I rose and busied myself with locking the scope onto the mount. Brax stood behind me, and I continued. "I knew it, though, and didn't care, really. I mean, it was me. Who I was." I gave him a quick glance, and he studied me in silence. "I was comfortable with myself and wasn't changing for anyone." I pushed my braid over my shoulder, checked the scope locks, then looked skyward. Finding the moon, I situated the eyepiece, zeroed the target, tilted the scope, and pressed my eye to it. Forced myself to breathe.

"I'm damn glad of that." Brax's raspy voice spoke with certainty; maybe a little admiration. Or surprise. And very close. *You're being stupid again ...*

"Well," I shook off my self-chastising and continued setting the scope. "I'm ... relieved you appreciate my individuality." I lifted my head and looked at him, and gave him a half smile. "Or maybe you just have weird taste in friends." I stepped out of the way and inclined my head toward the scope.

Brax's shoulder brushed mine as he moved to take my place, but he didn't comment. He lowered his head to the eyepiece and I studied his profile. In the shadows, his features were fierce, set, cut in stone like a gargoyle, maybe, and I was again disarmed by how brutal yet completely stunning he was. "Are you fucking kidding me?" he said in a low voice. Pulling his eye from the view finder, he grinned, then returned his gaze to the telescope positioned toward the moon's surface. "Christ, I've never seen anything like it, Gracie." Moments went by, and I waited in the dark as he scoured the stars. I felt thrilled Brax was intrigued. For some crazy reason, I'd hoped he would be.

"I guess we'd better pack it up," I finally said. "I don't want to abuse my privileges on the first day."

Brax straightened and made his mouth twitch. "You a by-the-book type of girl, yeah?"

I nodded. "Especially when it comes to my job. Yes." I reached for the scope, about to start unlocking the pieces, but Brax beat me to it. I watched, and to my surprise he'd really paid close attention. He broke every scope piece and mount part down perfectly. I crouched beside him and held open the bag while he loaded the pieces carefully inside. When he finished, he pointed.

"What's with the camera?"

I zipped the bag, Brax shouldered it, and we both rose. "Celestial photography," I answered. I started toward the platform door, and he followed. Inside the stairwell, the lights were dim. "Sometimes the lighting is perfect, and objects are sharp. I don't like to miss an opportunity."

He reached the bottom just ahead of me and he stopped. The space between us was non-existent, he was so close, and with me one step up we were nearly eye level. "Neither do I."

The surge of electricity between us pinged off the walls of the stairwell, bringing awareness to all of my senses. The scent of Brax's skin smelled clean, like soap, and it mixed with the faint aroma of fresh paint on the concrete walls. The warmth inside the stairwell brought a slight sheen of moisture to my arms, neck, face, and with each breath Brax released, it washed over me and cooled my skin. My heart slammed against my ribs, and we just stared. I couldn't move, frozen to the step I stood on. I knew I wasn't imagining it. Brax's gaze lowered to my mouth and stayed there long enough to make my breath lodge in my throat. Suddenly the scar through my lip seemed twice as large, and I tried to hide it with my teeth.

"Don't do that," Brax said. His thumb brushed over my scar, and he looked at me. "Don't hide that scar. Don't hide who you are, Gracie. Ever." *Scah*.

Brax's broad shoulders shifted, and his body leaned toward me. My mind was clogged, confused, but all I knew was I wanted his mouth on mine. I wanted him to kiss me. *Oh, God, he's going to kiss me ...*

The exit door opened, and I jumped back as Noah Hicks stepped inside. Luckily, his gaze was directly on Brax instead of me, because no doubt I had guilt written all over my face. "Hey, I was just coming to check out your scope." Brax had shifted back and stood tall, eye to eye with Noah. "But I see you've already packed it up. What'd you think?" he asked Brax.

Brax didn't answer right away, and I got the feeling he did it on purpose. "Fucking amazing," he finally said, then reached back and grabbed my hand. "We were just heading out. Thanks for letting me in, man." He moved past Noah, towing me behind him.

"It was an amazingly sharp moon tonight," I told Noah. "The platform is perfect."

Noah smiled at me, and I noticed then he had a dimple in his chin. "Wait until you check out the Mulligan next week. You're going to freak."

"No doubt," I answered. "See you tomorrow, Noah. And thanks."

"You bet, Olivia," he said behind me. Because Brax kept pulling me up the main hallway toward the entrance room.

At the door, Brax released my hand and we stepped outside. "What's a Mulligan?" he asked as we made our way to my truck. His bike was parked right beside it. His voice had an edge to it, like something bothered him. Was it because Noah had interrupted what probably was going to be our first kiss? Correction. Our second kiss. Or was I delusional about that? I couldn't believe I was even entertaining the thought. Hadn't it been my idea to remain neutral? Just friends? What had happened to me?

"It's the observatory's scope." We reached my truck and Brax stopped, looking at me. I pointed over my shoulder and grinned. "You know? The big one under the dome?"

Brax's eyes lifted in the dome's direction, then he settled his gaze on mine. Those blue ghosts had an angry flare in their depths. "I don't like that guy, Gracie."

I cocked my head. "Noah? Why—"

"Because I can see what you can't," he interrupted. "Students are off limits for TA's," he added. "I've seen more than one prick use that title to get laid. Just watch it with him."

I hadn't felt any weird vibes from Noah. Not at all. Then again, I hadn't felt any with Brax, either. Maybe my vibe-o-meter was way off? I unlocked my truck door. "I've been warned the very same thing about you, Brax." I gave him a solid, determined look. "I make my own mind up about people. And I watch it with everyone, don't forget."

He reached over then and slid my scope bag across the bench seat, then shoved his fingers through his hair as he studied me. "Yeah, you do, don't ya. You still hungry, Sunshine?"

"Stahved."

His lip turned upward. "Smartass. Let's go."

We'd just settled onto his bike when his phone rang. He answered it. "Yeah. Hell no, I'm on my way out. Are you fucking kidding me?" Brax pinched the bridge of his nose. "Yeah, all right." He half-turned to me. "Gracie, I gotta handle something. How 'bout I pick you up in thirty minutes at your dorm?"

I slid off Brax's bike. "You don't have to do that," I answered. "It's late and I—"

"It's only nine, Gracie. This won't take long." With his heel, Brax kicked the bike's stand down and he got off. He faced me now, a teasing smirk on his face. "You gotta eat, right?"

Who was I kidding? I wanted to go. I liked being around Brax. I liked how I felt around him. Even the nervousness. "Okay. I'll go change and meet you out front in thirty minutes."

In the dark parking lot of the Science complex, his teeth shone white as he smiled. "Be right back." He started his bike, pulled on his helmet, and waited for me to climb into my truck. I did, and we both left together. At the next intersection, he turned off to the left, and I watched his red tail light disappear.

Tessa turned her face toward me the minute I walked in. "What's up, chica?" she said with a grin. "How was nerd world at the observatory? Whoa—is that a body bag or what?"

I set my scope bag next to my bed and went to the small fold out closet to find something else to wear. I looked over my shoulder. "It could be a body bag. Nerd world was fantastic. How about you?"

Tessa sat on her bed with her long straight hair in a ponytail, applying some thick white cream to her face. "Sheer perfection. My biology professor is so fucking hot it's ridiculous." She peeked at me. "Why does it look like you're changing into something else?"

I threw my collared work shirt on my bed and pulled a brown tank top over my head. I shoved my arms into a long-sleeved plaid buttoned down. "Because I am. I thought you and the girls were going out?"

Tessa stopped her facial application in mid-rub. "We are. But seriously. After my most excellent advice you're still going out with *him*?"

I resisted giving my overly-dramatic roommate an overly-exaggerated eye roll. "We're just grabbing a bite to eat, Tess—no big deal, really. Actually, we were leaving right after the observatory but he—"

"He was at the observatory with you?" Tessa all but screeched. "Doing what?"

"Observing. What else?"

A pair of balled up fluffy socks hurled through the air, directly at my head. I batted it away.

"Look at me, Olivia," Tessa insisted, got up from the bed and came to stand right in front of me.

I finished snapping my shirt up and looked at her. "Yes, ma'am?"

After a moment, her eyes widened. "Oh shit. No way."

My brows tugged together in a guilty frown. "What?"

Like the Grinch as he stared with distaste toward Whoville, Tessa's gaze turned into accusing slits. "You *like* him."

I pointed at her brows. "You look scary when you frown like that."

"Olivia!" Tessa squealed. "I'm serious. What are you doing?"

My shoulder lifted to a shrug. "Eating supper. Then coming home to study." Even I could confess now how difficult it was to fend off a persuasive Brax. He was fun to be around, and the spark that seemed to flash inside of me whenever he was close to me? I liked it. Sure. I liked *him*. Didn't mean I was stupid.

Tessa flopped back down onto the end of her bed, grabbed a *Cosmopolitan* magazine from her purse, and started flipping madly through the pages.

"Look Tessa," I said, and sat down beside her. "I know he's a playboy. A big flirt. And he knows I know." Tessa looked up at me and I grinned. "He's funny. Makes me laugh. And I really don't think he's in it to hurt me." I considered my own words, surprised. "I haven't trusted a guy in a long, long time. Yet I find myself trusting Brax. I like being around him."

Her features softened. "Yeah, chica. I can tell. Just stay smart about it, I guess."

I gave her a light punch in the arm. "I will. Thanks."

Grabbing my faded denim jacket, I shoved my keys and cell phone in my bag, shouldered it, and headed out. I caught a few stares as I passed through the common room, and I knew it was because of Brax. Although my face heated as their eyes followed me, I decided that if I was going to go out with Brax—even just as friends—I wasn't going to cower. I'd suffered it in high school. I'd be damned if I was going to be a victim in college. With a deep breath I turned my full gaze on the group of girls staring me down, then pushed through the doors and stepped outside. I didn't look back to see their reaction, and although my heart raced a little, I felt better. I wasn't a coward by nature and it was damn time I stopped worrying about hiding. From Kelsy. From people. From the world.

The night air was thick, humid, and carried voices, music from neighboring dorms, and laughter. Taking a seat on the curb, I stretched my legs out, crossed my ankles, and waited there for Brax.

Twenty minutes passed as I watched girls straggle into Oliver Hall—some in small groups, others alone. No one spoke to me as they walked by, but I didn't speak, either. I checked my phone. Thirty minutes, and no text or missed call. Finally, after forty minutes, I rose and walked to my truck. Whatever Brax had to take care of was taking longer than either of us had thought. We both had early class, and my stomach was growling like a bear. Disappointment pinged inside of me, but I pushed it aside as best I could. I needed to eat, and it didn't look like Brax was coming. Since the cafeteria was closed, and I just didn't feel like another big whopping spoonful of peanut butter, I decided to drive to Hattie's, an all-night café about two miles out of Winston's main gates. I felt like breakfast. A really big one. I quickly sent Brax a short text.

Me: Hey, I guess you got caught up, but I'm stahved so going to grab a bite to eat. See ya in class ☺

Tossing my phone in my bag, I headed for my truck, hopped in, and made it to Hattie's in ten minutes. As I walked inside, I noticed the place was maybe half-full at almost ten o'clock. Most were other students, and a few regulars from town, I imagined. I spied an empty corner booth away from most of the other patrons and tucked myself into it. Just as the waitress handed me a menu, Brax slid into the seat across from me.

"Damn, Sunshine, you got no patience when it comes to food, do ya?" he said.

11. Letting Go

I GAPED AT BRAX. He still wore the same tee shirt and jeans he'd had on earlier, except now he sported a Silverbacks baseball cap.

And a brand new punched-out eye, along with a fresh cut on his upper lip. "Good Lord, Brax. What happened to you?"

He gave me a lop-sided grin, then got up and slid onto the bench next to me. He leaned his shoulder into mine. "Why, worried about me, sweetheart?" *Sweethaht*. He bowed closer, to read the menu with me. He still smelled good, and I tried to keep from falling against him. The effect he had on me was quickly becoming more ridiculous with each passing second. Part of me still wanted not to trust him so easily, but I just couldn't help it. I chanced a peek sideways at him and noticed how his dark hair curled out from his cap at the nape of his neck. It looked soft, and I clutched my fists against my thighs to keep from twisting those locks around my fingers.

"No, not worried," I said, and peered closely at him. "Who'd you make mad this time?"

Brax's chuckle was throaty and male. "No one, smartass." He looked at me, and those arresting eyes settled onto mine. "One of my frat brothers becomes an idiot when he's shit-faced. His girl broke up with him tonight so, you know." He shrugged and returned to the menu. "I let him get a few swings in, Gracie. Helped the guy let off some steam. No big deal. So what are you ordering?"

It felt strange, completely natural, and breathtaking having Brax sit right beside me in the booth. I hadn't been close to anyone, except family, in so long. It felt scary and invigorating. I drew in a calming breath. "Breakfast, of course."

Brax looked at me, ducked his head to meet my eyes. "Breakfast?"

"What will you darlings be having tonight? Oh, Jesus, son." The waitress was older, with a gravelly voice and pixie-shorn salt and pepper hair. She leaned closer to Brax, inspecting his beat-up face. "You want an ice pack or something for that?"

Brax gave her a bright smile. "Nah, it'll be all right."

"Tough guy, huh?" She grinned, and looked at me. "Go ahead, sweetie. What'll you have?"

"Apple pancakes and sausage," I said.

"And a large chocolate milk, please."

Brax looked at me then gave an approving nod. "Same for me."

"Nice choice, sweetie, although you don't look like you can hold it all.Be right back." The waitress left, and Brax turned sort of sideways in the booth, cornering me in.

"It looks painful," I said, and nodded at his eye. It was discolored and swelling fast. It'd be black and purple by the next day. I fidgeted with my hands in my lap, cracked my knuckles. Unladylike, I know, but I couldn't help it. Bad habit since I was a kid.

His gaze stayed on mine, but his grin was slow, sly and purposeful. He didn't answer,didn't respond. Just kept staring. Smiling. In the background, the clank of dishes and silverware and the low rumble of conversation barely infiltrated the intimate space Brax had created in the booth between us. I glanced away, then back to him, a little shy, a little curious. "Why are you staring at me like that?"

"Because you're just so fuckin' beautiful."

Shock and heat shot through me at his frank, crude, and incredibly sexy confession. I felt my skin turn hot from embarrassment, and I gave him a quick look.

"How hard did that guy hit you anyway?" I lifted my hand. "How many fingers am I holding up?"

His gaze didn't falter.

I fought a smile, lowered my hand. "You're crazy."

His mouth tilted. "Damn right I am."

I just shook my head, the impact of his comment sinking deep inside of me. I liked the way Brax made me feel. Then my phone vibrated in my bag. No one called me. Ever. Unless it was family. I fished it out of my purse. "Sorry, its home. I need to take this."

Brax continued to watch me. "No problem."

Jilly's name flashed across my tiny cell phone screen, and I answered it. "Hey, Jilly, is everything okay?"

"Hell, yes, everything's fine, darlin'." Jilly's sandy old voice washed over me, and I had to keep from laughing. He had a lot of drama for an old guy. "Is there somethin' wrong with a decrepit old man checkin' on his baby girl?"

My eyes lifted to Brax, who studied me closely. I knew he could hear everything Jilly said; everyone within earshot probably could. He was loud as sin. "You are not old and decrepit, Jilly. And of course not. Do you miss me?"

"Hell yes, I miss you!" Jilly exclaimed. "When are you comin' back home? I need someone to go target shootin' with."

I laughed. "Jilly, I just got here. I'll be home during fall break."

"Well, horseshit. That's more 'n a month away, darlin'."

My gaze rose to find Brax's lips twisting into a seriously cute grin. "I know," I appeased. "Maybe you and Mom can drive up and you can check out the Mulligan with me. It's sincerely a sweet scope."

Jilly heaved a big sigh into the phone. "Well, there is that, I suppose. Everything goin' all right there? You ain't turnin' all fancypants on me, are ya?"

Again, I giggled. "No, Jilly." I looked at Brax. His eyes were directly on mine. "Same old me."

"Good. Keep it that way. It's my bedtime now, gotta go. I love ya, darlin'."

My smile pulled at my mouth. "I love you too, Jilly. 'Night."

He grumbled and swore at something random as he disconnected the phone. I put mine away.

"And you can shoot?" Brax asked.

I eyed him. "Sure."

"I like you more by the second, Sunshine."

I lifted a brow. "You're easily impressed."

He chuckled. "The hell I am. I like that guy, though," he admitted. "Sounds as badass as his granddaughter. And he's apparently crazy about you."

I nodded. "He is, and he is."

"I can see why."

Just as my face started to heat up, the food came. "Okay, lovebirds, dig in." The waitress interrupted the moment and plopped two loaded plates of apple pancakes and sausage down in front of us. She followed it with a pot of steaming hot maple syrup, a small bowl of butter, and two large glasses of chocolate milk. The entire time she set the food down,

Brax kept his stare on me. The grin only grew wider.

"Wow," I said, leaning over my plate and inhaling. I smiled at Brax. "This smells so good." I plopped a gob of butter in the center of the stack.

"I'll give you a hundred bucks if you eat all that," he finally said.

I held out my hand to his for a shake, and he grasped it. His completely dwarfed mine; it was large and warm and calloused. And perfect. "You're on, Southie."

We dug in, delicious crispy-edged fried apple pancakes drowned in butter and hot syrup, and spicy sausage, and soon the uncomfortable shyness drifted out of me. "So how'd you get started in baseball?" I asked. I pulled a long sip of chocolate milk and waited.

A faraway look came over his expression, and I figured he was remembering things from a long time ago. He licked syrup off his thumb. It was the first time I'd ever recalled wishing like hell to be a thumb. "When I was a little kid I lived close enough to Fenway to hear the crack of a baseball against a bat." A fond memory must've flittered over his mind, and a ghostly smile lifted his mouth. "Me and my brothers used to sneak over, and the old guy at the ticket booth knew who we were and always let us in through a back entrance." He looked away then, like he was searching something familiar. "I got my ass beat more than once for sneakin' to the park, but I hardly

ever missed a game. Even when we moved."
Pahk. He looked over at me. "We'd catch the
train and ride it to Fenway. I loved everything
about that ballpark. Me and my brothers, we
didn't have to pay for anything. Hot dogs,
sodas, peanuts, the game." He winked. "All on
our eight year old charm. But it was the
sounds that drew me. Ball to bat. Ball to
glove." He dug back into his pancakes, and
my eyes were drawn to his inked knuckles and
tattooed arms. "The cracking sound they both
made." He looked at me, and kept chewing,
then swallowed. "I remember hanging over
the rail in outfield for the whole fucking
game, just to catch a fly ball." He drew a line
across his stomach. "Had a bruise straight
across here for a solid week."

I listened intently, hanging onto every
word. I could tell Brax was in his element. In
his zone. Before or after the bad stuff, it didn't
matter. Here, with baseball, he'd been happy.
I had a huge feeling though he'd faced a lot
harsher times than he was letting on.

He grinned as if he'd read my mind. "We
were poor as shit, and when good ole St. Nick
didn't bring me a glove for Christmas I stole
one from the thrift shop up the street from our
house. Took me a while to steal a ball. Hid
them both under my bed so my old man
wouldn't find them. After that," he shrugged
those broad shoulders again, "I just kept on
throwing. Every single day."

As I inspected Brax's very close profile I

tried to envision him as a little boy. It saddened me to think of him being mistreated, or going without. But I wanted to keep things light right now. I liked the spark I saw in those odd, clear depths. "I bet you were a big ole stinker. Charming your way into the ballpark with those eyes." I popped in the last bite of sausage and chewed, smothering a grin. "I bet you were all curls and teeth and pure deviltry."

Brax turned a bit, to directly face me. "So you're noticin' my eyes and locks and teeth, huh, Sunshine?"

"Ego, Boston, ego," I chastised. "We're in a crowded booth here, don't forget."

Brax laughed, shook his head, and draped his arm behind me on the seat rest. "Yeah, I had hair out to fuckin' here," he held his hands inches from his head. "Looked like a Wildman. So what about you? How was it growing up?"

I looked at my empty plate. "Like I told you before, my dad left us when I was little, and I don't remember him at all, really. But I remember after him." I fidgeted with the paper from my straw. "We all worked hard, even at early ages. My two older brothers, me, and my younger brother. We didn't have much. But as kids we didn't know it. My grandpa Jilly had just retired from the Rangers—"

"As in the Texas Rangers?"

I looked at Brax. "That's right."

"That's cool as shit, Sunshine. No wonder

he shoots." He nodded. "Proceed."

I smiled. "Jilly's a character—and one of my very best friends. Anyway, he'd just retired and so our income was limited. We broke horses for rich ranchers in the area. Jilly was untouched in his day. He could talk a horse into doing anything. My mom, too, and we'd get horses in from all over the state. My brothers and I were raised in the horse pen." I shrugged. "We always had food to eat. We always had a Christmas tree. Mom always made us birthday cakes and gave us plenty of love. The only time I really knew we were poor was when another kid at school would tell us so. Make fun of our clothes. Stuff like that."

"Kids can be mean little bastards." Brax's stare scored into me, like he could see deeper into that part of me usually reserved for the limited few and deserving people I'd allow in. As it had numerous times before, his gaze lowered to my mouth and settled there, and subconsciously I pulled my scar between my teeth. When his stare lifted, those eyes had turned rainy, smoky, fiery all at once. The look was so profound it made my breath catch in my throat, and I found I couldn't look away.

"What about astronomy, Gracie?" he asked, in that raspy voice. "Have you always loved it?"

I smiled then, and found it not so hard to look him in the eye. My stars were his baseball. "My whole life."

Brax's eyes softened, then he looked up, slowly exhaled, took his cap off and shoved his fingers through his hair. "Jesus Christ, girl," he muttered, then replaced his hat and turned to me.

I gave him a puzzled look. "What?"

His smile was again lazy and deep. "You're just so damned different."

We continued talking, and it was so easy and enticing and interesting that I'd lost track of all time. Of place, of purpose. We ordered hot cocoa with whipped topping, and talked some more. I could tell Brax skirted some subjects, fell lightly on others. I did the same, though, so I could hardly judge him on that. One thing I knew for sure: He'd experienced a lot of pain at some point in his life. I hadn't until the summer before my senior year, so I guess I had more to be thankful for than I'd thought. At least I'd had a loving family. I wasn't too sure Brax had. It'd been one of the subjects he'd eased over like a fresh pond of ice. Barely skimmed it. But I could tell. Could see it in those beautifully haunted blue eyes of his. Maybe one day he'd trust his secrets to me.

Maybe one day I'd trust mine to him.

For now, though, we learned the good stuff. What kept us going. What made us strong. And I was content with that. I think he was, too.

By two in the morning, the waitress interrupted us. "You two love birds want another pot of chocolate? Or do you wanna start on java?"

I shook my head. "No, thank you." I reached for my bag to get money for my portion of the bill. "It's so late. I'd better be getting back."

Brax stilled my hand with his. "I owe you a hundred bucks, remember?" He reached in his back pocket, pulled out his wallet, and handed the waitress his ATM card. She smiled at him, deep sun lines sinking in around her mouth and eyes. "That a boy, tough guy." She winked at me. "Be right back, darlin'."

We left Hattie's once she returned Brax's card, and he walked me to my truck. The early-morning air hung thick, warm but not uncomfortable, and a slight breeze drifted across the parking lot. Everything was quiet, and I fished my keys out of my bag and looked up at him. "Your eye is swelling pretty good," I said. "Do you have any frozen vegetables?"

Brax stared at me, then laughed. "Jesus, Sunshine, you can't still be fuckin' hungry."

"No," I smiled. "For your eye. A bag of frozen peas works the best. Melds to the skin better than a couple chunks of ice."

My back was already to my door; Brax eased closer to me, braced a hand against the truck. "You speakin' from experience?"

"I've had my share of black eyes." I quirked my head, inspecting the eye that was rapidly closing shut. "You'll be okay driving home?" He was close to me, leaning slightly in toward my body, and a thrill shot through me that made my insides hum, my skin grow warm. At the same time I was treading unknown waters, feeling unsure of myself, a little scared. This was exactly what I didn't want starting college; certainly didn't expect it, either. But was I being completely honest with myself? Hadn't I secretly and privately craved this? Dreamed I'd meet a guy, one who made me feel so alive?

Desired?

A slow smile and filtered moonlight transformed Brax's harsh features into something sexy, hungry, attentive. "Sunshine, I could ride that bike blindfolded." With his free hand he pushed my braid off my shoulder, and ducked his head to better see my eyes. "I'm not going to kiss you yet, Gracie." His hand reached for mine, and his thumb grazed the ring I wore. His eyes darkened. "But I will. When it's time."

I could barely breathe, much less speak. Somehow, I managed. "I believe you."

To look at Brax this close, after he'd expressed such an intimate confession, made every nerve ending in my body fire at once. It was difficult—yet I couldn't look away if I'd tried. Etched into his beautiful features were strength, determination, and struggle. Struggle not to kiss me? Did I even dare hope it?

Could I handle it if he did kiss me? Like, a real, intentional kiss?

Brax's fingers closed around my truck keys, reached around me so close I could've laid my head on his chest, and unlocked my door. "Get in, Gracie." I turned, and he stopped me, and I looked up at him again. "Before I fuckin' change my mind."

I eased into my truck, and Brax shut the door. I rolled down the window, started the engine.

"I'll follow you to your dorm," he said, then winked. "G'night, Sunshine."

"'Night, Brax."

I waited until Brax had straddled his bike and started the engine before I pulled out of Hattie's. My heart raced and thumped against my ribs the whole way back to Oliver Hall where I parked, got out, and waved goodbye to Brax as he idled, watching me until I'd slid my door key in and entered the common room. I heard the grumble of his pipes as he left the parking lot.

As I jogged up the steps to the second floor, a smile pasted to my face, I noticed my heart was light for the first time in over a year. For once, I felt my life just might change for the better.

12. Breathless

AFTER THAT NIGHT, I felt lighter. Despite having to look at Kelsy every day in humanities, even that tension eased up. He kept to himself and high-tailed it out of class the second it was over. Only occasionally would I catch him looking at me. The expression on his face was unreadable; a mixture of scorn versus longing, I guess. But with Brax beside me, I felt safe. Not so cagey anymore. And Kelsy left me alone. That was a plus in my book.

I began running, too, every morning before anyone else woke up. I ran alone, with just me and my thoughts, and as the days ticked by I felt stronger physically as well. My confidence was higher than it'd ever been. Working at the observatory was a dream. Steven was hysterical and a hard worker, and our shifts usually passed by pretty fast. Our first Night Sky Watch for our astronomy lab was approaching. Fun stuff. Exciting.

It had been almost two weeks since that night at Hattie's, and Brax's promise of kissing me still burned in my mind. The way he'd said it so bluntly, and looked at me? *Promised*? It'd taken me an hour to fall asleep that night. And my God, the way he had called me beautiful? The whole scene replayed in my head a thousand times. His bad-boy reputation be damned. I felt deep into my core he'd meant every word.

He hadn't kissed me, though. We'd grown closer—saw each other every day, during school and after—yet no kiss. Had he changed his mind? Lord knows I'd never have the courage to kiss him first.

But I sure did want to.

Most of these thoughts I kept to myself. At Tessa's unforgiving drilling I'd finally confessed to her that I really liked him. It didn't go over well at first. But after she'd been around Brax a few times with me, I think she saw he wasn't a complete beast.

It was a couple of weeks later when I lifted my cell phone off my nightstand and checked the time. Five a.m. A little earlier than I'd been getting up, but I'd had enough sleep and to lie in bed wide awake would just make me fidgety. Quietly, I crept out of the covers, pulled on the running shorts, tee shirt and footie socks I'd pulled out the night before, jumped into the bathroom for a sec and brushed my teeth, and rebraided my hair. As silently as I could, I eased out into the hall and headed downstairs. No one was up and about, and I liked it that way. The lights were dimmed in the common room, and I let myself out.

Outside, the air was still, breezeless, the sidewalks empty, and the pre-dawn sky was just starting to show a few streaks of radiance. A light mist hung through the oaks, making the old brick architecture of Winston appear haunting and ghoulish. I took off down the main street at a slow pace to warm up, measuring my breaths with each stride until I'd reached a perfect chorus of exhales and inhales. With each stride, energy shot through my feet and up my legs, my arms, and I picked up the pace. Early morning air filled my lungs; the heavy scent of pine and magnolia blooms saturated the slight breeze that passed through the trees, and I ran a little faster. The way a hard run made my muscles and lungs burn felt good, made my body feel alive and strong. Like I could conquer anything. Staying to the main streets, I found myself at Winston's sweeping entrance, where I turned and headed back.

"Are you stalkin' me now, Gracie?"

My heart jumped as I shot my gaze over my shoulder. The voice and body merged into Brax as he ran up behind me, and slowed to my pace beside me. He wore black shorts, black Nikes. Shirtless. He was absolutely shirtless. The hazy hue of the morning and his skin contrasted sharply to the black ink marked into his body and I found it hard to look away. His legs were long, his thighs muscular, his shoulders broad and he was light on his feet. His stomach was as chiseled as it'd felt when I held onto him while riding on the back of his bike. I sighed and shook my head, and took another quick peek at him. Godalmighty, he took the breath from my lungs.

"You scared me, dope," I said, and kept running. In that quick look I noticed one side of his chest had a verse inked into it, leading up and over his shoulder with various works of art down his arm. On the opposite rib cage, another verse.

Brax laughed. "You didn't tell me you were a runner, Gracie." *Runnah*. He closed in on me and bumped my shoulder with his. "Or I'd have looked for ya."

I picked up my pace a little. "I'm not a runner, really," I glanced at him. His eyes were directly on me. "I just like to run."

"How fast are you?" he asked, and pulled a little ahead of me.

"Fast enough," I answered. I quickened, passed him.

Our breaths mingled as we ran, and Brax glanced at me. "To Rigley Commons," he challenged. It was the main school centre park, a large grassy area where students reclined among statues and a mammoth fountain. "First one at the fountain—"

I shot out ahead of him and took off, pumping my legs and arms as fast as I could. I knew he'd catch me, but I'd make him work for it, anyway. I was fast—but I knew he'd be faster. I didn't look back, or to the side of me. I just ran as fast as I could.

Brax caught up. Slowed. Taunted.

"Pretty slick move there, Sunshine," he said, pacing just barely ahead of me to cock his head and look me in the eye. "Know what we call that in Southie?"

We both crossed the street and hit the outskirts of the park, the grass, and the fountain was dead ahead. I reached over and gave Brax a shove. "A cheater!" I hollered. He stumbled, and I shot forward in a burst of energy. Again, I didn't look back, I just focused on the fountain. Almost there—

My body suddenly left the ground in a swoosh as Brax dumped me over his shoulder and continued running. I squealed. "Brax!" My head bounced off his rock hard back until finally, he flipped me in his arms, and we were at the fountain. I looked up at him, mischief and deviltry in those crazy eyes. He leaned close to the water. "Know what we do with cheaters in Southie, Sunshine?" His breathing was somewhat rough, but not too labored to just have sprinted with a full grown person in his arms.

"No!" I pleaded. "Brax, no!" I wiggled and squirmed and tried to maneuver out of his arms. Those biceps and hands were like bands of steel. He wasn't turning me loose.

He held me over the water, and I squealed louder. "We dump cheaters in the drink!"

"No! I swear!" I laughed and writhed and twisted. "Please!"

"Jesus fuck, girl," he grunted as I tried to wiggle loose. "How much do you weigh?"

That did it. I pulled an old trick on him that I'd learned with my brothers growing up.

I went totally limp.

"Shit!" Brax grunted again and almost dropped me. When he tried to get a better hold on my full weight, I made my move. The moment my legs slid down far enough, I wrapped them around his and we both went down.

"Ugh, this fuckin' grass is wet!" He pushed me to my back and followed me over, arms braced on either side of me. That shocking face stared down, just like it had almost three weeks before, and I was just as taken aback. His dark waves, damp from sweat, crazy flipped in all different directions, and the half-moon scar at his cheek intrigued me, made his irrational looks more appealing than frightening. Before, I'd been scared. Now I smiled up at him. I could even say I trusted him. More than I'd trusted anyone outside of my family in over a year.

"What are you grinnin' at, gorgeous?" He braced on one hand, and with the other pushed several damp strands of hair from my face.

Brax's fingertips against my skin, his mere presence, set my insides on fire and high alert, and I realized how badly I craved his touch. And I definitely wanted his mouth on mine. I didn't care that it was six in the morning, or that we were sweaty and lying in dewy grass in the park's center and anyone could walk or drive by at any time and see us. I wanted him to kiss me, long and deep, kiss the breath out of me ...*Nutcracker!*

Brax's gaze was still on mine when the safe word popped into my head. The second it did, all of those ridiculous things Tessa had said about Brax that first night burst into my memory. A giggle began and bubbled up from my throat. I couldn't contain it, no matter how hard I tried. It was just so damn funny! The puzzled expression on Brax's face made me giggle even harder, and I squeezed my eyes shut to try and stifle it—

My mouth was seized then, and Brax's warm firm lips slanted over mine and settled in, sufficiently knocking the giggle right out of me. His hand slipped behind my neck, his thumb grasped my jaw, and he held my head still as he deepened the kiss, teasing me with slight tastes of his tongue, nudging my lips apart and sucking my bottom lip, caressing my scar. I lifted my hands and sifted my fingers through his damp curls. He inhaled sharply, and took my breath right along with it.

When Brax lifted his head and looked down at me, it was as it had been that first day. Shock and wonderment in his eyes mirrored my own. Finally, a slow, sly grin spread across those perfect lips.

"I always keep my promises, Sunshine," he said. "In the wet grass after a run wasn't my plan." He grazed my lip with his thumb.

"Guess I couldn't wait."

"I was thinking you'd forgotten about it," I admitted. I turned my gaze to the art and verse inked into the left side of his chest. "Or that you'd changed your mind."

"Look at me," he said. When I did, his mouth lifted at one corner. "I've wanted to do that since the first time I did it, and every day since." His brows furrowed. "You got that?"

I smiled. "Yeah, I got that."

A horn blasted from the street. "Get a room!" a male voice called out.

Brax grinned. "You ready to get out of this wet grass?"

I just kept smiling. "Not really."

His features shifted then; went from light to dark, softening in a sensual way that surprised me. "Why's that, Sunshine?"

Beneath the weight of his upper body, I shrugged. "Probably the ink."

Brax pushed up, grinning, and pulled me up with him. "I knew you was checkin' me out."

Brax ran with me back to Oliver Hall, and at the door he grasped my hand, winding his fingers through mine. "We have a fall game Saturday against Conyers State. I'm pitching," he said. I didn't think I'd ever get tired of that raspy, crazy accent. He grinned. "Wanna come watch us kick some ass?" He pulled me close. "Pizza after?"

A shiver shot from my head to my toes. "Sure. I'll ask Steven if he can change shifts with me."

People were starting to move through campus now, and the sounds of voices and motors starting up and doors opening/closing filtered in through the haze of my amazement at Brax's presence in front of me. He lowered his head and brushed his lips across mine, then grinned. "See ya in class."

I smiled. "Not if I see you first." I slid my key card through the slot and pushed open the door, stepping into the common room. I looked over my shoulder.

Brax laughed as he jogged across the parking lot.

When I turned back around, Tessa was standing in the middle of the common room, hair in a towel. Gaping.

"Holy mother of shit, did I just see Brax Jenkins kiss you?" she said.

I blushed. "You did."

She gazed out the window in the direction he'd run. "Well I'll be damned. An astronomy nerd freak of nature and two weeks is all it took to zap his magical porn radar weiner into an out of commission state of existence." Surprisingly, she grinned at me. "I gotta hand it to him, Liv. I've had my eyes on him. And other eyes." She gave me a light punch in the arm. "I'm not completely sold on him, but from the looks of it you've tamed the biggest man slut ever to grace Winston's campus, my friend. Kudos." As she pulled me toward the stairwell, she stopped. "But fair warning, chica. This is bigger news than you think, and trust me, it'll spread like butter on a warm tostada. Classic tattooed bad boy falls for straight-laced geek girl?" Her smile was tight. "I've seen it before. Epic. Brace yourself."

I gave her a questioning look. "What do you mean?"

Her brows lifted, and she blew out a breath. "You'll see."

13. Fallen

I WASN'T COMPLETELY convinced Tessa's *epic* and my *epic* meant the same thing, judging from her history of being overly dramatic. The idea had been planted into my brain, though. After I'd showered and dressed for class, and stepped out of the stairwell and into the crowded common room, I glanced around. Waited. A few looks, but nothing more than what I was already used to. I stepped outside, looked around, waited for *epic*. I hadn't been this suspicious since Y2-K. But nothing happened. No one gawked. No one rushed up to me with questioning eyes or accusing words. No scorned ex-lovers. No jealous hopefuls. Then again, it had only been an hour since Tessa's declaration. What was I expecting? I would've laughed at myself but I was too annoyed. Seriously? Epic? Was college just a big glorified immature high school? God, I hoped not.

Across the parking lot I saw Brax jogging in my direction, and my heart took a dip. He had such an easy lope; effortless and weightless at the same time as he maneuvered through other students headed to their vehicles. Most of the mist had lifted, but there still lingered a haze that made everything seem surreal. Brax wore his Winston baseball cap, ripped jeans, a white tee shirt, and distressed boots as he ran straight up to me where I stood at the end of the walkway. Without hesitation he flipped his hat around, grasped my face between his hands, and those ethereal blue eyes flashed. Just before he slanted his lips over mine. *Oh, dear God ...*

I melted against him, my hands against his chest keeping me upright, and as I inhaled I drew in his fresh-showered soapy scent. His fingers gripped my scalp, he nudged my mouth open, and his tongue swept against mine, tasted and played. Pulling back, he looked down at me, and his hands came to rest on my hips. A smile quirked his expression. "I couldn't get here fast enough to do that."

Two girls walked by then, their gaping gazes on me, but Brax's strong fingers slipping through mine drew my attention back to only him. He gave me quick kiss on the nose. "You ready to head to class?" He dropped his arm over my shoulder and pulled me close to him. "You're not saying anything, Gracie."

"I'm trying to breathe," I finally managed. Brax laughed and tugged me up the walkway.

I could listen to you talk all day, with that cute fuckin' Texas drawl." He leaned his mouth close to my ear, and his breath brushed over me as he spoke. "I'd rather kiss you all day, though. Wanna skip class?"

"No!" I said, but grinned. "You've lost your mind."

"Just so you know," Tessa said, suddenly on the other side of me. She leaned forward and looked over at Brax. "I've got my eyes on you, gringo." She pointed to him. "I'm watching. Like a hawk."

As we walked, Brax smiled at her. "Oh yeah, Tessa? And why's that?"

Tessa clutched her big zebra-striped bag to her side, and with her wedges on she was as tall as me. She lifted her jaw. "To make sure this isn't just some loco phase you're going through." She frowned. "You know—where the idea of being with someone like Olivia just fascinates you. Until it doesn't."

"Tess," I started.

Brax jerked to a stop and stared at Tessa. The people behind us on the walk nearly bumped into us. "What do you mean, with someone like her?" His voice was low and controlled. But I could tell he was angry.

Tessa met his gaze, not backing down, and she tucked her long straight hair behind her ear. "Come on, Brax. Everyone at Winston knows your taste in females. Olivia is polar opposite."

Brax turned to me, and his gaze softened as it swept over my face. With his arm draped over my shoulders, he pulled me closer, and a blush stole up my neck. "She sure is."

"I'm going to throw up now. Later guys," Tess started to walk away. "Hey, Brax, who's that dead-sexy first baseman of yours?"

Brax finally dragged his gaze away from me and looked at her. "Cory Maxwell? He's goin' through relationship hell right now."

Tessa's smile was white and ridiculously goofy. "I can totally be a rebound, no prob. Give him my number, will ya?" She twirled around and headed off to class.

Brax shook his head as we continued to class. "I like her."

I chuckled. "Yeah, I do, too."

In class, we'd moved on from Homer's *Iliad* to *Odyssey*, and although in the past couple of weeks I'd learned to just ignore Kelsy's presence, today I looked up. He was glaring at me, inconspicuously but still so. I quickly glanced back down at my notes, and when I chanced another look, he'd thankfully turned away. Perhaps seeing me with someone else had finally struck home; that he had no power over me anymore. Maybe it'd made him lose interest. I prayed it had.

For the rest of the day, though, Kelsy Evans stayed on my mind. Rather, the secret of mine he held. I'd waffled on just telling Brax everything; about what'd happened to me that night before my senior year, and everything after. Yet, I hadn't. Something inside of me still feared his reaction, and I couldn't explain that. What was keeping Kelsy from letting it be known just what a fraud I was anyway? Maybe fear of my brothers' retaliation? Brax's? The looks Kelsy had slipped me during class were of pure hatred most of the time, and I'd guessed it probably had something to do with the fact that I now was with Brax. I tried to push the dread away, bury it along with the horrible memories Kelsy had created from that night over a year ago. But on this day, it kept resurfacing. And the weight of my ring felt heavier on my finger than it had in a long time.

I'd just finished U.S. and Texas Government and was headed to the library to study when my cell phone vibrated in my bag. I stopped on the walkway, fished it out, and just seeing the name SOUTHIE on the screen wiped away my trepidation about Kelsy. I read the text and in no way could help the smile it put on my face.

BRAX: Hey gorgeous. Be out front of Oliver at six p.m.

ME: And why would I do that?

BRAX: Because u wouldn't wanna miss the bad ass pitcher waitin for u on a sick bike that's why.

ME: Ego.

BRAX: u like it

ME: yeah I kinda do

BRAX: u got a dress? Wear it if you do.

ME: u drive a motorcycle bone head.

BRAX: so? Bone head? That's gonna cost ya Sunshine.

ME: that's a weird request. But ok. Cost me? Not scared in the least. Anything else?

BRAX: Yeah. I can't wait to c u

ME: Me too.

BRAX: l8tr beautiful

ME: sweet talker

BRAX: ☺

The smile still pulled at my mouth as I entered the cool interior of Winston's massive library, and for the rest of the afternoon I poured over my notes for my first big test in Government in a small corner table in the history section. I loved the library and did most of my studying there. It was quiet. Peaceful. And there was just something about the smell of paper and books that set my mind free. By five p.m. I gathered my stuff and headed back to the dorm. Excitement fluttered through me as I pondered what Brax had up his sleeve for the evening. A dress? What in the world?

As I hit the front walk leading up to my dorm entrance, eyes followed me. Subtle at first, but soon I began noticing sets of eyeballs all over the place giving me the twice-over. Was this what Tessa referred to as epic? If so, I could handle it. They were probably just curious to see who Brax was now dating.

The thought skated through my mind that I was really just a novelty and he'd grow tired of me. He seemed so genuinely intrigued by everything I did, it was hard to imagine Brax was like that. Despite Tessa's initial judgment of him, I'd grown to know him and although he had a healthy dose of arrogance and ego, he was as real as they came. Straight forward, no holding back. I just didn't feel in my heart like he was leading me along just to get in my pants. He had his pick of a gazillion girls, on and off campus. So why bother with me unless he truly liked me. The thought made me feel so light on the inside, and my family crossed my mind. I couldn't wait to introduce Brax to them. Jilly would no doubt put him through the ringer, but Brax could handle it.

I took the steps in the stairwell two at a time and hurried down the corridor to my room. I shoved the key in and opened the door to find Tessa sprawled on her bed, books opened all over the place. I threw her a skeptical look.

"Now this is something new," I said, and dropped my pack to the floor. "What, did you find your parents installed a nanny cam or something to keep track of you?"

Tessa looked up from her studying and stuck out her tongue. "Very funny, chica." Then her eyes scanned the room. Searching.

I laughed and went straight to my closet and started sorting through my clothes. I'd only brought two simple sundresses, just in case I decided to go to church or, I didn't know.

Something came up that wasn't jeans-appropriate. Choosing the red floral shift, I tossed it on my bed.

"Where are you going?"

I peeked around my closet door. "I honestly don't know. But I'm meeting Brax downstairs at six."

"I still just can't get over it," Tessa huffed. "It's not that I don't think you're gorgeous or worthy—you know that, right?"

I smiled. "Yes, I know that. No need to explain." I grabbed a few under things and headed to the shower.

Tessa stopped me, and she set her pen down and sat up, sitting cross-legged on her bed. "What about your ring, Liv?" She nodded her head toward my finger. "Has sex even entered your conversations with Brax yet?"

Heat rushed to my neck. "No, it hasn't."

Tessa's eyes bugged. "You mean not at all? He hasn't even tried to—"

I gave an embarrassed laugh. "No, he hasn't."

"Okay," she said, and gave me a stern look. "You remember all that stuff I told you about Brax in the beginning? It wasn't all fable, my dear. Ask anyone. He's used to sex and plenty of it." She cocked her head. "That doesn't worry you?"

I studied my roommate for a moment. We'd grown pretty close in the short time we'd known each other. I mean, living with her day in and day out, I felt I could trust her. Yet, just like with Brax, I still hadn't divulged my secret to her. Was I making more of it than I should?

"Do you think of having sex with him?" she asked.

Now my face flamed. "God, Tessa," I said.

"Well? Have you?" she continued.

"Yes. Yes, I have considered it. At length. And all I can say is," I shrugged, "if it happens, it happens. Right now I don't feel pressured." I looked at her. "Not at all."

"Then you got nerves of steel, chica, because I've seen the way he kisses you," she shook her head and fanned her face. "Hot, mamacita. Sincerely."

I laughed lightly. "Yeah. That is true."

"What about your vow?"

I sighed, my finger twirling the familiar silver band. Should I tell Tessa? I wanted to, but the words wouldn't come. I sighed. "All I know is he makes me feel special, Tessa. I've never felt this way before. Ever." I shrugged. "I didn't pledge to become a nun. It's a pledge of choice. My choice. And he's not pressuring me. If our relationship evolves in that direction, I'll face it then. With Brax."

"What if he can't hold out?" Tessa asked.

The thought made my insides ache. "Well," I gave her a light smile. "Then I'll know I did the right thing by waiting."

A gentleness settled into Tessa's large brown eyes, and she gave a slight nod. "You are one tough woman, Olivia Beaumont. I truly admire you." She squinched her brows together. "But if that fucker breaks your heart his ass is grass!"

I laughed at Tessa as I jumped in the shower. It felt good to have her on my team, even though it was a little early to say my heart was truly invested. Funny, I hadn't wanted a relationship. It sort of just … happened. Unavoidable as breathing. Fifteen minutes later I stepped out, wrapped in a towel, brushed my teeth, and applied lotion. I slipped the sleeveless red floral shift with buttons down the front over my head, and it dropped to just at my knees. I padded out to my side of the room, grabbed my sandals, and sat on the bed. I looked at my legs with dread.

"What's that face for?" Tessa asked.

I shook my head as I applied lotion. "My legs are so beat up."

"How come?"

I looked at her and sighed. "It's what happens in a horse pen, Tess. They've taken a beating with me getting flung all over the place."

She waved a hand at me. "They look fine, chica. Disgustingly gorgeous, actually. No worries."

I pulled on my sandals, rebraided my hair, and grabbed my bag. "Thanks. I'll see ya later?"

"I'll be here."

With excitement pinging inside of me, I headed downstairs to meet Brax.

14. Daydream Believer

TWENTY MINUTES PASSED with no sign or
word from Brax. I'd settled on the edge of the
walkway, but the concrete was hard to sit on
for long. I finally stood, stretched and started
pacing along the concrete that skirted Oliver
Hall. The sun had dropped beneath the
horizon, but it was not yet dark outside. Just
that strange hazy gloom that fell between
afternoon and dusk, complimenting a sky
streaked lavender and ginger. It was peaceful
out, with very few students mingling between
the dorms. A breeze lifted the curls at my neck
and I inhaled, and continued to walk. I'd made
it almost to the opposite side of the dorm
when I stopped and scanned the parking lot. It
wasn't like Brax to be late. For anything.
Something must be holding him up—

"Liv? Now don't run off," Kelsy's deep
voice startled me from behind, and I whirled
around to face him. He stood there, hands up,
palms facing me. "I just want to talk, swear to
God."

I kept my distance and my eyes on him. "Just walk away, Kelsy. There's nothing to talk about." I searched for the easiest escape, and neither appealed me. The dorm entrance was further away than my truck. Escape? Why did I feel the urge to run? He wasn't going to attack me, for God's sake. Still, he made me uncomfortable. I cast a quick glance around the darkening parking lot. Mostly empty.

A low laugh came from his throat, and he shoved his hands into the pockets of his jeans. His head tilted toward me. "Nothin' to talk about? There's plenty, Liv. Don't shut me out." He took a few steps toward me. "Not again."

Anger pulled at my insides. "Again? What's wrong with you? Did our entire senior year conveniently exit your memory, Kelsy?"

He moved closer still, and I really had nowhere else to go except my truck. Run from him? I wasn't a coward, dammit. I wasn't. So I anchored my feet to the sidewalk.

"That's in the past," Kelsy crooned. "C'mon, Liv." He reached for me, close enough to grasp my bare shoulder. "God, look at you. That dress? You're so damn pretty. Liv, it's me. We've known each other since the fourth grade. High school was just high school. Stupid kid stuff. And I made a mistake." He grasped my other shoulder, dug his fingers into my skin and looked down at me. "This is a new start. A different life." A grin moved over his face. "We're grown now. All that other shit's forgotten." He tugged at my shoulders, pulling me unwillingly against his chest. His arms enveloped me. "C'mon, baby. Truce?"

I jerked back out of his grip. My brain spun out of control. Honestly, I couldn't do anything more than stare at him like he'd lost his damn mind. "That shit you've so easily forgotten about and shoved in the past almost ruined my life, Kelsy." My voice was husky, insulted, quiet, and it shook. I could hear it. Fear pinged inside of me, and I pushed it as far back into my inner shadows as I could. Had Kelsy gone crazy? How had he forgotten all the torment? Humiliation? Did he think he could easily dispose of the memories like he had his actions? The thought angered me to a fever, and I began to shake. With the palm of my hand, I pushed against his chest. Hard. "And finally, I'm starting to get on with my life. I'm not going to tell you again, Kelsy. It's over. Long over. Leave me alone, before it becomes an issue even your daddy can't control. I mean it." Satisfied that I'd made my point, I turned, scanned the darkening parking lot, and just headed to my truck. I wanted to get away from Kelsy. Period. Even if I had to just make a loop around campus. With my hand inside my bag, I fished for my keys as I hurried across the lot. Just as I reached the hood, I found my key. Where was Brax—

My arm was grabbed and Kelsy spun me around, pinning my back against the fender. I let out a grunt on impact, and my keys went flying and pinged against the concrete. He leaned forward, his body towering over mine. "Don't you walk away from me, girl." His voice was harsh. Painful. Guilty. His hair stuck to his sweaty forehead. His eyes flashed angrily. "You don't get to do that here. There ain't no reason why you can't hear me out, Olivia. I'm trying to be nice and civil and you're acting all disrespectful and bitchy." His head dipped toward mine, to look me in the eye, and panic dragged its claws against my insides. "I mean it, goddamit. Listen to me. I've told you a dozen fuckin' times I'm sorry for that night." His strong fingers grasped my chin and made me look at him. "Why can't you at least fuckin' acknowledge my apology, Liv?" When I did nothing but stare at him, his face darkened. "Why can't you just leave the past in the fucking past? Huh? Answer me, dammit." He slammed his fist against my fender, right next to me, and I jumped and squeezed my eyes shut. "I watch you in class every day, all lovely fucking dovey with that tattooed punk ass. It ain't right. Swear to God, I can't take this shit no more, Liv. I mean it—"

Suddenly his body just ... *moved*. It happened so fast, I barely saw Brax slam Kelsy's head, face-down, against the hood of my truck. Kelsy let out a yell, then swore. Brax lifted Kelsy's head by his hair and slammed it down again. He held him there, by the back of his neck, with Kelsy hollering to let him up. Only then did Brax look at me. He had a fresh shiner around one slightly swollen eye. His lip was busted. The features I'd found so disturbingly charming were now edged in fury. Anger rolled off him in waves, and then he turned away. He spoke to me, but he didn't look at me anymore. He kept his gaze fixed on the back of Kelsy's head. "Go wait by my bike, Gracie. Now."

I'd started shaking, and I couldn't stop. "No," I said quietly. My breath came in quick gasps, and I placed my hand on Brax's arm, gently closed my fingers. His skin felt warm, the muscles there tense and solid as strips of steel. I didn't want to let go. "Please, don't." My eyes drifted to Kelsy, his face turned to the side and pinned to the hood of my truck. "Let's just go."

"Let me the fuck up!" Kelsy grunted. "What's your fuckin' problem, man? Olivia, call off your goddamn mutt—"

Kelsy's words were silenced by the metal hood of my truck. He groaned, swore, but it was muffled by the pressure Brax was exerting.

"Back up, Gracie," Brax said. Still, he didn't look at me. His voice was quiet. Controlled. He wasn't letting Kelsy go.

I dropped Brax's arm and backed away.

Brax flipped Kelsy around and dragged him up by the neck of his tee shirt. Then he put a grip to his throat and jaw, pulling him closer. Kelsy took a swing at Brax and missed. Brax pushed his forehead against Kelsy's. "You touch her again and I will *fuck you up*." Brax turned Kelsy's throat loose, but still crowded him, nearly head to head. Brax shouldered him. Stared him down. But didn't say another word.

Kelsy pushed away, slinging his arms and swearing. Blood trickled from his nose and down his chin. His gaze slowly veered toward me, then he turned his head and spit on the ground. "She's not who you think she is, bro." Then he spun around, jogged across the parking lot and disappeared between the buildings.

Kelsy's words turned my insides cold, hollow, and I wanted to shrink into the concrete where I stood. Humiliation made me speechless, made me weak in the knees, and I didn't know what to do or where to go. I just wanted to crawl in a hole and be left alone. Be forgotten about. Run away. Tears burned the back of my eyelids, my throat. Brax had witnessed everything. Had heard everything. He'd find out about me now, about what'd happened, and how I'd lied over and over to cover the truth. Is that why I was being punished? For the lies?

Jesus God, how had this nightmare followed me to Winston? How had I thought for even a second that I could put it all behind me? That Kelsy would just leave me alone?

In the next instant warm, strong hands grasped both sides of my face and stilled my shaking body, forced me to look up. Brax pressed his forehead to mine, and everything else around me shut down. "I'm sorry I wasn't here, baby," he whispered against my skin.

The air became as still as my breath. There was nothing but Brax. He stood there, his head pressed against mine, saying nothing, yet being everything I needed just then. My breath slowed, and my fingers gripped his forearms.

"It's okay," I answered. "I'm glad you're here now." I swallowed hard. "About what Kelsy said?"

He pulled back, just a fraction, and looked at me with a fierce intensity that made my body tremble even more. "I know all I need to know about you, Olivia Grace Beaumont." He tilted my head, ever so slightly to the left, and his lips hovered over mine. "Everything."

The word brushed across my mouth like a whisper, and he kissed me, his full lips settling over mine, staking claim, and me allowing it. Slowly, I slipped my arms around his neck, my fingers in his hair, and held on.

Footsteps hurrying across the parking lot broke us apart.

"Guys, what happened?" Tessa said, breathless. I turned to see her bending over at the knees, sucking in air. "Someone banged on our door and said Brax was down here kicking some guy's ass. Guess you didn't notice the audience of girls on the walkway?" She looked at Brax. "Kudos, gringo. I think I like you a little more now."

"That was no ass kicking," Brax clarified. His arm was around my shoulders, pulling me to him, and I could feel his heart thumping against my ear. "That was just a fuckin' warning."

Tessa's worried and curious gaze drifted to mine. "What the hell, Olivia?"

"It's okay," I told her. I straightened, pulling slightly away from Brax's protective embrace, and smoothed the front of my sundress. Embarrassment over the whole situation started to settle in. I hid it with an assuring smile. "I'll tell you about it when I get back." When Tessa lifted a brow, I added, "Promise."

"I'm gonna hold you to that, chica," she said, and started heading back to the dorm. She threw up a wave. "Deuces." We both stood there watching her in silence, before Brax pulled me to him and kissed my temple.

"Gracie, if you don't feel like going—"

I looked at Brax, and shook my head. "No, I do. I'm fine, really." My fingers reached for his, and I tangled them together. "I'm sorry you had to even see any of that. But I'm not sorry you stepped in." I stretched to my tiptoes and kissed his cheek. "I'm far from being helpless, trust me. He just," I looked away, then back into Brax's intoxicating stare. "Caught me off guard. Thank you."

His gaze remained steady on mine; I could tell he wanted to ask more, but held back. There was something else there, too. Something troubled. Unreadable.

"I'd have hurt him, Gracie."

"I know." Only then did I notice Brax's top lip was busted. I pulled closer, peering at it, and grazed it lightly with my fingertip. "What happened this time?"

"Nothin', sweetheart," he answered. "Just a friendly tussle."

"Kinda like medieval warriors, huh?" I said, brow raised.

Brax laughed. "Yeah, somethin' like that." He shot a glance across the parking lot, then looked at me. "Let's take your truck. We're headed to the sports complex." He grinned. "I'll drive."

Still feeling a little shaky, I was glad for both requests. "Okay."

Brax reached behind me and opened the truck door and, just as I turned to climb in, he grabbed me by the waist, faced him, and lifted me up, setting my bottom on the seat. I scooted to the middle, and he hopped up. "That's far enough, Sunshine." When I handed him the key, he shoved it in the ignition and turned it over. My pipes rumbled to life. The total guy smile that plastered his face made me roll my eyes.

"This tank is a fuckin' beast!" he hollered. Then he draped an arm over my shoulder, pulled me against him, and we took off. My eyes drifted to Brax's hand on the steering wheel, and I noticed the letters inked into his knuckles. Who in their right mind would ever cross him?

We pulled into the sports complex and Brax drove around to the back lot, behind the pavilions, grandstands and baseball diamond. There were several other cars and trucks, and Brax parked next to a restoration-in-progress 1970's model Camaro. I recognized the year, the work. My brother Jace'd had one just like it.

"Looks like the beast is here. Good." Brax said. He nodded toward the car. "That's my first baseman's ride." He opened the door and reached for my hand to help me out. "It's a work in progress."

I stepped out and Brax closed the door. "So he's the same one who duked your eye out before, and the dead sexy first baseman Tessa was talking about?"

"One in the same." He tugged my hand, and passed me a sly grin. "Ever been in a batting cage, Sunshine?"

"I guess I haven't," I answered. "So why exactly did you want me to wear a dress to a batting cage?"

We hit the concrete walkway leading into the pavilion. Inside, it smelled of leather and wood and something I would dare label male. Brax grasped my chin and stared at me, his lip quirked. "Because there's just something that appeals to me about a gorgeous girl in a dress swinging a baseball bat." His eyes raked over me, just before he settled his mouth against mine. "Jesus Christ, you are so beautiful," he whispered against me, and I shuddered. His lips were firm, warm, and moved with just a slight, simple claim that made my body feel weightless. When Brax pulled away, he stared down at me, and I stared back, barely able to breathe. From the intense expression I'd almost accuse him of having the same trouble as me. He inclined his head. "Come on."

Brax led us up to a set of double doors, and when we pushed through it opened into another smaller entry room, the walls covered in baseball team banners. An older man, probably in his eighties, seated behind a counter and wearing a Winston's Silverbacks hat, glanced up. A grin split his weathered face.

"Well, look who it is," he said. His voice, gravelly and deep and thoroughly Texas, resonated off the walls. "The Yank with the hundred mile an hour fast ball. Nice lip you got there, boy. Looks a lot like Cory's."

"Hundred and one, and Cory's face way worse." Brax corrected. He pulled me next to him, and the old man's eyes lighted on me. "Henry, this is Olivia Beaumont." Brax inclined his head. "This is Henry 'The Crook' Johnson." Brax leaned over to my ear. "King of the stolen bases in his day." Though an innocent gesture, his warm breath against the shell of my ear made me shiver a little. I wondered if Brax noticed. If he realized the reaction he stirred within me by just his breath grazing me, he didn't let on. My reaction seemed ridiculous, but unstoppable at the same time.

I gave Henry a warm smile and held my hand out to shake his. He grasped it, firm but gentle, and the mischievous glint in his green eyes belied his aged exterior.

"So you're the one," Henry said, gave a low whistle and eyed Brax. He dropped my hand. "You weren't kiddin', were you?" His gaze returned to mine. "Nice to meet you, darlin'. The boy here's been non-stop gabbin' about you for two solid weeks." He leaned on his elbow. "Said the very first time he saw you he almost stopped breathin'."

"Thanks, Henry."

Henry grinned. "My pleasure, son." He winked at me. "You two can take booth four, next to Cory. And no fightin' in the booths."

"Nice to meet you, Henry," I offered, and smiled.

He gave a nod. "Hope to see you around here more often, darlin'."

"Maybe."

"All right, put your eyeballs back in their sockets, Henry," Brax teased, and led me through the doors to a long row of side-by-side narrow batting cages. We stopped at booth four, and beside us in the next cage stood a giant in a batting stance, facing the pitching machine. When it spit out the pitch, the giant swung, and the sharp cracking sound made by the ball as the bat tore into it rung in my ears.

"Hey, man," Brax said. "I got someone I want you to meet."

The giant rose and stepped back off the plate, pressed a button on the wall and turned to face me. A partition of chain link separated us. He pushed his batting helmet off his forehead, and hazel eyes—one with a slight discoloration close to the cheek bone—regarded me closely. Easily six foot five if not more, and shoulders as broad as, well, my whole body it seemed. I couldn't believe Brax walked away with only a split lip. Sandy-colored hair flipped up from under his hat in the back. Strong jaw, athletic build. Or, in Tessa's exact words, dead sexy. She was right. He was. And by the lines between his brows he didn't appear to be extremely happy to meet me.

"This is Olivia," Brax said. "Cory Maxwell, my freakishly large first baseman."

"Hey," I said. I held his gaze, refusing to turn from his scrutinizing stare. Maybe he was just in a bad mood because he wasn't over his girlfriend yet? He could still be frazzled from the tussle, too.

"Hi," he said curtly, with a quick nod.

"I really love your car," I offered. "My brother used to have one similar." Although I had to wonder how he folded all that length into a Camaro.

Something sparked in his eyes, but diffused quickly. "Thanks." He looked at Brax, then inclined his head to the plate. "Gotta get back to this."

"Sure thing, Beast."

And without another word, he pushed something on the wall, snugged his batting helmet down and a ball flew in his direction. He swung with enough strength to take someone's head off.

"Come on, Gracie," Brax said. I saw a hint of something in his eyes, too. Disappointment? Guilt? It was gone too fast for me to decipher, and then he slipped me that heart-stopping smile and I couldn't do anything more except concentrate on standing upright. "Watch me hit a few first, then you can try."

He handed me his Silverback's hat and stepped into our booth. I watched in awe as Winston's bad boy grabbed a batting helmet off the wall, a bat from the corner of the booth, and punched the start button. He hunkered into his batting stance, and when the machine pitched a fast ball, Brax's swing was a mighty one. The bat and ball connected with a deafening *thwack*. He threw a grin over his shoulder and hit five more, over and over. His body was a powerhouse of ink and muscle and energy and strength, all channeled into a wooden bat to make the ball explode out of the end of it. Every muscle in his arms tightened, defined, and his tee shirt pulled taut over a broad chiseled back. For a fleeting second a thought burrowed into my head, making me wonder exactly what it was that made a guy like Brax Jenkins so attracted to me. I may never understand it.

"Alright Sunshine," Brax said, breaking me from my thoughts. He stepped off the plate and hit the stop button. "Your turn."

I stepped inside the cage, and he handed me the bat. "Hold this." He jogged out to the pitching machine, and then ran back in the easy, bow-legged lope I'd started really looking forward to watching. He grinned, removed his helmet and eased it onto my head. "I readjusted the settings so you're not swinging at fast balls to start with." *Staht*.

I eyed him. "How do you know I can't hit a fast ball?"

His mouth pulled, amused. "You said you'd never been caged before."

"Never needed a cage. I had three brothers and an empty hay field."

"Well," he said, hit the button on the wall and stepped back. "Let's see what you do with a fifty mph. Then we'll go from there." He didn't move out of the cage, but stayed off to the side. I could feel his eyes boring into me as I took my stance and stared at the pitching machine. Waiting. The ball pitched, I swung. *Thwack*! *Thwack*! *Thwack*! I hit three in a row.

Brax punched the stop button. "All right smartass, let's work on something here."

I smiled. *Smaht ass*. "But I'm hitting them."

Brax moved behind me, close. "Get in your stance, Gracie."

I did as he asked, and he moved closer, the length of his body pressing against the length of mine. His hands found their way to my hips, and he straightened them to the position he wanted. "Right here," he said. "Now back up, stop crowdin' the plate." He nuzzled my neck. "Only I can do that."

I laughed softly, but it was to mask any other uncontrollable girly sound that might escape my mouth. His arms reached around me. "Now hold up your bat." I did, and he covered my hands with his. "Down just a bit. Right there. Now grip it tight with them long fingers, Gracie. Strong grip."

"Okay," I breathed. I peeked down, at the ink and muscles banding his forearms. He was close, his front to my back. I thought I was going to let out an audible sigh. One that Brax would definitely hear. I pinched my lips together, just in case.

"All right, when that ball comes at you, swivel your hips with your upper body." He moved me in the way he meant, his arms and hands over mine on the bat. "Use the strength of your whole body when you bat." He kissed my ear. "Got it, gorgeous?"

I chanced a peek at him. "I got it, smooth talker."

The door slammed beside us, and we glanced over to see Cory Maxwell shoot us a look of ... disdain? He shook his head, his gaze glaring at Brax, then turned and strode toward the pavilion.

"He seems really mad," I said. "Is he going to be okay?"

Brax pressed his stubbled jaw to mine, kissed me there. "Yeah. He better be." He nuzzled me again, and a thrill shot through me. "All right, Sunshine. Let's see what you can do."

We hit balls for about an hour, and each time it was my turn Brax decided there was some new basebally secret move or stance or way to hold the bat he needed to show me. We both knew it was flirtatious fun; I wasn't going to need this baseball knowledge for anything. But it was fun. More than fun. To have Brax's body against mine, his five o'clock shadow scrubbing my neck, his lips teasing my ear?

He had me at *swing batter-batter, swing*!

We didn't stay out too late; at my insistence. And although we grabbed a light supper at Hattie's, Brax never brought up Kelsy or the parking lot incident or what Kelsy had meant by the words *She's not who you think she is, bro.* And I was so glad. On one hand, I'd wanted to tell Brax everything. And, I almost did. I'm not sure even now what held me back. Humiliation? To be frank I was sick to damn death of humiliation.

I decided that I was going to tell him, but not now. Not this night. In the parking lot at Oliver Hall, he pulled up and parked my truck next to his bike. We got out, and Brax leaned me against the fender and kissed me. He cradled my head with his big hands, swept over my lips with his and moved over them in such a seductive way I started to sway. But when I slipped my hands around his neck, twisted my fingers through his soft curls and kissed him back? He groaned against my mouth, urged the kiss deeper, and swallowed my breath. I felt the rough cut on his lip with my tongue; he tasted my old scar. By the time we came up for air, we were both quivering.

He walked me to the door and slid the card for me, and pulled me against him, my cheek against his chest, his chin on the top of my head. "What are you doing to me, Gracie?" he said quietly.

I said nothing, but my only thought was *whatever this is, I don't ever want it to end.* Somehow, I'd caved. My heart was invested. Brax meant something to me. And I prayed like crazy it was just as real to him.

15. Infamy

Brax: Wake your ass up, Sunshine.

I grinned as I stared at his text. What a charmer.

Me: I've been up, Boston. I had celestial homework on the rooftop. What's up?

Brax: I'm running late. Celestial you say? Sounds sexy. Meet u in class?

Me: Of course. Everything sounds sexy to you, weirdo. Last one there's a rotten egg.

Brax: A dare? You're on. But it'll be worth more than eggs, sweetheart.

Me: We'll see.

Brax: L8R beautiful.

Me: You're crazy.

Brax: I know.

I set my phone down and glanced over at Tessa, still curled up in a ball on her side, buried in the covers. She'd come in late last night, long after Brax and I had said goodbye. "Tess? Are you okay?"

She turned her head and one eye cracked open as she peered through a mossy mass of tangled hair. She groaned. "I don't feel so good, chica. I'm going to skip class."

I stared and shook my head. "For shame. Can I get you anything?"

Tessa pulled the covers completely over her head. "Yeah. A hammer. Then you can bonk me on the head with it."

I laughed lightly and continued getting ready for class. Steven had agreed to take my shift so I could go to Brax's baseball game Saturday, and I'd taken his shift for tonight. Excitement coursed through me at watching Brax pitch. I could barely wait.

Pulling on a pair of jeans, a cami top and a three-quarter sleeved snap up shirt to wear over it, I hurriedly dressed, pulled on my All-Stars and grabbed my pack and bag. One final glance at Tessa's huddled form beneath the covers, and I headed out. I hit the stairwell and jogged down to the first floor, but the second I entered the common room, I noticed quite a healthy amount of heads had turned my way. A little self-conscious, I wondered why they were all looking at me. Making my way to the front door, I stepped outside and noticed more students in the parking lot. As I walked, heads turned. What was going on?

"Hey, Olivia." A hand reached for my arm, and I turned to find a girl named Becca from my astronomy class. In her expression I immediately saw pity. "Do you know who did it? Pretty lame."

"Did what?"

She pointed. "Isn't that your truck over there?"

I followed her gaze and pointed finger to where my truck was parked. Several people stood around it, holding their cell phones up. My feet started moving before my brain kicked in, and I started pushing my way through the gathered students toward it. With my heart in my throat, I finally got close enough to see what the fuss was all about. White letters slashed across the hood, fender. Pushing ahead of the people who stood gawking and taking pics, I could do nothing but stare, horrified at the vulgar words scrawled against the blue paint.

Gutter Fuck.

Embarrassment washed through my body, and anger, shock, almost paralyzed me. A few voices filtrated through my brain as I continued to stare. *Oh shit, man, that's harsh,* and *Oh. My. God.* I didn't look up. Didn't look at anyone. I just turned, pushed through the crowd and headed back to the dorm to find something to wash it all off. Eyes followed me, of course, all the way back through the common room, and I eased up stairs and into mine and Tessa's dorm. She lay sleeping, just as I'd left her. Quietly, I grabbed a few older towels I'd brought with me specifically for washing the truck, and just as I was slipping back out the door Tessa stirred.

"Something wrong?" she asked feebly.

"No, go back to sleep," I said. "Sorry to wake you." I closed the door and made my way back outside. Thankfully, most of the crowd had dispersed, probably hurrying off to class. But a few other gawkers remained, and for some reason, that irked me. They looked at me as I climbed into the bed of my truck. I held their gaze, annoyed and saying nothing, then knelt down to the toolbox, unlocked it and pulled out the plastic bucket I had stashed. I hurried to the side of our building to the water spigot and filled it up. When I returned, I just dropped to my knees, dunked the towels, and started working on removing the vulgar words. Whoever had done it had graced my tailgate, hood, doors and fenders with the same phrase: *Gutter Fuck*. Who'd done it? The most likely person to come to mind would be Kelsy. But I'd seen the flash of fear in his eyes when Brax had pulled him off of me in the parking lot. Would he really risk it?

Behind me, comments and snarky laughter didn't go unnoticed. I heard it. But I wasn't going to react to it. I was too focused on just getting the job done, and trying not to cry from mortification in the process. Or, from anger. At least the damn shoe polish was coming off. I kept on scrubbing, ignoring the comments, until my arm started to ache. I'd just returned with a new bucket of clean water and was working on the tailgate when a voice startled me.

"What the fuck, Gracie?"

I glanced over to see Brax standing behind me. His features were taut and frightening, fury rolling off him like smoke as he slowly walked around my truck. I continued washing the polish off in silence. He rounded the truck, swearing, then dropped to one knee, grabbed a sopping towel, and started on the hood. He swore some more. Brutal curses that made me cringe each time he spit them out. I thought he might even be madder than me.

After a few minutes passed he dropped beside me and stilled my scrubbing with his hand. "Look at me."

I stopped, looked up. The intensity of his eyes—so light they almost appeared pale gray—socked me in the gut. It was almost as though he saw inside of me then, saw what those horrible words meant, how they related to the true me. The me he really didn't know about yet.

"This is fuck crazy bullshit, Gracie," he said, then ducked his head to look me more squarely in the eye. Or, to make sure I saw him clearly. "You hear me? And none of the pricks taking phone pics and sending them all over the goddamned campus bothered to offer you any help?" He pinched the bridge of his nose and stared between his feet, then looked up. The expression on his face could only be described as ferocious. "I'm going to find out who did this." His knuckle lifted my jaw, and he peered closer, deeper. "Do you have any idea—"

Brax stopped his words in mid-sentence, and something dark and frightful flashed in his eyes. His gaze moved across the lot, toward the direction we'd have taken to class.

He simply dropped the sopping wet towel on the concrete and took off running.

"Brax! Don't!" I hollered. But he didn't stop. I knew exactly where he was running to. Humanities. And I prayed he didn't snatch Kelsy out by his throat.

"Holy fuckballs, what happened here?"

Tessa stood, still in her boxers and tee shirt, her hair a wadded mass on the top of her head. She spied the one remaining door we hadn't cleaned off yet. Her eyes widened.

"How'd you know?" I asked. Then bent down to finish cleaning.

"InstaGram," she said. "It's all over campus. Was that Brax taking off just then?"

I nodded. "Yes, and I hope he doesn't do what I think he's going to do. His fuse is like a half inch long. He's got a scholarship to think about."

Tessa knelt beside me. "Shit. Are you okay?" She bumped her shoulder against mine. "Does this have anything to do with that dude you told me about last night?"

I let out a long breath and looked at my roommate. I'd told her a little about the history between Kelsy and me. Not the entire thing, but enough. "Yeah, it probably does. And yes, I'll be fine. More embarrassed this morning when I first found it, surrounded by tons of students taking pics of it with their phones."

"Holy God," Tessa said, and looked around us. A few students still remained, standing in clusters, unable to stop staring. Standing on her tiptoes, she peered into the bed of the truck, reached in, and turned to the onlookers. "Hey, brainless fucks. How 'bout you stop staring before I stab you in the eye with this tire iron here." She held it up and waved it with intent to use, and despite my mortification over what'd happened with my truck I couldn't help the smile tugging at my mouth. Tessa was formidable. A true frightening warrior in plaid shorts. With a grunt she tossed it back into the bed and picked up the towel Brax had discarded. "Douchebags," she mumbled. "I swear I hate people. I'll help you finish up this damn mess. So Brax. He was pissed I take it."

"Yeah, seemed like it." I wrung out the towel. "I hope he doesn't do anything stupid. Putting something like this before his scholarship would be lunacy. It's not worth it."

"I can't believe I'm saying this," she glanced at me. "But honey, I think you're worth more to him than anything. Including his scholarship."

I sighed. "I just don't want him to get into trouble."

"Well, trust him, Liv. He didn't get this far by being an idiot, right? Besides," she grinned. "He has a reputation to uphold. Can't go fuckin' that up now, can he?"

I gave the tailgate a final wipe and grinned at her. "You're the best."

Tessa grinned. "I know. Now let's get this done before I have to hurt some lookie-loos."

"You're so brutal," I teased.

"I got your back, chica. Don't you forget it."

I never would.

I finished out my day of classes without seeing Brax. He'd sent me one text saying he'd meet me after work. He didn't mention Kelsy, and I didn't ask. I'd save it for later. I endured several stares as the day progressed, and when I slid into my desk in astronomy, Steven was there, waiting. His already-shaggy brown hair flipped over his ears, his head lowered to his notes. When he saw me, his head lifted and he leaned toward me.

"I just heard. Man, are you okay?" His brown eyes studied me, wide and concerned.

I eased his mind. "Yeah, I had some help washing it all off."

"Pretty harsh words," he said. "Do you know who did it?"

I shrugged. "I have an idea." I dug in my bag for my comp book.

"Does it have anything to do with that guy

you're dating?" He regarded me closely.

"What do you mean?"

Steven busied himself shuffling papers. "I don't know. He's got a rep you know." He gave me a hooded look. "A lot of girls like him. Maybe one's jealous?"

I nodded. "Could be. But it's over now, so I guess I won't worry about it."

He squeezed my shoulder. "Well, next time text me if something happens and I'll come help you take care of it."

I couldn't help but smile at Steven then. "I sure will."

The rest of the day passed pretty fast. I knew my truck pics—along with me scrubbing the words *Gutter Fuck* off of it— had gone viral via InstaGram. I thought the circulation had started and ended at Winston. Until my little brother Seth called me during my fifteen minute break at the observatory. I'd just finished setting up the mega-pieces of a celestial puzzle for the children's exhibit when I stepped into the employee's break room and checked for a message from Brax. Instead, a missed call from my brother. So I called him back.

"Hey, little bro. What's up—"

"Why didn't you call me?"

I sagged against the wooden window sill and closed my eyes. "Please tell me you kept quiet about it. It's been handled."

"Has it? Really? 'Cause I heard another little rumor. One that includes a certain douchebag attending the same college as you."

Seth's voice sounded years wiser than his ripe old age of sixteen. Usually a sweet guy, quick to horse around, his character did a complete rotation when it came to two women in particular: our mom, and me. He was that guy you did not breathe an indecent word to about his mother or sister. It simply didn't work for him. "Does Mom and Jilly know? Kyle or Jace?"

"Not yet." Seth sighed into the phone, and I could envision the dimple sink into his cheek as he frowned. "Who's the guy with the ink?"

My heart leaped. "Just … a friend. He was helping me."

"You're a terrible liar, sis. Who is he?"

I pinched the bridge of my nose. "He's … really nice, Seth. I trust him. Please don't tell them yet."

"Fine. Then tell me who he is."

My gaze drifted to the space between my feet. "I met him my first day here. He's a baseball player. From Boston."

Seth was silent for a few seconds. "Are you guys dating?"

I let out a gusty sigh. "Yes."

"Does he know?"

I knew he meant details about my senior year, and about what had happened with Kelsy. "No, he doesn't—"

"Olivia, Jesus."

I glanced at the clock on the wall. "Hey,

my break's over. I'll call you back tonight." I pushed off the sill and found my pack. "Please don't mention it to Mom and the others. I swear he's a good guy. Okay? Please?"

"Godalmighty, sis," Seth breathed. "Okay. Call me back tonight."

"I love you," I said.

"Love you, too."

As I stashed my phone in my pack, I ground my teeth. Great. There's no telling how long it'd be before the rest of the Beaumonts would know about not only the vulgar words on my truck, and Kelsy at Winston, but about me dating Brax, too. In a normal life at least half of that wouldn't really be a big deal. But my life stopped being normal about a year ago. Hopefully, Seth could hold his tongue for a little while longer. Truly, it was a big IF.

For the rest of the evening my thoughts ran rampant, scurrying across my brain like five thousand beetles rattling around in my skull. My head hurt. One second I felt okay, like the whole incident that morning was over and didn't really bother me. The next second brought thoughts of Kelsy and high school crashing down over me. Not having talked to Brax all day probably aided in that headache. I couldn't wait to get off work and just … see him. The thought of it eased my mind, and I pushed through my tasks at the observatory. I'd just stepped out of the break room at the end of my shift when Noah Hicks stopped me in the hall. His expression was grave; I knew he knew. And he knew I knew he knew.

"You should've told me," he said. His smile was warm, genuine, and it softened his eyes. "Do you want to talk about it?"

I shifted the weight of my pack and smiled. "You know us geeks are targets for pranks like that," I said. "I'm already over it. But thanks."

"Olivia that was no typical prank," Noah clarified. "But if you change your mind, I'm all ears."

I returned the warm smile. He was nice, personable, and I could see it in his eyes. He sincerely meant it. "Thanks, Noah. I appreciate it."

"I think you're a lot tougher than you look," he called after me.

I threw a grin over my shoulder. "I try to be anyway."

As I made my way to the entrance, butterflies kicked up in my stomach in anticipation of seeing Brax. For a moment I wondered if he'd even be waiting on me; I hadn't heard any more from him. Worry clawed at me; worry that maybe he'd heard something about me. Or that Kelsy had told him something I should've already told him myself. Maybe he'd decided I was too much drama, too high maintenance? The butterflies turned to ache as I pushed open the doors of the observatory and stepped outside into the night air. What if Brax had decided I just wasn't worth all the trouble?

Beneath the street lamp next to my truck, I saw him, straddling his motorcycle, waiting for me, and my pent up breath and worry eased right out of me. He looked up and was off his bike, jogging toward me in that easy lope that I never tired of watching, and my eyes drank in the sight of his long muscular legs closing the space between us. My heart sped up as he grew close, and at the last second, just before he reached me, he flipped his ball cap around, bill to the back, and gathered me in his arms. His body enveloped mine, and his scruffy jaw buried against my neck. I sank into him, my arms slipping around his waist and marveling at the muscles bunched there. When his lips settled over the skin of my throat the erotic gesture sent a shiver down my spine, and I melted a little more. How had I come to crave this with him? To so vehemently crave Brax? What was even more astonishing was that he seemed to crave me, as well. In less than a month? Could it even be real?

"I thought I was going to have to come in and drag your ass out," he said against my skin. His mouth moved to my jaw, then my chin, then grazed my mouth. Then, he pulled back and looked at me with those light, ethereal eyes. "Let's get outta here."

Sliding the pack off my shoulders, Brax led me to my truck. "We'll take my bike," he said, and waited for me to open the door.

"Where are we going?" He hadn't mentioned the incident from this morning. Hadn't mentioned Kelsy. And I hadn't heard of any fights or trouble after Brax took off this morning, determined to get to the bottom of the vandalism on my truck. What had happened once he'd left me?

He tossed my pack onto the bench seat, then closed and locked the door. He grasped my hand and threaded our fingers together. His were long, warm, slightly calloused, and dwarfed mine, and I decided I more than liked the feelings he caused within me whenever he touched me. However slight the gesture, it stirred a physical response deep inside that I now longed for; hungered for. I knew he struggled at times; I could see desire in his eyes, feel it in the depth of his kiss, the desperation in his touch. I marveled at his control. I marveled at my own. As he pulled me toward his bike, the expression he threw over his shoulder at me nearly stopped me in my tracks. Mischievous. Sexy. Promising. "You'll see."

We rode through campus, my arms wrapped around his stomach and holding tightly. The warmth from his skin seeped through the tee shirt he wore and sank into me, and I loved that feeling, too. It reminded me of safety, protection, desire, all tightly bound within the tattoos and muscles of the most unlikely of scarred heroes. Dare I call him mine?

Brax changed gears and slowed the bike as we pulled into a darkened sports complex, winding through to the baseball diamond's parking lot. At this time of night all the lights were off, and Brax came to a stop close to the dugout entrance. He braced the bike as I climbed off, then with his heel he kicked the stand and swung his leg over. Immediately, he turned to me and unclasped the straps to my helmet.

"It's so dark," I said quietly. "What are we doing here?"

He set both our helmets on the seat of the bike then grasped my hand and looked down at me. The full moon had already come and gone, so the celestial illumination was next to nothing. Brax's face was swallowed in shadow. His voice washed over me; raspy and familiar. But when he smiled, his teeth slashed across his face. "You're about to break the law, Sunshine. Now come on."

"We're breaking into the ball field?" I whispered, and pulled back on his hand. "Brax, we'll get into trouble."

His body brushed mine. "Only if we get caught." Humor laced his voice, and he pulled me gently. "Come on, Gracie. Let loose a little." We got to the dugout gate, which was chained and about seven feet high. Brax pulled me close, lowered his head and brushed my lips. "Trust me, sweetheart. Can you climb a fence?"

"Oh lord," I whispered, looking around nervously. "Of course I can."

His hands moved to my hips. "Well, get your skinny little ass over the gate then, will ya?"

"Brax, I swear," I murmured. Then I heaved a gusty sigh, stuck my fingers through the links and shimmed up and over the chained gate. Brax followed behind me with grace and very little effort, and dropped to the ground. His hand found mine and pulled.

"Your reluctance is too fucking cute, Gracie. Besides, adrenaline is good for the heart," he whispered. "Now quit your bitching and follow me."

"I'm not bitching," I insisted in a hushed voice. "I'm voicing my concern over your delinquent decision, is all."

Suddenly and in the darkened dugout Brax jerked to a halt and scooped me up in his arms. I stifled a squeal, and he chuckled. "Keep it down, keep it down," he warned. He bent and grabbed something as we passed the benches, and then rounded a corner and started walking.

"I can walk, you know," I insisted. It only made him chuckle again.

"Yeah, but I like you right where I got you." He pulled me close against him, and I tucked my head in the crook of his neck. He walked for a few seconds more, then stopped. His warm breath brushed my temple. "All right, keep your eyes closed. No looking." He set me down.

Not that I could see a solitary thing anyway, but I still let my lids fall. "Yes, sir."

Brax busied himself close to where I stood, laughing softly to himself. I wanted to peek, but I refrained, just on the off-hand he'd catch me. Then, he was there, his body crowding mine in a way I felt positive only Brax could do. Even blinded, I felt him swoop in, melding us together as he enveloped me, one arm around my waist pulling me snugly against him, the other cupping the back of my head as he steered his mouth over mine. My hands found their way to his hair and entwined my fingers through the soft flips and curls I found so appealing. His lips, so expert and full and firm and pliable moved over my jaw, my lips, and his tongue tasted me in such an erotic way that I couldn't help the groan that he coaxed from deep within me. He pulled back and whispered in my ear.

"Christ, girl, you're killing me." He kissed my nose, then my body went airborne once more as he lifted me, his arms catching me behind my knees. "Keep those beautiful eyes closed, you hear me?"

"I will," I whispered. Then, my body began to drift downward as Brax lowered me to my back on the ground. My fingers flexed and I encountered a blanket beneath me.

"Be still," he ordered. I did, and he straightened my legs, my arms at my side. I felt him lay beside me then—not directly side-by-side, but just his head. With my eyes closed it seemed a strange feeling, his roughened jaw against my temple. But I waited in silence. I didn't have to wait long.

"Open your eyes."

I blinked several times as I focused straight up above me into the vast, pitch-black blanket of Texas sky littered with a million blinking stars. The night sky was cloudless and perfect, and my face broke into an unstoppable smile. "Brax," I muttered. Even I could hear the awe in my voice.

"Impressive, yeah? Even though you've seen it a hundred times?" he asked.

I turned my head to look at him, and found he was looking at me, too. The darkness shaded his features but I could still make them out; slightly crooked nose, arched brows against fair skin, with the longish curls he usually kept pushed back falling over his forehead. Although I couldn't see it, I knew his sharp gaze searched my face, too. He was beautiful, strong, and stunning. I smiled. "It's always perfect."

"I don't fucking deserve this. With you." He had one arm behind his head, and he rolled onto his side so that he now braced himself with his elbow. I did the same. His words took me off guard, shook me. I wasn't expecting to hear that from him. We were face to face, inches apart, our bodies pointing in opposite directions, yet we remained intimately close. To me it still wasn't close enough. With his free hand he grazed my jaw with his knuckles. I thought he'd kiss me then, or more. But he didn't. He simply stared, explored my face, throat, shoulder, with deft, long fingers that left my insides humming. When he spoke, his raspy voice was quiet, controlled, serious.

"I want to know what happened with Evans, Gracie," he said. "I want you to trust me."

16. Confessions

I COULD BARELY BREATHE. I wanted to trust Brax so badly it hurt. Should I? How wise would it be to trust someone with such a dark piece of my past? Even more was, how wise would it be to keep that dark seed locked away inside of me? It would only grow like a tumor until it spread from that secret hiding place, malignant and brain-infesting and all-consuming until all that remained was an embittered, fragile, ugly shell of a woman. I missed my old carefree self. I missed her so much. Brax was slowly bringing that part of me back and I knew it.

Brax's fingers brushed my cheek, then grasped my jaw, lifting my gaze that had drifted away to meet his. I inhaled, drawing in his clean scent. "I've been in that dark place, Gracie. I know what it's like to keep secrets." He laughed softly, void of humor, filled with sarcasm. "Trust me, I've got my share of them." He caressed my lips, my scar with his thumb. "But I don't want you to shoulder yours alone anymore. I can see whatever it is in your eyes, hiding, every time I look at you. And I fucking hate it."

So very close, I let my stare settle into his, and in my next breath it consumed me with trust, hope for a peace I hadn't experienced in, well, over a year. Everything that drew me to Brax Jenkins merged and connected at once, and I knew then that it was meant for us to meet. Meant for us to belong. I drew in a long, cleansing breath, and let it exhale slowly. "Promise me something then, Brax."

"Anything." This he said without the first trace of hesitation.

Timidly, I lifted my hand and let my fingertips brush over first the scar at his cheekbone, where it lingered despite the slight flinch I'd felt. He didn't stop me, though, and I fingered the roughened skin there, noticed the difference between it and his otherwise smooth texture. Then, I traced his perfectly shaped lips, and another scar so similar to my own. Like he'd done to me, I grasped his jaw, the stubble like sandpaper against the pads of my fingers. I liked that.

"You have to promise me that, no matter what I tell you, you won't act on it. At all." I pulled his face closer to mine, and as I stared at my hand holding his face, shadows merged our bodies into one. "I swear it's the only way I'll do this, Brax."

His hand reached for mine, and he brought it to his mouth, pressed his lips over my knuckles, then my fingertips, one at a time. "I don't think I like the sound of this." He kissed my fingers again. "But for you, I promise." He held our hands up between us, pressed palm to fingers, and then laced them together. And waited.

This was it. To not go forward with this, with trusting Brax? It meant I was a grade-A coward in the worst way possible. According to Jilly there was no such goddamn thing in existence as a cowardly Beaumont. I breathed. Then began.

"By the summer before my senior year, Kelsy and I had been dating for almost a year. We'd known each other since the fourth grade, when his family moved to Jasper." My eyes watched Brax's as he studied me, fierce and with every ounce of concentration evident in the shadowy blue depths. I smiled, and it was a mixture of good memories and deception that belied the humor tugging at my mouth. "Kelsy's from a very affluent Texas family from Dallas. His father is a successful attorney with statewide connections and a shocking amount of power, political and otherwise. And Kelsy, boy," I shook my head. "Kelsy had charm. Charisma. Respectful to adults, and all the guys looked up to him. All the girls swooned at his feet, including me. He," I tried to decide how to describe it, and couldn't. "He just had that thing that made every girl at Jasper High wish to God she was me." I let out another whispery laugh. "His parents weren't too happy about their son dating a poor ranch girl, but they left him alone about it. Kelsy sure had me fooled, though. Had everyone fooled, actually, only they just didn't know it. Still don't. Everyone except my grandpa Jilly. Nothing gets by him. Ever. Anyway."

Brax's body had grown tense; I could tell by the slight pressure he'd started exerting in squeezing my hand. He wanted to speak, and I believed it was extremely difficult for him not to, but he didn't say a single word. Just listened. It was a lethal silence though; deadly and dangerous. Even his breathing had stilled. In anticipation of what I'd say, maybe? Inside, I shook like crazy. This was it. I hadn't told a soul about that horrible nightmare of a night that I barely remembered. But I was going to tell Brax. Trust him.

I continued, carefully choosing my words. "Like I said, it was the summer before senior year. It was Saturday, a typical August Texas night, blistering and sticky, and our graduating class had gathered at Marshal's Pond for a huge party. It'd been kept a secret, of course, since there was a lot of under aged drinking going on." Dread began nagging at me as I remembered details, and I stared at Brax's chest now, focusing on the rise and fall as he breathed, and it urged me to push past the pain and continue. I swallowed. "I'd lied and told my mom I was sleeping over at Carrie Yeoman's house, and she'd believed me without question. I'd never lied to her before, but Kelsy said we couldn't miss our own class party. And I knew I'd never be given permission to go. So I did it." I may have been pretty toasted, but I recalled his angry face, jaws clenched, cheeks reddened. He was so mad at me. I drew a deep breath. "We'd been at the pond since four in the afternoon, swimming, drinking beer, having a swell time. We had a bonfire once it got dark, and the fun continued. Just a bunch of teenagers goofing off, making memories." I stared down at the blanket now, a small space between Brax's shoulders and mine, and forced myself to breathe as the memories flooded back. When I lifted my gaze, Brax's stare held me steady, so profoundly, even under the cover of darkness. I could see clearly enough to notice the depth at which he listened. And it gave me a strength that surprised me. "I remember only a few things after the darkness came. One, was Kelsy's insistence that I have one more drink. I'd had enough and could tell it, but he was so damned adamant." I shook my head. "He started to get angry, telling me I was going to ruin our fun, that we'd only have shitty memories of our class party. I caved. He left, brought me a drink. Everyone had their trucks backed up to the bonfire in a huge circle, and we sat on the tailgate of the Beast, the very same truck he drives now. I remember … drinking the whole thing. You know, typical red plastic cup." I shook my head again. "The next thing I remember was my lip being sewn up in the emergency room—"

"Jesus *fuck*! He hit you, Gracie?" Brax pushed off the ground, clasped both hands behind his neck and paced the pitcher's mound. "Jesus *fucking* Christ!" He returned and stopped beside me. "I'm going to fucking kill him," he growled. Crouching beside me, he ducked his head, and he grasped my face with both his hands. They were shaking. "Tell me the rest, Gracie." He dropped his hands and waited.

Fury fell off him in pulsing sheets as more curses followed, and I pushed up to sit cross-legged. His reaction made me rethink my decision to tell him everything. I didn't want Brax to go nuts on Kelsy. He'd get into trouble. Maybe even lose his scholarship. Kelsy Evans wasn't worth it. Not at all. I swallowed hard, pushing that part of my nightmare into a darkened corner in my mind. "He didn't hit me, Brax. I tripped." He hadn't hit me, at least that's what he'd sworn to my brothers. But I had no memory of anything after that red cup, except the emergency room. A burning between my legs. And having my lip sewn up. Brax laced his hands behind his neck and paced. Swore. After seeing his reaction now? It'd been a good call not to tell him the one part that I felt sure would ignite his fury like a stick of dynamite.

I blinked away tears. "He confessed only to my brothers that he'd spiked my drink. But after the beating they gave him," I said, shaking my head. "Kelsy's father went ballistic. Kelsy, of course, denied spiking my drink with anything. Then there were the pictures others had taken of us—of me—at the party." I gave a short laugh. "It was quite apparent I was having a good time, hanging all over Kelsy and acting like ..." I shrugged. "Like so many other girls do at parties. Like a complete fool. Everyone saw it and there was no denying it." I breathed again. "Kelsy claimed my brothers caught wind of the party and came for me, found me drunker than a skunk and then jumped him for letting me get that wasted. Kelsy's father not only threatened to drag the Beaumont name through the dirt with a public trial, but that my brothers would surely go to jail for assault and battery. I believed every word of it, too. Like I said— Kelsy's father is extremely powerful." I gave a hollow laugh. "My brothers—they are so damn hardheaded. They were willing to risk everything—even their whole future—to defend me. I begged them. *Begged*. Pleaded with my mom, Jilly, not to do it." I looked at Brax. "Not to go fight Mr. Evans in court. To just ... let everything be forgotten about, and settle everything quietly, just between us and Kelsy's father. I'd do anything to keep my family's name out of the dirt. And they reluctantly agreed." I pushed my hands into my lap. "My senior year left little to be desired, and I'm relieved it's over. Everyone loved Kelsy and it was easy for them to turn against me for causing so much trouble." I shrugged again. "I was shunned. You know, poor ranch girl versus the ever-so-popular lawyer's kid. But I'd worked my ass off to get where I was academically. Senior year I submerged into my studies, ignored the taunts and accepted the solitude, worked twice as hard, and I received this scholarship and employment. My brothers were safe and not facing jail time, and that was the most important thing to me." I let out a long sigh, amazed by Brax's silence. "Nothing else mattered. Which is why you have to keep your promise."

Brax sat now, knees bent up with his forearms resting on them, his head hanging down and staring between his feet. He sat that way, wordless, for several moments. Then, his head rose. His fingers found mine, and he stroked my ring. "What made you decide to wear this?"

I looked at the ring and marveled at its sudden weightiness. I shrugged. "After Kelsy, despite the ugliness that followed, I was still heartbroken. He was my first boyfriend." I twirled the ring around my finger, ashamed to be withholding details from that night. But I had to. One day, I'd tell Brax. But not now. He would no doubt run off half-cocked and do something crazy, get himself in trouble with the law. Or with Kelsy's father. I looked at him. "My oldest brother Jace bought it for me. Said it would send a message to idiot dickheads who tried to bother me. I've worn it ever since." I met his stare. "What it stands for to me now is choice. Abstinence until *I* say otherwise." I brushed the blanket with my palm. "I know I'm atypical, Brax. Most girls my age have casual sex like there's no tomorrow. I'm sorry, but that's just not me. I'm ... simply not causal."

Brax slowly exhaled, nodded, then rose to his feet and started walking. At first I thought he was going to keep on and leave me there. I wouldn't blame him; I'd been lying to him from the moment we first met. Still was, if I dared tell myself the truth. Fear struck me, and that sensation of panic made my breath catch. My eyes watched him in the darkness as he stopped, put his hands on his hips, and stared at the ground. Then he walked back, sat behind me, and wrapped his arms completely around me. He pulled me between his thighs, nestling me against his chest, and rested his chin on my head. Only when his lips brushed my temple did some of my alarm alleviate. He reclined, lowering us both to the blanket and tucking me against his chest. The steady beat of Brax's heart thumped against my ear, and it was a soothing sound that comforted me. My hand skimmed the hard muscles of his chest, and rested there. My exhale was audible, and I closed my eyes.

"You've put me in a fuck-bad position, Gracie. Fuck-bad." Brax's voice resonated beneath my ear, and it was husky and strong and perfect. It wasn't accusatory, his statement; it was sheer fact. I knew I'd placed him in a predicament. I hadn't meant to, but there it was all the same. My head, resting on Brax's chest, rose with his slow, deep inhale; lowered on his exhale. Darkness surrounded us as we lay on a blanket near the pitcher's mound in the deserted baseball field. "I grew up as one of Boston's derelicts. Born, then thrown the fuck away. A Chinese restaurant owner on Braxton Street found me when he took out the garbage. His name's Yen, and he still sends me a box of fortune cookies and a Christmas card every year." *Fohtune. Cahd. Gahbage.* "The cops called me Braxton Doe, since I was found on that street. Better than John Doe, I guess. Anyway, the name stuck." His arm held me close against his body, and I felt him tense at his own words. I stilled as much as my breath did as I listened, and Brax's uniquely sharp Boston accent washed over me with words more painful than I ever expected. A pain Brax still tried to hide. "I grew up in foster care, and I remember a lot of shady families. I ran away dozens of times, started fightin' for cash in back alleys, runnin' with low-lifes." I remained silent as he lifted my hand, grasped my finger and grazed the scar at first, his cheek, then his throat. "See these, Gracie, I earned in a bar fight at the ripe old age of fourteen with one of my foster fathers. A real grade-A prick, that guy. Nothin' but a loser drunk who beat his wife and own kids, but thought rippin' my throat out with a broken bottle was a little more rewarding than using his fists or a belt. I stopped that thought process of his real fuckin' fast, and with the same broken lager bottle he'd used on me." I held my breath, already knowing his next words. "I killed him, Gracie. Killed the fuck out of him."

I didn't know what to say so I said nothing. I didn't fear him; instead I felt a deep, guttural pain. I moved my hand to cup his scruffy jaw and held it there, my thumb moving over the day-old stubble, and waited for more confessions. They came.

"The courts demanded that I be locked in juvie until I showed some sort of remorse because at the time I didn't have not one fuckin' ounce of it. That sorry sack of useless shit had beaten his wife to within a hair of her life; and me countless other times. That night I followed him to that bar, and was gonna jump on him when he finally stumbled his drunken ass out." He gave a low, sarcastic laugh. "But one of his buddies dragged me in off the sidewalk, threw me at my foster father. My foster father was a big guy and a mean ass drunk, and he shoved me, started beatin' the holy shit out of me, and his friends just let him. No one bothered to stop him. Then he cracked that lager bottle across the bar, just like on a fuckin' movie, and took two swipes at me." He laughed again. "Fuckin' took me off guard, seein' how wasted he was. After two swipes, with my face and throat bleeding all to hell and back, I kicked him in his goddamn nuts, he dropped the bottle, and I picked it up." A long, pent up exhale blew across my forehead. "He took a swing at me with his bare fist. I ducked, and took one just like it, only with the bottle. I'll never forget his face that night as he realized what'd just happened. Got his jugular and the bastard bled out right there in the bar. Right in front of me as I watched." He turned his head and looked at me. "Does that repulse you?"

I stared at his face, my fingers still on his jaw, and was not that surprised by my answer. "Not at all."

A sigh of relief, maybe, escaped Brax's lungs, and he pulled me closer. "I wasn't sentenced for that, but I had a lot of goddamn rage that I couldn't control. Started fights— with everybody. Other kids. Cops. I stayed locked up in juvie until the Jenkins adopted me when I was almost seventeen. They're decent people. Let me play baseball, encouraged my studies. To this day I can't believe they risked it." His laugh resonated with self loathing. "Risked a crazy fuck like me."

Once more I found words to be hollow and senseless. I let my fingers lower to his chest, then raked them over his arms, knuckles. "Your tattoos," I began. "What do they mean?" I'd noticed the script was in a foreign language and as intricately detailed as the art work.

"Here, sit up," Brax said, and pushed us both to sitting. Reaching over his head, he pulled off his tee shirt. My eyes had adjusted to the dark well enough that I could see arms, chest, abs chiseled straight out of a block of stone. First, he held out his fists, indicating the letters inked into the knuckles. "I did these myself, and as you can see they're a little sketchy. I was twelve and had just started fighting." He laughed. "Man, I thought I was one bad ass little fuck."

"What about this one?" I touched my fingertip to his ribs, where an inscription lay scrawled in black.

He looked at me. "Aut viam inveniam aut faciam. It's Latin. It means I shall either find a way or make one."

I was stunned by Brax's fluid shift in language. I moved to another one where a mystical black creature with a bird's head and skeleton wings twisted around his shoulder and down his arm, and melded into more script. I grazed it lightly. "This one?"

"A phoenix. Luctor et emergo. I struggle and I emerge."

I moved to his other arm, where another mystical creature with an eagle's head, wings, and a lion's body entwined his forearm. "Here?"

Brax held his arm up. "That's the gryphon, merging into a cross. And here," he lifted his arm higher and pointed to the underside of his bicep. "Temet nosce." He looked at me. "Know thyself." He cocked his head to the side and touched the inked words trailing away from the jagged scar at his throat. "Vincit qui se vincit. He conquers who conquers himself."

I nodded, understanding each one of his marks. Then, Brax twisted, turning his bare back to face me. Another Celtic cross was inked between his shoulder blades, and within the lines, more script.

"Non ducor duco. I am not led, I lead."

My fingers traced the cross, and in the dark encountered multiple raised slashes embedded in Brax's skin. "What are these?" I asked quietly. I knew the answer before he said it, and my stomach turned. Brax had just yanked open old wounds. I'd kept hidden my most horrible one.

"Memories of foster parents past," he said with a harsh laugh. He turned back to face me, and ducked his head, looking me in the eye. "I drag a lot of shit around with me, Sunshine. Lucky you, you're the only one who really knows I'm a derelict delinquent with a juvie record and no fucking clue who my parents are. And if you can't stomach being with me, knowing all that? Then I need to know. Now. Because I don't know if I can take any more fucking heartache—"

Emotions burst within me, and I grasped Brax's face in my hands and sealed my mouth over his, hushing his words before he could finish them. A low groan escaped his throat and resonated against my lips as he kissed me, and I'm not sure if I pulled him down to the ground or if Brax took me there; maybe it was both. I laid on my back, with Brax's upper body pressing into me, one arm cradling my head, the other resting on my stomach. He took over the kiss and his mouth devoured mine, hungry, surprised, and somehow I felt his pain ease out of him with each sweep of his tongue, each taste, each playful nip. His hand explored my ribs, my hip, and he deepened the kiss, causing a searing, needy turmoil inside me. I kissed him back with just as much hunger, my fingers twisting in his hair, then moving over the flexed muscles and raised scars of his back with light caresses, pinning him to me.

Never wanting to let go.

Brax's mouth moved over my jaw, throat, and across my collar bone, and my head dropped back to offer more. But he didn't take it; his lips returned to mine, controlled, and then he stopped, mouth to mouth, breath to breath. One heavily muscled thigh held mine down, and I felt the evidence of his desire pushing erotically against me. Surprise at my lack of fear gripped my insides. I desired Brax, and I wasn't afraid. My heart beat so hard then, and my breath came fast. Then, he kissed me once more, slowly, tasting each corner, scraping his tongue against mine. He pressed our foreheads together, intimate and close.

"I fucking want you so bad it hurts," he said, out of breath and in a husky whisper. "But not here. Not like this. And not now."

My heart exploded then; my arms encircled Brax's body, and I nestled my head into the crook of his neck. I knew then that I loved him. That I was *in* love with him. Knew it with every fiber within me. That scared me more than offering my false virginity to him. For now, I'd keep the sentiment safe, locked away inside of me. A new secret, because it was way too soon to confess it otherwise.

We laid together for a while longer, wrapped in each others arms and staring at the mass blanket of stars above us. Finally, after we'd both drifted off to sleep more than once, Brax lifted me up, pulled on his shirt, and we drove back to my truck. With my arms wrapped tightly around his stomach, my thoughts ran crazy wild and replayed every moment, every breath, every kiss. I couldn't get enough.

As he always did, Brax followed me to my dorm where he gathered me in his arms and kissed me breathless at the door. He pulled back, studying my face.

"You know enough about me now to realize I don't have the strength to keep that promise I made you." His stare was profound, sincere, protective and frightening all at once. "Whatever Evans did or did not do to you was wrong." He lifted my chin with his knuckle and ducked his head closer. "But what his father did, and condoned? Bailing his loser son out like that? Threatening your brothers for defending you? And what Evans continues to do to you now, here?" He shook his head, and anger lit his eyes. "It's fucking unforgivable. Evans claims he didn't graffiti your truck, and trust me, I pressed the issue. I'm still not sure I believe him. He doesn't scare me and neither does his prick father." His lips caressed mine once more. "Just so you know." He swiped my key card and gave me a light shove inside, and the door closed behind me. From inside our gazes held tight through the glass, and he just started backing up, his stare matching mine, and I wondered if he was in as much awe as I was. Under the street lamp I saw his beautiful mouth curve into a smile, then he turned, straddled his bike, and I stood there in the common room of Oliver Hall and watched as Brax disappeared into the night. I knew then if Kelsy screwed up, nothing would stop Brax. God, if Brax found out the rest of the story? About what happened beyond the drinking that night at the pond? Neither me, Kelsy's father, nor the authorities would stop him. It was simply an unsettling yet bald-faced fact.

As I crept into bed I marveled at the absolute contentment, mixed with limitless fear that filled me. Was it truly real? Was Brax? I prayed to Jesus and begged him to make it so. It'd been fate on that first day at Winston, when Brax Jenkins had slammed into me on the front lawn. What else could it have possibly been? As I replayed every conversation, every shocking admission and every sensual kiss we'd shared, I drifted off into a deep, satisfied slumber. And for the first time in a long, long time, my heart was full.

17. Almost Perfect

"I GOTTA ADMIT, LIV. He's not what I thought he was. Well. Minus the short fuse and cocky attitude. Both of those traits he definitely possesses."

Through my shades I peered at my roommate, seated beside me in the bleachers as we watched Brax pitch the long-anticipated late afternoon fall home game. Tessa wore her long straight hair in a high ponytail, her eyes rimmed by large framed Hollywood-style tortoise shell sunglasses that went fashionably perfect with her skinny jeans, snug red top and pumps. I raised one brow. "So what changed your mind?"

Tessa shrugged, and a smile crept across her tanned face. "I've noticed several things during my weeks of in-depth scrutiny of Winston's reputable man slut, which he was, by the way. That famous magical porn radar wiener wasn't an urban legend. He's just ... changed now. But the one thing in particular is the way he looks at you. Not just sometimes, but *every* single time. He's so into you, Liv. It's like," she inhaled, exhaled in a Tessa-drama fashion. "I don't know. Like there's no one else in the universe except you. Those freaky eyes soften and fill with absolute wonder, every single solitary time you appear anywhere within his range of sight. You're all he sees." She rested her head on my shoulder. "Like Tarzan sees Jane. Sheer bewilderment." She sighed against me. "You're so damn lucky." Her head popped up and she smacked my thigh. "Shit! Brax is up to bat!"

A contented smile fell across my mouth as I tore my gaze across the bleachers to home plate. Brax dropped the bat over one shoulder and glanced my way, and his mouth broke into a bright wide grin.

"See what I mean?" Tessa said in a whispery voice.

"Yeah," I answered back. A shimmer of excitement coursed through me. "I sure do."

Everything since the night of confessions, things had been almost perfect. Almost in that we had large chunks of time during the day that we couldn't be together. I had work; he had baseball. I had astronomy. He had fraternity. We saw each other every day, though, and I still couldn't believe I'd met someone like him. It was thrilling and terrifying at the same time. I kept secretly expecting it to end; for something to happen. Anything. But it hadn't. I hadn't told my family about Brax yet, but I would. Maybe he'd want to come home with me for Thanksgiving?

I settled my gaze on the game. Two men on base, two outs, and Brax crowded the home plate as he owned his stance, thighs spread wide and knees bent, fists gripping the wood and bat held high above his right shoulder. The pitcher threw a fast ball, and Brax swung and missed. He jerked, spit, and slammed the bat against home plate.

"Oops, he's pissed now," Tessa said.

He settled into his stance once more, the pitch fired across the plate and this time when Brax swung he nailed it. The bat cracked against the ball, firing it like a cannon down the left field line. Two runners crossed the plate, but my gaze remained on Brax's powerful body as he rounded each base at top speed, finally stopping at third. Tessa and I leaped to our feet, clapping and hollering with the rest of the crowd. The third base coach slapped Brax on the shoulder, then Brax turned, found me, and held his arms out wide in his famous *look what I just did* gesture. I laughed.

"What a freaking hot dog," Tessa claimed. "Oh! Oh shit!" She linked her arm through mine and yanked me back and forth. "Cory's up!"

I laughed again. Tessa had it bad for Cory, and had been pretty bold about letting him know it, too. But after the break-up he'd endured, he wasn't biting the bait Tessa kept chunking at him. It didn't seem to deter her one little bit. We watched as Cory belted it into corner right field. Brax crossed home plate and Cory made it to second. Winston was ahead seven to two. Tessa's brother Cole strolled to home plate.

"Holy fuck, he's so full of himself," Tessa griped. "Look at that strut!" Then she cupped her hands to her mouth and hollered. "Batter, batter swing, big brother!"

Three strikes later and Cole slung the bat to the ground, and the inning was over.

"Oh, hells bells, he'll be in a mood tonight," Tessa said.

My eyes followed Brax as he jogged out onto the pitchers mound in that easy, arrogant swagger that screamed confidence and sex appeal. The last three innings flew by as Brax struck each batter out. His long, powerful pitches used every ounce of energy from his body as he wound up and threw. It was an amazing sight to watch. One I didn't think I'd ever grow tired of. As the last pitch fired into the catcher's mitt, before the umpire called the strike, Brax leaped into the air. Tessa and I did the same, clapping and yelling. Game over. Silverbacks had won.

"I need to talk to you for a minute, Liv."

Tessa and I both jerked around. Kelsy stood behind us, one row up. Two guys stood on either side of him. Kelsy's eyes stayed on mine. I turned away, just as my heart leaped into my throat. "Just walk away."

"It's important."

I looked back at him. What was he thinking? After Brax had threatened him in the parking lot that night, Kelsy had left me alone. Why would he come to Brax's game and confront me? "You're just trying to cause trouble for Brax. Be a mature adult and just leave. I don't have anything to say to you." I glared at him, hard, trying to force him to see the logic. He didn't budge. Just stood there, staring at me.

"She said to leave," Tessa snapped. "Are you loco, gringo? Do you think your monkey squad there is going to stop *him*?" She jerked her head in Brax's direction. I'd told Tessa as much as I'd told Brax. Not the complete truth but enough that Kelsy was forever on Tessa's shit list.

Kelsy's gaze darkened as he flashed a glance at her. "Whoever the fuck you are, shut up."

Without missing a beat, Tessa let loose a string of Spanish expletives, waving her arms and bowing up. Tessa didn't take crap off of anyone. Especially a man. She took a swing at Kelsy but the guy on his left blocked her.

"Get your hands off me!" Tessa demanded. The guy let her go.

Her rants didn't faze Kelsy. He ignored her. "Olivia, I'm serious."

"I am too, Kelsy. Leave." I regarded him angrily. He knew Brax would react and possibly get into trouble. He was doing this on purpose, just to goad him. "I mean it."

"Oh shit," Tessa mumbled. "Liv, here he comes."

I turned to find Brax pushing through his teammates, his face drawn in fury. He broke free and started running directly at us. I shot my gaze between Kelsy and Brax; Kelsy not budging, and Brax gaining ground. I started down the bleachers, hoping to divert Brax away. It didn't work. When he reached me, he didn't stop but his eyes, hooded by the bill of his Silverbacks hat, turned to me for a flash second.

"Wait here."

My head turned to watch him take the bleacher steps two at a time. I could do nothing but stare helplessly as he never slowed down, Tessa backed out of the way, and Brax's fist connected with Kelsy's face. Kelsy kept backing away from Brax, with his hands held up in front of him. Brax charged him, chest to chest. I thought Brax was going to break Kelsy's nose with his forehead.

"What part of 'leave her the fuck alone' don't you get?" Brax growled. His eyes were dead-on fastened to Kelsy's and only a few inches separated them. Kelsy's nose had started to bleed from the first hit. One of his friends grabbed Brax's shoulder. Big mistake. Brax elbowed him in the mouth so hard I heard the crack four bleacher seats down. A big blur flashed by me. Cory Maxwell reached both of Kelsy's friends and shoved them back. The guy Brax just elbowed was bent over at the waist, holding his mouth.

"Jenks," Cory said. He stood behind Brax but didn't touch him. "He ain't worth it, son. Let's just get the girls and bust."

Brax ignored him and shoved closer to Kelsy. He didn't say anything, just … crowded him. Then, surprisingly, Kelsy spoke. To me.

"Why don't you ask your boy here about his dare, huh, Livvy? I'd love to hear—"

Whack! Brax popped him right in the mouth.

Kelsy's head snapped back with the force of Brax's hit and his hands flew to his face. "Fuck!"

I hurried up the bleachers toward them. "Brax, stop it! Let's go."

Brax turned his head, ever so slightly, acknowledging my presence, my words. But he didn't look at me. His eyes remained on Kelsy, staring him down until Kelsy moved past him and hurried off the bleachers. His buddies trotted behind him.

Brax's harsh stare followed them down, and it wasn't until Kelsy had disappeared around the concession stands that Brax looked at me. "Did he touch you?"

"No," I answered. I knew Brax's rage had tripled toward Kelsy after my half-confession and I knew Brax was just trying to protect me. What I wanted to do was shake it off and forget about it. "He only wanted to talk." I slipped my fingers through his and lifted his hand. The middle knuckle was bleeding from where he'd hit Kelsy. "But he's gone now, and like Cory said. He's not worth it. You know he's only trying to egg you on. So let's go eat." I pulled him close and pressed my lips to his, smiling against them. "You kicked ass on the mound, Boston."

Like a sieve, I felt the tension slowly drain out of Brax. His hands found my hips and those ethereal eyes clashed with mine. "You noticed."

"Wow. It's like a freaking magic show or something, the way you tame the beast." Tessa's sunglasses hid her expressive eyes, but I knew they danced with mischief. "Can we go now or are you two going to make out right here? 'Cause I'm starved."

Brax's mouth lifted and a dangerous spark glinted in his eyes. His fingers dug into my waist. "Decisions, decisions."

"If you're riding with me then let's skin outta here," Cory said as he started down the bleachers.

"Not so fast, fellas." A tall man in his early forties waited by the dug out. He looked directly at Cory, then Brax. "What's with the fists, son?"

"It's cool, Coach," Brax answered. "Handled and done."

The coach's skeptical gaze swept over Brax. "I've heard that one before." He gave a quick look at Cory. "Make sure it doesn't happen again or you're benched."

"Yes, sir," Brax answered. "No more fists."

The coach trained his eye on Brax. "I mean it, son."

Brax didn't say anything as the coach walked away. I looked up, and Brax tapped me on the nose with his fingertip. "No worries, sweetheart. You hear me?"

I nodded, but the worry remained.

"Shit. That's all you need, bro. That fuckin' temper of yours is epic. Can we skin outta here now?" Cory said.

"Yeah," Tessa chimed in. "Come on, you disgusting lovebirds. There's a pizza and a pitcher of beer with our name on it."

Brax's stare held mine for a handful of seconds longer, ignoring the playful taunts of our friends. In his eyes I thought I saw hesitance; something a little darker, maybe. It was so fast, I couldn't be sure. But before I could question it, he tilted his chin and tugged my hips. "Let's get out of here."

We rode in the back of Cory's work-in-progress Camaro with the windows down, Metallica blasting through the stereo and Tessa singing at the top of her lungs. Brax held my hand, our fingers entwined and resting on his muscled thigh and it felt comfortable, secure. Yet I'd noticed a shift in him as we rode; a quieter, more withdrawn Brax, and I wasn't exactly sure if Kelsy's presence was the sole reason behind it. I wondered about what Kelsy had said. Something about a dare? I held my tongue, though. For some reason I wanted to ask him about it in private. Not in front of Tessa and

Cory. Coming from Kelsy Evans, it had to be something ridiculous. He was purposely trying to make me mad.

After we'd settled into a booth at Milani's Pizzeria, along with most of the other Silverbacks baseball team, Tessa, elated to be parked in a booth beside Cory, leaned forward and flicked her straw paper at me. "Liv, what was it that brainless jerkoff said to you earlier? Oh yeah. Something about a dare?" She looked at Brax. "I'd heard a rumor about Kappa Phi fraternity dares when I was a senior in high school." Her gaze drifted to me. "I'm talking loco dares, chica. Like stuff you see on Jackass. My brother said it was just that. Bullshit rumors. Kinda disappointing, really." She wiggled her perfectly arched brows. "Like finding out there's no Santa Claus."

Well, so much for me waiting to ask Brax about it in private. Cory's gaze darted to Brax's, and I felt his body stiffen beside me where our thighs brushed together. A hooded, smoky sheen glazed over Cory's chocolate brown eyes, then his mouth tilted in a rare grin. "Sorry, Tessa. Just another famous Winston urban legend." The muscle in his jaw flinched. "Dares are just as bad as hazing. Against school policy."

"Bummer," Tessa said. Our pizza came, and the topic was dropped. Brax returned to his usual obnoxious, arrogant, charming self, yet not completely; at least in my eyes. That subtle hesitancy remained, and I was pretty sure only I noticed it. Maybe Cory, too.

After Cory dropped us off at the dorm and Tessa waved goodbye, Brax, still in his clay-stained Silverbacks uniform, walked to his motorcycle and started the engine. I stood close by in silence, the old familiar taste of dread on my tongue like I knew something bad was about to happen. He wasn't acting the same. Not the confident Brax I'd known since day one, not the zealous Brax who could barely keep his hands off me. I couldn't help but wonder if I'd done something wrong. Despite heavy make-out sessions, we'd not taken it to the next level. I knew Brax wanted to; felt the urgency in his touch, in his kiss. I knew he'd refrained because of my ring. Had that become too much of a burden on him? I mean, what hot-blooded twenty year old guy withheld from sex, no matter that a ring existed? Or ... Jesus, maybe he hadn't withheld at all. Thoughts of the girl from the seafood restaurant that first night out with Brax returned. Old fears. Self doubt.

But then he reached for me, tugged me by my hand as he sat against his bike with his legs spread wide, and nestled my hips between his muscled thighs. With hands splayed over my waist, his gaze drifted; over my shoulder, my chest, my mouth. Everywhere but my eyes. Fear stabbed me in the gut like a sliver of broken glass, jagged and sharp and lethal. Something felt so off. So, so off. Part of me wanted to turn tail and run as fast as I could, away, away. Away from any possible hurt. The urge to protect myself, to throw up steel armor around my heart to keep all pain from worming its way in, nearly choked me. My body quivered. I tensed. I wanted to hide my fear. I didn't want Brax to see the weakness he'd created within me.

But then Brax pulled me to him with a frustrated exhale, wrapped those powerful tattooed arms around my whole body, and buried his face against my shoulder. His lips pressed to my throat, warm, firm, possessive and I felt the tension ease out of his body once again. Confusion webbed my brain, and at the same time my fear eased, too, as Brax's mouth dragged slowly along the column of my throat, grazed my jaw, then his kiss consumed me, and I wanted it. I wanted this, wanted him, so badly that I felt pressure in my chest, heat where our bodies touched, an ache that I couldn't describe. I couldn't say it. God, I wanted to, but I just couldn't. My fingers threaded through his hair, kneaded the muscles in his neck as I kissed him back, and I couldn't help the groan that escaped me.

Out of breath, Brax broke the kiss, resting his forehead against mine. We breathed in silence, and then he kissed my nose. "'Night, Sunshine. See ya in the morning."

I let my hands fall from his hair, and grazed the top of his thigh. "Good night," I responded, still breathless, a little hurt, a lot confused by the sudden end to our kiss. I turned without another word and walked to the dorm's entrance, slid my key card and didn't look back as I crossed the common room. The rumble of Brax's exhaust trailed after me as I hit the stairwell and climbed to my room.

Tessa's steady stream of excited chatter about how hot Cory was and how sculpted his abs were and oh what an Adonis ass he had kept my mind occupied until she finally fell quiet, exhausted, in her bed. With a couple of astronomy chapters to read before class the next day, I sat against the wall with a pillow behind my back and my knees pulled up, book balancing on top like a mini-shelf. Concentration on my work proved challenging; all I could think about was Brax, us, and what seemed to be changing. Was it changing? Or had my self-confidence taken a nose dive again? Tessa's tinny voice interrupted my thoughts.

"Hey," she said while yawning. "What do you think dickface really meant about the dare, anyway?" She rolled onto her side, braced her head with her palm, and looked at me. "I mean, seriously. That was weird. To risk getting his face bashed in by Brax? Sadistic as all holy hell if you ask me."

The words in my text book blurred as I stared, thinking again. What *had* Kelsy meant by the dare? He'd known Brax would see him, would charge him. That was an awfully risky chance to take on a Winston urban legend. Was there a deeper meaning to it? God forbid, some truth? The last thing I wanted was to sound like a consumed-with-worry girl. Especially to Tessa. So, I hid that worry. "I guess I don't know," I finally answered. "Maybe he was hoping to get Brax into trouble with the coach? That sounds something like he'd do." And, that was true. And something completely like Kelsy Evans.

"Douchebag," Tessa muttered. "'Night, Liv."

I heartily agreed as I returned to my studying. "'Night." But I fell asleep wondering about the possibility of a dare. Dare for what?

Surprisingly, Kelsy left me alone after that. Every once in a while I'd catch him tearing a glance away from me in humanities, but there were no further shocker visits, no sudden need to have a word with me, and I was glad. Thoughts of Brax's violent past plagued me at times, though, but not in a fearful way; at least, not fearful toward me. More for what he might do to Kelsy if my secret was fully exposed; if he knew what Kelsy had really done to me that night. The one thing I'd decided to do was make sure that didn't happen. As long as Kelsy just ... got on with his life and stopped hounding me, it'd be okay. We could both just ... get on with our lives. I mean, if I could get past it, certainly Kelsy should be able to. And just when I thought Kelsy was our only obstacle, I discovered another one.

Our astronomy lab class had just concluded the first of two night observations, of which we'd gathered with our lab partners and logged our findings on the platform of the observatory. Eight of us had signed up, and Noah had led the observation. We had to complete two for the semester, and combined, along with our log, was worth twenty-five percent of our final grade. Steven and I had both brought our telescopes and were just packing them up. I heard a giggle and noticed Noah speaking to a pair of girls who'd remained behind the other lab partners.

Steven cleared his throat. "During my observation of the human female I've noticed Noah Hicks brings that insanely obnoxious and primitive behavior out in most cases," he said, then quirked his head and looked up at me with a grin. "I've concluded that the female species is simply beastly and unpredictable. I'm surprised you're not on the Noah Hicks bandwagon."

I gave Steven a disapproving fake frown. "Who are you now, Dr. Sheldon Cooper?" I continued loading up. "Steven, if I did have primitive beastly behavior I sure wouldn't just let it out for everyone to see."

"Let what out for whom to see?" Noah said behind me. "Exactly?"

My gaze flipped around to Noah, who watched as I packed up my gear. His lip twitched.

Good Lord, busted. I gave a nervous laugh. "My primitive beastly obnoxious side." I flashed a glare toward Steven.

"That's something I'd have to see for myself." Noah knelt beside me and began breaking down the tripod. "How's the log coming along?"

My braid slipped over my shoulder as I leaned across and tucked the body of my scope into the bag. "We picked up cloudy nebulus tonight. Saturn."

"Yeah, and a few cool shots of the Milky Way with Olivia's camera." Steven shouldered his scope bag and pulled his car keys from his pocket. "I've got an online Stargazer's meeting to attend in twenty minutes, plus about a pound of chemistry homework. So I'm gonna head out." He flipped me a thumbs up. "Nice job, lab partner of mine. See ya in class."

"Bye." I gave a short laugh. I really liked Steven a lot. Like me, he was a geek to the nth degree.

Noah leaned close, and a slip of a breeze picked up his cologne and it wafted toward me. He smelled good; polished, crisp, well groomed. After tucking my tripod away he turned and sat on the ground, his forearm resting on his knee, his head turned toward the sky. I noticed how sharp and square his profile was; like a statue chiseled from stone. Not in a bulky, muscular way, but in a David sort of way. No wonder all the girls lost balance whenever he passed by. "Did you ever find out who damaged your truck?" he asked without looking at me.

"No." I zipped my bag and sat down beside it, turning my stare toward the heavens.

"It could've been any number of random people, I suppose."

He let out a quick laugh. "I'd be willing to bet another girl did it," he looked at me. "Just because of the guy you're dating." He shrugged. "Girls can be pretty vindictive."

I knew that better than Noah thought. "Luckily they used shoe polish." I searched the vast blanket above me, kept my eyes trained there. "It came right off."

"Yeah," he continued. "But those words were pretty harsh, Olivia." I felt his eyes on me, and embarrassment heated my face. I looked at him, and his eyes appeared completely black. "Listen, I know it's none of my business, but," he searched for words. "I guess I hate to see people,"—he shrugged—"nice girls, I mean, get in over their head."

"In over my head?" I didn't know where he was going with this, but an uncomfortable feeling nicked me; something that usually didn't accompany Noah.

He exhaled, looked down at the platform, then lifted his gaze. "Brax Jenkins. You two seem ..." He laughed again. "Well, you know." He rubbed his hand over his jaw, then his close-clipped hair. "Dammit. I'm over-stepping my boundaries here. Just be careful, Olivia. If you ever need anything, you have my number." He flashed an embarrassed kind of smile. "Us nerds have to watch each other's back, you know."

"Gracie, you ready?"

I jumped at Brax's unexpected presence on the platform. I leapt to my feet, grabbing my bag. Guilt washed over me as my eyes met his; anger and pain flashed over his features. The words weren't mine, but I felt responsible for them just the same. Brax walked over and shouldered my scope bag, and I nervously searched for something to say. "Uh, yes. Actually. Just finished up here."

While his hand found its way to my lower back, his gaze shifted to Noah's. A hostile flare shone there, and although his words were for me, he threw that hostility at Noah. "Let's get out of here."

Noah rose, cleared his throat and shoved his hands in his pockets. "See you in class, Olivia."

"See ya," I answered. Brax guided me to the stairwell, tension radiating off of him.

"And hey," Noah added. We stopped, but Brax's gaze remained forward. I looked over my shoulder. "We're expecting the Draconids to be spectacular, with very little moonshine to block the view." He grinned. "It'll be … great for your log."

I nodded. "Thanks."

Silently, Brax led me down the stairs, out the main lobby and, by the time we hit the exit door, I thought he would self-combust. We made it to the parking lot before I couldn't take it anymore. I knew he'd heard what Noah had said.

"Brax, I'm sorry. I don't know—"

"What was that, huh, Gracie?" Brax, my scope bag still on his shoulder, began to pace. The anger rolled off him in sheets, and his face was a mixture of emotions. In the lamplight I noticed hurt was one of them. "You're discussing us with *him*?"

"No, I—"

"He's got no right in our fucking business, Gracie." His eyes were so angry, so inflamed, and it stung to be on the receiving end of such a stare, in more ways than one. "None." He wiped his face with his hands. "Fuckin TA. He doesn't know me." He glared at me. "The only reason I didn't break his fucking nose is because I didn't want you to get in any hot water. Period."

The sting of his anger, seemingly toward me, sifted into defensiveness. "Are you mad at me?"

When he stood close, his body engulfed mine. He grew louder. Angrier. "You were discussing us, Gracie. Me. With that prick. Yeah, I'm pissed."

Irritation flushed over me. "I wasn't discussing anything, Brax." My voice quieted, and I felt hurt. "What he said to me was unasked for, unprovoked. Out of the blue."

Brax drew closer, his head lowered, eyes focused and accusing. "You didn't bother to correct him."

His blame singed me, and I felt an icy dread sludge through my insides. I retrieved my truck keys from my pocket. "You didn't give me time to. Can I have my scope please?" When he just stood there, I turned and walked to my truck. Brax was right on my heels. Once there, I unlocked and opened the door.

"*You're* pissed? Are you serious?" Sarcasm and disbelief hung in his voice. "I'm the one who walked up to find you and dickhead all cuddled up on that platform, gazing at the stars and talking about how you needed to be careful with me." He barked out a laugh. "Give me a fucking break, Sunshine. Even you can't be that naïve."

White hot emotions careened into me then; fury, pain, and the realization that Brax had a serious problem with jealousy. Much like Kelsy. I lifted my scope bag from Brax's shoulder and slid it across the bench seat in my cab. I climbed in after it.

"Whoa, whoa," Brax then said. He grabbed my waist with both hands and pulled me back. As I stood there, my heart raced; my breath hurt to move through my lungs. And I hated that for the first time since falling for Brax Jenkins, I wanted to get away from him. "You're going to leave, just like that?" he asked.

I turned in his hands, my back to my opened truck door, and I looked up into beautiful, frightening, astonished eyes. "For whatever reason, Noah took it upon himself to warn me about you. I had no control over it. That's what you heard when you walked up, Brax. I was just as stunned as you to hear it." I took my hands and pushed his off my hips.

"But what stuns me even more is how quickly your anger turned on me." Twisting, I jumped up into the cab of my truck. Tears stung my eyes but I kept them from falling. "I'm not nearly as naïve as you think I am."

I yanked on my door to close it, but Brax caught it, held it open. "Gracie, wait. Don't go. I'm sorry."

Sadness made my gaze heavy. "So am I." This time I pulled, and Brax let the door close. I started the engine and put the truck in drive.

Brax slapped the fender, making a tinny thump. "I said I'm fuckin sorry!" he yelled. "Gracie!"

Pain made me react, made me want to just escape and, although not the mature response, there it was. Tears pushed past my lids now, and I angrily swiped them away. It was just a stupid fight, I knew that; but it was our first. It didn't feel good. Not at all. Dammit, I didn't want him to see me cry.

I pulled out of the parking lot. I didn't look back.

18. Almost Paradise

SOMEHOW, I KNEW BRAX would follow me; the round headlight in my rear view mirror was all the proof I needed. I knew he had a right to be angry, but for some reason it offended me that he seemed to take that anger out on me. As if I'd had anything to do with Noah's proclamation of Brax's bad reputation.

No sooner did I pull into my parking spot, kill the engine and open the door was Brax already off his bike and standing there. He opened the door. "Jesus fuck, Gracie, please." I sat stone-statue still in my truck, staring out the windshield, my knuckles turning white as I gripped the wheel. His voice held pain; more than what was caused by our fight, or by Noah's warning, or even by his accidental intrusion on the conversation. I let out a pent-up sigh, watched as a tear fell onto the thigh of my faded jeans.

"Baby, Christ God, I'm such an idiot. Please don't cry." Brax's calloused fingers grasped my jaw, forcing my gaze to his. Embarrassment swamped over me and I

blinked, trying to convince my treacherous
eyeballs to stop leaking. But Brax's
roughened knuckle brushed away the trail of
dampness. He crouched down then, the
material pulling taut over his muscled thighs,
the tee shirt snugged over his broad shoulders,
and he looked up from his lowered position.
His hands now rested on my knee. He
squeezed it, slightly, exhaled and stared at the
ground between his feet, then back up to me.
"You gotta believe me when I say I'm sorry,
Gracie. I lost it back there." He glanced away,
thinking. "I thought he'd convinced you I was
no good." His eyes seared into mine, and I
saw doubt there. A lot of it; more than what he
probably meant for me to see. "I thought you
believed him."

Brax's confessions from that night on the
ball diamond came rushing back, and I was
struck by the force of the fears he still had
buried deep inside. Abandonment seemed an
empty description. In many ways he was the
strongest person I knew; his turmoil growing
up had made him a survivor, valiant. Yet a
part of him, no matter how small it might
seem, lingered inside of him like a small,
frightened kid—scared of being left alone in a
dumpster to just ... stop existing. It saddened
me; it didn't make me pity him, but just the
opposite. I respected him for showing me this
vulnerable side of Braxton Jenkins, for letting
me in, and I was positive not another soul in
Texas had witnessed it. I wondered if it meant
something. If he might care for me as much as

I secretly cared for him. I reached for his hands then, where they still gripped my knee, and threaded my fingers through his strong ones. My voice felt unsteady, shaky. "I draw my own conclusions, Brax. About everyone, and everything. That doesn't just include you. It *especially* includes you." I chose my next words carefully. "I don't typically let people in"—I pressed one of my hands to my heart— "here. So trust me, if the rumors I heard about you from the get-go didn't scare me away, nothing will." His fingers tightened around mine, and I saw instant relief flood the harsh planes and unique features that the shadows tried so hard to hide. "Noah was wrong for what he said. Even he admitted having overstepped his boundaries, and he was right about that. And I have no idea what caused him to feel the need to warn me about you." I peered closely at him. "I don't need any more warnings. And I don't like being yelled at, Brax, or accused falsely. I understand you felt like you'd walked up on something between Noah and I, but you didn't. That's not me, not the kind of person I am." I smiled then, and I saw regret soften his unusual eyes. "I'm different. Remember?"

Brax stood, his body filling the space left by my opened door. With one arm, he braced his weight against the frame and leaned in. His hand lowered, pushed my braid over my shoulder, then grasped my jaw and drew his mouth over mine. "I know you are," he whispered, and his lips brushed feathery over mine. Then, he nudged my mouth open as he deepened the kiss, and the gentle swipe of his tongue, so possessive and erotic, made my lips tingle. Without thinking, I eased across the bench seat, Brax slid behind the wheel, pulled the door closed and laid me back, our tongues and mouths fusing, tasting. My heart raced out of control. God, that kiss could have gone on and on.

Or maybe even further. And just when I thought it would, Brax stopped, his big palms resting against the bare skin of my ribs, our breathing in sync and fast and deliciously fogging up the windows. He instead helped me from the cab of my truck. Walked with one arm around my shoulders as he carried my scope to the dorm entrance. Kissed me again and swiped my card. Gave me a little push inside after we kissed some more. Watched me until the shadows swallowed me up in the darkened common room. Even inside the stairwell, the rumble of his muffler sounded, and I listened to it as it carried him further away. It was a double-edged sword, that distinct sound; one of comfort, of familiarity. And then, one of departure, an echo of Brax departing. Leaving. Fading away. That sound and thought thumped heavier in the pit of my stomach than it should have, and I didn't understand why.

Over the next week we'd left September behind, and the first day of October brought about a subtle change in the atmosphere at Winston. Not so much in temperature; I mean,

Texas was Texas, and if we were blessed with even the occasional cold front, we were lucky ducks. Regardless of the weather, though, the early sightings of fall, and pending Halloween, brought out the mischief in people. Girls tried to wear sweaters or long sleeves, simply because it was *that time of year* to do so. Frat and sorority parties grew in numbers. The Sigma Chis had an on-going rival with the Kappas, and pranks were traded back and forth. Colorful flags of pumpkins and changing leaves hung from the Lambda house. Football games became the thing to do on weekends, and were either preluded, preceded, or both, on game day with public acts of harmless humiliation. Underwear on car bumpers. Bras taped to windows. Someone from the Sigmas dressed as a Reaper and stalked students as they hustled from one class to another. They seemed immature, but all in good fun.

Until I became the butt of one.

Again.

My poor truck.

Noah and Dr. Callandar had left Steven and I in charge so that they could attend a weekend conference in Fort Worth. We'd not only finished setting up a new expo of a simulated and extremely cool Draconid meteor shower in observation room two, with a fall of stardust and mist and extraordinary planetary geekness, but we'd also knocked out a major log entry and experiment for our astronomy lab by breaking down the parts of a spectrometer to show its function and relativity to studying light and the stars.

"You know our project is a beast, right?" Steven said, locking the front entrance to the observatory behind him. "Aced it."

I laughed. "Yeah, it is, and we did." Steven always parked around the side of the building, in the opposite lot facing Main Street, so I threw up my hand and waved as he trotted down the steps. "See ya Monday."

"Yep," he answered, and I watched the darkness gobble him up. From the shadows, he called out. "Hey, where's your boyfriend?"

I turned and answered. "Fall baseball game with North Star State. He's coming over later. We're scoping Draco from Oliver's rooftop." Draco meaning the constellation. It always blew my mind when I encountered someone who'd never been shown a constellation, and Draco was by far my favorite.

"Sweet. Just making sure I didn't miss any girly break-up clues. See ya!"

I started down the ramp and wound my way to my side of the observatory. I glanced up and sighed. Such a perfect night, totally clear with no glaring moonshine. Stars flooded the heavens, and I thought this might be one of the most perfect constellation nights ever.

The moment my eyes clapped onto my truck, I knew something was wrong. Not situated in the brightest of light, at a quick glance it looked okay. Until you noticed the tires.

Or rather, the lack of them.

It stopped me stone-cold in my tracks. Not a sound did I mutter as I stared, disbelieving. Barely a breath. Certainly no words. At first. Then it sunk in. What had really, truly happened.

I lowered my head, stared at my shadow stretching across the pavement of the observatory's empty side parking lot. And swore.

"Shit, shit, shit!" I spat. I stood for a moment, hands on my hips, just ... gawking. My gaze shot around the parking lot. Who in their right mind would drive up this close to the observatory and remove all the wheels and tires from my truck and stick them in the bed? But they had. All four of them, off. Concrete blocks took their place, and held up the frame.

Shit!

I blew out a long, frustrated, pissed off sigh and stomped across the lot. Of course this would happen on a night Brax wasn't here to meet me after work. *Perfect.* I peered through darkness, to where the halo of street lamp ended, and listened. I didn't hear anything. Nor did I see anything. No camera phones. No giggling. Nothing.

Then, a burst of laughter erupted from the shadows, and it set off, I don't know, at least a half dozen more fits. Male and female, from what I could tell. A few flashes went off. I turned my back and ignored them. I couldn't help but wonder who it was. At least *gutter fuck* had been left out of the equation.

In the distance, music rocked from one of the campus frat houses, and the football game must've ended by the sound of a stream of horns blowing and people hollering. I swore again, just as an engine started in the darkness, at the far end of the lot and close to the main road. Away from lights, I couldn't make out the model. I could tell it was a truck, but that was all. I turned away once more, before someone got an even better view of my face. The last thing I wanted was to become another overnight viral sensation. I just wanted to get finished and get gone.

This wasn't going to be easy. Doable, but not easy to accomplish alone. "It's not going to fix itself by you just staring and huffing about it, Beaumont," I muttered to myself out loud. And, my inner self was absolutely right. Luckily, I knew how to fix the problem or I'd have to spend a chunk of money to call someone out to do it for me. Lowering the tailgate, I leapt up, unlocked my Lockbox, and dug out my tools and jack. Placing them on the concrete by the front driver's side, I pulled one wheel and tire out of the bed, rolled it to the front, and set to work.

By the time I had three of the four wheels back on, the roar of exhaust tore through the air. Cory's Camaro flew across the parking lot, and hadn't even stopped before Brax threw open the passenger side door and leapt out. In his cleats he jogged toward me, and beneath the bill of his Silverbacks ball cap, his expression was dark and thunderous. Orange clay stained his right thigh and backside, no doubt where he'd been sliding. Cory killed the engine then unfolded his big self out of the driver's side and followed Brax over. His uniform looked as dirty as Brax's.

"You okay?" Brax asked, and his eyes fixed onto mine until I answered.

"I'm fine now," I said. I wanted to diffuse the anger I saw brewing in Brax's expression. "Earlier, though, wow." My lip quirked up and I lowered my voice. "I said dirty words. Out loud, even. Did you guys win?"

Well, that sort of did the trick. The darkness fell, and Brax's mouth lifted in one corner, and he gathered me in a full body hug. "Did you now?" he said into the crook of my neck. "I'm sorry I missed that. Yeah, we won. Why didn't you call me? Or Tessa?"

"Because. Tessa went home for the weekend and you were at your game." I shrugged. "This is a pain, but I can do it myself. How'd you guys know?"

"Are you sure you wanna be an astronomer?" Cory asked. "Because you've become a local star." He shook his cell phone at me. "Viral."

My head dropped back and stared skyward. "Ugh, great. My brother's going to see it and rat me out."

Brax's face appeared over mine, and he brushed his lips against my mouth. "I like your brothers, then." He glanced over my head at the truck, then looked at me. "I can't believe you can fuckin' change your own tires."

"Hmm," I answered. "The skills I possess." I shook my head. "Mind-blowing."

He nestled his lips against my throat, and his teeth grazed my skin. I shivered. "What a sick chick I got, huh, Maxwell?"

"So right, Jenks. I'm pretty jealous, actually. You only got brothers, huh, Beaumont?"

I laughed at Cory, who'd slowly taken a shine to me after that first day in the batting cages. He only called me by my last name, which I found hilariously cute. "Sorry, buddy. Just brothers."

"Mother?"

"Dude," Brax teased. "Power down."

Cory just laughed. "Okay, you two weirdly conjoined twins cut the cord and let's get this hooptie back together." He looked at Brax. "We've got some assholes to find."

My gaze shifted from one ball player to the other. "What do you mean?"

Brax moved to the bed of the truck, gathered the last wheel and tire in one hand, and leapt down. "You don't think we're just gonna let this ride, do you?"

"No chance," Cory chimed in.

"Seriously, there's no need to make a big deal about it," I urged. "It was a fall prank. Nothing more. Girls and guys, a whole group of them. Not just one person. No big deal.

You don't need to go punch someone's face in because of it."

Brax's head appeared around the tailgate, his hair curling up from the back of his cap. "Doesn't matter. You've already been pranked once."

"Yeah, and it was a royally fucked up tasteless prank," Cory said.

"Twice pranked? On my girl?" Brax returned to putting the wheel and tire on the back right side. "Sorry. Hell and fuck no, Sunshine." The sincere protectiveness made his accent heavier than usual, and I'd be lying if I said I didn't like him referring to me as his girl.

I left it at that, mainly because I knew there'd be no changing either of their minds. They were as hard-headed as my brothers. Within minutes, Brax had the tire on and Cory loaded the concrete blocks into the bed of the truck.

"Later," Cory said, and his Camaro door squeaked as he opened it. "You good, dude?"

"Yeah," Brax answered, and retrieved his duffle from the backseat. "Be there when I'm there, bro."

Cory flashed me a grin as he slammed the door and stuck his head out the window. "See ya, geek girl."

I returned it. "Not if I see you first." He sped off, his tail lights fading into the night.

Brax pulled me against him, buried his chin into the hollow of my neck, his lips settling on the sensitive skin there. "You gonna let me shower at your place before you show me this Draco thing or what?"

The sensations he stirred within me as his warm breath brushed over my throat made my knees quiver a little. Along with the thought of Brax in my shower. My eyes drifted shut. "You're not going to go kick some butts first?" My voice cracked, and I slipped my arms around his waist.

Brax's deep chuckle shook me back to consciousness. "And miss the sky dragon and making out with my girl?" He nuzzled me once more. "That would be a hell and no." He tugged me toward the truck, and my stomach flipped in anticipation of the night ahead. I was filled with amazement that Brax had been able to bring me to this place; a place where my high school trauma no longer stabbed me, or self-doubt lingered. It had blessedly vanished. And my heart had opened up wide enough to trust him with the secret I'd been holding onto. Right now, he believed me to still be a virgin. Tonight, I'd tell him the whole truth. He'd been honest with me. Now, it was my turn. It'd be his last chance to bail, and that thought alone made me so very nervous. But I had to do it. It was time.

His lips brushed the soft shell of my ear. "Let's go, Sunshine," he whispered.

And I melted inside.

My nerves, though, continued to twist in turmoil as we climbed the stairs to my dorm room. Brax took the key from my fingers, unlocked the door. Inside, the walls seemed to close in on me, his presence large, looming, yet, strange as it sounded, suffocating. In a good way. In an ... appealing way. The moment he stepped into the bathroom and turned on the shower, I raced around my room, toeing my All Stars into the corner, kicking out of my work pants and pulling my Mulligan Telescope tee shirt off. I stood facing my small fold out closet, pondering my choice. My fingers brushed a favorite pair of soft faded low riders and a burgundy thin strapped cotton cami, and I hurriedly slipped both on. On my bed I waited while he showered, no less than thirty feet away, and yet some of my trepidation eased as he began a not-too-shabby Slim Shady rap. The louder he got, the harder my mouth tugged. Finally, the water stopped, I pulled on my boots and re-braided my untamable hair.

Brax emerged from my bathroom, hair wet and curling and messy, shirtless and barefooted with only a pair of well-worn jeans slung low over his hips. And all those cut in stone muscles, tattoos and Latin scriptures stretched taut ...

My breath left me, and it actually hurt to pull it back in. My dorm room filled itself to the gills with Brax Jenkins and all his raw male hunger; so thick I could feel it pulsing off the walls as much as the steam wafting from the bathroom. He swaggered over to where I sat and plopped down beside me, and my body sank into his weight. As he pulled on clean socks and boots from his duffle, his head turned sideways, watching me with eyes so profound I began to fidget. Brax's muscles flowed like liquid metal beneath his skin with each movement, and I noticed the thick roping veins that snaked from his hands, up his forearms, his biceps. On his face, throat, and back lay the scars; the evidence of the beatings he'd endured, and the Celtic cross between his shoulder blades that represented his salvation. It fascinated me. Brax fascinated me.

He rose, and pulled me with him. "You want me to grab the scope?"

"Not this time," I said. As he pulled his long arms into a white buttoned-down shirt, I reached for the big folded quilt and two pillows off my bed. Just as he finished the last two buttons, I piled the pillows into his outstretched arms. I carried the quilt, and grabbed the wrench and flashlight I kept on my bedside table. "This is all we'll need."

A slow, sly smile stretched across his face. "Is that so?"

I gave him a nervous fake scowl, and held the door open. "Yes, that's so. Now come on before it gets too late, wise guy." I led him out into the hall and locked my door behind us.

"Wise guy. I like that." Brax's raspy chuckle reverberated off the walls of the stairwell as we climbed to the rooftop. When I pushed open the door to the roof, turned the flashlight on, held it with my teeth and jammed the wrench in the crack at the bottom, he laughed again. "Who are you? Mission Impossible? I guess this is something you do all the time?"

"Maybe." The night air had the slightest of crisps to it; not chilly by any means, but not as scathing hot as August. Finding my usual spot, I spread the quilt out, dropped to my knees and smoothed the corners. "It usually only takes me one time to learn a hard lesson." I turned my face toward his. "I got locked out once and was stuck on a rooftop for hours." I sat back on my heels and inclined toward one side of the quilt. "You can drop those there."

He did, and I situated them right where I wanted. Then I crawled onto the quilt, flipped over and laid flat on my back. My gaze was straight up, right at Brax's as his stared over and down at me. Inside, I was jittery; hopefully my exterior proved a little cooler. I patted the space beside me. I drew a slow, inconspicuous breath in. Released it. "Right here, Boston."

Although a smile pulled at his mouth, his stare remained bottomless as it held mine. He dropped beside me, straightened his long, lean body out and I stuffed one pillow beneath his head; took another for myself. Our heads, bodies were side by side. I looked at him. "Comfy?"

A line bunched between his brows. "No. Come here—" He reached for me, but I pushed him back and giggled. It didn't stop him. He grabbed me, pulled me half onto his chest, his arms around me. "This is better."

I scowled at him, although I more than loved lying like this, against him, so intimate. "Brax. Do you want to see Draco or not?" I studied his face, so close to mine now; noticed each sharp edge, planes and angles of his cheekbones and jaw cast in mysterious shadows, and thought I'd never seen anything more beautiful in my life. Such a contrast in reaction to the very first time we met. I had to force myself to breathe. "Well?" My voice was quiet, but not as shaky.

Leaning up, he brushed his lips across mine. "I want to see Draco."

I narrowed my eyes. "Okay then." He settled me back down beside him, but I leaned my head closer to his shoulder, and he laced his long fingers through mine. The night sky was perfect; moonless, cloudless, each star twinkling, the markers brighter than the rest. Raising my arm straight up, I pointed to the sky. "Okay, what do you see?"

Brax inhaled, exhaled. "I see stars, Sunshine. A lot of them."

"Is that all?"

He was quiet for a moment. "Some are brighter than others."

I smiled in the darkness. "That's right. Can you see a pattern? A distinct shape?"

More silence as he studied the heavens. "Am I supposed to?"

I gave a soft laugh. "Yes." I lifted our joined hands between us. "Point your index out like mine and follow the ends of our fingers." He did. "Memorize each spot our fingertips pause at, and then mentally draw a line from each star. Kind of like an Etch-a-Sketch. Ready?"

"Always."

I snuggled closer. "Okay. Here we go." I began pointing, our index fingers snugged together. "See that bright star there?"

"Yes." His lips brushed across my temple, sending tingles over my skin.

I concentrated. Hard. "Okay, that's our starting point. Now we move down, then over, then back up," I continued. "We've just traced the tip of Draco's tail. Now keep your eye on our fingertips and move up, up, up." I could clearly see Draco's entire body, but I'd been looking at it my whole life. "Can you see it yet?" I moved our hands over the star points until the entire dragon had been traced, then lowered our arms. I turned my head slightly, watching Brax's features as he searched the sky.

The minute he found it, I knew.

Slowly, he sat up, his face turned heavenward. He didn't say anything for several moments; but his eyes roved over the night sky. "It's right there," he said. With his own arm stretched out, without my help, he dragged his fingertip through the air, marking each of Draco's stars. "Holy shit, I see the whole dragon, Gracie."

I sat up beside him. "I knew you would."

His fascination at seeing the beauty of Draco twinkling in a black October sky sent a thrill of contentment rushing throughout my body. That he thought something I loved so much was so … interesting? It was hard to believe. "Breathtaking, isn't it?"

He didn't answer at first; his gaze was locked onto the stars of Draco. But then his stare left the heavens and turned to me. In the darkness, those ghostly eyes softened as they searched mine, and the scar on his cheekbone appeared like a jagged smudge of soot in the shadows. "Hell yeah, it is." His hand cupped my jaw, his thumb brushed over the scar on my lip. "I can't believe it's been right here this whole time."

My breath lodged in my throat, and no matter how hard I tried, I just couldn't look away as he lowered his head and pressed his lips to mine.

19. Redemption

Brax SLOWLY PUSHED ME back, his body hovering over mine, bracing his weight on his elbow as his lips explored further. He kissed my mouth fully, drawing my bottom lip in and sucking, his tongue tangling with mine and causing a surge of excitement blended with fear, desire, and I clutched his forearms. Urgency laced his breath, and a low groan escaped as his free hand found the bare skin of my stomach, his fingers dragging roughly, yet gently, over my ribs. I wanted this. I didn't want him to stop. But I had to tell him the truth first.

I pushed my hand over his and stopped his movement. When he pulled back and looked at me, his expression was unreadable. Waiting. His unusually beautiful features were etched in stone.

"I have to tell you something, Brax," I said. My voice was whispery soft, and a little unsteady. "I should've told you before now.

But I was … scared." I lifted my hand to his jaw, loved the roughened sand-papery feel of his day-old stubble. "But now it's necessary."

In the shadowy light, his eyes flashed question, uncertainty. He didn't say anything; not a single word, but his hand remained possessively against my bare stomach.

I stared at his Adam's apple, the strong column of his throat marred with the scar that carried a reminder of his violent past. "The night with Kelsy—our senior class party at the pond." My gaze moved to the portion of his chest exposed by the opened buttons of his shirt. I swallowed, inhaled, and raised my eyes to meet his. "I'm not a virgin, Brax. This ring," I moved my hand between us, held up my finger. "It's a personal choice I made after that night." A soft laugh escaped my throat as I looked away. "It's my one and only time and I don't even remember it. Not a single second of it. I only remember that last drink." Brax's silence frightened me, but still I went on. "Then … being somewhere else, away from the others, on the ground, face down in the dirt, the pain in my lip, and … other places." The recall of humiliation brought fresh tears to my eyes, and I'd leave most of the sordid details out of the story. "Through the darkness I could see my brothers beating Kelsy." Brax's hand moved to my hip, and his fingers gripped me there as he listened in silence. "I remember thinking they were going to kill him, and I was so damn scared of that." I squeezed my eyes shut for a second as the memory crowded me. "Kelsy was crying, begging them to stop and saying how sorry he was. That he'd been drunk—was still drunk and only slipped me one pill in my drink, just to loosen me up. He hadn't meant to hurt me, he'd said." I let out a long sigh. "Later I remembered getting my lip sewn up in the emergency room, and then the … female examination, and how painful it was—"

Brax pushed up and sat beside me, knees pulled up, his forearms resting against them. He stared straight ahead, into the darkness. I sat up, too, close to him, but not touching. I kept quiet, staring at the blanket I sat on and inadvertently rolling the deceitful silver band around my ring finger. What did Brax think of me now, I wondered? Revulsion? Anger for keeping it from him? I had no choice now but to continue. "Rumors surfaced about what happened that night, and especially when Kelsy's father got involved. Kelsy made sure he wasn't going to look bad, though. I guess when it came down to me or him, he won." I stared at Brax's broad shoulders and tapered waist. Still, he looked straight ahead. "I was shunned by people I'd known my whole life. Labeled a slut. And had I not wanted this," I spread my arms wide, indicating Winston, "so desperately, I may have let them win. But I did want it. I worked hard for this scholarship. So I just …" I pushed out a breath. "Dealt with it."

Brax rose then, and strode to the chest-high wall at the ledge of the roof. Clasping his hands behind his head, he stared into the night. I stood too, and took a place beside him. I found I was suddenly speechless then, and humiliation flooded me. I didn't know what to say.

Brax turned then, and leaned back against the wall, spreading his thighs wide and pulling me between them. With strong fingers he gripped my face, tilted my head, sought answers with just his eyes that flashed a palpable fury before speaking. "That prick raped you. That's what you're fuckin' telling me, Gracie?"

The word was an ugly one; I hated it. A part of me still refused to believe that's really what Kelsy did. "I'm telling you that he didn't force me. According to the dozens of phone pics that circulated around school? I was more than willing." I couldn't meet his gaze now. "I just don't remember—"

Brax's hands gripped my shoulders, his fingers digging in. As he towered above me, he stared down, and the ferocity in those wraithlike eyes held more power than I'd imagined. He was so, so mad. "Gracie." He shook me. "Look at me, dammit." He drew closer. "Would you have had willing sex without the Ecstasy?"

I looked at him, and didn't hesitate. "No."

A cold, icy hardness fell over Brax's face; it shifted everything into something primal, full of raw rage. "Then that's rape, Sunshine. And I don't give a fuck about him or his powerful father." His fingers dug into the bones of my shoulders. "He'll pay for it." Blue eyes hardened to shards of glass, and his raspy voice held no threat, no excitability. Only a savage, raw quiet guarantee. "That's a fuckin' promise."

Raising my hands, I held his face. "I didn't tell you all this to gain your pity, or for you to jeopardize your scholarship, your future, just for you to seek revenge for my sake." I fastened my gaze to his, wanting him to see what I tried so hard to explain. He went motionless, eyes searching mine. "I didn't want anything left unspoken between us. No secrets. You told me your past. This is my mine, Brax. I don't want it dug back up. I want it to stay buried, back in that old life of mine. I lived it once, and that was more than enough. You see," I pressed close against him, pulled his face closer to mine. "You saved me. You led me out of a dark enclosure, a place I'd grown pretty comfortable hiding in. A prison, where I'd lost who I was." I smiled, and it felt good. It felt real. "You set me free, Brax Jenkins." Pushing to my tiptoes, I brushed my lips over his, but barely. "You stole my fear, then my heart. You made me want to feel again—"

Brax crushed his mouth against mine, and the violent possessiveness in his kiss shocked me, thrilled me at once. His arms completely encircled me as he pressed us together, engulfing my body. With those perfect lips he nudged mine open, traced the sensitive seam, then pulled my bottom one in as he sucked it with a slow, erotic taste that forced a groan from my throat and a fire to smolder in my lower belly. My fingers entwined through the curls that hung soft and messy at his collar, still damp from his shower, and I breathed in his scent; Brax swallowed my exhale, the sensation leaving my insides quivering, wanting more. His big hands slid over my backside, pulled me hard against him, and an ache so violent burned at the feel of his hardened state of arousal. He pulled back, his eyes searching mine, and without words I dragged my fingers down his arm, reveling in the hard muscles and strength beneath my palm, entwining our hands. We moved, both knowing what the other wanted, I think, and Brax bent and swept up the quilt and pillows with one hand. Silently, we left the rooftop, entered the darkened stairwell, made our way to my dorm room. My fingers shook as I pushed the key in the door, and Brax took it from me, lowered his mouth to my ear. His warm breath brushed over the shell, the sensitive skin of my neck, and I shivered.

"Do you want me to stay, Gracie?" His quiet gruff voice washed over me.

I nodded, turned my mouth to his, hovered my lips close, but not quite touching. "More than anything."

Silently, Brax unlocked and shoved the door wide for us to enter. He closed and locked it behind us. Threw the quilt and pillows on my bed, then waited for nothing else; he took my hand, led me through the hazy dark to my single bed, turned me around. His fingers squeezed mine, strong, protective. While his fingers grasped the hem of my cami, he leaned close, whispered in my ear. "Hold your arms up." I did, and he lifted my shirt up and over, and dropped it to the floor. His hands moved over my arms, lingering at my shoulders, then traced my collar bone with his thumbs, trailed down my ribs and I felt the roughened calluses of his pitching hand as it skimmed my skin. The yard lamp at the corner of the building shined through my window, and its sallow rosy shaft fell across Brax's face and I found the stark contrast between his beauty and brutality a drug to which I'd become addicted. I couldn't tear my gaze away. My fingers found their way to the buttons of his shirt, and as nimbly as I could I loosened each one until the edges hung free. Hesitantly I pushed the shirt over his wide shoulders, pulled each arm out and let the material fall to the floor next to my cami. I had no idea what I was doing; I only knew I wanted to touch him; feel the ridges of muscle beneath my palms, and his mouth on me. He scooped me up in his arms, put a knee into the mattress and lowered us both, and he rolled over me, bracing his weight on his elbow, much like we'd been on the rooftop, but so much more intense. Wraithlike eyes left mine and traveled slowly down my throat, my chest, and stomach, where his hand came to rest. He dragged his fingertips over my navel, across my hipbones, and with expert fingers loosened the five buttons of my jeans. I watched as his head dipped low, his lips pressing against my lower stomach, sending tingles of sensation scattering over my flesh when he licked then sucked the skin there, his tongue swirling over it, making me writhe beneath him. My fingers found their way into his silky dark curls, his taut neck, the corded muscles there. His mouth trailed upward, dragging those perfectly shaped lips and velvety tongue over my skin as his fingers dug into my ribs, and my eyes drifted shut as I twisted my hips, inching closer to him yet not nearly close enough. The anticipation was excruciating and painful and delicious.

Brax's tongue tasted and licked and suckled as he kissed the sensitive flesh of my breasts that rose above the lace of my bra. He kissed the hollow of my throat, settled his lips over my pulse that was rapid-fire fast. As fast as my breath. He moved to my ear. "As much as I've fantasized seeing you in nothing but those boots, they're in the way," he whispered. "Hold still."

Words would not push past my vocal cords, so I just waited and watched as Brax sat up, bent over at the waist, and in seconds I heard his heavy boots hit the floor. He twisted, grabbed first one foot, relieved it of my boot and sock, then the other, and he moved back up to my waist. "Raise up." I did, and he eased my jeans over my hips, tossing them to the floor and leaving me in nothing but my bra and panties. He flung his big body next to mine, and the bed dipped with his weight and I bounced beside him. I couldn't help but giggle.

"Oh, you finding something funny with my moves, Sunshine?" he teased, and his mouth and fingers dug into my sides, my belly, my neck, and I squealed as he tickled me.

"Brax! No! Stop it! Please!" My giggles were unstoppable. "Please! I love. Your moves. Not. Funny." I gasped.

He threw one jean-clad leg over both of mine, pinning me as he laid half on top of me, and looked down. His longish curls twisted messy and perfect over his forehead, his teeth gleaming white as he smiled a long, silky lazy smile that was hidden mostly in shadows.

I lifted my fingertips to his chest, caressed his lip that carried a scar just like mine, and it was then my gaze landed on my ring. It had meant something to me, and had eased my pain in more ways than one. But I no longer needed it. I eased it off, Brax's eyes watching closely, and I set it on my nightstand. Then I slipped my hands round his neck. When I tugged, ever so gently, Brax's gaze went from jovial and mischievous to stormy. "Tell me what you want, Gracie."

My smile was sincere, my voice a whisper and I was scared and brave at once. "I don't know what I'm doing, Brax," I confessed.

"But I know I want your mouth on mine. Your tongue tasting me. And your hands on my body." His eyes turned to liquid metal in the hazy shadows. "I want to feel you so bad I actually ache."

With a groan he crushed his mouth to mine, rolled over and pulled me on top of him. While his tongue wrecked havoc, his teeth nipped, and he sucked my bottom lip. His hands gripped my backside, palming my hips, and the thick bulge grinding against the juncture of my thighs shocked me and made the ache turn to a wicked burn beneath my panties. I didn't know what I was doing; I knew what I wanted, though. And I knew it was right. I pushed up then, leaving Brax lying on his back and staring up at me in what looked like wonder, and I slid off his hips and moved my fingers over the buttons of his fly. It took me a minute but I worked them all loose, and wordlessly I pulled them off his long, lean legs. He sat up then, and we were face to face on my bed, and he reached for my braid, slid the elastic off the end and threaded his fingers through my hair until it fell long and loose down my back. Over and over, he let it slide between his fingers. Then reached behind me, unclasped my bra, and pushed the thin straps off my shoulders, freeing my breasts.

"Christ Jesus, Gracie," his raspy voice spoke quietly, somewhat pained. "You're so fucking beautiful it hurts."

His harsh confession almost made the air jolt to a stop. Breathing became impossible; only I knew we were too far apart. Sliding one thigh, then the other over his lap, I straddled him, his erection hard and pressing against me in the most intimate of ways yet ... not quite there. Not satisfied, not close enough. His hands fell over my breasts, and with my hands I held his face. "So are you." Perched high enough that I had to look down at him, I pushed his hair back with one hand, fingering the puckered scar at his cheekbone, then I pressed my mouth to his in a feathery, timid kiss. Unsure. Completely sure. "I've never wanted something so bad in my life, as I want you."

With a guttural groan he palmed the back of my head and again crushed our mouths together in a primal kiss; he devoured me, suckled my lip, tasted my scar with his tongue, and his hands left nothing untouched. He turned me onto my back, followed me down, and while driving me insane with his teeth nipping at my lips, his other hand edged my panties down, and then his fingers were inside of me and I sucked in a surprised breath. Brax drew it in, swallowed it, and kissed me deeper. His fingers moved, touching places I never knew existed, and the sensation nearly brought a yell from my throat. I writhed against his hand, trying to close in, wanting something deeper, something more. My own fingers pushed at the boxer briefs he wore; snug over his muscular buttocks. I couldn't reach, couldn't get them down far enough, and Brax turned me loose just long enough to help me. He laid atop me, with nothing but skin touching skin, his tongue tangling with mine, his hands everywhere. Still I burned, I ached, and I arched against him, seeking relief. My mind wasn't thinking any longer; it just reacted, and my hand reached between our bodies until my palm sought the velvety steel of his erection. I wrapped my fingers over it, amazed, frightened, and the burn caught fire. Brax let out a groan that sounded as tortured as how I felt.

Then his upper body disappeared over the edge of the bed, and when he sat up I knew he'd retrieved a condom from the wallet in his jeans. He ripped the package off with his teeth, removed the thing, and his hand disappeared into the shadows as he slid it on. He returned to me, his body over mine, his lips settling against my lips in a gentle, thorough kiss. "Are you sure you want this, Gracie?" he whispered against me.

"I want *you*," I answered. And I knew I did.

Braced above me on his elbows, he nudged my thighs open with one knee then entered part of the way. I sucked in a breath and dug my fingers into Brax's back, my heart racing, my breath painful as it lodged in my lungs. He stilled then, waiting, kissing my mouth in a slow, erotic dance that intensified the longing and ache between my thighs. His mouth moved to my ear as he gently began to rock.

"I've wanted you for a long time, Gracie Beaumont," he whispered gruffly. "Dreamed it even. I can't believe you're mine."

The tight fit of Brax inside of me eased as he moved, until he filled me, and it was delicious and addictive. His gaze never left mine as he rocked slow at first, then faster, and I moved with him, my legs wrapping around his waist and my fingers digging into his shoulders as I held on. His mouth found mine, then he tore it away with a groan and buried his face in my neck.

A slow, gradual sensation began to build at my core, slowly emerging from a place so hidden within me I didn't know it even existed. The more Brax moved, the more intensified it became until he thrust again, sending a delicious surge through me. "Brax," I cried, and I dug my fingers into his skin. Like a mirror shattering from the sun behind my eyelids, I exploded, gasped and writhed with the rhythm as the waves fell over and over and over my head. Brax's groans rumbled against my neck, his fingers dug not painfully into my hips, revealing his own release, and my mind scrambled to make sense of anything, everything. He slowed, grew still, burrowed his mouth into the crook of my neck and tried to rein in his ragged breath. Contentment and wonder flooded me; everything about him made my insides sing, and a smile settled over my mouth in the dark.

Brax found my lips with his and kissed me with a gentleness that belied the fury he'd grown up with, and he held my entire body with his; legs entwined. At last, he pressed his lips to my temple, kissing me tenderly, and then he looked down at me, and his eyes shined in a way I hadn't noticed before. He said only one word, and that word made me shiver.

"Mine."

He dragged his lips over mine and it was a possessive kiss, and I found I liked that. I breathed him in. "Mine, too," I whispered.

Brax rolled off and pulled me with him, snugging my body tightly against his; he held me close within the muscles of his arms, and my cheek rested against his stone-like chest. I splayed my fingers over his stomach, tracing the defined cuts of muscle, the sharp V's at his hips. As my eyes closed, and I reveled in his warmth, I decided then I could stay just like this for the rest of my life. Right here, in my bed, wrapped in nothing but Brax. On a contented sigh, I drifted off into a deep, fulfilled slumber.

20. Broken

My eyes fluttered open, and I blinked through the early morning gray haze of light filtering my room. Rain fell, a constant fall of dreary outside my window. A draft moved over me, and I glanced down at my bare shoulders. I was naked, beneath my sheets. Brax and I had made love. My hand reached for him but only found a cold, empty spot beside me.

I jolted up, clutching the sheet over my breasts as I scanned the shadowy corners of my silent dorm room. "Brax?"

No answer.

After quickly checking my cell phone and finding no missed calls or texts, my gaze fell on his duffle bag, sitting zipped against the far wall. Maybe he went out for breakfast? He hadn't mentioned early baseball practice, and he knew Steven and I had traded shifts and I had off today. Like me, he usually went for a morning run. But in the rain? And wouldn't he have awakened me? Something nagged at me, though, bit into me, deep down. Disappointment? That had to be it. I'd assumed I would wake up tangled in Brax's strong arms and legs. Where had he gone?

Memories of our lovemaking crashed over me; I recalled every single touch, every single kiss, and how his lips caressed me. Details scorched into my brain for eternity. A smile turned my mouth up, and I rose, pulling the sheet with me and wrapping it around my body as I made my way to the shower. Maybe he went out for coffee, and I'd been in such a dreamy state of contentment I hadn't heard him leave. Tilting my head back, the steamy water poured over my face, and I noticed a delicious burn between my thighs. Another smile tugged at me as I remembered what caused it. *Lord, so that's what the fuss was all about.*

With my wet hair wrapped in a towel, I tugged on the jeans Brax had expertly flung to the floor, chose a clean tank top out of my drawer and pulled it over my head. Rubbing my wet hair vigorously in the towel, I let my unruly locks hang long and limp to air dry as I pulled my physics book out and laid on my stomach across my bed to study for the mammoth exam I had coming up on Monday. Time ticked by; my concentration was next to nothing. An hour. An hour and a half passed and no word from Brax.

Finding myself re-reading the same pages twice, three times, I flung the book aside and grabbed my cell phone. After trying to reason with myself about why not to sound pathetic and text Brax, I lost the battle and sent him a short message.

Me: Hey, Boston, you there?

I waited, staring at the tiny screen on my unfashionable old flip phone, but after fifteen minutes with no response from Brax, I decided that to sit around the dorm room would do nothing except allow my mind to wander. And wonder. So I gathered my physics book, my pack, and headed to the library to study. Wherever Brax was and whatever he was tied up doing, he'd surely text me when he finished. Meanwhile, I had to study. No choice.

The campus was as still as the air when I cut across the lawn and started toward the massive three story brick Winston library. I'd slipped on a long sleeved shirt that snapped down the front, along with a hoodie to keep away the light rain still falling. Not exactly chilly, but more so than usual, especially with the dampness. I couldn't help but dart my gaze all over as I walked, looking for Brax. Where in the world was he? After the night we'd shared it seemed so unlike him to just … leave me alone. It was Saturday. Where could he have gone?

I reached the library and climbed the steps, and pushed into the cool interior, peeling off my hoodie as I did so. Smiling at one of the librarians I'd come to recognize as she busied herself behind the horseshoe entry desk, I hurried past her and made my way to a quiet back corner table in the astronomy section, where I hung my jacket on the back of a chair and sat alone. Fishing my text from my pack, I opened it up, took a deep breath, checked my phone. No message. I turned the volume off, leaving it on vibrate. No getting around it, Brax was heavy on my mind, and despite how whole he'd made me feel the night before, doubt began worming its way into my brain. I closed my eyes briefly, forcing out negative thoughts before they had a chance to latch on. I was being ridiculous. Something came up, he didn't want to wake me, and he left quietly. Whatever had kept him, he'd been unable to use his phone. Could be any number of things, I reasoned. Physics, Beaumont. Big test coming up. With a frustrated silent swear at my new distraction, I dug into my studies.

Physics held my attention for a while; at least until nearly noon. One of my strong subjects, I made sure I covered all the notes and pages I'd flagged to study. But I'd had enough, and after I'd lifted my phone a hundred times, just to make sure I hadn't missed a quiet vibrating message from Brax, I packed my stuff up and left.

Now I was getting worried. A sick feeling gnawed at my insides as I crossed the campus. Still overcast and gray out, the rain had slowed to a barely-there drizzle when I entered my dorm. The moment my eyes rested on my bed, visions of Brax and I from the night before flooded me. But he'd been gone by morning, and I hadn't heard from him since. I dropped my pack on the floor, next to his duffle, then plopped down on my bed. I stared at my hands, recalling how I'd touched him, how he'd felt against my skin.

I was driving myself nuts.

Deciding I couldn't just sit around the dorm and pace, I yanked off my jeans and boots, trading them for running shorts and a tee shirt. The common room was empty, save for one girl who sat reading a novel on the sofa, and I pushed out of the door and started up the sidewalk at a fast pace. Fast, in hopes of out-running the fear now digging at me. The drizzle falling didn't deter me; it actually kept my mind occupied as I ran along Main Street, circling the observatory, and skirting the park. It felt good to make my muscles burn, so I kept going, until I found myself at the sports complex. I wasn't surprised to find it desolate; it was a rainy, dreary, Saturday afternoon. People were holed up in their apartments, their dorms, their houses. Watching TV. Studying. Painting their nails. Gearing up for Saturday night parties. So where was he?

Deciding to circle the complex, I began a quick-paced run around the walkway. No one was out; the complex was deserted. Only me, the crazy one, had decided running in the rain was a great idea. By now my hair was sopping wet, the heavy braid bouncing off my backside like a soakened hemp rope, and the faster I ran, the deeper my lungs burned. I ran for over two hours; my skin was slick from rainwater, my clothes drenched. Finally, I stopped beneath the mammoth cottonwood tree close to the ball diamond, pulled my phone out of my pocket. I had one message, and it was from Mom.

Hey, sweetie, I miss you. Give me a call when you get a chance. Xoxo

Shoving my phone back into my pocket, I took off, this time leaving campus. I ran through the main entrance and turned toward town and just … kept running. Few cars were out and about, and the rain continued to fall in light sheets that left me soaked to the bone. I didn't care. Something was wrong; I could feel it. I swear I could.

My Nikes smacked the wet concrete as I ran past an old white wooden church, its spire jabbing the heavily clouded sky. I turned onto the side street, circled around, made my way back to campus. I was jogging along the run path at Rigley Commons, the park where Brax had kissed me by the fountain, when his voice jolted me from behind.

"Gracie, wait up."

I spun around, and the moment my eyes rested on Brax, relief washed over me. I hurried off the path toward him where he stood beside the massive fountain, and I couldn't help the grin that took over my face. "Hey, you. Where'd you—Brax, good Lord!"

I stopped in front of him, where he stood motionless at the fountain, and I inspected him closely. Shock and fear tore at my insides as I took in his busted and bleeding eyebrow, cut lip, and white tee shirt splattered with blood. More blood stained the front of his jeans. When I looked at his fists, I saw they were busted up and bleeding, too. He wouldn't look at me. "What happened?"

It was then, when Brax's eyes finally lifted to meet mine, that I felt it. Like someone just suckerpunched me in the gut. "We gotta talk, Gracie." His voice was edgy. Strained. So not Brax.

I stared at him then, through the lightly falling drizzle, and my insides clenched. "What is it?"

He wouldn't touch me; wouldn't even come close to me. A good three feet separated us. Fear kept me frozen in place as I waited. He looked away first, to some unknown point, then lowered his gaze to the ground. Then slowly, to me. I felt the change in his character just as surely as I would a shift in temperature.

"This won't work."

Disbelief shocked the breath right out of my lungs. I could do nothing but stare. No way had I heard him correctly. "What won't work?"

"Fuck," he muttered under his breath, and

glanced away. He grasped the back of his neck with both hands. "You and me, it won't work." He looked at me then. "You're a nice girl, but I don't do relationships, Gracie. Especially nice girl ones. Never have."

My breath left me, like I'd dropped from a tree and landed on my back. It hurt to breathe, and I hardly knew how to react. What to say. Shame flooded me. I'd opened up to him. Trusted him. "Ok. You don't do relationships. So all this time, and then last night was—"

"Nothin'. It was nothin', Gracie." His sharp bark of laughter made me wince almost as much as the frigid stare of his eyes. "Just a good old fashioned college chase and fuck."

A mixture of heat and numbness sifted through my skin. I couldn't feel my lips. Nausea pitted my stomach. I looked at him; at his battered face. "You don't mean that." My voice sounded weak, and I hated it.

"I mean every fuckin' word of it."

A myriad of emotions clamped around my throat and squeezed. I felt tears, somewhere deep inside my ducts, but they wouldn't flow. My eyes stayed dry as a bone. I didn't know what was going on; what had happened. Something epic had happened, but Brax wasn't telling me. Whatever it was, it'd won. Had beaten him.

I stepped closer to him, and he didn't move. I looked up, into those ghostly eyes, watched the rain drip down his soakened curls and trail down his face, and saw nothing but bitter cold as he stared back. Yet anger—raw and primal—rolled off of him in waves, a contradiction to his hurtful words. Either way, he'd made a decision. And I wasn't about to beg. For anything or anyone. I steadied my breath, tried to keep from showing him how my heart had just been torn in half. I managed to hold my composure, and forced my eyes to remain locked onto his. I studied him for a moment, making sure he saw me, too. Something flashed in his eyes. Regret? I guess I'd never know.

"I'll leave your bag outside." With one, long final stare, I turned and started across the lawn. I didn't look back to see if he followed; I couldn't. I'd shown weakness once in my life. To hell with that. I'd never show it again.

By the time I made it back to Oliver Hall, I jogged up to the entrance, slid my key card and hurried inside. I took the steps two at a time, making my lungs burn just a little more, before I reached my room. Inside, I grabbed his duffle bag, ran back downstairs, and to the curious eyes of two girls seated on the sofa, I opened the main door and set Brax's bag on the walkway. I didn't look to see if he was waiting. Instead I turned and jogged back to my room. Inside, I peeled out of my wet clothes, stepped into the shower, and beneath the searing water I let the suffocating pain come. I bent over at the waist and sobbed until my throat was hoarse and the water ran cold, and I forced my emotions to run just as icy. It didn't work, really. The moment I stepped out, wrapped up in a towel, and faced my dorm room alone, grief swamped me. Shame. More humiliation. And the ultimate sting of rejection. It hurt. It just goddamned hurt. I'd cried so much in the shower, I had nothing left. Only a hollow pain in my stomach that wouldn't ease up.

My phone rang then, and I hurried to it. My heart sank as I answered it. "Hey, Mom."

"What's wrong?"

The hole in my stomach felt jagged, ripped. I wanted to cry, just at the sound of her voice. But I had no tears. I inhaled. I wanted the comfort of my family, but I couldn't talk about it over the phone. "Can I come home?"

"Baby, what's the matter?" she asked, her voice panicked. Then, she sighed. Almost as if she'd guessed. "Never ask such a silly question. Of course come home. I'll be waiting on you."

I wasn't usually a runner; not the kind that hid from problems. But this ... unexpected whirlwind of emotions with Brax? Just thinking his name made me hurt. But staying clammed up in the room we'd just made perfect love in hours before? I couldn't do it. Quickly, I dressed in my old favorite jeans, tank and a button up. I pulled on my boots, plopped my hat on my head, stuffed a few things to wear in my pack, grabbed my scope bag and headed out. At the door I stopped, scrawled a note to Tessa and left it on her bed. I knew my roommate was going to react badly to news of me and Brax and I'd rather her hear it from me in person.

When I stepped out of the entrance, I noticed Brax's bag was gone, and the pain bit a little deeper. I made it to my truck, tossed my stuff inside, and thanked God my tires were still intact.

My thoughts scrambled as I sat in the parking lot, gripping the wheel as if my life depended on it. Home would ease this pain, wouldn't it? Jesus, it *hurt*. After so long I'd finally let someone in. Gave Brax not only my trust, but my heart. Whether he knew it or not, I was in love with him. Was I truly nothing more than a glorified chase and fuck? Really? Had Brax the capability to say such endearing things to me, to look at me with such wonderment, and to react to my touch with such ferocity then turn so cold, callous, with no regards to my feelings? After the secrets we'd shared; after he'd called me *his*? How could he have changed his mind so fast? I turned the engine over, threw the gear into drive, and left Winston behind.

By the time I hit the city limits, my tear duct system had replenished.

I cried all the way to Jasper.

21. Southern Comfort

WHEN MY HEADLIGHTS FELL on the familiar graveled driveway of our small ranch, my gut twisted inside, and a homesickness I hadn't been aware of made my heart even heavier. It hadn't been two full months away from home, yet it felt like years. The yard lamp cast a faded yellow arc over the porch swing, where Mom sat, swaying gently back and forth. She rose and started down the steps as I climbed out of the cab, where she met and enveloped me in a tight embrace. She smelled of her favorite honeysuckle shampoo and leather, and the familiarity of it washed over me. I squeezed her tightly, and my tears fell on her shoulder.

"Oh, baby," she said into my hair. Grasping my face in her hands, she studied me with concern edging her soft brown eyes. "What in the world's happened?"

I let out a frustrated sigh. "It's a long story."

A wise smile touched her mouth. "I've already got a pot of coffee on and ready, darlin'."

Shouldering my scope bag, Mom picked up my pack and we set them inside the front door. Grabbing two cups, she made our coffee, blond and sweet, she'd always called it, and we sat together on the porch swing. At two thirty in the morning, only the creak of the chain, the wind rustling through the cottonwood trees and the chirping of crickets broke the air as I told her all about Brax Jenkins. Sadie Beaumont listened quietly, with no interruptions; a solid presence, a strong shoulder. God, how I needed all of it, and it released a flood of emotions I'd been fighting so hard to keep penned up.

"I opened up to him," I said, so quiet that it barely rose above a whisper. With the toe of my boot I gave the swing a push. "He was so fiercely protective, so furious toward Kelsy." I shook my head and looked at my mother. "His eyes hold everything, Mom. When he looks at me, it's like he sees way deeper than just the surface. It's like he sees what I'm really thinking, really feeling. It doesn't make sense inside of my head, or my heart, for him to break it off like this." I stared between my feet, at the worn wooden planks of the porch. "Especially after last night. I told him everything about what happened that summer with Kelsy. And then we," I stopped my words, and tears filled my eyes again. I pushed my hands against my heart. Briefly, I remembered the ring that no longer sat on my finger. "You know it actually hurts here, Mom. Like real pain." I squeezed my eyes tight, pushing out the tears. "I tried not to like him. I tried so hard." With the back of my hand I dried my eyes. "I fell in love with him, Mom." I shook my head, picking at the hole tearing through the knee of my jeans. "Can you believe I was such a stupid girl? I can't believe I left for college and immediately became so involved with a guy." I met Mom's gaze and gave another half-hearted laugh, then exhaled. "Sure wasn't planned."

My mom pulled me to her shoulder, kissed the top of my head. "Well honey, it never is." She looked at me, wiped a tear with her forefinger. "But I will say this. For Brax to break things off, and especially after all of that," she said. "Either the boy's got a frigid heart and such deep-seeded problems you *never* want to get involved with—trust me. Or, there's something going on here that you're not seeing. Boys do stupid things, I know that." She turned my face to hers. "And right now I'd like nothing more than to punch him right in the eye." She let out a long, tired sigh and gave the swing another push. "But one thing we Beaumonts have always known. Only the good Lord looks out for us. Him," she patted my knee. "And each other. I know it hurts, sweetie. I've known that hurt before and it's nothing but a sonofabitch." She turned sideways in the swing. "But you worked hard to get where you are right now. You're the strongest person I know." Her eyes grew glassy in the sallow light of the yard lamp. "You can't let Brax or Kelsy or anyone else ever take it away from you, Olivia Grace. And I'm not talking about just your scholarship." She pressed her hand against my chest. "I'm talking about what's in here, baby. Your ferocious lion." She cupped my face. "You go ahead and grab its tail, give it a hard yank." She smiled. "Piss it off. Then you kick a path through all the crap, hold your pretty head high and proud, and shove your way through the muck. That's how you survive this. Trust me, darlin'. I know."

I studied my mom's features; each fine line that fanned out from her soft brown eyes, the high cheek bones, her strong, determined jaw, and the arched brows that made her face so expressive. She'd suffered plenty in her life; our dad had left her high and dry with three kids and a barely-surviving horse ranch. He'd broken her heart; not her spirit. And knowing all that, seeing the kind of strong woman she'd turned out to be? It lifted me. Lifted my spirits. Gave me strength.

I threw my arms around my mom's neck and hugged her so tight. Almost as if her strength could seep through her skin and sink into mine. I pressed my face against her neck. "Thanks, Mom," I said softly. "That's so what I needed."

"What in the damn hell is goin' on out here?" Jilly pushed the screen door open and it creaked as he stepped onto the porch. The

Texas Rangers tee shirt was rumpled and
faded; he had on his favorite plaid sleep pants
tucked into his crusty old cowboy boots.
When he focused on me, then Mom, he
frowned. "Lil' Bit, what the—I don't like the
looks of this. Why didn't you two wake me
up?" He nodded to our discarded coffee cups.
"You got any more of that?"

Mom got up and gently pushed Jilly into a
rocking chair close to the swing. "Sit. I'll
bring you a cup. And she arrived in the middle
of the night, that's why." She grabbed ours
and headed into the house.

Jilly's aged stare measured and weighed
me silently. Then after a few moments, he
shook his head. "The middle of the night, eh?
It's a goddamned boy, ain't it? Well, you
gonna just sit there or get up and hug your
grandpa?"

Even though I still hurt, Jilly's gruff yet
correct assumption made my mouth tug into a
half grin. I got up and wrapped my arms
around his neck, and sat back down. "Sort of."

He grunted, rubbed his big, gnarled hands
over his knees. "Sort of my ass. Who is it,
what'd he do, and do you want me to make
some calls?"

I shook my head as I looked at my fierce
grandfather. Making a call meant phoning
friends within the Texas Rangers. "No, Jilly.
No calls necessary."

"I swear you people are lunatics." My
baby brother Seth joined us on the porch, and
he walked straight over to me and plopped

down next to me on the swing. He draped an arm around my shoulders. "Does this have anything to do with your truck being vandalized? Or that guy you're dating?"

"What'd you say, boy?" Jilly asked, then looked at me. "Lil' Bit?"

I looked at my brother. "Big mouth." I sighed and gave my grandfather an assuring smile. "Just a college prank, Jilly. Someone jacked my wheels and tires and put my truck on concrete blocks. Threw the tires in my bed and videoed the whole thing. Posted it on YouTube. Totally separate incident."

Jilly swore under his breath. "Well, I don't like how this college horseshit is going at all, Lil' Bit." He started to rise. "I'm gonna make some calls."

"Sit down, Dad," my mom ordered as she stepped out onto the porch carrying a tray of coffee mugs. "There'll be no calls, you hear me?" Her eyes softened in that knowing, mom way. "Olivia will be just fine. The last thing she needs is a pack of ornery old Rangers showing up on campus."

"Well I ain't budgin' off this porch until somebody tells me what the hell's goin' on," Jilly said. "And I mean it."

The hard lines and weathered face of my grandfather's profound stare as he waited for my story made me know for a certainty I wouldn't get off the porch any time soon. At least until I told him and my brother what had caused me to drive from Winston in the middle of the night. So I began, feeling a little stronger after talking to my mom, and of course leaving out some of the more delicate details that a man of any age need not hear. Especially a protective little brother and a really protective ex-Texas Ranger of a grandpa.

Jilly and Seth listened quietly—a miracle in itself—and by the time I finished, and they'd given their two cents worth a line of gold pushed at the treetops as the sun began to rise. Seth pulled me to his side in the swing.

"Nothin' like some good ole hard labor to kick that heartache's ass," he said with a crooked grin. He lifted my hand, turned my palm over, and ran his thumb over it. "Man, Jilly, you should see how soft these things are." He lifted his face, and I noticed for the first time a slight shadow of stubble patching his chin. "You can help me de-poop the stalls this morning."

"We were all going to work on a few new colts later," Mom added. "It'll do you some good to ride them in the round pen. And spend time with your brothers."

She was right.

After we all had a short nap, Seth and I hit in the stalls, and he eyed me over the back of one of the new colts. A pretty little paint, his ears were pricked forward listening to every word Seth said. My brother's eyes met mine, and it struck me how good-looking and mature he seemed to have grown in the couple of months I'd been away.

"So this guy," Seth said as he shoveled manure into a big pile in the center aisle. He stopped, balanced his weight with his elbow on the handle. "This inked baseball player tough guy from Boston. You're in love with him, huh?"

The words were a sock to the gut; it hurt to hear, but I breathed through it. "Yeah," I shoveled, tossed, shoveled again. "I suppose so."

"I don't buy it."

I stopped mucking and looked at him. "What do you mean?"

Seth shrugged his broad shoulders. "I don't know, sis. From what you say he seemed completely into you. And from what you say about his background?" He shrugged. "Then an abrupt kiss-my-ass-I'm-not-into-relationships?" He laughed, spit on the ground, and shook his head. "Sorry, sis. Sounds sketchy to me. I ain't buyin' it."

"Well," I continued my chore. "It is what it is and I don't have the heart or energy to pursue it." I met his gaze. "It hurts too much. It hurts like crazy, Seth."

The muscles in Seth's jaws clenched as he turned a surprisingly mature sixteen year-old stare on me. His deepening voice softened. "I can see that."

We finished the stalls and brushed the horses down before Kyle and Jace showed up. Both were mad as hell about the vandalism on my truck—both times—and even madder that

I hadn't told them about it. It was nice to have their support, honestly. But I no longer wanted to linger on the subject of my broken heart, my vandalized truck, or any of the above. And working hard seemed to help start the healing process. After Mom's breakfast of fried eggs, bacon, biscuits and homemade strawberry jam, we hit the pens and started on the four colts. When it was my turn, my brothers except Jace, my mom and Jilly all found perches on the fence while I eased into the saddle. The colt immediately nutted up at the pressure from my backside, and ripped around the round pen. I held on, coaxing and squeezing my thighs around him, trying to calm him, but he wasn't having any of it. Not this day. Just when I thought I'd bail, he threw me—hard. My face plowed into one of the posts, and my brother Jace skidded on his knees in the dirt beside me.

"Lil' Bit, you okay?" he asked. He moved my braid and helped me to sit, then grasped my jaw, inspecting my injury.

"Yeah, I'm fine," I said. I welcomed the pain in my face. It drew away from the ache in my heart.

Kyle hopped down and bent over at the knees. "You're gonna have a nice shiner there, darlin'."

I didn't even care.

By late afternoon, all four colts had been ridden, put up, brushed. Mom made pot roast and potatoes, and it felt good to sit around my familiar dinner table with my family beside me. So good that I knew leaving in the morning would be more difficult than it had been the first time. I knew I had to study, too, and I hated to see my two older brothers leave so early. Both lived within a fifteen minute ride from the ranch, but Mom must've known I wouldn't be able to study with them around and told them to skedaddle. One of her favorite words. Ever.

On the porch, with my textbook and notes spread out on the swing, I read and studied until the fading light made it too difficult to see. I stretched, yawned. Thought about Brax, winced at the pain it caused. At the hurt I knew would still be there once I got back to campus. Then the screen door creaked open, and Jilly walked out.

"You stare at those books long enough yet?" he asked, but took the rocking chair anyway.

I grinned and closed the text. "Yes sir, I have. Just finished up."

"Hmm." Jilly wore his long white hair pulled back into a low ponytail, and almost always wore a hat. It perched now on his head, and he pulled it down, closer to his brow. Jilly had kind eyes; soft brown and always with a twinkle. Which belied his extreme toughness. To his family, though, his heart was wide open. "Sky's supposed to be clear tonight. Only God's thumbnail to get in the way."

My mouth twitched at my grandfather's none-too-subtle hint. "Sounds perfect to me."

Jilly looked at me, square in the eye as he always did. "Let me tell you somethin', Lil' Bit. And I want you to push aside the pain in your heart long enough to hear me." He rocked back. "I know you're feeling about as low as you can feel right now. Heartaches hurt like hell. There's no way around that." He pushed his hat back, and I could see his expression clearly; sincere, angry, and full of wisdom. "The only boy good enough for you darlin' is one who'd sacrifice everything to have you. I'm talkin' everything important to him, just to keep you. No matter the cost. Otherwise," he rubbed his jaw, "he ain't worth his weight, pound for pound, in pure solid horseshit. He just ain't, Olivia Grace. You remember that."

I rose from my seat to throw my arms around my grandfather, squeezing him tight, drawing in his familiar, comforting scent. His big rough hands patted my back, and he hugged me, too. "I'll remember," I said. "I love you, Jilly."

Jilly cleared his throat. "I love you too, Lil' Bit. Now come on." I let him loose and he rose from the rocker. "Let's go put that big scope in the barn to use before the sky clouds up and we won't be able to see a damn thing."

Jilly and I watched the sky for some time that night. Neither of us brought up my heartbreak or Brax again. And I was fine with that. What'd needed to be said, had been. My family provided a deep comfort within me that nothing or no one could possibly ever replace.

Later, Jilly, Mom, Seth and I played a few rounds of Texas Hold 'Em, and chatted about plans for Thanksgiving. A family in need had been chosen at church and I was going to help Mom and a few others prepare the whole turkey dinner to take to them the night before. It was something our church did every year, and I remembered not all that long ago that our own family had been chosen. It was a good thing, and we looked forward to it every year.

Before I turned in for the night, Seth had knocked on my door, sat on the edge of my bed, and caught me up on local stuff. He told me about a girl he was interested in, how he was acing his classes without hardly even trying, and how he'd won three more shooting trophies. He looked at me then, shadows falling on his handsome face in the dim lamp light of my room, looking older than his years. "You gonna be okay, Bit?"

I cocked my head. "When did you get all grown up and sweet and stuff?"

He softly punched my arm. "I've always been this awesome. Now I mean it. Are you?"

I gave my brother an assuring smile. "Yeah, brat. I will be."

I hoped I was right.

The next morning I left my family on the porch and drove straight to class. It was a long drive. I felt better; truly, I did. Jilly's words, my mom's comfort, and brothers' support all converged and made me stronger. But the hurt was fresh. Deep. And I knew realistically it

wouldn't simply ... go away, just like that. I
mean, how could it? Despite the hurt, the slap
in the face, I'd fallen in love with Brax. True
love, my mom said, doesn't fade overnight.
She was right. It hadn't. And I was stuck
dealing with it. At least now, though, I
believed I could. Slowly. Over time. But trust?
Boy, that one had taken a big ding. I wouldn't
hand that out so easily again. Ever.

Butterflies ripped into me as I stepped into
humanities. I forced my eyes to avoid the
seats Brax and I usually took in the far corner
of the auditorium; instead I turned down
Kelsy's aisle and grabbed an empty chair four
seats behind his. Far away from Brax, and
behind Kelsy, with an easy shot up the aisle to
escape both directly after class.

The moment I slid into my chair, Kelsy
stepped into the room. My gaze drifted up and
I was shocked to see his face had been
recently beaten. One eye was mostly swollen
shut, with red and purple bruising all around
it. His jaw was bruised. Lip split. A cut to the
forehead. His gaze caught mine for a second,
and he noticed my own blackened eye. He
said nothing and folded into his chair, his back
to me. I couldn't help wondering what—or
who—had done that to him. And why.

Brax didn't come to class. Part of me felt
relieved. Almost like something heavy had
just been lifted off my chest, and to be honest
that bothered me. The other part was ... I
don't know. I couldn't label it. The second

lecture was over I was ready, and darted up the aisle and out of class.

"Liv, wait!" Kelsy's voice sounded behind me, but I ignored it, hurried past other students hustling to class. My blackened eye caught some curious glances, but no one stopped me, no one spoke, and I hurried to my next class. I didn't want to talk to Kelsy, not at all. I kept my head down, fearful of accidentally running straight into Brax, of falling apart and letting the wide split of my broken heart bleed all over the place for everyone to see. I didn't see him, and Kelsy didn't pursue me, either. By the time I started my physics exam, I could actually focus on it. Luckily it was a subject I loved. Most of the content I'd studied in one form or another on my own, since it was relative to astronomy. After I finished the exam, the professor pulled me aside.

"Ms. Beaumont?"

I stopped and looked at him. "Yes, sir?"

His gaze moved to my eye. "Is ... everything all right?"

"Oh," I said, and my fingertips brushed the tender skin. "Yes, sir, I was thrown off a horse, is all."

He inclined his head to the door, dismissing me, and I hurried outside. I'd just made it to my truck, had the key in the keyhole, when his voice stopped me cold.

"Gracie."

My hand froze on the door handle, and my

breath left my lungs, leaving me weak, dizzy.
I didn't turn around. I said nothing. Just stood
still, gripping the metal. I forced myself to
breathe in. Out. In again.

His hand went to my shoulder and turned
me around.

I didn't look at his face; I kept my eyes
trained on his chest. I knew he stared at my
blackened eye.

His knuckles brushed my jaw, tilted my
head up. Made me look at him. "What the hell
happened to you?"

His concern angered me, and I then
couldn't look at him anymore. I shifted my
gaze over his shoulder. "What do you want,
Brax?" My voice didn't quiver. Didn't reveal
tears. It was as even and impassive as I could
muster. I also noticed his bruises, his
blackened eye. I'd almost forgotten about it.
So many emotions had flooded me that day.
Just as they were now.

Anger flashed over his face, hardening his
jaw, the lines between his brow. "Did
someone do this to you?"

"No. A horse." I turned away, opening my
truck door.

"I just wanted to make sure you're ok."
His voice eased, apparently relieved.

Forcing my strength, I looked at him. Just
seeing his unusual face, and all the memories
it brought back, crushed me, and I sucked in a
breath as though I'd been slammed in the gut.
I prayed he couldn't see the raw pain that
scratched and clawed its way to the surface.

My lips went numb, I wanted to scream and yell and ask him why. Why did you go through two months of slowly dragging me out of my carefully constructed shell, only to stomp on my heart? Was it seriously just for a good old-fashioned college fuck? But I didn't. I somehow held it together. I leveled my gaze to his for a painful fraction longer. A feat in itself. And I said the only thing I could say. "I'm no longer a concern of yours." With that I shut the door, and surprisingly, he stepped back. Didn't beat on my door, swear or demand me to hear him out. He actually allowed it. Without another glance, I started my engine, put the truck in drive and left Brax Jenkins standing in the parking lot.

22. Brax

I STOOD THERE AND watched her take off
through the parking lot. Watched 'til her truck
disappeared from sight. I scrubbed the back of
my head. And just stared. Had I really
expected any other reaction from her? I guess
I'd hoped for ... what? Forgiveness? The pain
in her eyes felt like a goddamn kick in the gut,
and it was so real I almost had to look away.
I'd put it there, that hurt in her beautiful eyes.
She'd trusted me. Laid her goddamn soul wide
open and bare to me, just as she had her body,
and I'd taken both. Swear to God, I couldn't
fuckin' help myself. If only I'd known what
I'd later that morning found out. If only
what'd happened ... had happened sooner.
Before we'd had that night together. Would I
have done anything different? Would I have
been able to refuse her? No. Why? Because
I'm a selfish prick. End of fucking story.

I started running, heading to the batting
cages to meet Cory, and my mind filled with

her image. It filled with everything Gracie. The way her eyes were wide, soft, and shaped so that they tipped up a little in the outer corners. Full lips that I'd—Jesus Christ, I could've kissed them for hours. Hair that fascinated me when worn in her usual braid; sucked the life out of me when I'd unraveled it, let it hang long over her bare back, shoulders. I shook my head, trying to fling those images out. They wouldn't budge. I guess it'd be my punishment. It's what I fuckin' deserved.

I'd planned to stay away from her— Christ, I didn't want to hurt her any more than I already had. But when Cory'd texted me asking about her banged-up face, I had no choice. I had to see for myself, see *why* her face was banged up. *I'm not your concern anymore.* Damn. She might as well have shoved a knife in my heart. Those words had stung. Hurt like hell. Bad thing was Gracie'd never know how much they'd hurt me. It had hurt like hell to say the things I'd said to her before, seeing her face twist in pain and confusion. They'd all been lies. Unavoidable lies. And she'd never know how deeply she touched me. No one in my life had made me feel that way. Only her. And I'd lost her.

She'd never, ever know that I fucking loved her.

It wasn't even possible. Kelsy Evans' father had made that crystal fucking clear.

A horn blasted behind me, and when I turned Cory passed by, his hand stuck out the open window of his car. He knew. Knew some of the fucked up situation. Most of it, anyway. I'd had no choice but to leave some of it out, for Cory's sake. Gracie had been right about one thing. Evans' prick father was one twisted fuck. The less Cory knew about what had gone down, the less shit would fall on him. Or the Beaumont's. Jesus Christ, I couldn't let Gracie's family suffer because of me. Bad enough the goddamn Kappa dare still existed. I was responsible for it, too. I regretted the hell out of that one. I hadn't known Gracie when I took that challenge. But this thing with Evans? That was a whole different set of balls. Cory knew how I truly felt about Gracie. That much I'd confessed to him. And I'd sworn him to fucking secrecy. Cory Maxwell wouldn't say a word.

I couldn't afford him to.

I yanked my beanie down further over my forehead and picked up the pace. I liked how the jolt of my feet against the pavement sent a shockwave through the muscles in my legs, made my lungs burn, and I ran faster still. Rounding the corner I hit the sidewalk and straightaway toward the sports complex. People passed by, recognized me, blew their horns. Yelled out the windows. I ignored them all. None of them really knew me. Only liked the thought of me, what they believed me to be.

When I reached the cages, Cory was parked, leaning against the door of his Camaro.

"Bout time you got here, douchebag." He shouldered his pack. "You see her?"

I bent at the waist, hands resting on my knees, catching my breath. "Yeah. Said a horse threw her."

"Is that it?" He started toward the entry, and I followed.

"No. She told me she wasn't mine to be concerned about anymore."

"Man, you should just tell her." Cory stopped at the door. "Stop fuckin' around and just tell her. We'll figure things—ugh, Christ!"

Cory grunted as I grabbed him by the shirt, slung him away from the door and shoved him against the brick wall. I pushed my face close to his. "You know I fuckin' can't. That means you can't either." I shoved him again, hard, and stormed through the doors.

The minute I hit the entryway, old Henry looked up. He didn't move; barely changed facial expressions. But he knew I was pissed.

"Take it easy on my cages, boy," he said as I passed by. "You got hellfire in those crazy eyes of yours today."

I said nothing as I pushed out into the walkway, stepped into a booth, and grabbed a bat. Slinging my beanie off, I yanked a helmet over my head and slammed my fist against the start button on the wall. Squared up to the plate. Waited for the pitch. It came, firing out of the pitching machine at ninety-eight mph, and I swung the hell out of the bat. The familiar slam with the baseball sent vibrations shooting up my arm. I crouched, swung, hit. Over and over, I didn't miss a pitch. Just kept swinging as hard as I could.

"We need that arm you're rippin' on," Cory said behind me. "Take it easy, man. You pitch tomorrow."

Anger fueled my swings. I could care fuckin' less about that damn game. Again. Again. The harder I hit, the better I felt, and I swung until the machine quit pitching and I ran out of breath. I dropped the bat and flung off my helmet, squatted and held my head in my hands. Cory stayed behind me, silent. Finally, I rose and stared out across the pitching bay. "This is more than some dumbass college dare, Cory." I wiped my forehead against my shoulder and looked at probably the only real friend I had. "More than her tires being snaked, and more than some goddamn insulting graffiti. It could fuck up her life, man." I shook my head, spit, looked at him again. "I can't let it go."

Cory looked at me, then away, then back at me. "Son, you've got to make a choice. Either talk to the girl and tell her everything— which would be they way I'd go. A girl like that doesn't come around often." He rubbed his jaw then shrugged. "Or let it the fuck go."

I stared off, beyond the pitching bay. I hadn't known the full depth of what'd happened to Gracie before that night. What that prick fuck Evans had done to her, and the shit senior year that'd followed. And when I left Gracie that morning, I hadn't truly known what a psychotic bastard Evans' father was, either. But I damn sure found out.

Thinking about it now smoked a hole in me so deep I felt like I was going to fucking explode. But I was crammed in a corner where Gracie would suffer more if I pushed the issue. If I tried to change things. Jesus fuck, how did this all get so goddamned turned around? Dammit to hell.

I looked at Cory, bent down, grabbed my beanie, and pulled it on my head. "Guess I'll just let it the fuck go."

23. Green-Eyed Monster

OCTOBER DRAGGED BY. Humanities class was a test of endurance since Kelsy sat in front of me, and Brax off to the side in the back. I was acutely aware of Brax, though, and my concentration during lecture just pure out sucked. Thank God it was the only class I had with either. Blessedly, both had left me alone. Some twisted, in love part of me, though, wished every day Brax would just pop up out of nowhere, have a reasonable and forgivable explanation for what he did, and we could resume our relationship. I missed him. Really and truly missed him. I couldn't help it.

He'd changed, too. At least, from what I'd noticed. Before he'd been rowdy, full of life, endearingly rude. If that made sense. Now, even several rows over and forward, I could sense his anger. He was like a big pot of molten metal, ready to boil over at any given moment. It'd only take a toe to push it over. A slight shove. And I had no idea why.

One thing I did know, however. Every night I worked, a single headlamp followed me to my dorm. It stayed far back, in the shadows, until I'd made it to Oliver Hall's entrance and slid my key card. By the time the door closed behind me, the headlamp was gone. I knew it was Brax, and it just added to my puzzlement. No phone calls, no texts. I tried not to dwell on it, but it was hard. Damn hard. Hardest thing I'd ever attempted to do.

The week before Halloween I was sitting in the library, studying. I had texts opened and scattered all around me on the table only I occupied. Then, something dropped onto my book.

"Tell me that's not utter perfection."

Tessa's voice startled me, and I picked up the small plastic card she'd dropped. I turned it over in my hand then scowled at my roommate, who'd plopped into the chair next to me. "Tessa, that's a fake ID."

Her full lips, covered in shiny lipgloss, pulled taut over her white teeth. "Wow. You do have a lot of gray matter up there." She pointed at my head. "Of course it's a fake ID, doofus. How else can you get into MacElvee's? Lord, girl," she snapped her fingers. "Get with the program."

I stared at the ID, then squinched my brows together. "Tessa, it says I was born in nineteen eighty-nine."

She rifled through some of my opened books. "So? Mine says eighty-eight." She smiled broadly and tapped the end of my nose like a child. "They never check. Besides, you're going out with us tonight." She laid her head on my shoulder. "Please? I'm tired of you sulking around, staying clammed up in the dorm room, and here in this stuffy old library. Or at the nerdservatory." She looked at me and batted her long lashes. "You gotta get out, chica. Put that douchebag behind you. *Live*." I started to protest, but she pressed her fingers against my lips. "Shut up. I don't want to hear it. Not one more lame excuse." Her perfectly arched brows drew into a fake frown. "You promised a long time ago, Beaumont. You don't work tonight, and you've been studying all afternoon. Seriously. I know you're a geek, but you're a pretty cool geek whom I've grown to kinda love. Time to pay up. We're going and that's that. You need a beer."

My lips pulled into a smile I couldn't stop. "I do not need a beer. But okay. I'll go."

Tessa squeaked, then hastily covered her loud mouth with her hand. "Yay! We'll leave at eight. And I'm dressing you." She leaned over, kissed my cheek, and waved. "Later, babe."

"Wait, Tessa, no," I said. But she threw a grin over her shoulder and kept on walking.

By the time I got back to the dorm it was nearly six p.m. Tessa was there. Waiting on me. Like a predator. I scanned the room quickly, and sure enough, she had one of her own outfits spread out on the bed.

"Okay, before you say anything, just hear me out," she began, and she met me at the door, pulled my pack off my shoulder and tugged me to her bed. "Seriously. You're adorable. I mean that in a," she glanced to the ceiling, thinking, "holistic, wholesome, Mary Poppins kind of way." She tweaked my nose. "You and your E.T. shirt are just so darn...cute. But I'm gonna bling you up a bit, chica. Nothing drastic, I swear."

I searched through the objects of clothing on her bed. "You want me to wear this little gauzy thing?" I asked. "Tessa, I have banged up legs. They're not pretty and smooth enough for this." I eyed the other pieces: a white tank top, and a nearly see-through shirt with a laced-up back. The skirt was tissue-paper thin, short and floral. Pretty, but on me?

"You're ridiculous. Put this on. Your legs are fine."

"I'm wearing my boots."

Tessa grinned, and it made me feel she was up to no good. "That's the idea, my darlin'. Now get ready. I still have your face and hair to work on."

"Good Lord. Please don't slut me up."

"I'm not going to slut you up, weirdo. Just let me have my way. For once?"

It didn't take long to trade out my jeans and button-down shirt for Tessa's outfit. I looked in the mirror. The upper half wasn't too bad. But the skirt. "Tessa, this thing is short!"

"Come out and let me see!" she hollered.

I inched out of the bathroom, and she squealed. "Shit, you're hot! Turn around."

I did. "I am not hot. It's…unnatural looking on me. I look like a hootch. And I'm not trolling for guys, Tessa." I turned back around and gave her *the look*. "I'm just going to hang out with you girls for a little while."

Tessa rolled her eyes. "I know that. No reason you can't make the boys drool while you're just hanging out." She grinned. "Right? Now come here. I'm not finished. And you do not look like a hootch."

She pushed me onto the bed, and I gave her a meaningful glare. "Do not make me look like a clown. I mean it."

Tessa bonked me on the top of my head with her blush brush. "You are so weird it's not funny. Now be still."

After a torturous hour of hair pulling, facial tugging, and an occasional punch in the arm, Tessa had me exactly like she wanted me. To my surprise, I did not look like a clown. Or a hootch. More make-up than I'd normally ever wear, but it was ok for a change. One night out. That was it.

"Your eye shadow looks smoky fab," Marcie said as we all walked up the ramp to MacElvee's. "You should wear it more often."

"She is a non-believer in make-up and all things uber-girlie," Tessa said. Then grinned at me. "But it does look stunning on you."

I just shook my head as we pushed into the bar. Friday night, the place was packed. Wall to wall with Winston students, as well as what

Tessa had deemed *local infiltrates*. I was sandwiched between Tessa and Kelly as we shuffled to the back. Wooden rafters stretched overhead, and the dark walls were decorated in an old western theme, with horse blankets, old saddles, and spurs. Tessa grabbed my hand as she spied an empty table and pulled me through the crowd. Already I felt out of my element, the music was thunderous, the patrons loud, and a drone of conversation and laughter made normal speech pointless. I rose on the toes of my boots to settle into the bar chair, and at the same time my hand kept the hem of my gauzy skirt from riding up too high.

Tessa laughed. "God, you should see your face! Pure terror!" She shook her head. "You're drinking a beer, chica! You gotta loosen you up! Excuse me? Hello?" Tessa flagged down a young guy with a black apron on. Mid-twenties, cute. He gave Tessa a wide grin. "Yes, ma'am?"

"A pitcher, garcon. Pretty please." Tessa's smile flashed white.

His eyes drifted to me. "You girls got your ID?"

"Of course," Tessa said. She fished hers out of her big Zebra bag, and the rest of us followed suit. After the waiter glanced at each one, he nodded. "I'm Ash, one pitcher coming up." I watched him make his way to the bar, disappearing through a sea of people. I met Tessa's gaze as I stuffed my ID back into my bag. She wiggled her brows.

"God he's scrumptious," Kelly said, and tucked her hair behind her ear. "Liv, he was checking you out big time."

"He sure was," Tessa agreed. "Marcie? Did you see it?"

"I did." Marcie threw me a grin. "I think I feel a pang of jealousy."

I laughed back. "No, he was not," I insisted. "You guys are imagining things." He was cute; tall, broad shoulders, shaggy brown hair that fell to his shoulders. Brown eyes. But he just wasn't Brax. And I just wasn't ready for this. *Dammit*!

"Hey, Tess, there's that giant you're so in love with," Marcie said.

Without thinking about it, I turned my head. And my eyes clashed with Brax's. I jerked my gaze back, started fumbling with a napkin.

"Shit a brick," Tessa grumbled under her breath. "We've been in here a gazillion times and this is the first time I've seen him in here. Liv," she said. "I'm sorry. Ignore him. But I can't. Be right back."

"No—Tess! What are you doing?." But Tessa was already gone. Godalmighty, what was she up to? I drew a slow breath in and tried to calm my jittery nerves just as Ash returned with our pitcher and four glasses. I looked at him, and he was already looking at me. Smiling. He set the pitcher and glasses in the middle of the small table.

"Enjoy," he said, but was only looking at me when he said it.

I gave him a hesitant grin. "Thanks." Just then, Tessa returned.

He didn't walk off. Instead, he turned directly to me. "Ash."

"Thanks, Ash." I had no idea why he was so puzzled by me.

"I haven't seen you in here before," he said. Those brown eyes were liquid pools and deep, and no doubt most girls fell right into them. I might have, had I not still been reeling from a crushed heart, and the crusher was less than twenty feet away.

I gave an embarrassed smile. "No, you haven't."

He cocked his head, as if studying me. "You work at the observatory." His gaze moved from my hair to my legs unavoidably poking out from Tessa's skirt. "I guess I didn't recognize you at first. You know, out of uniform."

"Ash, order's up!" Another waiter hollered across the bar, and he turned.

"Yep!" he called back. Then threw me another grin. "See ya later."

As he sauntered off, Tessa, Marcie and Kelly all squealed at once. Tessa squeezed my knee under the table, and I jumped.

"Oh my God girl, he's so into you!" Tessa said excitedly. "He said 'See. You. Later.' You know he's a Sigma Chi, right? A senior, too. Uncanny how I found that out so fast, don't you think?"

"Cut it out," I said in a harsh whisper.

"What did you do, Tess?"

Tessa poured beer into a glass and pushed it into my hand. "I only warned Jenkins to stay away from us or I'd call the cops. Now bottom's up, chica," she said. "Relax. Hot Sigma Chi Ash the senior is after you." She clinked her glass to mine. "Smooth sailing from here, my darling."

"You said you'd call the cops? And us, with our fake IDs?"

"Shh! Are you loco?" Tessa said, followed by a string of Spanish none of us understood. "Now lick your glass, Liv. Ash is watching you. God, he makes my ovaries quiver."

Kelly and Marcie looked at me then burst out laughing. I shook my head at their giddiness and Tessa's vulgar humor. Seriously, Ash probably pushed that line on all the girls. Besides—I wasn't going to hook up with the bartender. I forced myself not to think about Brax being directly behind me, and it wasn't an easy feat. I didn't really like the taste of beer, but I raised the glass to my lips and let the cold brew slide down my throat. I didn't have to look over my shoulder to know Brax watched me. I could feel that profound stare burning into me like a red-hot branding iron and it was so intense that I had to fight to ignore it. But after a few minutes, whether it was the brew or the atmosphere and giggling friends or all of the above, I relaxed a little. We laughed. People watched. Finally, Kelly called it quits.

"Okay, knuckleheads," she said. "I have to get up early in the morning. And since I'm the DD, I say it's time to scram. It's past midnight."

"God you're such an old lady," Tessa accused. "But I still love you."

We gathered our bags and I eased off the stool, still careful that my skirt didn't fly up. The crowd had thinned out quite a bit, and I couldn't help but peek over my shoulder. Brax and Cory had already left. I felt relieved. I felt disappointed Brax hadn't approached me. *Stupid girl ...*

We'd just stepped out the door and were heading down the ramp when a voice from behind stopped me. "Hey—I didn't get your name."

"Olivia Beaumont," Tessa offered, and gave me a little shove in his direction. God, I was going to pound her in the noggin later for that.

Beneath the outdoor lamp Ash's smile was wide, warm—and predatory, if I had to label it. Maybe the shadows playing across his face gave me that impression. I didn't know for sure. He held out his hand. "Well, Olivia Beaumont, it's nice to meet you."

I reached for his hand, and he enveloped it with his. "Nice to meet you, Ash—"

Suddenly a body shoved between Ash and I, and I was staring at the back of Brax's head as he faced Ash. I heard Tessa swear, then Brax turned his body around and faced me.

Those eyes that would never stop shocking me stared down, and even in the shadowy light I could see the fury in them. "I gotta talk to you, Gracie." His voice was raspy and low and edgy, and he'd had more than his share to drink. He placed his hands on my hips and started to turn me around. "Now."

"Dude, what's your problem?" Ash said.

Brax ignored him. "Let's go."

"Wait a minute," I said, confused. "Brax, what are you doing? I'm not going anywhere with you."

"She doesn't want to talk to you, bro," Ash said, and grabbed Brax's shoulder, spun him around.

Brax launched a punch, his fist to Ash's jaw. So fast I almost didn't see it. "Back the fuck off," Brax warned. He turned to me, his eyes angry and pleading at the same time. "Gracie, now."

"Brax, you're drunk. Leave her alone," Tessa said, and grabbed my arm. "Come on, Liv."

"You heard the girls," Ash said, facing Brax. He rubbed the spot Brax had walloped. "Leave her alone, man."

I didn't have time to even pull in a breath before Brax had slammed his fist into Ash's face. His head snapped back with the force of Brax's hit, and he stumbled, but then Ash, who was the same size as Brax, threw back and the two went at it. Brax lit into Ash full force until they both hit the concrete.

"Stop it! Brax!" I yelled. But he wouldn't stop. He kept hitting, and hitting hard. Punch to the ribs, to the head. Ash fought back, landing punches to Brax's face, but Brax's fury gave him an edge.

Finally, Cory's big body stepped in and dragged Brax off of Ash. Tessa pulled on me. "Come on, girl. Let's go while Cory has him."

"Get the fuck off me, man!" Brax yelled at Cory. "Gracie, wait!"

Tessa pushed me into Kelly's car and as we drove away, I stared out the window. Brax, still held by Cory, caught my gaze. God, he was mad, so angry. He swore, shoved Cory off of him, and before I saw anything more I turned and faced forward.

"Jesus God!" Tessa said. "What a beast! Are you okay?"

I nodded. "Yeah, I'm fine." But I wasn't. Not at all.

"It's a good thing you guys didn't work out," Marcie said, peering at me from the front passenger seat. "He's crazy, Liv. A complete psycho. Did you see how he beat the hell out of that guy? He didn't even know him! You don't need that kind of crazy."

While Tessa, Kelly and Marcie regaled the whole drama, I rested my head back and noticed how the moonlight bathed everything in silver as we passed. I sucked in a long breath, closed my eyes, and also noticed how, even though it probably shouldn't, my heart ached for Brax. The sight of him, the sound of his familiar raspy voice, his presence close to me. The angst in his voice. I still loved him. And for some unexplained reason, I thought he loved me, too. Past the hurt and anger and alcohol making his ethereal eyes fiery, I saw it.

So why had he done this? Why had he shut me out? Only to step in between me and Ash? A guy I didn't even know? A guy Brax didn't know? It made no sense. Ash could press charges and Brax would be in so much trouble with the school. God, what was he thinking?

After Kelly dropped us off at our dorm, Tessa and I got ready for bed. In the dark, Tessa said, "You know he's absolutely zero good for you. Right?"

The Brax I knew—or rather thought I knew—was good for me. I'd felt it clear to my bones. How could it have been fake? "I'm so confused, Tess. I just don't get it. Or him."

"I don't know what's going on with that boy, but two things I know for sure. One, he's still crazy about you. Otherwise, he wouldn't have bothered to jump poor Ash. Who, by the way, is fine as holy fuck. No kidding. And two, he's loco. And chica, it don't matter how much a guy loves you. If he's crazy, it'll only lead to more heartache. Or worse."

I let out a long sigh. "I know. Thanks, Tessa. 'Night."

"Goodnight, darling. Dream of Ash. Totally into you."

Instead I thought of eyes so light they seemed silver, of scars and soul-searing tattoos and a crappy childhood and a perfect smile. Then, I cried myself to sleep.

24. Wrecked

"**Y**OU'RE GOING TO THAT brainless Halloween Blitz? Tonight? Woman, if I'd known that's why you wanted to cut out of here two hours early I'd have said no way. Then I would've driven you straight to the loony bin. You've gone kookoo. For Cocoa Puffs."

I gave a light laugh. "You're probably right." Steven and I had just finished leading a group through the new Draconids exhibit. I sighed. "To be completely honest I was sort of pushed into it."

"By your aggressive but extremely hot roommate?" Steven grinned. "Don't tell her I said that. Wait, yeah, tell her. No, never mind. Don't."

I chuckled. "I won't. But yes. She has a way with words."

"Why are you kookoo? Exactly?"

We both turned, and Noah joined us. He looked at me. "What have you done, Olivia?"

"She's going to that obnoxious Halloween Blitz put on by the Sigma Chis and Kappas," Steven said. "The one they do together every year."

I sighed. "Guilty."

Noah's gaze held mine, and I could see disappointment there. I knew he'd disapproved of Brax but just never said anything. Not that it was his place to. "You just be careful, Olivia. Those parties can get pretty rowdy."

"No worries there," I assured. "I'm the least rowdy person you'll ever meet."

"That's why you had that black eye, right?" Steven said with a grin. "'Cause you're so un-rowdy?"

I glared. "I was thrown from a horse, goof."

He shrugged. "See? Who does that? Rowdy people."

Noah laughed, but it was soft and half-hearted. "Seriously, Olivia." He closed in on me then, sort of blocking Steven, and the look in his eyes was filled with sincerity and a little worry. "There's usually a lot of drinking. A lot of pranks. Like," he looked up, thinking. "Stephen King, Carrie pranks. Pig blood dumped on poor prom queen pranks. So please." His large hand squeezed my shoulder. "Watch yourself."

I gave Noah a smile. "Thanks, boss. I will."

We finished our work after that, and I

ignored Steven's disapproving head-shake as I left the observatory. Although it was still somewhat daylight outside, I knew a single headlamp wouldn't be following me back to the dorm. Still, I checked my rear-view mirror, and for what reason other than habit, or possibly hope, I didn't know. The second I stepped into mine and Tessa's room, though, she squealed, leapt off the bed and grabbed my hand.

"You know what's so phenomenally epic about Halloween parties?" she asked.

"Not really."

Tessa popped me in the head. "Disguise, chica." The smile on her face was pure devilment. "No one knows who you are if you do it right." She patted my hair. "Which is why we're going to do you famously right. As long as you're still wanting to do this?"

I inhaled, exhaled. "Yeah, I'm sure." I looked at her. "I have to know, Tessa. He plagues me." I stared at spot of carpet between my feet. "Day. Night. He's in my brain." I looked up. "Boring a hole in my noodle, and I'm sick of it disrupting my life. I want to ask him why. Why ... he did what he did."

"And you think that will settle you? And that he'll tell you?"

I shrugged. "I don't know. Maybe by catching him off guard, he will."

Tessa inclined her head to the bed. "Well have a seat and let's get started." A mysterious glint sparked in her eyes. "I've just the costume for you, darling, so let's get our asses moving. We're meeting Marcie and Kelly at eight and I've got a small miracle to perform here."

"Wow, how comforting."

Tessa smacked me once more. "Shut your cake hole and be still."

Two hours later, I stood in front of the mirror, shocked. Lifting my hand, I grazed my cheeks with my fingertips. "This is not really me."

Tessa laughed. "Yes it is, and stop touching yourself." She snorted. "Eww, weird. Anyway, I told you I was a miracle-maker. Just getting all that crazy ass hair you have semi-tamed and up in that stack was a miracle in itself. Now slip these wings on and you're all set."

What stared back at me from the bathroom mirror was more than a miracle. It was a piece of living, breathing fantasy art. As I held my bare arms out, Tessa slid a pair of gauzy, white feathery angel wings over my arms and hooked them together between my shoulder blades. They were short and appeared to stick straight out of my spine. Paired with the slinky silvery blue mini dress and silver strappy heels, I looked as though I'd fallen out of some alternate heaven. Tessa had applied glittery silver shadow to my eyes that swept out at the corners to swirl over my cheekbones, long false lashes, and silvery blue lipstick. I definitely did not look like me.

"Are you sure about this?" I asked. I looked at my roommate, with her painted Day of the Dead face and short black mini dress. "Brax might not even be there."

"Perfectly sure," Tessa assured. "And if he's not, Ash will be and we'll have a great time. Now let's go."

Butterflies rammed my insides as we loaded into Marcie's Range Rover and headed over to the Sigma Chi house. This was so totally out of character for me; not only with the costume, but the approach. I hated that Brax's abrupt and painful split from me hurt so bad—bad enough that I had a difficult time concentrating on my studies. I wanted—no, needed—to know why. He owed me that much. And for once, I wasn't going to stand for anything less. Could I have tried to obtain this information without the whole blitz gig? Probably. But despite Brax's harsh exterior and brass accent, he was far more intelligent than most granted him. And my simply approaching him would never have worked. He would have made excuses. This way, he'd probably have a little alcohol in him, and he wouldn't know it was me until it was too late. At least, that was my rationale. I hoped to God it worked because I couldn't take much more of this. The not-knowing. The endless what-if that beleaguered me at every turn, awake or asleep. It was driving me nuts.

By the time we pulled up into the already-jammed yard full of vehicles at the Sigma Chi house, my nerves were fried. My gaze scoured the parked cars. I didn't see Cory's Camaro. I didn't see Brax's bike. And part of me felt relieved. God, I was so confused; I didn't know what to do. And it was driving me insane.

Halloween night proved to be classic; full moon, dark clear skies, and the temperature had dropped to the mid-fifties. I shivered as we climbed from the Rover, my arms and legs bared to the elements. Orange and black lights had been strung from the front porch; all manner of monsters and zombies and slutty costumes littered the lawn, and laughter cracked the otherwise still night.

"Come on, chica," Tessa said, and looped her arm through mine. She tugged me along as we hurried across the lawn to the front porch, and I pressed against her as we entered the house. Metallica blared from the surround sound, and it was literally wall-to-wall with people. Tessa scoured the crowded room, then looked at me. "Over there!" she hollered. "Let's go!"

In a line, Tessa, Marcie, and Kelly, with me sandwiched between Tess and Marcie, wormed our way over to the far wall facing a small cleared area where a make-shift stage and mic stood. The noise deafened me: laughter, music, loud conversation. Couples dancing, making out. It was like a scene from an old eighties college slasher movie.

"Okay, Kelly, let's go get drinks," Tessa yelled. "You guys hold our place!"

Marcie and I watched the girls weave through the crowd until they disappeared.

"This is so wild!" Marcie hollered happily. "Oh my god!"

I laughed and shook my head, not nearly as enthused as Marcie with the party environment, and involuntarily I began to search the party-goers for Brax. Death—literally, someone garbed in a Death costume—made his way through, goosing females with his foam sickle. I prayed he stayed far away from us. Still, my eyes explored, and it was so hard to distinguish people. How would I ever find him? How stupid was I? I'd dressed up so he wouldn't recognize me. Didn't I for one second think he'd be difficult to find, too? Lord.

A disco ball twirled from the ceiling, and flickers of light darted through the semi-darkness, and it was then someone took the stage—which was nothing more than a few stacked pallets. A spotlight swung toward him. He was dressed in a full-suited black tuxedo and his face was painted in black and white, like a skeleton. He cleared his throat and banged his hand against the mic, and the music lowered.

"Ooh, this must be the costume contest I heard about!" Marcie leaned close and said loudly. "Epic!"

"Excuse me, assholes, could you all please shut the ever-living hell up? I have an announcement." The chatter lowered, too. "Why, thank you. Now, as you might have heard, the typically fucktabulous Jenks failed miserably at what most would've considered an easy task. But then again, he's a Kappa, not a Sigma." He shielded his eyes against the spotlight, searching the crowd. Jenks, if you're out there, you sadden me, bro. And here we all had applauded you for completing your Kappa Phi Dare before time was up. Instead, you were duped, which is really kind of embarrassing, given your rep, man." He shook his head. "Goddammit is all I can say, my friend. Godfuckingdammit."

Boos filled the room. Dare? I looked at Marcie, who shrugged, and my eyes went back to the skeleton at the mic. What was he talking about? My eyes scanned the crowd, searching for Brax. I didn't see him in the throng of partiers filling the room. It was then I noticed a few other guys dressed in tuxes with skull face paint. What the hell?

Just then, Tessa knocked into me and grabbed my arm. Her eyes were wide, filled with worry. "Olivia, we have to go. Now." She began to pull me.

"No, Tess, wait—"

"Olivia!" Tessa said. "Brax—oh my god, it was all a hoax!" She tugged harder. "I'll explain later. Come on!" I resisted, though, my eyes still searching for Brax.

The skeleton speaker continued. "So since Jenks nailed the poor little self-proclaimed virgin cowgirl, only to find out she's the Gutter Fuck—remember that live feed, guys?" The crowd roared, and the skeleton laughed, and my stomach dropped to my feet as realization slowly penetrated my frozen brain.

"We had to challenge a Sigma Chi brother to a new task." He scanned the crowd again. "Bro, if you're out there, you're disqualified!"

"Olivia, dammit, please!" Tessa yanked hard on my arm, but I stood my ground. More boos filled the air, and a girl approached the skeleton speaker and said something in his ear. He then looked in my direction, then directly at me, and then I noticed Kelsy standing beside the girl. He draped his arm over her and grinned.

"Oh, fuck me, will you look over there!" the skeleton yelled. The spotlight swung toward me, and I squinted at its blinding brightness.

"Oh, shit," Tessa growled.

The guy laughed and pointed with his mic. "Now that's a good sport right there, guys. Cowgirl, you lost your cherry a long time ago, but you got one big set of balls, darlin'! Gutter fuck? You look like an angel to me! You busy next weekend—ugh!"

The skeleton went down as Brax lunged out of nowhere, swung, and made the guy's head jerk sideways with a forceful fist to the jaw. Brax wasn't in any sort of costume like the other fraternity brothers. He was in jeans and a tee shirt. The crowd erupted, the light swung off of me and onto the two frat brothers. A sea of partiers closed in around them as they fought, and I could no longer see Brax. Only his fist as he raised it, smashed it back down.

The words sunk in as the crowd erupted into cheers. My head swam, and everything around me blurred. *Poor little unsuspecting self-proclaimed virgin cowgirl.* I was Brax's dare. Bang 'em and leave 'em. From that very first day, Brax had lied. No wonder he'd taken off and left me. My gaze then lifted and Brax had left the fighting circle and was there, staring dead at me, not two feet away, his chest rising and falling harshly with heavy breaths. I felt frozen, unable to move and cold as ice inside. Unable to breathe. Those haunting blue eyes of his stared hard at me, unreadable, frightening. In the next second, Tessa shoved him and began guiding me toward the door. People knocked into me, my body jerked, but I didn't really feel anything. Suddenly, I felt as though I was trapped, caged in an airless box, and I yanked my arm from Tessa and pushed through the crowd. Behind me, above the laughter and humiliating chanting of *gutter fuck*, I heard Brax's frantic, guttural yell.

"Gracie! Stop!"

I didn't stop, though, and when I hit the front door the chilly night air slapped my bare arms and legs as I rushed onto the porch, past other partiers and down the steps onto the lawn. I ran, best I could in Tessa's heels, those gauzy little angel wings flapping at my shoulders, until a force stopped me in my tracks. Steel fingers wrapped around my wrist, my body spun around. Brax stood there, his strong hand holding onto me, his face contorted into fury and pain.

"Gracie, Jesus, I'm so fucking sorry. You don't know the whole story." He stepped toward me, not letting go of my hand, his voice edgy. "I tried to stop it, swear to God. Please. Just hear me out."

Brax's words hit me like a solid punch to the gut. Shock and anger that he'd been a part of such a low prank churned inside of me, turned to hurt, more humiliation. He'd known about it all along. I'd come to this stupid Halloween Blitz to approach Brax, to find out the truth, and the weight of his deception pressed heavy and suffocating against my chest.

I was sick of being a door mat. The butt of jokes. Of being disgraced. Of giving my trust and having it yanked away.

Every raw emotion within me collided, and without another thought, I closed my free fist tight, reared my arm back and swung as hard as I could. My knuckles connected with Brax's steel-boned jaw, and his head snapped back in surprise. My hand exploded into white-hot pain, but I didn't care. I didn't give a damn, not anymore, and tears free-fell down my cheeks as I leveled my angered gaze to Brax's.

"You can *shove* your lame apologies!" My voice held even, steady, belying just how rattled I truly was.

"Jesus, Gracie, your hand!" He reached for it, and I pulled back.

I turned, tried to run, and he caught me, pulled me hard against him. The heat from his body seeped through the gauzy material of the dress I wore and clung to my skin, and part of me still wanted to lean on him, melt into him. I wanted all of this to be wrong, a big mistake. I wanted it to have never happened at all. But it had. And I'd been had. Again.

He shook me. "It's not what you think! Listen, dammit!" Brax pleaded. His fingers dug into my shoulders as he steadied me, anchored me to the spot of grass I stood in.

"No! You listen!" I said, shrugging out of his grip. From my peripheral I noticed people from the party passing slowly by, as they walked in and out of the Sigma house, watching our argument. Tessa stood there, too, waiting. Maybe I'd end up on YouTube again, and they'd all get some satisfaction from one more public humiliation out of me. It'd be the very last. I cradled the throbbing hand I'd punched him with. "I trusted you, Brax. I believed everything you'd said, despite my hesitation. Despite your thuggish looks, I never believed the rumors." More tears burned my eyes, and I could do nothing more than shake my head and laugh. "God, was I so wrong about you. You're no man. Just a stupid boy with no *goddamn* sense." My voice caught then. *Breathe*.

"You weren't wrong about me." he growled, scrubbed his face with his hand. "This is fucked up, was taken way too far and you've gotta hear me out—"

"I don't have to do anything." Somewhere deep inside of me, I found a shred of courage. A little more self respect. I stepped closer to him, tilted my head, ignored the hurt I saw in his crystal eyes that matched the deep ache in my heart. "Just pretend you never met me, Brax." I cocked my head, studied him. "Leave. Me. Alone." I turned and began to walk away, but he once more followed me, grasped my uninjured wrist and swung me around to face him. The panicky pain I saw etched into his features made me flinch.

"I tried, Gracie. But I just fucking can't."

He'd tried? What did that even mean? Confusion spiked through my brain but I held eye contact, as hard as it was to do that, and yanked free of his grasp. "My name's not Gracie." The cold, flat finality that resonated in my voice surprised me. From the ashen look on Brax's face, it'd surprised him even more.

"Olivia, are you okay here?"

Noah Hicks' voice sounded behind me, and he eased his body in front of mine, mostly blocking Brax from my view. "Walk away, man. You don't need to make things worse." Noah's shoulders stiffened as he addressed Brax.

Brax said nothing, pushed his fingertips into his eye sockets, then locked his fingers behind his neck. "Fuck!" he swore under his breath.

Then he charged Noah and the two went down fighting. Noah was athletic, but no match for Brax. Noah grunted as Brax's knuckles connected to his jaw. "Brax, stop it!" I yelled. "Stop!"

Brax was like a rabid dog, taking his frustrations out on Noah fist over fist. Cory's big frame pushed forward and he pulled Brax off. "Whoa, man, take it easy, take it easy."

Noah rolled up from the ground and took my hand. "Come on," he said. "I'll get you out of here."

"You won't fucking take her anywhere!" Brax fought to break Cory's hold—and almost did. Although Cory was a big guy, the strain was evident in his face as he struggled to contain Brax. Finally, he did, pinning his arms behind him and holding him tightly against him in a backwards bear hug. "I can't hold him forever," Cory said to Noah. He cocked his head. "Get outta here."

I looked once more at Brax's face. His eyes. Silently, they pleaded with me. Begged me for something, some unknown thing. Noah draped his arm over my shoulder, and I turned away.

"Gracie, wait. Please, just listen to me. Hear me out. Let me the fuck go, man! Gracie!"

I didn't look back as Noah guided me to his Mustang parked along the walkway. He opened the passenger side door and I climbed in. Just as he slammed the door shut, I heard Brax's tortured cry as he called my name, cutting through the chilled night air, and it struck me in the gut. Something about all of this felt so damn wrong. All of it. None of it. Everything. I tried not to look, tried not to torment myself by seeking Brax out, but I couldn't help it. He was there, still held captive by his best friend.

Behind Brax and Cory stood Kelsy Evans, his arm draped over some girl dressed as a seductive nurse. Even under the shade of darkness, I saw his stupid grin of victory.

I closed my eyes.

As Noah pulled away, I glanced at his face. With a busted lip and a swollen eye, he stared straight ahead and maneuvered his car away from the Sigma house.

"Thanks," I offered. "I'm ... sorry for all the drama. I'm sorry you were hurt. This—it's not who I am, Noah. It seems to follow me."

He looked at me, a fast glance, then returned his stare to the road. "It's okay. And I know this isn't you, Olivia." He reached over and patted my knee, then returned his hand to the wheel. His hair was messy from the tussle with Brax, and his tee shirt was torn at the collar. "It'll all blow over." He gave a grin, then winced at the cut on his lip. "It always does."

We talked for a while, just driving around, until finally, Noah took me back to the dorm. He walked me to the entrance. "If you ever need me, Olivia, just call." He smiled, and it was genuine and unthreatening. With his hand he straightened my crooked fairy wing. "I mean it."

"I will. Thanks, Noah."

I watched him drive off and, despite all that had happened, the humiliation, the hurt, the *shit*, my eyes darted through the darkness. Seeking a familiar headlamp from an even more familiar motorcycle. There was nothing. The lot was empty, save my old truck and few other lone vehicles. And I wasn't sure if I felt relief or disappointment.

With a heavy heart I slid my card through the key lock and entered the dorm.

25. Anguish

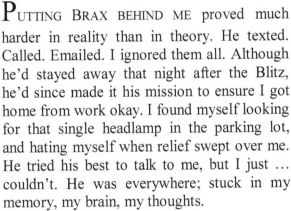

Putting Brax behind me proved much harder in reality than in theory. He texted. Called. Emailed. I ignored them all. Although he'd stayed away that night after the Blitz, he'd since made it his mission to ensure I got home from work okay. I found myself looking for that single headlamp in the parking lot, and hating myself when relief swept over me. He tried his best to talk to me, but I just ... couldn't. He was everywhere; stuck in my memory, my brain, my thoughts.

My humanities class.

Right along with Kelsy.

I sat away from them both and tried my best to concentrate on my studies. It was as if my brain had its very own clump of gray matter at its beck and call. Against my will my gaze would slip over the room and seek out Brax. Every single time it happened, he caught me. He'd have his gaze fixed on me, too, and a look of anguish and helplessness would wash over his distinctive features as his eyes silently pleaded with me. I hurriedly turned away every time. It was almost unbearable. My emotions were so raw, conflicted, at war with one another and me, jammed right smack in the middle. It drained me. Made me tired. Uninterested with school. Sad. I missed Brax. Missed the way it'd been ... before. His voice. His accent. His playful teasing. All of that clouded my recent memory of the embarrassment and pain I'd endured once I'd discovered his true intentions at that stupid fraternity Blitz. Maybe it made me feel better to have a shred of hope that some of it had been real. How could anyone be that callous? That shallow? The truth of his deception was plain and evident. Black and white. Cut and dry. So why did I still carry hope? Was it the pleading of his voice I heard in my head, over and over again? Begging me to listen, to understand he'd tried to stop it? That I didn't know the whole story?

Stupid girl.

As soon as class was over, though, I'd have my bag already clutched in my hand and I'd hurry out the door and down the stairs, never giving Brax a chance to catch me. Kelsy, blessedly, didn't even try. He had his seductive nurse girlfriend from the Blitz at his side constantly now and had apparently moved on. I was old news, no longer a conquest. In my heart I knew he thought he'd won. Let him think it. He was the very last thing I needed to worry about. I was glad his obsessive behavior was turned on anyone else other than me. Poor girl.

Over the next two weeks before Thanksgiving break I seriously struggled. Tessa was right there for me. She, Marcie and Kelly tried their best to convince me to go out with them again, but I had zero interest in going to bars. Strangely enough, Ash's fight with Brax hadn't deterred his pursuit of me, and after getting my cell number from Tessa, he'd texted and asked me out. I was flattered, but uninterested, and declined. Then I threatened to strangle Tessa for giving my number out. She promised not to do it again.

A week before break I was closing at the observatory with Steven when all hell broke loose. Noah and, regrettably, Dr. Callander, were both present and in the lobby. Steven and I were turning all the lights off in the displays in the back.

"I need to speak to Gracie Beaumont. Now."

Brax's booming voice, a little slurred, resonated off the walls, and Steven and I exchanged a worried look.

"Uh oh," he said quietly. "That sounds like trouble. Maybe you should stay back here with me?" He glanced at the doorway. "Let Professor Callander handle it."

I nodded, but moved closer to the doorway so I could hear a little better. Steven moved with me. Inside, my heart pounded.

"Son, you've been drinking," Professor Callander said in a strong voice. My stomach dropped at the accusation that was more than likely completely true. "Ms. Beaumont is not available. Leave now and I won't call campus police."

Brax's disbelieving laugh cut through the air. "She's here. She's always fucking here so go get her. She was supposed to be off an hour ago."

"I'll give you one last chance, son," Professor Callander advised. "Leave."

"I'm not your son. Hicks, you know she's fucking here. Tell her I'm waiting for her outside. Never mind douchebag, I'll tell her myself. Gracie! You might as well get out here and talk to me. I ain't leaving this time till you hear me out! I'll be waiting by your truck."

The double glass doors in the lobby slammed, and I jumped where I stood.

"Shit," Steven muttered. He looked at me. "You can't go out there. He's drunk."

I closed my eyes briefly. Godalmighty, he was drunk. And all he'd wanted to do, ever since the Blitz, was tell me his side of the story. Why hadn't I just listened?

I looked at Steven. "I don't want him to get into trouble." I sighed. "If the professor calls the campus police on him, he will get in serious hot water with his coach."

Steven's brows knitted into a frown. "So? He should've thought about that before boozing it up and coming here to harass you."

I sighed again and shook my head. "I'll just go talk to him." I put my hand on his shoulder. "Thanks for being such a good friend."

"You're welcome. But this won't end good, Olivia," he said. "Do you want me to come with you? I don't think he'll punch me out like he did Noah."

I glanced over my shoulder as I hurried out the door. "No, it's okay. Thanks."

Steven followed me, though, and the second I entered the lobby, I almost ran smack into Professor Callander. Noah was right behind him and I knew they were both headed to find me. Noah's pensive expression stopped me in my tracks.

"Professor, I am so sorry," I started. "I can explain—"

The professor was older, with graying hair and a long mustachio, but had the gentlest brown, honest, no-nonsense eyes I'd ever seen. In a firm grip, he squeezed both my shoulders. "Olivia, I know you are. And I understand this isn't your fault. But," he cleared his throat and leveled his gaze to mine. "I can't place this program or the observatory at any risk, whatsoever. And that boy, I'm afraid, is a risk." His eyes softened. "I'm sorry, Olivia. You're a fine, promising astronomer, and I abhor this decision. But I'm going to have to let you go."

My mouth, cheeks, face went numb with shock and disbelief. I couldn't say anything. Only stare. Let me go? I was getting fired?

"Um, Professor Callander," Noah said hurriedly. "I'm sure this can be worked out."

"I wish it could be," Professor Callander said to me. "But in this instance I have to think of the department."

"I," I found my voice. Small, not as determined as I'd have preferred. "I promise, Professor, this won't ever, ever happen again."

Again, the older man's eyes softened. "Yes, Ms. Beaumont. Yes, it most certainly will."

My heart sunk. "I'm … sorry." Without knowing anything better to say, I made my way to the employee lounge.

"Oh, man, Olivia," Steven said, walking alongside of me. "Oh, man. This totally sucks. It's not even your fault."

In the lounge, I grabbed my pack and turned to my friend. "It's okay, Steven. Thanks." I gave him a small smile, then thought better and wrapped my arms around his neck and hugged him. "For everything. I'll see you in class."

"Are you gonna be okay?" he asked. His cheeks flushed red.

I met his gaze. "Yeah. I'll be fine." I wasn't, by far. But what could I do? Save face, keep my pride intact, and leave. That's what I could do.

Professor Callander was gone when I entered the lobby, but Noah stood by the door, waiting on me. "I'll talk to him, Olivia. He's made a rash decision."

I stopped and shook my head. "No, he didn't. I mean, I wouldn't want me working here, with my drunk ex-boyfriend showing up making obnoxious demands." I forced a smile. "Thanks for taking up for me, Noah. I appreciate it. But I'll be fine."

Noah exhaled slowly. "Olivia. Jesus. I'll walk you out—"

I held up a hand. "Seriously. It's okay. I prefer to go alone."

"He's drunk."

"And I'm not. He isn't going to hurt me, Noah. That much I know."

Noah nodded. I could tell by the worried look in his eyes he didn't believe it. "I'll be right here if you need me."

I pushed out of the lobby doors, barely hearing Noah's words past the fury and chaos rushing in my ears. I walked fast, purposefully, toward my truck. Brax's motorcycle was nowhere in the parking lot, but there he was, crouched down by my front left tire, inspecting it. When he heard me approaching, he rose and started toward me, palms facing up.

"Gracie, listen—"

"No, Brax, you listen." I stopped just so we stood toe to toe, and I looked up at him. "Because of you, I just lost my job. You know, the one I use to live on and send money home to my family in order to help keep our struggling ranch afloat." His face paled, and my voice quivered, and I hated it. But I couldn't control it.

"Are you fucking kidding—they fired you?" He ran his hand over his head, swore under his breath. "Jesus Christ, I'm sorry. I never meant—" He turned, his eyes wide. "I'll straighten that out, Gracie, swear to God."

I shook my head. "No, you won't. You'll only get yourself into trouble because Professor Callander was a half inch from calling the campus cops on you. Just ..." I closed my eyes, sighed, opened them. "You leave me alone, and I mean it. Stop calling. Stop texting. And stop," I waved my hand. "Being here. In my life." I settled my gaze on his. "I don't want you around me, Brax. At all."

Although I caught the waft of liquor, Brax wasn't sloppy drunk; he still knew exactly what he was doing. In two steps he was right in front of me, grasped my shoulders, lowered his head, and fixed that ethereal gaze on mine. As he frowned, the scar on his cheek pulled. "God, you don't really mean that, Gracie."

I didn't. God knows I didn't. But I couldn't handle this anymore.

I couldn't handle Brax anymore. I felt like it was sink or swim, fight or flight. Him or me. And for once, this time, it was going to be me.

With a deep inhale, I steadied myself, forced my insides to be cold, hard, unfeeling. All of which were as big a lie as the next. "I wish I'd never even met you. Just ... go away, Brax."

He jerked as though I'd hit him, and I instantly regretted my choice of words. In his eyes I saw a flash of emotions; pain, desertion, rejection. But he'd hurt me. He'd betrayed me, set me up for a big public display of humiliation. At the cost of what? A frat prank? Seriously? Neither of us was good for the other. In our wake, chaos and disruption followed. I needed that like I needed a hole in the head. It was better this way. Brax with his Silverbacks and his various girlfriends and player's reputation; me, my family, and my studies. Period. At least, that's what I spent hours trying to convince myself of.

Brax stared at me for a long time; so long that I thought I was going to have to make the first move to step away. In his eyes I saw pain, his soul, and that disturbed me more than anything else. Darkness and the light pole I was parked beneath cast his scarred face into sharp planes and shadowed angles. But I could still see him, plain as day. He swallowed. The muscles at his jaws flinched. Then he dropped his hands from my shoulders.

"Sorry you feel that way, Sunshine. Because you're the best fucking thing that ever happened to me." He turned and started walking away. "See ya 'round, Gracie," he said without turning back.

I watched silently, those familiar broad shoulders, his cocky, bow-legged swagger, until the shadows swallowed him up.

Only then did I allow the tears to flow. And when they came, they rushed, like a deluge, and I slowly climbed into my truck and drove back to the dorm. Tessa was gone when I got there, probably out with the girls, and that was actually a good thing. I didn't want her seeing me a mess. Not again. All this drama was exhausting, and I was tired of it. I got ready for bed, climbed beneath the covers, and clicked out my light. Then cried some more. Finally, my body depleted, the tears subsided, and I fell into a restless sleep.

Over the next two days, I did a lot of pretending. I pretended my heart wasn't ripped in two. I pretended it didn't really, really matter that I'd lost my job. And I pretended that Brax's presence in class—especially the way he completely ignored me now—didn't bother me. Lies. I was full of them lately. Bottom line, though, was simple enough. Brax had betrayed me. Not just that, but after knowing what he'd known about me, from high school, what I'd gone through? I still couldn't believe it.

Neither could I shake his pleading words in my head. *You don't know the full story. Just let me explain ...*

If there had been a good explanation, or a good story behind his betrayal, I'd closed that door the night I told Brax I wished I'd never met him. Harsh, but it had certainly done the trick. Not one text, or one call, or even a single glance had he graced me with. It's what I'd asked for, right?

Then why did I feel so shitty? Why did everything feel so wrong now?

It was the day before Thanksgiving break, and I was sitting in humanities, staring at the words in my notebook until they all swirled into a big blur. Some students had already left to go home for the holidays, so the class wasn't as full. I was taking notes for the test we'd have after break when the pen I was using ran out of ink. Blindly, I reached into my pack to fish out a new one and noticed my cell phone vibrated as my fingertips brushed over it. No one ever called me during the day. Well, except Brax, and since two days ago, he'd stopped. Curious, I grasped my old phone and flipped it open.

Four missed calls from Mom.

Totally unlike my mother. Instantly, my insides froze, and a bad, bad feeling pitted my stomach. I rose from my seat and without thinking, hurried out of the classroom. In the hallway, I dialed home. My mom picked up on the first ring.

"Baby," she said. "I'm sorry to call you in class—"

Mom's shaky, faint voice immediately set me on edge. I knew something was bad, awful wrong. "What is it, Mom?" I couldn't hide the panic in my own voice.

From the corner of my eye, a body emerged from the classroom, and Brax moved close to me. He didn't touch me, just stood by. Waiting. I lifted my eyes to his, fixed on mine.

"It's Jilly," Mom said, and her voice cracked. "He's ... bad, honey. You need to come home. Now."

"How bad?" I asked, the panic rising. "Mom, you're scaring me. What's wrong with

Jilly?" I started pacing, my throat constricted. I could barely swallow. "Tell me."

"It's his heart, honey. He's had a massive heart attack," Mom said. She cried now. Cleared her throat. "He's in the ICU at Jasper Memorial. You need to come on home, Olivia. Okay?"

I found the wall and sagged against it. "Is he awake? I mean, or is he in a coma?" Tears stung my eyes and my voice shook as the words stumbled out of my throat. "Mom, please."

"He's awake, honey. But his heart has sustained a lot of damage. Just ... come home."

Brax moved closer to me. "Okay, Mom. Okay. I'm coming. As soon as I grab some stuff from my room. I'll be there."

"Drive straight to the hospital," Mom said quietly. "Be careful, baby."

My hands shook, and I felt my phone slipping from my fingers, but suddenly, it was gone and in Brax's hand. Still, he kept his distance. He ducked his head to look at me. "What's wrong, Gracie?"

"My, uh, grandfather." I looked around, a little dazed, unsure what exactly to do next. This couldn't be happening. Jilly? Sick? He'd never been sick a day in his life. I started walking to the exit door. He was awake, though, so that was a good thing. Right? "I ... gotta go."

"Whoa, whoa," Brax said gently, and

grasped my arm. "Hold on." He stopped me, lifted my chin, forced me to look at him. "What's wrong with Jilly?"

Tears filled my eyes, and confusion webbed my brain. "Heart attack." The words cracked as they exited my mouth, and I hated them more than I'd hated anything in my life. I started back for the class room to get my pack. "I gotta go."

"Wait here," Brax said. "I'll get your stuff." He left, and I stayed put, my mind whirling in a thousand different directions. Before I knew it, Brax slipped back out of the class with both our bags slung over his shoulder. He grasped my elbow. "Come on."

Reality struck me. Brax. "No—what are you doing? I ... don't need your help." I pulled away from him, confused, now running.

Brax stopped me, gently pulled me against him. I fought at first, then ... didn't. I allowed him to hold me, and I sobbed. I was so scared. And he felt so ... comforting. His hand cupped the back of my head, and I liked it there. After a moment he ducked again to fix a determined gaze onto mine. "You ain't drivin' nowhere, Sunshine, so forget it. I'll drive you."

I shook my head. "No."

Brax's eyes softened. "Sorry, Gracie. I know you sort of hate me right now, but this ain't happening." He shook his head. "I'm driving you home. No arguments." His hands found mine, and he lifted them between us.

"See? You're shakin' like a leaf. You're not getting behind the wheel."

Ahguments. The familiarity of his harsh Boston accent washed over me, and I knew he was right. I hadn't let my mom know how upset up I was, but I couldn't hide it from Brax. Not in person. I felt as though I was going to shake right out of my boots. I had no time to worry about trust, betrayal, or anything else. I needed to get home. And I wasn't sure I could do it alone. "Okay." I looked at him. "But I have to go now."

"Come on."

As we walked, I barely noticed Brax making calls on his cell. One I knew was to Cory, and after that my mind went in five thousand directions. Was Jilly going to be okay? Old, cranky Jilly? Nothing could get that ornery old ex-Texas Ranger down. He'd been shot five times in the line of duty. Kicked and thrown by wild horses. He was made of piss and cast iron. Wasn't he?

By the time we made it to my dorm, Tessa and Cory were both there and met us at the front door. Cory handed Brax a packed duffle bag. Tessa hurried toward me.

"Are you okay with this?" she asked. Her eyes skimmed over me as though I'd been hurt, or in a car wreck. "Liv?"

"I'm okay with it," I answered, and I knew she'd meant with Brax taking me home.

"Well, come on, I'll help you throw some things together," she said, and grabbed me by the hand and led me upstairs. She had my pack on the bed, unzipped, and helped me gather clothes. "Is your grandpa going to be okay?" she asked.

"Yeah," I answered, and forced a smile. "He's, uh, tough as nails. He'll be okay." I felt numb, like I was watching someone else go through the motions of gathering a toothbrush, sneakers, and clean panties. I just wanted to leave. Go. Now.

Finished, Tessa shouldered my pack and looked at me. "Come on, chica, let's go." She bumped my shoulder with hers as we walked.

"All right," I answered.

Downstairs, Brax took my bag and we headed across the parking lot. Tessa pulled me into a tight embrace at my truck. "Call me, okay? For anything, any time." She kissed me on the cheek. "I mean it, Liv."

"Thanks, Tessa," I said quietly. "I will."

Brax helped me across the seat, then slid behind the wheel. He slammed the door shut, rolled down the window. Cory towered over Tessa, his arm draped over her shoulders. I'd been so consumed with myself lately that I hadn't processed the fact that they'd started seeing each other. "Let me know something, bro."

"Will do." Brax started the engine and as we pulled away I barely saw Tessa waving.

We drove in silence through town, and when we hit the Interstate Brax hit the gas, and my truck surged. Exhaust pipes rumbled. And I closed my eyes and prayed.

26. Promises

Despite how fast Brax drove it was a long ride back to Jasper. Halfway there he pulled into a Petro-Stop for fuel; while he pumped gas I ran inside to use the restroom and grab some coffee. A cold front had moved in, the weather dropping into the thirties. My breath puffed white ahead of me as I made my way to the passenger side of my truck. I handed him one of the steaming cups as he climbed behind the wheel.

"Thanks," he said, and slammed his door shut. He reached over, his cold fingers caressing my knuckles. His eyes searched mine. "You okay?"

I felt raw, exposed, and frankly, I didn't care anymore. I didn't even look away from him. "I'm scared." My throat tightened. I forced myself to swallow past the enormous lump there.

The muscles in Brax's jaw flinched. "I know you are. Sit tight. I'll get you home."

Brax didn't force conversation; he didn't

force anything. In silence we sipped our coffee, and I stared out the window and it struck me how bleak the scenery was. Leafless trees, brown grass. Occasionally I'd slip a glance at Brax. His features were tense, eyes straight ahead on the road, the gas pedal to the floor. He'd sense me looking at him, and his gaze would turn to mine, hold for a few seconds, and wordlessly he'd return to the road ahead. At some point, he'd reached across the seat and grasped my hand, lacing our fingers together, and I let him. It calmed me a little, and it felt right. We drove that way for a long time.

Finally, we hit the town square of Jasper, only a handful of blocks away from the hospital. Butterflies slammed into my gut as I directed Brax, and by the time we'd parked and were walking through the lobby it was just after noon. Brax had shortened the drive by thirty minutes.

I'd been to the ICU at Jasper Memorial before when Kyle had needed stitches in his head after getting bucked into the fence. He hadn't needed a unit bed but apparently it had been the only one available. With Brax's hand wrapped tightly around mine, I led him down a series of hallways to the waiting room. Mom and Seth leapt to their feet as soon as they saw us.

"Olivia," Mom said, and gathered me in her arms. Her body felt warm through my brown down puff jacket, and Seth leaned over and kissed my forehead. "Hey, baby."

"How is he?" I asked. My eyes searched my mom and brothers, and the worry I saw in both made my stomach feel sick.

Mom's tired eyes sought mine. "He's tired, sweetie. He's awake, in his right mind, and made sure we knew his wishes." A tear fell down her cheek. "His exact words were, *Don't let 'em hook me up to all that techno medical horseshit*." She smiled, but it was the saddest expression I'd ever seen on my mom's face. "Crazy old fool."

"They can't do anything for him?" I asked.

Mom shook her head. "Heart's too far gone. Blockages and damage from here to hell and back."

My mind raced, and my stomach ached. "Did … they say how long?" The words felt heavy, wrong on my tongue.

She smiled wanly. "Only the Lord knows that, honey." She inclined her head. "He's been asking for you." I noticed her gaze fall behind me, and I turned.

"Oh, Mom, Seth, this is Brax Jenkins. He … drove me."

Seth's hand shot out and he shook Brax's. "Thanks, man. We appreciate it."

"Glad to do it," Brax answered Seth. He looked at Mom. "Ma'am."

Mom gave him a smile. "Nice to finally meet you, Brax." She pressed her hand against his shoulder. "There's a snack machine down the hall."

Brax nodded, and our gazes held for a few seconds before Mom and Seth led me out of the waiting room and down the hall to the locked door leading to the patient rooms. Seth pressed the intercom button, told his name, and the door opened.

"Honey, Jilly looks a little worn around the edges," Mom said quietly as we walked by several curtained rooms. "Don't be scared, okay?"

I was already scared, sick, and hated that we were all here. Seth stopped at room 113, and pulled the curtain back. As my eyes adjusted to the dimly lit room, my other two brothers rose from their seats. My gaze fastened on Jilly, lying in the bed. Oxygen tubing in his nostrils. Covers pulled up and folded neatly across his chest, arms straight by his sides. An IV hung beside his bed on a pole and ran into his hand. He looked pale, eyes closed, barely breathing.

"Lil' Bit," Kyle said quietly, and he and Jace both enveloped me.

I moved out of their arms, though, and made my way to Jilly's side, and I slipped my hand into his cool one. Running my thumb over the big veins and callouses, I still couldn't believe we were here, and he was sick.

"'Bout time you got your little fancy pants college ass here," Jilly whispered, and my eyes jerked to his. They were open now, a little glassy, and ... tired. His weak voice hardly sounded like it belonged to my loud, boisterous grandfather. "You here to bust me out, Lil' Bit? The food here tastes like horseshit."

Despite the tears welling up in my eyes, I couldn't help but smile. "Yeah, I bet it does." I gently tugged his hand. "Come on, Jilly. I got the truck running by the emergency room exit."

Jilly gave a light laugh, but it was weak, barely there. "Just give me a minute. I gotta find my drawers first. Fool nurses took all my goddamned clothes." He blinked, and I hardly felt the pressure as he squeezed my hand. "Damned ticker ain't worth a shit either, darlin'. Guess I ate too many pork rinds."

A sob caught in my throat. "Jilly," and I leaned over him, rested my head against his chest, and slipped my arms around him. "Stop it."

Behind me, I heard Mom's sniffles. Tears fell from my lids onto Jilly's hospital gown, and somehow my weakened grandfather found the strength to lift his arms and embrace me. "Quit all that cryin' now, girl. You're getting my damn dress all soggy."

I hugged him tighter. "No."

Jilly gave another weak laugh and let his arms fall to his sides. "Come up here, then. I got somethin' to tell you. And I ain't got the strength to talk much anymore." He sighed, and I lifted my head from his chest. "I'm damned tired as hell."

For the first time in my entire life, my grandfather looked frail. Like he couldn't wrangle a horse to the ground. Or drink a man half his age under the table. Or beat anyone's ass. He looked old. Before my eyes, he was fading, like a gas light running empty. How could this be happening? It wasn't real. It couldn't be. I leaned close, my ear to his mouth.

"I ain't gonna be around to make sure the man you choose is good enough," he whispered. "You don't accept anything less than the one who puts you first, Olivia. Above anything else."

Through tears I pulled back and looked at Jilly, and his eyes were clear and tired at once. His gray brows furrowed. "You hear me, girl? Nothin' less than first."

"Yes, sir," I choked out. "Brax is here. He drove me from Winston."

Jilly's eyes narrowed. "Good. Ya'll get out. Send him in. Alone."

Surprise made me pause, blink. But I knew better than to question. "Yes, sir."

I exchanged glances with my family, then we all headed out to the waiting room. Brax was sitting in a chair, legs sprawled, elbows resting on his knees, fingers laced. When we walked in, he looked up, and his gaze found mine. He stood.

"Jilly wants to see you, son," my mom told Brax. "Alone."

Brax stiffened, squared his shoulders, and nodded. "Yes, ma'am."

"Just through there, third room on the left," Mom said.

Brax drew in a long breath, then disappeared out of the waiting room. I sat between Mom and Kyle, and none of us spoke a word. Mom held my hand. Kyle had his arm around me. What in the world could Jilly be saying to Brax? I hoped Brax looked him in the eye. Jilly despised any man who couldn't look him in the eye.

"So are you two okay now?" Mom asked. "He seems like a decent boy. Dropped everything to bring you here."

"I don't know what we are, Mom," I answered. "But yes, he is a decent boy." I looked at her. "I don't want to be here." Kyle's arm tightened around me. "None of this is right."

"I know, baby," Mom said softly, and rested her hand on my knee. "I know."

It was a few minutes later when Brax came walking back into the waiting room. His eyes again found mine, his expression unreadable. He took a seat across from me and kept silent. But every time I looked at him, he was looking at me, too. I thought he probably didn't know how to take all of this in; my family, the hospital. Facing Jilly alone. I was pretty sure he'd never experienced anything like it before.

Throughout the night we took turns sitting with Jilly. Each time I entered his room, he looked weaker, paler, and as I sat beside his bed on my third visit, holding his hand, he squeezed. Barely. It was the last time.

Jilly died at four forty three a.m. I knew this because he had a big clock on the wall that clicked so loud, I could hear each second as distinctive and clear as if someone stood thumping a watermelon. Jilly hadn't opened his eyes for hours, and I stared at the little hollow dip in his throat where his pulse had slowed. His chest had stopped rising and falling. My mom sat on the other side of the bed and she'd noticed it, too. We all had.

I laid my head against my grandpa's chest, hugged him and cried.

"Dammit, Jilly," my brother Jace said from the foot of the bed. I didn't dare look at him. Or any of my brothers. We all knew how the other felt, and our grief hung in the air like a thick fog. I wanted it to go away. I wanted Jilly back. It was too fast, too soon. I wasn't ready for this.

The staff allowed us time to mourn and say our goodbyes, and then it was time to leave. We all dragged out into the waiting area, and the moment we stepped into the room, Brax jumped to his feet. His gaze drifted from my mom, to my brothers, to me, and without words, he knew. I could see it in his eyes, and how those strange blue orbs softened. I walked to him, and without even thinking, allowed his embrace.

"I'm sorry, Gracie," he said against my temple. "Damned sorry."

My tears fell, and I shook, and Brax's arms tightened around me. "I am, too," I said against his chest. He held me that way for a while.

We followed my family home to the ranch, and Brax held my hand in silence the whole way there. The sun was just starting to rise, edging the tree line as we pulled onto our drive. When Brax parked, he left the engine running and stepped out. My mom and brothers walked over to meet us.

"Gracie, I'll get a room in town," Brax told me. It was cold out, and his breath puffed white in front of him.

"Nonsense," Mom said. "You'll stay here and I won't hear any more about it."

Brax looked at me, and I gave him a nod. I was positive he wasn't sure what to do, but there'd be no arguing with my mom. "Thanks, ma'am."

"Sadie." My mom gave him a wan smile.

Brax smiled back. "Sadie."

Mom, my brothers by her side, left us at the truck and wandered into the house. Brax grasped my hand. "Are you okay with this? Swear to God, I'll go if you're not. It wasn't my intention to make you uneasy." His nose was turning red from the cold.

"I know that. I'm fine with it," I answered. My voice sounded hollow. Shallow. Soft. "Thanks. For being here."

His wraithlike eyes regarded me. "Thanks for letting me."

We stared in silence for a moment, then Brax reached behind me and grabbed our bags from the bed of the truck. "Ready?"

Suddenly, realization crashed over me, leaving me short of breath, panicky, and I leaned against the truck. "Not really," I said quietly. A subtle shaking began in my body, and it rapidly grew. Tears welled up, spilled out and fell in frozen little trails down my cheek. Inside the house, everywhere, was my grandfather. How could he be gone? *Oh, Jilly ...*

Brax dropped the bags and pulled me against him. I went easily—a little too easy, maybe—and his warmth, the strength in his arms embraced and comforted me. I cried into Brax's shoulder, and he stroked my hair and held me close as grief flooded me.

The next two days blurred by. Two older men, a little younger than Jilly, had shown up at the ranch the day after Jilly's death. Retired Rangers, they'd served with my grandfather and assured Mom his funeral expenses were taken care of. I could literally see the relief wash over her. Meanwhile, chores still needed to be done and horses needed to be cared for, and we all pitched in to get it done. Brax was right there, mucking out stalls and feeding animals, and his rough Boston mannerisms seemed to take a step back as he conformed to life at a ranch. The second he'd finish one chore, he'd ask for another. Yet as busy as we all kept, the pain stayed. Laid heavy on my shoulders—on all of us. Jilly's presence was everywhere ... and nowhere. It was so weird, him being gone. Sometimes I'd look up a little too fast and I'd think he was there, leaning against the horse pen, his booted foot propped on the bottom rail, his hat pushed back and a stream of dirty swear words flooding from his mouth.

Neighbors brought more food than fifty people could eat in a month. Every few hours, another car or truck would slowly make their way up the drive, dropping off casseroles and cakes and homemade bread.

"Is there a food committee or something?" Brax asked.

I looked at him. "The food? No," I answered, and shrugged. "It's what we do. It's death. Birth. Marriage. Divorce." I smiled. "It's ... Texas."

I couldn't sleep, so I sat in the family room by the fireplace, watching *Walker, Texas Ranger* because Jilly and I had watched every single episode together. Brax watched it with me until I fell asleep from exhaustion. Vaguely, I remembered being carried to my bedroom and tucked in. I woke up thinking it was all a bad dream, and Jilly was in the kitchen scrambling eggs. It wasn't, and he wasn't, and sooner or later I'd have to get a damn grip on it.

The services were unlike any I'd ever attended. Jilly's was a Ranger's funeral, and Mom was presented a Lone Star flag and a silver Ranger's star. No less than thirty active and retired Texas Rangers were present, each with a Winchester rifle they shot off in his honor. Jilly would've hollered for sure. I couldn't seem to stop the flow of tears falling, but Brax stood beside me, holding my hand, squeezing it if I wavered even the slightest. Kyle had lent him clothes for the funeral, and he wore black slacks, dress shoes, and a blue shirt that made his eyes nearly glow. It wasn't a long service, but I thought it would never end. I stared at Jilly's casket at the graveside service, at the Lone Star flag draped over it, and I still couldn't believe it. I just wanted the day to be over. Finally, it was.

Thanksgiving Day was a dismal event. But because Jilly wouldn't have wanted a house full of sour pusses crowding his table, we celebrated just like we normally would have. Only we didn't dare roast a turkey, or make the first morsel of food. Friends and neighbors took care of that, too, and soon we had to start making room in the freezer for things. Jace blessed our food and dedicated the day to Jilly's memory. It was a Thanksgiving I'd never forget. It was one I wished I could. Yet beside me, Brax sat. Never out of sight. Always comforting.

"Let's go for a walk," I said, later that evening. "I need to stretch my legs."

"Lead the way," he answered. We both rose from the sofa.

"You two bundle up good," Mom said, and she smiled at Brax. "You might be used to Boston weather, sweetie, but this is about as cold as I've seen it get in Texas."

Brax flashed my mom his famous smile.

"Yes, ma'am."

Mom shook her head, a slight grin tipping her mouth, and turned back to the stove to make tea.

In the foyer, we both pulled on knit hats, scarves, and jackets, and headed outside into the chilled night air. The yard lamp cast an amber hue over the porch, and we started down the steps. Our breath frosted and billowed out before us on each exhale as we walked the path to the barn. My hands dug deep into my coat pockets, seeking warmth. Brax walked close, his arm around my shoulder. I wanted to just melt into him. Forget everything that had happened before now. Because compared to losing Jilly, it was … I don't know. It seemed stupid. Immature. Not worth the worry. Right? I mean, Brax was here, with me now. He didn't have to be. He didn't have to even offer. But he had. Question was, could I ever trust him again? Would it always be a thorn in my gut, digging away at me?

"Gracie," he started. He was quiet then, and I looked up. His eyes were on mine, and he struggled with his words. "I want to tell you the whole story. Everything. But," he glanced up, toward the sky. "I don't want you to think that's the reason I came here." He stopped us both, grasped my shoulders, and looked down at me. "It's not. At all."

Sincerity shined in the reflection of light in his eyes. "I believe you." To my surprise, I did, too.

Relief passed over his gaze, and he nodded and we started up the path. I watched the earth pass beneath my boots as we walked. "But only if you want to tell it."

"I do." He drew in a long breath, exhaled. "There are things you need to know."

I guided us off the path and turned toward the barn's side entrance. "Let's go sit in the loft," I offered, and a fond memory passed through me. "Jilly always knew to look here if he couldn't find me. It's my thinking spot."

I let us in the side entrance, and the familiar scent of hay and horse and sweet feed swept over me. A couple of horses whinnied at our presence, and I led us to the ladder at the far end. I climbed up first, Brax right behind me. In the loft, I crossed the wooden floor to the swing door, unbolted it, and pushed it open. When I sat and dangled my legs out over the ledge, Brax did the same. We were still and silent for a few moments, staring out across Beaumont land in the darkness. Stars littered the clear November sky.

He turned where he sat, looked me square in the eye. "I chose you for the dare, Gracie. The second I saw you walking across the lawn, I knew it had to be you."

27. Conflicted

MY HEART PLUMMETED AT Brax's confession. I didn't know what to say. Didn't know where to look. I wanted honesty? Well, he was giving it to me, double-barrels. I stared at my hands, laced my fingers. I said nothing, just waited for him to continue.

"All those rumors about me, Gracie? They were true." He looked out over the field, and I slid a glance at his profile. Strong. Handsome. Perfect. "Getting women to fall for me? It was like a drug. The chase, an adrenaline rush." He looked at me then, and shadows obscured half of his face. "When I first laid eyes on you? In that hat, and those boots? Carrying that box across the grass?" He shook his head, but kept his gaze on mine. "I thought it was just another game. Another chase." The muscles flexed in his jaws. "You suckerpunched me, Gracie. Never been hit so hard in my whole life." He brushed his knuckles over my cheek. "You're just so damn different."

Butterflies churned in my stomach, and I found I couldn't look away. Still, I kept silent. Brax dropped his hand. "The night we were together, someone got me on their iPhone leaving your dorm. At first, I denied everything. They wouldn't go for it. Then I tried to convince the guys to drop the dare, or drop you from it." He let out a short laugh, sarcastic, angry. "When words didn't work, I used my fists. That didn't work, either. Egged them on, actually." He looked at me. "They wouldn't leave it alone. You fascinated them almost as much as you did me. And that ring?" He brushed his fingers over where that slight silver ring used to rest. "It just made the dare that much more exciting. And the more of a big deal I made of it, the worse they got." His gaze moved to the sky. "Evans got word to the Kappas that you weren't a virgin after all. I got to thinking that it'd all die down after the Blitz. Figured they'd grow the fuck up and move on. Evans didn't help matters. He prodded. Made it flame." The crystal stare moved back to me. "Then you showed up at the Blitz." He again shook his head, and his breath frosted out in a puff of white. "Cory found out you were there and I'd tried to get to you before they announced everything. Christ, I'd never felt so shitty in my entire life. And I lost it." A look of raw emotion flashed over his eyes. "I realized long before that night, at what you really, truly meant—" He sighed. "Mean to me, Gracie. When you drove away with Hicks?" He blew out another gusty sigh. "Ate me alive. And I'm sorry for not only starting the whole fucking dare thing," he laced his fingers through mine, "but for not stopping it. The last thing in this world I'd ever want to do is hurt you."

Thoughts ran cross-road style in my head as I tried to process everything Brax told me. I knew he meant them—I could see the sincerity in his eyes. He was being honest. Yet something held me back. I couldn't put a finger on it, and it infuriated me.

"The morning I left you? Christ, you were lying there, so fucking peaceful, with your hair all around you. You made it hard for me to breathe, Gracie. It was the hardest fucking thing I'd ever done in my life, leaving you there alone." He looked away, struggling for words, then stared back at me. "I had no idea when I left that I wasn't coming back to you."

My insides froze. "What do you mean?"

Brax let out a harsh breath. "Cory called me. Said Evans was drunk as all holy fuck yelling outside the Kappa house." His eyes hardened. "About you and some video he had." The muscles tightened in Brax's jaw. "I slipped out of your room and hauled ass over there, ready to put a stop to the whole fucking thing. Sure enough, Evans was there, letting everything he knew about you out." A sadistic curve settled over his mouth. "I beat the fuck out of him that morning, Gracie. If Cory hadn't pulled me off, I might have killed him."

My heart seized, and I shivered. I'd known there were cellular videos of me acting stupid at that party with Kelsy. "What happened?"

Brax stared straight ahead for a few seconds before turning a full gaze on me. "Evans' father happened."

Icy fingers of dread clutched at me. "What?"

"One of Evans' dick buddies had called his father before I'd even shown up. Said his boy was in trouble. He, uh," he scrubbed his jaw. "He brought a few thugs of his own. Pulled me off Kelsy and beat me pretty good." Brax looked at me. "He told me it'd be in your best interest if I left you alone. Stayed away from Kelsy. That with the pictures and video he had of you, he could make sure your life at Winston would be pure hell." He looked out of the loft. "He said he even knew a few people on the scholarship board. Said if I didn't leave his boy alone he could make you look real bad. And after what he'd already done to you and your family, I fucking believed him."

Words escaped me, and it grew harder and harder to breathe. "Oh my ... God."

Brax traced my jaw with his thumb, and his eyes, filled with worry and pain, sought mine. "I knew I couldn't chance it. Risk you getting hurt, in any way. So I left." He sighed. "Then, the more I dwelled on it, the more the selfish part of me kicked in. I thought I could handle whatever trash shit Evans threw at us together. I couldn't stay away from you. I missed you so fucking bad, it hurt. And I wanted to explain what had happened." He shook his head. "Maybe even go to the cops or something. I just couldn't let you keep on thinking I was a soulless prick who took advantage of you."

I let a long, pent up breath slowly release from my lungs. "I believe you," I finally answered. Brax's eyes remained guarded, though, never leaving mine. I exhaled, fought back tears as my own realization flashed before me. "But, Brax," and at that moment, fear crossed his gaze, and I hated it. "I gave you my complete trust. After everything I'd gone through with Kelsy my senior year, I overcame it all by believing in you. What we shared that night? It meant way more to me than you can imagine." I stared at him. "And I gave it to you. Willingly. I didn't think that would ever happen. When you broke it off?" The too-recent memory crowded me. "God, it hurt. Hurt so bad, Brax."

"It was not casual to me, either, Gracie, please," Brax insisted. "Far from it. It was so goddamn real, it scared the hell out of me. I'd never experienced anything like it. Like you." He lifted our joined hands to his lips, brushed a cold kiss over my knuckles, and my heart plummeted once more. "I'm sorry for letting you think, even for a second, that what we had wasn't real. I'm sorry for letting Evans and his father convince me into breaking it off with you, instead of telling you what had happened. It was stupid. A fucking mistake. And I'm asking for another chance."

My brain and my heart tangled. I wanted to trust him fully; believe in him. Part of me did, one hundred percent. But that other part had doubts, and not all were caused by Brax's betrayal. It was residual, a dirty sheen of self-doubt left over from my days with Kelsy. I knew then if Brax and I were meant to be, we would be. But I didn't want to go into that relationship half-cocked. I wanted no doubts. No second guessing.

Jilly's dying words rang in my ears. *Make sure you come first, above all else.*

I forced bravery into my stare, and it was a hard thing to accomplish. It'd be so easy to just say okay. To deal with my own doubts. But I couldn't. I'd promised Jilly. "I just can't give it to you right now, Brax. I just … need time. To sort things through."

The pain in his eyes rocked me, and he nodded, looked away. "All right." His voice was hoarse. "That's fair. I can give you time." He squeezed my hand, but didn't look at me.

He didn't understand, though. I knew he didn't. I barely understood myself. And I wasn't going to fill his head with a load of crap, with explanations and empty reasons why I couldn't just give him another chance. "Thank you for being here for me during all this. It meant a lot to me. To my family."

Again he nodded, and this time he looked at me. The hurt in his eyes almost unraveled me. "You have a great family, Gracie. I'm glad I got to meet them. Jilly especially."

The thought crossed my mind about Jilly's private meeting with Brax. "What did he say to you?"

A somber smile touched Brax's mouth, and he let me hand go. "Sorry, Sunshine. That one stays with me. For now."

We stayed at the ranch for two more days and helped Mom, Seth, Kyle and Jace with, well, everything. Brax was up at the crack of dawn each day, chopping wood, helping feed the horses, and he even helped Mom give a few vaccinations. He was still charming, miraculously watched his Boston potty mouth, but a change had come over him, ever since that night of confessions in the loft. Ever since I'd denied him a second chance. He kept his distance, for the most part. There beside me, yet not really. I chose not to share with my family what had transpired between Brax and Mr. Evans. My mom and brothers had suffered enough my senior year. I wouldn't drag all that hell back up and them through it.

When we left the ranch, Brax hugged my mother goodbye, shook my brothers' hands. No one suspected that I'd just hurt him. At least, I didn't think they did. I hadn't wanted to hurt him. My heart had begged me to change my mind. But my brain had decided not to ever be stupid again. And I'd listened.

The ride home wasn't completely uncomfortable. There was no hand holding, no random brush of Brax's knuckles against my skin, and no in-depth stares from eyes that no doubt would always haunt me. When we reached my dorm, he parked my truck, and walked me to the door. There he surprised me, and even with girls going in and out of the dorm, he kissed me on the cheek, and then said goodbye.

As I watched him jog across the parking lot and out of sight, my heart sank. I'd made this choice, this smart, highly intelligent decision of self-preservation. I had no idea what the future held as far as Brax and I were concerned; I only had control over myself. And it was there, standing in the lobby of Oliver Hall, that I decided not to waste a single second trying to decipher my own decisions, and whether they'd been the right ones. I had a semester to finish. Not just finish, but excel at. After all that had happened—Mr. Evans' threat to destroy my life at Winston, my broken heart, and Jilly's unexpected death—I had a lot of ground to cover.

The first week of December flew by. True to his word, Brax had somehow managed to convince Professor Callander to give me my job back at the observatory. Noah had been waiting for me in astronomy and gave me the good news. And when I'd shown up at work that afternoon, and thanked the professor, he just looked at me with those gentle brown eyes, and nodded. "I'm sure you won't disappoint me, Olivia," he said. He hadn't mentioned Brax at all.

After work, my heart and brain divided once more, and as Steven and I parted ways at the front entrance, my eyes scanned the parking lot for Brax's bike. I continued to check my rear view mirror for it the whole way back to Oliver Hall, but I never saw it. Not once. And when I climbed into bed, amidst Tessa's non-stop chatter about her and Cory's weekend plans, I checked my phone. My text messages. Nothing from Brax. And I was disappointed. I willed myself to stop being so obsessive, and to stop thinking so much about Brax. To stay on track and get my grades back up. Easier said than done.

Over the next two and a half weeks I stayed crazy busy. When I wasn't in class, I was at the library. When I wasn't at either of those places I worked overtime at the observatory. Brax's presence in humanities made life nearly impossible, but I did it. He was nice. Cordial. And would most of the time scoot out of class ahead of me. I'd step out of the building in time to see him jogging to his next class, in that bow-legged swagger that he had. And while Kelsy didn't directly bother me anymore, I'd notice a sly grin on his face. One that reeked of victory, of power over me and my family. It made me want to charge him and slap it right off. I didn't, though. I'd decided he wasn't worth it.

Brax didn't call. He didn't text. But every once in a while, I looked at him in class. And he'd be looking right back at me. And I'd see in his eerie eyes a somberness that shook me.

It drove me completely crazy. I almost called him. More than once. But each time I'd pull up his name on my out-of-date flip phone, my finger would hover over the call button, and I'd snap it shut. He was driving me internally kookoo. And it'd been my decision for it to be that way. I'd denied him. My fault. Told him I'd needed more time to sort things out. Well, I'd had time, and Brax had made sure I'd had it, too. I wasn't sure now that it'd been the right decision. But what was I to do about it now?

The last day of class before Winston let out for the Christmas holidays, Brax was absent. I'd made it to class early, hoping to speak to him. I wondered what he planned on doing for the holidays, and thought about inviting him home. My eyes stayed glued to the doorway, waiting, and when he didn't show, my heart sank. I could've called him, or texted him. But I didn't. After saying goodbye to Tessa at the dorm, I loaded my scope and pack into the truck and started for home. Disappointment followed me. Made me a little gloomy, even. Not only was I facing my first Christmas without Jilly, but I missed Brax. Truly missed him. I'd turned him away, and he'd gone without another look-back. I'd blown my chance, I supposed.

The day was gray, cold, but the miles flew by and before long, I pulled into the ranch's winding drive. No sooner did I kill the truck's engine did my cell phone ring. I grabbed it, hoping it was Brax. It was Tessa instead.

"Oh. My. God," she said immediately. "Chica, are you home yet?"

"Yeah," I answered. "Just got here."

"Good. Go straight inside and check your email. I've sent you a link." She paused. "It's Brax. And it's freaking bad."

Fear froze my insides. "Okay. Let me get inside."

"Call me right back. You have to see this now."

I hurried inside, and Mom greeted me at the door. "Hey, baby," she said, and I hurried right by her. "Where's the fire?"

"Tessa just called. Something's happened to Brax." I set my bag down, fished my laptop out of my pack, and took it over to the sofa.

"And it's on your computer?" Mom asked.

"Apparently," I answered. She sat beside me and I pulled up my email. A YouTube link. I clicked it, and my stomach dropped as I waited. I called Tessa.

"Are you on it yet?" she asked.

"Yes," I said. Then my eyes widened as the video began. A bar. Brax, in a Winston baseball jersey.

"Is that Brax beating the horse snot out of …?" Mom stared closer at the screen. "Kelsy Evans?"

"It is." He was, too. Like rabid-dog fighting and beating the holy hell out of Kelsy. I stared hard, studied it. Replayed the video. "That's not recent."

"Nope, it's not," Tessa agreed. "Apparently it happened after your truck was vandalized with shoe polish. Kelsy denied it, but Brax said he knew Kelsy did it. Then a few days ago he got wind there was this video of him beating the shit puss out of Kelsy in a bar." Tessa drew in a breath, pushed it out. "Cory said some girl took the video. Kelsy found out about it, convinced the girl to send it to him, and as soon as she did, he bragged to Brax, saying he'd make sure he never played baseball for Winston again. Brax ignored him until Kelsy threatened to not only upload that one, but also a video of you from some party."

"Oh, God," I said, stunned.

"Cory said Brax went to his coach and told him everything. He dropped out of the Kappas and moved out of the frat house. Coach confided in a Winston attorney about yours and Brax's video and has threatened Kelsy's father with a slander case. Brax is a seriously balsy gringo, my friend. I mean, talk about self-sacrifice. He just laid his whole baseball scholarship on the line."

I felt sick to my stomach. Had Brax done all that? For me? Had he lost his scholarship? "Hey, Tessa, thanks for letting me know. I ... gotta go."

"Okay, you know where to reach me if you need me."

We hung up and I sat back, and looked at my mom. "What a mess."

With gentle fingers she pushed a long hank of hair from my eyes. "Yes, darlin', it is. So," she patted my knee. "What are you going to do about it?"

I leaned my head back against the sofa cushion and closed my eyes. "I have no idea."

"Did you ever find out what it was Jilly said to him at the hospital?" Mom asked.

I gave a wan smile. "Brax wouldn't tell me." I looked at her. "You wanna know something, Mom?"

"I sure do," she answered.

I told her about mine and Brax's discussion in the loft, and how he'd asked me for a second chance and I'd denied him. I told her my reasons, and how they didn't seem to hold much weight any more. "What should I do?" I asked.

"Well then," she said. "If it were me, I'd have to give Brax that second chance, darlin'. Before you miss your own."

Mom was right. And over the next two days my mind pondered it. All of it. It was a big pill to swallow. Jilly's larger-than-life presence was gone, yet not. I could still hear his laugh. His deep, graveled voice as he swore at random things that irritated him. And when I glanced at his favorite chair, I envisioned him in it. All of that grief warred with my thoughts of Brax. I wanted to set things right with him. I did. Yet I didn't call. Didn't text. I don't know what stopped me, but something did. Something inside of me held on. For what? It was so … stupid. Every time I thought about calling Brax—which was, like, every hour—I stopped myself. Embarrassment? Shyness? Did I want him to make the first move? Seriously? He'd just risked his baseball career and scholarship in my honor. Was courageous enough to challenge Mr. Evans. And I was embarrassed? That wasn't just stupid. Jilly would call that being a grade-A dumbass.

While I ran every scenario over in my head, I worked like a demon with my brothers at the ranch. Jilly had been older but he'd more than carried the weight of a man three times younger. We had a lot to catch up on, and I didn't slow down for a second. It helped, really. To deal with Jilly's death. And with my ever-growing ridiculous dilemma over what to do with Brax. Dammit. I knew what to do. I was just scared. Scared to take that dive. I was starting to get on my own nerves, with all that scariness, waffling behavior. Beaumonts fight for what's theirs. For what's right. And for what they want. Enough was enough.

That night I laid in bed, cell phone in my hand. I'd had enough. I was tired of fighting it. Tired of wondering what to do. I knew what I had to do. I flipped open my phone and with my stomach in knots, called Brax.

It rang, and I smiled at his ringback tone. *Take Me Out to the Ballgame*. It played out, and Brax's voicemail took over as quickly as my disappointment at him not answering the phone. My self-righteousness had finally bitten me in the ass. Double-jawed, as Jilly would say.

I left a message. "Hey, Brax, I, uh, missed you in class." I blew out a breath. "No, I mean, yeah, I did, but what I mean is." I sighed. "I'm an idiot. I miss you. Please call me back?"

He didn't, and I fell asleep with my phone in my hand.

The sound of an ax connecting with wood pulled me out of a deep sleep the next morning as I blinked open my eyes. A shadowy, hazy light fell over my room, and I knew it was super early. The realization that Brax had never returned my call socked me in the gut. Was he finished with me? Had I pushed him away? I patted my covers and found my phone. No missed calls. No texts. I continued to hear the chop-chop of the ax outside, and it started grating my nerves.

What had gotten into Seth? I'd told him I'd chop wood with him at first light. I grumbled to myself as I climbed out of bed, jerked my feet into my boots and over the cuffs of my Winston sweat pants. Brushed my teeth, stuffed a knitted hat over my head and pulled on my down coat. I pushed out into the frigid December morning where the sun hadn't even cracked the horizon yet, yanking the zipper of my coat up to my throat.

"Jesus, Seth Beaumont," I grumbled as I hurried down the steps. "Why didn't you wake me up—"

At the bottom of the porch steps, my words fell away. My heart raced, my eyes widened and I stood there, gap-mouthed, gaze fixed on the wood pile. Not Seth Beaumont.

Brax swung the ax, embedding it into the chopping block. He leaned on the handle, his

Boston Red Sox cap on backwards; his thick leather Winston Silverbacks baseball jacket zipped to the neck. In the haze of early morning, his pale skin stood stark against dark brows and dark scruffy jaw. Even from where I stood, his eyes held a radiance that made them almost glow. Gloves covered his inked knuckles. Winter clothes covered the rest of him. Yet I could do nothing but stare in silence. He literally stole my breath.

The smile on his face started slowly, tipping the corners of that beautiful mouth upward, and he took a step in my direction. My heart nearly shut down at the predatory expression.

"Your mom called. Asked if I wanted to come for Christmas." He kept walking, that sexy, baseball player's swagger, his eyes fixed on mine, and I stayed frozen to the porch step. Finally, he stopped, barely a foot away. His frosty breath billowed out in front of him on each exhale. I don't know why I thought that sexy, too, but I did. "Mind if I stay?"

28. Sacrifices

BRAX WAS SO CLOSE I could smell the sharp soapy scent on his skin. I forced myself to breathe. Then, to speak. My mom called him? How did she get his number, anyway? "Why didn't you call me back?"

His gaze moved over me, from my boots to my hat. Then fastened on my eyes and his smile only widened. "I almost did. I played that message over a dozen times, just to hear you say you missed me." He moved closer, took my hands. "I'd already talked to your mom, but I don't know. I guess I was scared you'd change your mind if you knew I was coming. Thought it would be easier, face-to-face. So?"

I cocked my head, wondering what he meant.

He tucked my hands into his coat pockets. Pulled me close, and gave me the most arrogant, beautiful smile. One dark brow lifted. "Do you want me to stay?"

I couldn't tear my gaze from him. "I saw the video. Tessa called and told me what you did." I closed my eyes for a brief second, then looked at him. "Please tell me you haven't lost your scholarship, Brax."

"I haven't, Sunshine. It's all squared," he promised. "I came clean with the coach. All I have to do is keep my 4.0, stay out of the bars." *Bahs*. "But it would've been worth it." A smile touched his mouth. "Well worth it, though, to have that prick Evans' balls on a pike. He won't bother you again."

"You have a 4.0?" I asked.

Brax covered his heart with one hand. "You wound me, sweetheart. Of course I do."

"So that's why you missed the last day of class? Squaring things up with your coach? And you're not in any trouble?"

Brax's eyes lit up in a silent laugh. "Yes to all of that, Sunshine."

Hope seized my heart; I couldn't help but smile back. This could really work. Brax. Me. It felt real now. "I suddenly feel inclined to use my safe word."

Brax looked away, then back. "What is that thing, anyway?"

"Nutcracker."

"Is that so?" He removed first his left glove, then the right. He dropped them on the porch step.

"Yeah, it is." My breath caught, just before he lowered his head, held mine still with both hands, and swept my lips with his. Fire sparked between us, and my hands left his pockets and slipped around his neck, tangled in his hair. With a groan, Brax deepened the kiss, his tongue grazing mine and setting my insides on fire. We kissed that way, in the twenty eight degree air on that December morning, for a long, long time. Until someone cleared their throat.

"You call this chopping wood?"

I took my time ending the kiss, saw the heat in Brax's eyes as he stared down at me, then slowly we turned and faced my baby brother.

"Get a room, why don't ya?" he said with a grin. "Mom said coffee's on." He stepped back inside, the door cracking shut.

"Gracie," Brax said. He gently grasped my head, forcing me to hold his stare.

"Yes?"

"I'm sorry. For everything." He inhaled, exhaled. "Except for one thing."

I tilted my head. "And what's that?"

"Knockin' into you." Brax's smile transformed his harsh features into something heart-stopping, beautiful, and I nearly lost my breath. "That was Fate, Sunshine. A day I'll thank God for, every single day of my life."

I thought my heart would burst, and I brushed his scruffy jaw with my knuckle. "I lied when I told you I wished I'd never met you." Tears stung my eyes. "I can't imagine my life without you, Brax Jenkins—"

Brax's mouth descended on mine, and his kiss was reckless, desperate, and so damned sexy my cheeks grew hot. He pressed his forehead to mine, and we close-stared for several seconds.

"So all you have to do is keep your GPA up and quit beating the horse snot out of guys, right? And you keep your scholarship?"

We both turned to find Mom on the porch. She grinned.

"Yes, ma'am. That's the deal."

She gave a short nod. "Swell. Now get your butts in here then and have some pancakes. We have a Christmas tree to cut down later." She wagged her brows. "Decorations and lights. My dad wouldn't want it any other way."

Brax pulled me close, thought better of it, then swept me up into his arms. "Your mom said swell." He kissed me on my nose. "She's about as cute as you are."

"One of our favorite Jilly words," I snuggled against his warm chest. Contentment and joy filled my body as Brax carried me up the steps and into the house. Although Christmas without my grandfather would leave a mark, Brax had just made it a whole lot easier to accept.

My brothers came by later and we all headed down to Crom's Christmas Tree Farm to pick out the Beaumont tree. We were down one man—Jilly—who usually griped and complained over at least twenty trees before agreeing on one. But we were up one man— Brax—who loved and wanted every single tree we picked out. It was like watching Christmas through the eyes of a child who was just old enough to feel the Christmas spirit. Those crazy blue orbs sparkled with more mischief than any toddler I'd ever seen. He helped my brothers cut a ten footer down and load it onto the top of Mom's Suburban. I was pretty sure Brax had never had a Christmas quite like the one he was having now.

Back home, we trekked through the woods behind the barn, on our annual hunt for the perfect misletoe. Kyle spied it first.

"Dude." He pointed to a giant cluster of green in the top of a mostly-barren hardwood. "Perfection."

"And you're gonna shoot it down so I can kiss your sister?" Brax cupped his eyes against the glare. He looked at me and winked. "Fire away, bro."

Kyle did, and the massive ball of evergreen tumbled to the ground. At the ranch, Brax helped me string it up on the porch.

And then we tried it out. And tried it out again.

Brax wrapped his arms around my body, pulled me close, buried his mouth against my neck. "I think this mistletoe thing works. I can't seem to keep my hands off you," he whispered against my skin, making it tingle. "I hope your brothers don't clobber me." *Clobbah.*

"I hope my mother doesn't," I said, breathless. The look of fear in his harsh features made me burst out laughing.

"Nutcracker!" Brax hollered. *Nutcrackah!*

I fell into an unstoppable fit of giggles. Not only from his adorably sexy accent, but sooner or later I'd have to tell him just exactly what the safe word entailed.

Brax helped decorate the tree. He climbed the roof with my brothers and strung hundreds of lights—including strategically placing our twenty-five year old Santa and reindeer on the eve closest to the chimney. Yet whenever we were near each other, his eyes were on me and they burned, literally lit up. It made me feel cherished. Desired. Loved, maybe? He hadn't said the words. I sure felt them.

On Christmas Eve, we all gathered for the traditional standing rib roast meal, the watching of *It's A Wonderful Life*, and the opening of one present each. Brax totally surprised me with an official Boston Red Sox jersey with *Beaumont* and his number on the back of it. I'd gone shopping with Mom and had picked him up a book on constellations from the bookstore. I'd had to make him put the book down, and it gave me a good feeling inside, knowing he was interested in my interests. And visa versa. I now wanted to share a special place with him. We drank nutmeg eggnog. Spiked with rum. I'd never realized what a storybook Christmas we always had. Every year. Not a spoiled Christmas, with loads of presents. But family. Tradition. I wouldn't trade them for the world, those memories.

"Where are we going?" he asked, walking as close to me as possible, his arm around my shoulders. Slung over his opposite shoulder, my scope.

"You'll see," I said. I was actually a little melancholy about the place. Jilly had made it for me years ago. High above the barn loft, a trap door led out to a platform made especially for stargazing. We reached the barn, climbed the two sets of ladders to reach the platform, and when we stepped out onto it Brax sucked in a breath.

"Man, Gracie," he'd said in a low voice. "This is wicked."

"Jilly built it for me," I told him. "Years ago. We used to watch every single meteor shower of the year from up here."

I spread out a blanket, Brax set up the scope, and we laid there for a long time, staring at the crystal clear skies and glittering stars.

Suddenly, he pointed. "What was that?"

"Let me see," I said, and moved to look through the eye piece.

"I don't know," he said, snuggling close to my ear. "Looked like a sleigh or something." His hand slid under my jacket, resting against my stomach.

I giggled, and turned to look at him. "You got me."

We laid facing each other, and he kissed me. "Yeah, and I'm keepin' ya, Sunshine." His lips touched mine, his tongue swept over and over, and my hands found their way to his jaw and I kissed him back.

"I'm f-f-f-ucking f-f-freezing," he said against my mouth, and moved closer, his hands now finding their way beneath my thermal shirt to my bare skin.

I squealed. "Brax! No! Your fingers are like ice!" I squirmed, and he continued his assault until finally, his hands warmed against my body, and he trapped me with his heavy thigh. Bracing himself on his elbow, he looked down at me; his gaze searched mine, seemingly moving over every inch of my face. With his free hand, he brushed my hair out of my eyes. He was quiet for a long time.

"You take my breath, Gracie Beaumont," he said, his voice husky. His intense stare burned straight through me, I shook, and he kissed me so deep and with so much emotion, a surge of joy filled me and swept away all trepidation I'd ever felt.

"What'd Jilly say to you that night in the hospital?" I asked again. "If you can tell me now?"

He snuggled closer. "He told me not to play around with your heart. That if I really wanted you, I had to prove it, or else walk away. To sacrifice." He kissed me again. "And he also said if I hurt you again he'd find a way to come back and kick my horse's ass." He grinned. "I told him he'd never have to worry about that. Ever." *Evah.*

I could so hear my grandpa saying those ornery words. God, I missed him.

On Christmas morning, Brax crept into my room and woke me up.

"Gracie," he whispered, shaking me. "You

gotta wake up, Sunshine."

I cracked open my eyes and there he was, his Boston Red Sox hat turned around backward, an excited grin plastered to his face.

"Now," he pleaded.

"If my mother catches you in here she's going to beat you with her broom."

He lifted a brow. "Your mother sent me in here."

I sat up, shaking my head. "By the way, I've been meaning to tell you thank you."

Brax tugged on my arm. "For what?"

"Watching your usual Southie potty mouth around my mother."

He shrugged. "Tryin' to clean up the act a little, is all."

I rolled out of bed. "You're scared of her."

"Wicked scared of her." He grinned.

I laughed, and we walked out into the family room, where our ten foot tree was sparkling with lights. Underneath, a few more presents than when I'd last checked. I eyed Brax with suspicion. "What'd you do?"

"Merry Christmas, guys," Seth said, just walking in.

My other two brothers stuck their heads from the kitchen. "Merry Christmas, Lil' Bit. Brax."

We all exchanged gifts. Brax was nearly squirming by the hearth for me to open the small box he'd handed me. I knew it wasn't anything overkill, like a ring. But it was …

something.

"Gracie, you're killing me," he said. "Open it already."

I did, and inside the box was a thin silver chain, complete with the tiniest charm. A silver telescope. I flung my arms around his neck. "I love it! It's perfect!"

He looked at me. "I know."

My cheeks flamed, and I reached around him and handed him a brightly wrapped box with a burlap bow I'd made myself. "Your turn."

Brax turned those ghostly eyes on me. "What'd you do, Gracie?"

"Open it."

He did, and when he pried off the box lid, he stared. "No way."

I glanced at my brother Jace, who'd helped me pick it out. "Yes way, Boston."

"Ah, man," he said, and withdrew the straw Stetson. "Close your eyes, Gracie. You know," he winked. "For effect."

I rolled my eyes and closed them.

"Okay."

I opened them again to find the hat pulled arrogantly down over Brax's brow, a perfect fit, and a smoldering expression on his face. He crossed his arms over his chest.

"This is what I call *the fury*," he said. His brows pulled down, lips puckered.

"More like *the pimp*," Kyle said.

We all burst out laughing.

Brax stayed with us throughout the rest of the holidays and helped catch the ranch up on repairs, chores, and even helped us break a few new horses. He helped Jace and Kyle fix the roof, a few rotted boards on the barn, and several places of fence that needed mending. On New Year's Eve we shot off Jilly's Winchester, and Brax kissed me for the entire minute leading to the New Year. Seth, Kyle and Jace shot off fireworks, and although I missed my grandfather desperately, I was washed in a new kind of joy.

Desperate, true, forever love.

I couldn't have been any happier, save Jilly being around for it. I think he'd approve, too. Of me. And of Brax. Of us. Yet neither of us had admitted it.

The days zipped by, and in a blink it was time to head back to Winston. It felt weird not being able to say goodbye to Jilly. I guess Brax could tell something was up.

"What's wrong?" he asked, walking out to my truck.

I shook my head and explained. "It's just so … strange. Not seeing Jilly. Not saying goodbye."

Brax brushed his knuckles over my cheek. "We'll say goodbye on the way out, Sunshine."

After I hugged my mom and brothers, Brax tightened the tie-downs securing his motorcycle in the back of my truck and we pulled out of the drive. Brax drove us to the cemetery on the outskirts of town. We'd all visited on Christmas Day, but still—it felt wrong not to visit again, and he'd read my mind. Brax gave me a few moments alone at Jilly's grave. The dirt was still fresh-looking and new. I ran my fingertips over the headstone, traced the Ranger's star etched into the marble with my thumb.

"Thanks, Jilly," I whispered. "And you know why, you old badger. I love you."

On the way back to school, Brax drove, and we both wore our hats and sang with Kansas and the Eagles to the top of our lungs. But when he bypassed Winston's front gates, I looked at him.

"Sorry, Sunshine," he said in that familiar raspy voice. "But you're comin' home with me tonight."

My stomach dropped. "Am I going to need my safe word?"

Brax turned up a single lane drive, up to a house, and around the back to a small apartment. He killed the engine and gave me *the fury*.

"Definitely so," he said, his voice low.

I laughed, but he silenced me with his mouth, and the kiss lingered, deepened, and finally, he pulled away. "I wouldn't keep you against your will," he said. "Do you want to stay?" He kissed me again. "Christ, I want you to stay."

I leaned forward and pressed my lips to his. "I do, too," I whispered against him.

Wordlessly, he opened the door and pulled me out with him. He shouldered our bags and my scope, grabbed me by the hand and pulled me up a flight of outdoor steps that led to an above garage apartment. He looked at me as he unlocked the door. "Henry's renting to me for a fair shake. Plus he gave me a job at the cages." We pushed into the apartment, and Brax kicked the door shut with his foot. He locked it, set our stuff down, and pulled me to him. "Small, but private." He grinned, and stared at my lips. I'd noticed a dim lamp in the far corner that cast a hazy light over the single room apartment. "And all mine."

I peeked over his shoulder. We stood in a small but complete kitchen. Tiled floors. A bed in the far corner, with a chest of drawers, and in the center, a sofa, coffee table, TV against the brick wall, and a Bucks stove for heating. One door led to, I assumed, the bathroom. I grinned at Brax. "Perfect, Southie."

"I think so," he said. "Gimme a second. I'll get this place heated in two." He wiggled his brows. "This thing gets wicked hot."

Brax crossed the room to the Bucks, knelt down and I followed. I stood there, noticing how sexy the Stetson looked on him, with his dark curls hanging out the back. At how his jacket pulled taut across his broad shoulders; how his jeans pulled snug across his thighs, and how fast his hands, fingers worked the fat lighter, the matches. He fascinated me, in every possible way. It wasn't long before he had logs burning, and he kept the trap door open to the stove and stood. When he saw me, saw how close I'd come to stand behind him, his eyes smoldered, fixed on mine, and he reached for me. "You are wearing way too much, Sunshine." His fingers grasped the zipper to my down jacket and pulled. As it opened, he slid his hands inside and swept his mouth over mine, and I did the same to him. Inside his leather coat, his body warmed my icy fingers.

"God, woman, you're freezing," he whispered. "Come here." Taking me by the hand, he led me to his bed where he yanked all the bedcovers off at once. He piled two pillows in my arms and we dragged everything over to the stove and threw it down on the floor in front of it. He smiled at me. "Sit."

I did, and he followed and threw himself down beside me. We faced the stove, only a few feet away, and I held my hands out to reach the warmth. He did it, too. I wanted him to touch me, kiss me, and, well, everything. My insides were writhing with need, and the sensation excited and confused me at once. Brax must have sensed my frustration because he looked at me, and the fiery gleam in his eyes made me pause.

Then I reached up and yanked his hat off. Tossed it on the floor.

A slow smile grew on Brax's beautifully scarred face from the corners out, and he flipped my hat off, too, and in one smooth motion peeled my arms out of my jacket, followed by his, and laid me back against the comforter. Bracing his weight on his elbows, he hovered over me. His gaze dragged over my features, one at a time, and my heart slammed against my ribs at the seductiveness of it. With nimble fingers he unsnapped the buttons on my shirt and opened it, revealing my thermal, and he placed his palm over the left side of my chest. Over my heart.

"You can trust me with this, Gracie," he said quietly. He said nothing more, just stared at me with those eerie eyes filled with desire. And something else.

"I know," I answered, and I brushed my fingertips over the dark scruff on his jaw. "I think I always knew."

Brax stared at me for a long time, then slowly lowered his mouth to mine. When our lips met, the turmoil inside me quickened, and my hands found their way around his neck and I pulled him closer. He kissed me so thoroughly, tasting the corners of my mouth, my top lip, the bottom one, his tongue grazing mine and me savoring it. My lips were numb, my heart beat fast, my nerve endings on fire from his touch. Brax's hands moved over my clothed body, and it wasn't nearly close enough. He wasn't close enough, and I desperately tugged at his shirt, the buttons of his jeans, and pushed at his boots with mine. My body writhed beneath his, and he took the cue. Our movements weren't slick, smooth, or movie-worthy. We jerked and yanked each others clothes off, awkward and fast, and it wasn't until we had every stitch off that we were satisfied. Brax lay over me, one heavy thigh trapping both of mine, and his hand moved in the gentlest caress from my face, to my collar bone, to my breast. As he touched, he kissed; when I exhaled, he inhaled, swallowing my breath, and he traced strong fingertips over my stomach, my navel, my hips. His touch set my nerves on edge; I felt hot, and the desire inside of me grew to a pitch that had me frenzied. He unraveled my braid, his hand burying in my hair. My fingers dug into the muscles of his broad back, his biceps, and we moved in sync, fever pitch for fever pitch.

At once he was between my thighs, and Brax grabbed his discarded jeans. He lifted a small wrapper to his mouth, tore it with his teeth, and stretched a condom over his hardened length. "Don't close your eyes, Gracie," he said, then leaned over, dragged his mouth over mine. "Watch what you do to me."

When I drew my next breath Brax pushed into me, and I gasped but kept my eyes on his. He filled me, exquisitely, and I lifted my hips a bit to take him in just a little more. Not close enough. I wrapped my legs around his waist, and he let out a groan that sounded almost painful.

"Jesus, Gracie," he said hoarsely, and started to move against me. His mouth descended on mine, and his kiss matched his thrusts, and I saw the desire in his eyes because I didn't close mine. I watched. He watched. And we moved together, faster, and a slow, tumultuous storm grew in strength between us until the waves crashed over us both, simultaneously, one after another until I bucked and became breathless.

"Brax," I whispered. My hands gripped him as he sagged against me, and I tasted the salty sweat of his skin as I kissed his shoulder.

He raised his head and looked down at me, pressed his lips to first my forehead, then my mouth. He kissed me long. Thorough. Sweet.

"God, Gracie," he whispered, then completely enveloped my body with his arms, rolled off to the side and pulled me tightly against him.

We laid together, my head against his chest; his rapid heart beating against my ear. I knew I loved him. I felt he loved me.

Neither of us said it, though.

I wondered about that.

But as contentment washed over me, so complete and absolute, I decided not to ponder it too much. It—Brax—felt too right to worry. I closed my eyes and drifted fast asleep, wrapped in Brax's arms.

29. Forever

"YOUR FOLKS ARE COMING, right?"

I smiled and kissed Brax on the nose. "Yes. They're coming. They're probably already in the stands."

He grinned, wagged his brows, and cockily pulled the bill of his Silverbacks hat low. "They'll see how wicked bitchy I pitch."

I shook my head. "Your ego, Southie. It's a biggun."

"You like it."

"I do."

Brax pulled me into a tight embrace, lowered his mouth to mine.

And devoured it.

I kissed him back, no hesitation, no shyness. He made me that comfortable.

Our kissing turned smoldering, and we fell against Brax's front door. His hand moved to my hip, around my buttock. "How am I supposed to concentrate on the mound,

Gracie?" he said, taking small nips of my bottom lip.

"Just think of what'll be waiting for you after you win," I said, breathless.

A knock on the door at my back startled us both.

"Hey! We know you're both in there. Probably naked and making out," Tessa's tinny voice sounded from the other side of the door. "Game day, guys. Come on! It's freezing out here!"

Brax pulled back slowly, my bottom lip in his mouth, and he gave it one last taste. "Hold your ponies, Barnes," he said, grinning. His eyes never left mine. "Be out in a sec."

Two weeks into the new semester, and everything was absolutely perfect. Brax and I didn't have any classes together, but we still had lunch every day. He worked at the batting cages when he wasn't at early spring training, and I at the observatory. We studied together, spent as much time together as possible, and although I hadn't moved into his apartment, I stayed there a lot. Henry didn't mind. Brax hated to ever see me leave.

We were as close as a couple in love could be.

Except, we'd neither said it.

Brax had changed. I probably had, too, but his was noticeable. To me, anyway. Although he'd defend me in a sweet minute, that angry side of him had disappeared. He wasn't quite as rough around the edges. I don't know … it was as if he'd found peace, maybe? I'd liked to think I was that peace. He'd certainly been for me. Besides. Kelsy Evans had all but vanished. I was pretty sure he'd flunked his semester. Or his father had pulled him from Winston in order to duck trouble. Either way, I never saw him around school and that sat perfectly well with me.

"Come on!" Tessa complained from the other side of the door. "Cory, tell your pitcher to move his ass!"

"Move your ass!" Cory hollered.

Brax kissed me once more and grinned. "Let's go before I punch him in the throat."

We all headed out to the Winston baseball diamond in Cory's Camaro. The middle of January was chilly and sunny and perfect. My family had driven in to watch Brax pitch and have dinner. The only thing missing was Jilly. And I knew he was there in spirit.

Brax and Cory's cleats clicked across the parking lot as we hurried to the dugout, where Brax swept me up and kissed me once more.

"Kick ass," I said, grinning, and kissed him back.

"You know I will," he replied.

Tessa ran with me up the bleachers, where I found Mom and my brothers. I introduced everyone, and we waited for the game to start.

"Come here, Lil' Bit," Jace said, and pulled me next to him.

Kyle reached around Mom and smacked me in the back of the head. "This better be good," he said, a mischievous smile tugging at his lips.

I grabbed his knee cap, and he squawked. "Just you watch."

"All right you guys," Mom said. She tugged my braid. "Behave."

The game started, and Brax fired three fastballs in a row for the first strike out. I watched in fascination as he collected, stretched, and pitched. It was a thing of beauty, to me. The ball popped the catcher's glove so loud it sounded like gunfire. He had a grimace on his face that showed every ounce of strength he used to shoot that pitch, too. I thought it was the sexiest growling face. Ever.

"Damn that boy," Seth said low. "Jace."

"I know," he agreed. "Son of a—"

"Hey," Mom said.

"Wait 'til you see him bat," I added.

After three consecutive outs, the Silverbacks were up to bat. The first two batters hit singles, leaving Brax with runners on first and second. He found me in the stands, pointed his bat right at me.

"God he's cocky," Kyle said. "I like that."

I only grinned.

"Could you be a little more sickening?" Tessa teased. "Chica, please."

My brothers laughed.

Brax crowded the plate on the first pitch and swung. He loved to hit fast balls, and that's exactly what had crossed the plate. His bat cracked the ball, sending it out to the left field corner. He took off in that arrogant, bow-legged swaggering run. One player scored, one was on third, and Brax made it to second by sliding. We all jumped to our feet and hollered.

"Okay, baby," Tessa yelled as Cory strutted to the plate. "You know what to do!"

"He's a moose!" Seth commented. "Is he even human?"

Tessa grinned. "Mostly."

On the second pitch Cory smacked the holy hell out of the ball for a homerun, sending Brax and the other guy over home plate. Again, we all cheered.

"Okay, here comes big brother," Tessa said.

Cole hit a single, and after four more batters, the inning ended. We were up five to zip.

By the sixth inning the score was nine to two, Silverbacks. The crowd in the stands was ecstatic, and Brax was at his best. Pride filled me, and I was glad that my family was there to witness it. The day couldn't have gone any better.

Brax made his way to the mound, picked up the chalk bag and tossed it a few times, then threw a few pitches to the catcher. The seventh inning began, and Brax fired his first pitch. It was then a muffled drone caught my ear, coming from the visitor's side of the stands. Ignoring it, my attention was fast on Brax, the fluid motion of his athletic body, his perfect pitching form.

"Oh, hell," Tessa murmured beside me. "Liv?"

"What?" I responded. I didn't look at her. My eyes were glued to Brax.

Tessa's elbow dug into my side. "Liv!"

"Tess, I swear—" I stopped, mid-sentence, as the drone caught my attention again. It'd grown louder, more distinct, and it made me look away from Brax, to the visitor's section. I saw him then. Kelsy Evans, his buddies. And the words rose above the cheers of the Silverbacks fans.

Gutter-fuck. Gutter-fuck.

Realization punched me in the gut, and my eyes darted back to Brax. I knew the second he heard it, too. He'd just thrown a pitch—it'd no more left his hand when his head turned to find me.

And that's when it happened.

The ball cracked against the bat as a line drive shot out of the batters box and straight for the mound.

The ball hit Brax in the temple as he searched the crowd, and he dropped so fast to the ground he looked like a rag doll.

My breath left my lungs and I leapt to my feet. "*No!*" I started down the bleachers as fast as I could move. From my peripheral I noticed my brothers moving, too. To the visitor's side. My eyes stayed forward then, on Brax's body. Unmoving. Still as death. I slammed into the fence by the dugout. Cory was already at the mound, kneeling beside Brax. He was quickly joined by the catcher. Soon all of the starters were hovering over him, and I couldn't see anything except his cleats. No movement. My heart nearly stopped.

I tried to open the dugout, but I couldn't budge it. Locked. "Let me in!" I yelled.

Mom and Tessa came to stand beside me, and Mom put her hand on my shoulder. "Back up, sweetie. EMS is here. He'll be okay. He'll be fine."

Mom had to pull me back; I couldn't tear my eyes away from Brax's cleats. It was the only part of him I could see, and I wasn't losing sight of him. Oh, God. *Oh God!* "Mom," I said, frantic. My voice quivered. "That ball ... it had to be going at least ninety."

Mom stroked my hair. "I know, honey. I know. Just ... wait."

EMS quickly cleared the area, made the players back up as they brought a stretcher next to Brax's body. Still, he didn't move, not an inch. Not a breath. I strained my eyes, trying to see his chest move. I didn't. Or couldn't.

All because Brax heard that stupid chant, started by Kelsy Evans.

The crowd was silent as death now; you could hear a pin drop. The EMS guys hovered over Brax, but I couldn't see a thing. My fingers squeezed the chain linked fence as I stared hard, and tears fell down my cheeks. I didn't care. I could barely breathe.

It was the longest eleven minutes of my life. I held my breath for most of it. Behind me, I heard random people in low voices saying, *Is he breathing? Is he going to be okay?* I prayed with my eyes open, fixed on Brax's motionless body. That was a hard hit. Straight to the temple. *Jesus God, please be okay!*

Suddenly, I saw it. His hand moved. On his own. Hope surged inside of me, and I wanted to crawl over that chain linked fence, drop to the other side and run like hell to that mound. EMS, with Brax's body now strapped to the stretcher, raised it to full height. Then Brax's arm lifted, higher than before, and he gave a thumbs-up.

The crowd roared.

Relief swept over me like a violent wave, and I exhaled my pent-up breath. Mom and Tessa hugged me. Suddenly, my brothers were behind me, too.

EMS didn't move, though. One of the guys bent down, over Brax. Then he walked to the dugout. I saw then that Brax had a black neck brace on, and my nerves shot high.

"Just for precaution, sis," Jace said close to me. "You know that."

I exhaled again, and kept my gaze trained on Brax. The EMS guy jogged back to the mound and handed something to him. His arm lifted to his mouth. His throaty, raspy Southie voice came over the loud speaker.

"Gracie—you're gonna have to find higher ground for me to see you, sweetheart," he said. "I got this damn thing on my neck."

Sweethaht. My heart leapt.

"Here," Kyle said, and led me to the bleachers. "Go up a few."

I did, and turned back to the mound.

"Better!" Brax said. "Can you see me?"

The crowd was dead silent and looking right at me. I waved to Brax so he knew I could see him.

"Gracie, I got something to tell you, and I've been wanting to tell ya for a long time, but now seems to be it. Crazy, huh?"

I stood frozen in place, waiting, breathless.

His voice boomed over the intercom once more. "I'm in love with you, Gracie Beaumont. Do you hear me? I love you!"

Tears filled my eyes as the entire stand of baseball fans cheered, and a content and full feeling nearly made my heart burst. I cupped my hands over my mouth and hollered back once the crowd quieted. "I love you, too!"

I couldn't see his face clearly, but I saw his hands go to his face, heard his raspy laugh come through the speaker system. "Pardon my French, Ms. Beaumont, but can you get your ass down here?"

With the crowd cheering, my mom crying, and my brothers helping me along, one of the coaches opened the dugout door and I rushed through it. I ran all the way to the mound and stopped just at the foot of Brax's stretcher. The grin on his face stretched from ear to ear, and he waved me closer. He lifted the mic to his mouth. "Come here, Sunshine."

I did and, with the crowd on its feet, roaring, I leaned over Brax and our eyes fixed. "Say it again," he said.

The crowd was so loud, I could barely hear myself speak. I leaned over the mic. "I said I love you, Brax Jenkins!"

"Woohoo!" he hollered into the mic. "Did you hear that? She loves me!"

And with the stands at a low roar, cheering and hollering, I kissed Brax. He kissed me, too. Until the EMS guy had to pull us apart. He, too, was grinning, though.

"Ride with me to the hospital?" Brax said, squeezing my hand.

"Absolutely," I replied.

Cory had come to stand beside me, towering over me. Brax briefly looked at him. "Win the game, bro," Brax said.

Cory grinned. "You know we will."

And with a strength that made relief sweep over me again, Brax gripped my hand, threaded my fingers through his, and I walked alongside his stretcher to the ambulance. My mom, brothers, and Tessa were there, too.

Jace surprised me and leaned over Brax, said something quiet in his ear. When he rose, Jace winked at me, then looked at Brax. "Beastly pitching, man," he said.

Brax grinned. "Thanks, bro."

After they loaded Brax into the ambulance, I climbed in and perched beside him. The ambulance started to move, and I grasped his hand. "You scared me to death," I said. "Don't ever do that again."

He couldn't move his neck because of the brace and, as expressive as he was, I knew it bothered him to keep so still. He squeezed my fingers instead. "I'm in love with you," he said again. "You're forever, Sunshine."

I looked at his unique face, both eyes already growing purple from the hit, and I realized how lucky he was. I was. We both were. My eyes scanned his tattooed forearms. His knuckles, and the letters inked into them. *Goin Down.*

I was goin down from the second I'd met him.

And I knew I'd found my forever, too.

"I'm in love with you, too, Braxton Jenkins." Tears filled my eyes. "Forever won't be nearly long enough."

"Sweetheart," he said, his eyes holding mine. "Forever is for fuckin' sissies. Pardon my French, but let's go for eternity, yeah?"

I grinned and squeezed his hand. *Forevah. Pahdon.* I'd made the right choice all right.

And sometimes, what seemed like the stupid choices turned out to be the only choices.

STUPID BOY BY CINDY MILES
Book 2 in the
Stupid in Love series

Brax Jenkins and Olivia Beaumont are the most envied couple at Winston College—but the so-called "virginity dare," orchestrated by Brax's old fraternity, almost tore them apart. Now, a new dare is taking shape, and it's sure to set the campus ablaze with crazy new rumors and chaos.

Winston's "It Girl" Harper Bell isn't just president of Alpha Delta Phi—she's also a master at keeping her ugly past a secret. So, when the Kappas' dare hits closer to home for her more than anyone realizes, she devises a competition of her own as payback. Three sorority sisters will seek out a notorious bad boy, train him to be the perfect boyfriend, seduce him almost to the point of no return, and promptly—and publicly—break his heart. Always up for a challenge, Harper targets the biggest player she can find: Brax's wickedly handsome foster brother Kane McCarthy.

But, Harper discovers there's much more to

Kane than girls, games, and partying. His easy smile belies the quiet, old soul reflected in his deep brown eyes. All it takes is one night, one secret laid bare, and one kiss from Kane to shift Harper's world on its axis. Suddenly, the girl who's always walked a straight and narrow path can't think of anything else except losing control.

ACKNOWLEDGEMENTS

WITHOUT THE FOLLOWING PEOPLE, Stupid Girl wouldn't exist, and from the bottom of my heart, I thank you. My husband Brian, daughters Tyler and Lyndsee, son Kyle, my mom and dad, sisters Sheri, Tracy, and my bro-in-laws Jerry and Jordan, and my extended family, for always believing in me. My best friend and sister writer Lily Dalton, who is always there for ideas and support, and who has made me believe I can do anything I set my mind to. Sister author and cord twin Leah Brown, who has been there with me from the beginning of my writing journey and who loves Jon-Erik Hexum as much as I do. My sweet friend Jan Williams-Watkins and her son Joe, for all things love, baseball, and inspirational. My wolfpack of friends—you know who you are and I love you. My fabulous agent, Deidre Knight, for loving Brax as much as I do, as well as everyone at the The Knight Agency, for believing in this project. My editor at TKA, Jamie Schlansky, for her phenomenal job of editing the book and making so many wonderful suggestions. And a special thanks to Jia Gayles, for all her hands-on marketing wizardry! For Keith Urban and the song that inspired me, *Stupid Boy*. And finally, for Frauke, whose amazingly crafted Stupid Girl cover is simply magical. And, to God. Thank you all.

AUTHOR BIO

CINDY MILES GREW UP ON the Vernon River in coastal Georgia. A best-selling author and a full-time writer, she lives and continues to be inspired by the Gothic Revival and Georgian architecture, the moss-draped squares, ancient cobbles and surrounding coastal marshes of Savannah.

Visit her online at www.cindy-miles.com, on Facebook, Twitter, and Goodreads.

Made in the USA
Lexington, KY
16 March 2016